IN.

FOR INFORMATION ABOUT PERMISSION TO REPRODUCE SELECTIONS FROM THIS BOOK, WRITE TO
TRADE.PERMISSIONS@HMHCO.COM OR TO PERMISSIONS, HOUGHTON MIFFLIN HARCOURT PUBLISHING COMPANY,
3 PARK AVE, 19TH FLOOR, NEW YORK, NEW YORK 10016.

WWW.HMHBOOKS.COM

LIBRARY OF CONGRESS CATALOGING-IN-PUBLICATION DATA IS AVAILABLE
ISBN   978-0-358-34554-1 (HBK)
ISBN   978-0-358-34556-5 (EBK)

PRINTED IN CHINA

SCP 10 9 8 7 6 5 4 3 2 1

FOR EDWARD AND LIZZIE

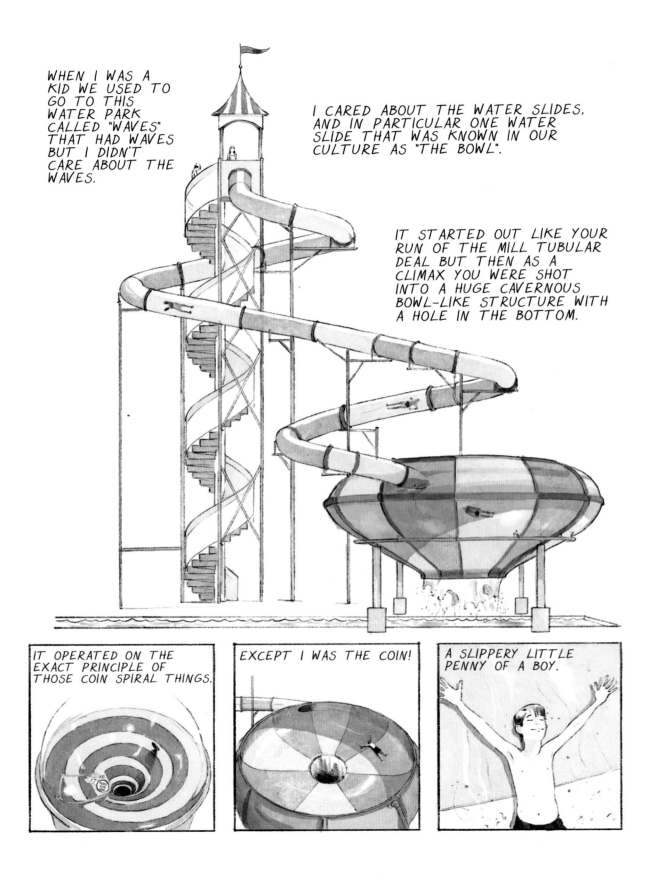

WHEN I WAS A KID WE USED TO GO TO THIS WATER PARK CALLED "WAVES" THAT HAD WAVES BUT I DIDN'T CARE ABOUT THE WAVES.

I CARED ABOUT THE WATER SLIDES, AND IN PARTICULAR ONE WATER SLIDE THAT WAS KNOWN IN OUR CULTURE AS "THE BOWL".

IT STARTED OUT LIKE YOUR RUN OF THE MILL TUBULAR DEAL BUT THEN AS A CLIMAX YOU WERE SHOT INTO A HUGE CAVERNOUS BOWL-LIKE STRUCTURE WITH A HOLE IN THE BOTTOM.

IT OPERATED ON THE EXACT PRINCIPLE OF THOSE COIN SPIRAL THINGS.

EXCEPT I WAS THE COIN!

A SLIPPERY LITTLE PENNY OF A BOY.

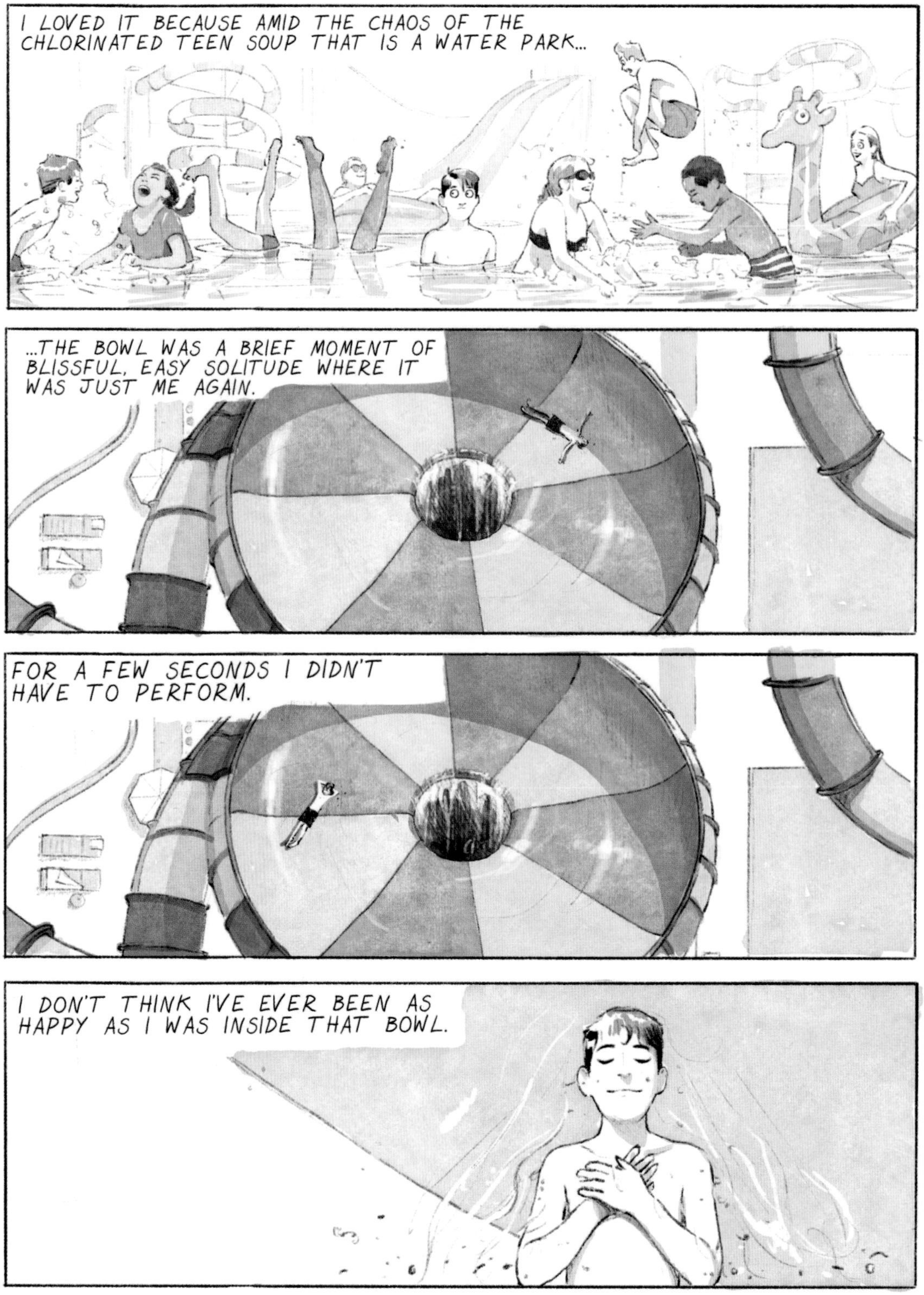
I LOVED IT BECAUSE AMID THE CHAOS OF THE CHLORINATED TEEN SOUP THAT IS A WATER PARK...
...THE BOWL WAS A BRIEF MOMENT OF BLISSFUL, EASY SOLITUDE WHERE IT WAS JUST ME AGAIN.
FOR A FEW SECONDS I DIDN'T HAVE TO PERFORM.
I DON'T THINK I'VE EVER BEEN AS HAPPY AS I WAS INSIDE THAT BOWL.

ONE WEEKEND AT WAVES, ME AND THE GUYS WERE PUTTING OUT THE VIBE IN THE SHALLOW END WHEN I, CONCEALING MY EAGERNESS, SUGGESTED WE CHECK OUT THE SLIDES.

MY STUPID FRIENDS TOOK THE BAIT AND BEFORE LONG I WAS SLIDING FEET FIRST TOWARDS THE BOWL'S WET EMBRACE.

THE TUBE OPENED UP AND I WAS BACK WHERE I BELONGED.

BUT SOMETHING WASN'T RIGHT. IT FELT DIFFERENT.

I WASN'T ALONE.

THERE WERE OTHER PENNIES IN HERE.

MY FRIENDS SOON FOLLOWED BEHIND ME AND WITHOUT VERBALLY DECIDING IT, WE HEADED BACK TO THE CHANGING ROOMS.

THEY TOO MUST HAVE HAD THEIR MOMENT WITH THE CHILDREN OF THE BOWL.

BUT NONE OF US SPOKE ABOUT IT.

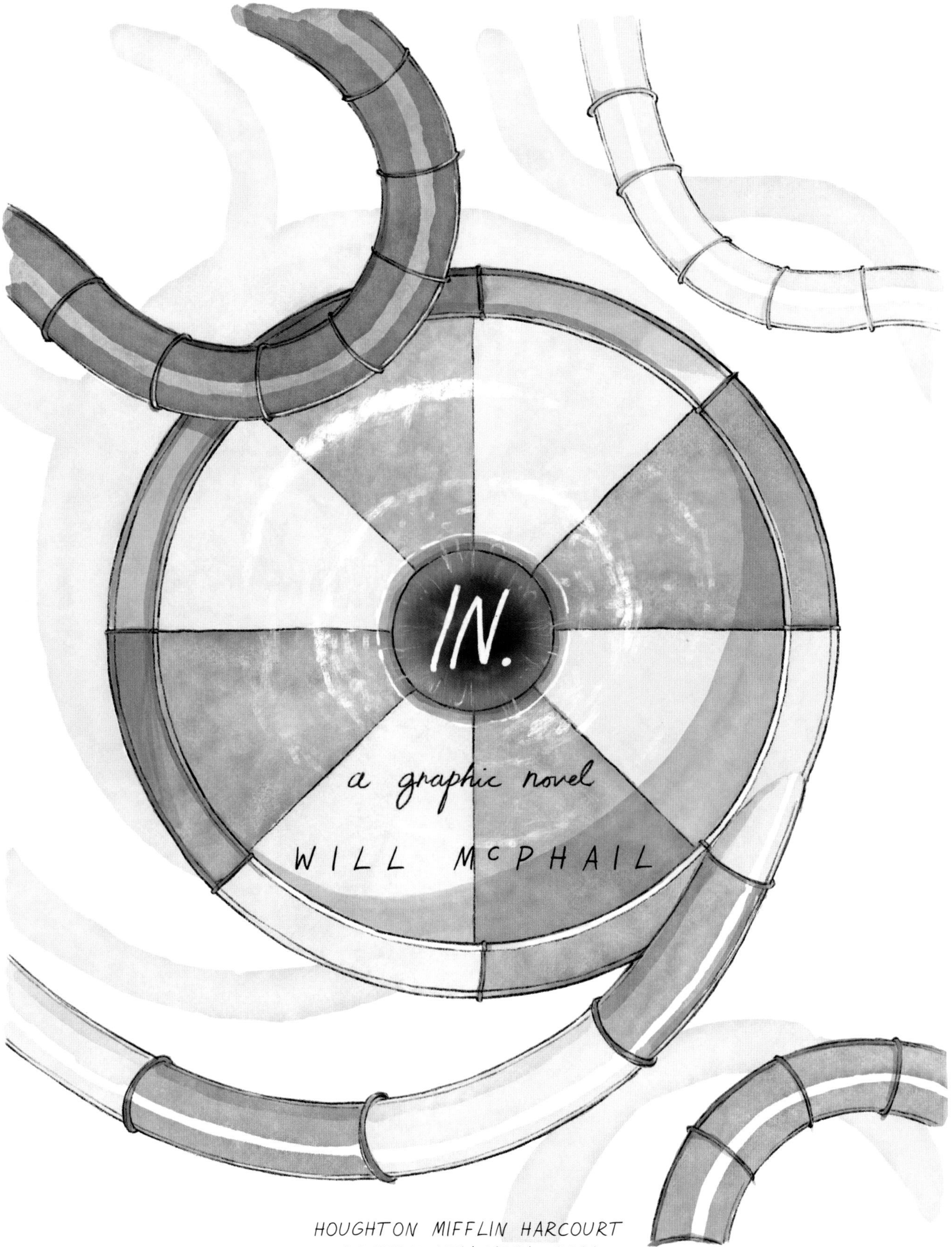
IN.
a graphic novel
WILL McPHAIL

HOUGHTON MIFFLIN HARCOURT
BOSTON NEW YORK 2021

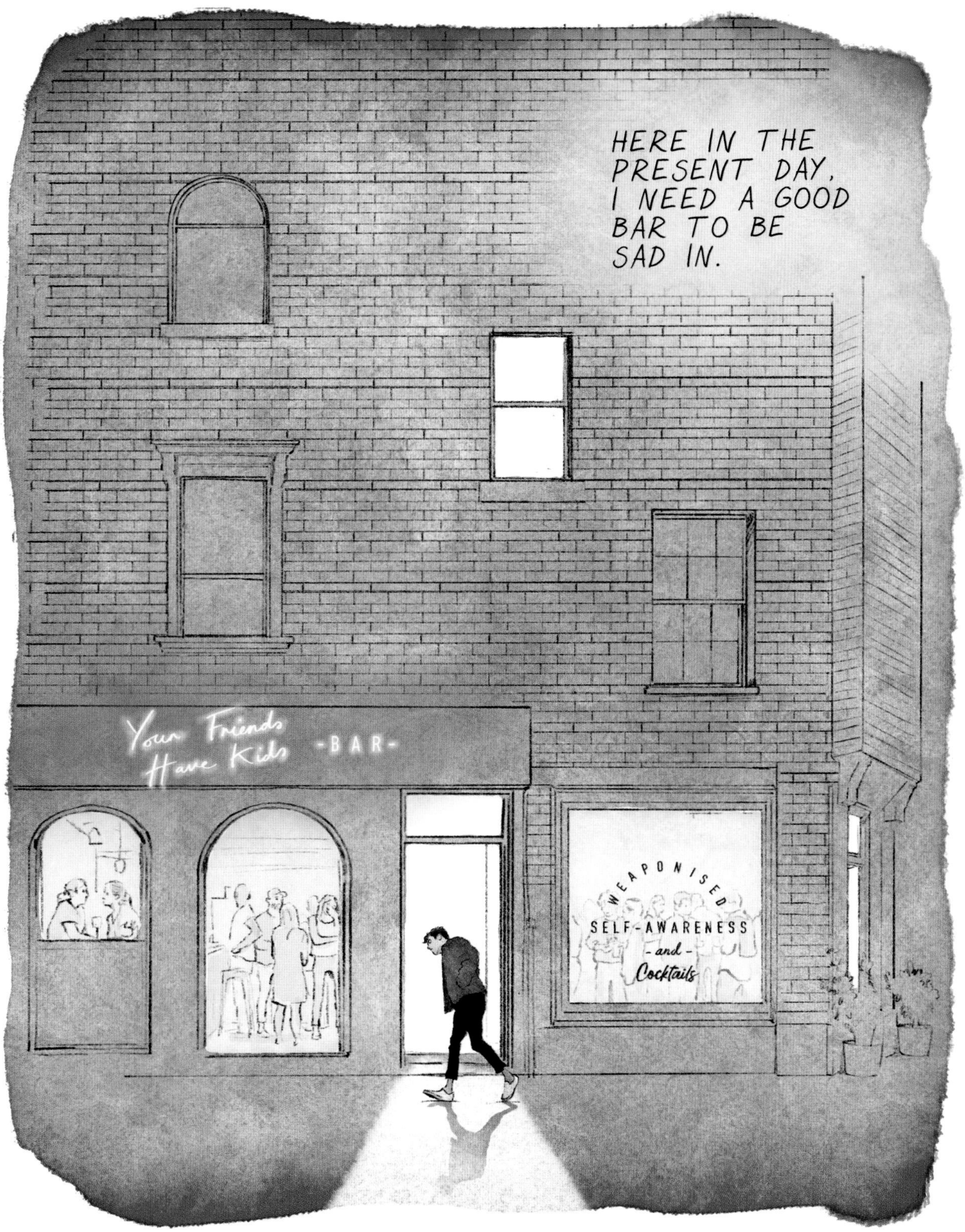
HERE IN THE PRESENT DAY, I NEED A GOOD BAR TO BE SAD IN.
Your Friends Have Kids -BAR-
WEAPONISED SELF-AWARENESS -and- Cocktails

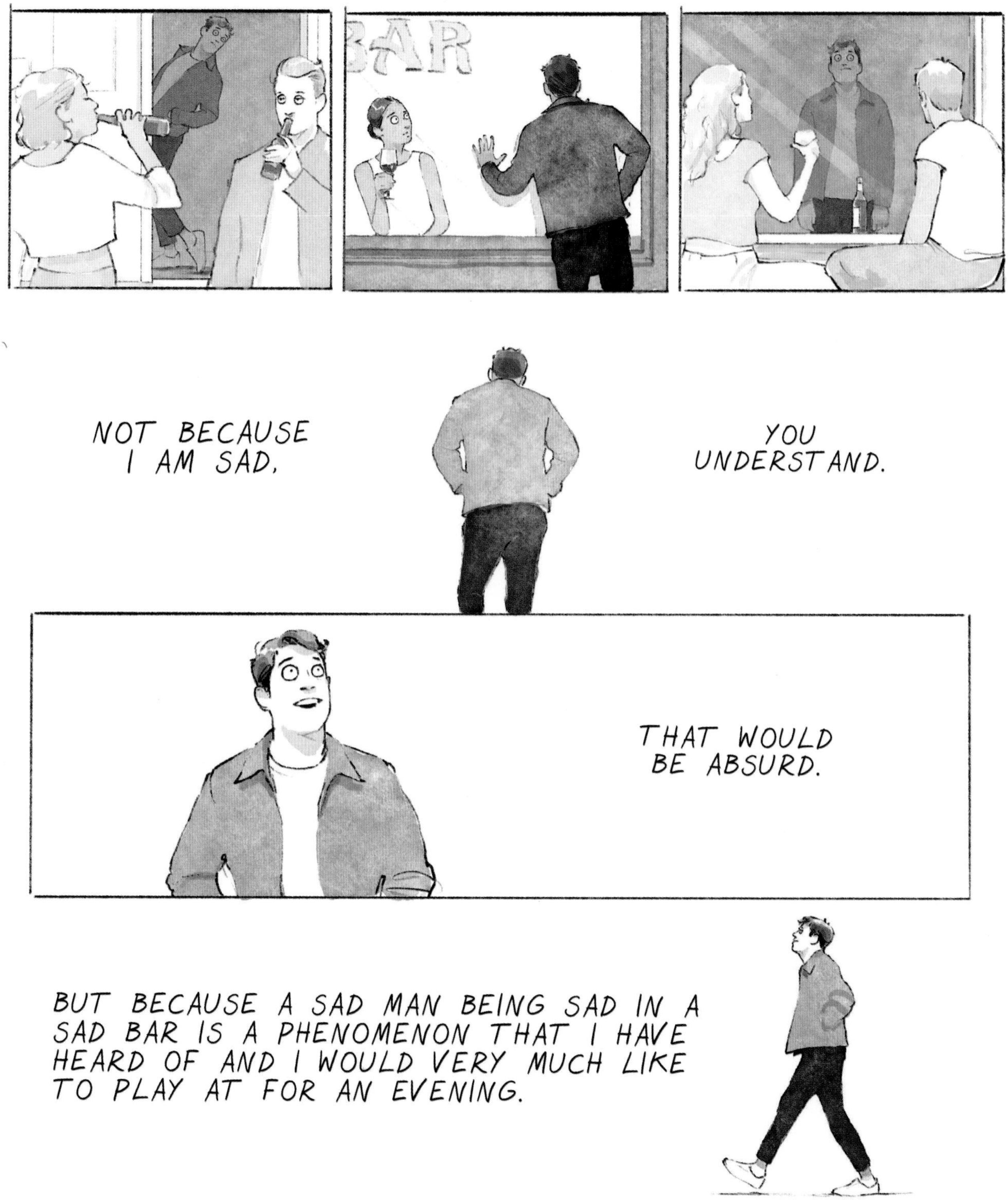
BAR
NOT BECAUSE I AM SAD,
YOU UNDERSTAND.
THAT WOULD BE ABSURD.
BUT BECAUSE A SAD MAN BEING SAD IN A SAD BAR IS A PHENOMENON THAT I HAVE HEARD OF AND I WOULD VERY MUCH LIKE TO PLAY AT FOR AN EVENING.

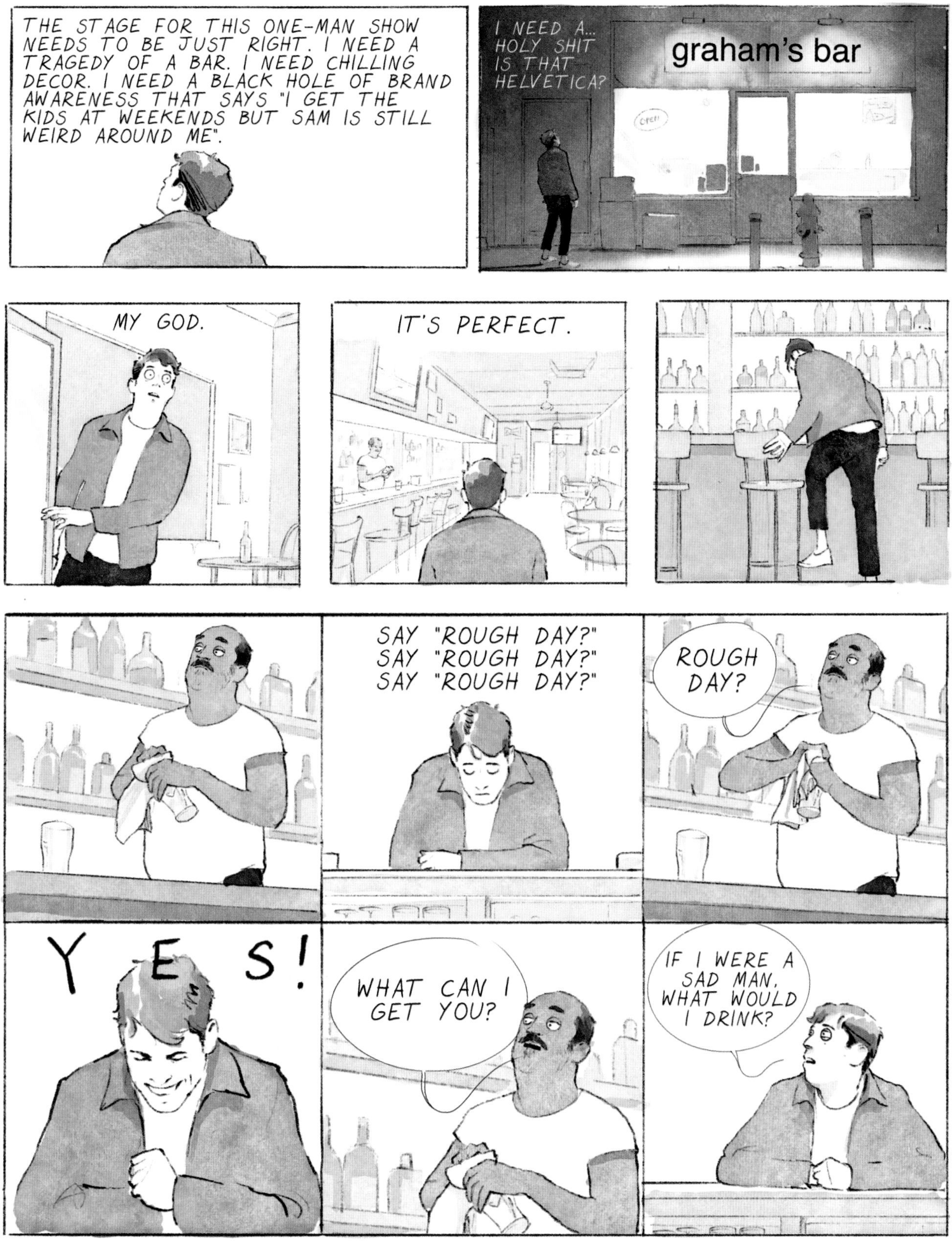
THE STAGE FOR THIS ONE-MAN SHOW NEEDS TO BE JUST RIGHT. I NEED A TRAGEDY OF A BAR. I NEED CHILLING DECOR. I NEED A BLACK HOLE OF BRAND AWARENESS THAT SAYS "I GET THE KIDS AT WEEKENDS BUT SAM IS STILL WEIRD AROUND ME".
I NEED A... HOLY SHIT IS THAT HELVETICA?
graham's bar
MY GOD.
IT'S PERFECT.
SAY "ROUGH DAY?" SAY "ROUGH DAY?" SAY "ROUGH DAY?"
ROUGH DAY?
YES!
WHAT CAN I GET YOU?
IF I WERE A SAD MAN, WHAT WOULD I DRINK?

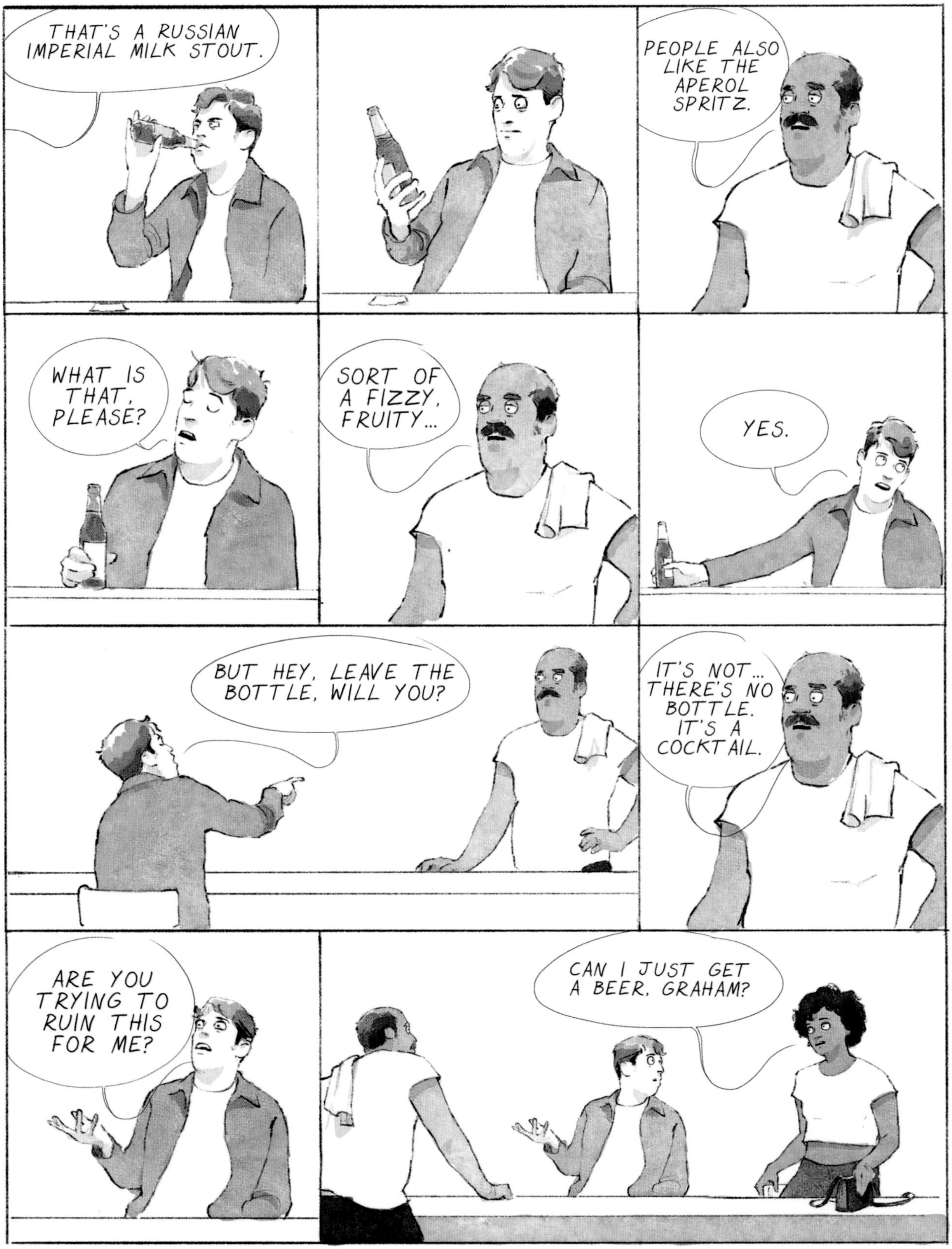
THAT'S A RUSSIAN IMPERIAL MILK STOUT.
PEOPLE ALSO LIKE THE APEROL SPRITZ.
WHAT IS THAT, PLEASE?
SORT OF A FIZZY, FRUITY...
YES.
BUT HEY, LEAVE THE BOTTLE, WILL YOU?
IT'S NOT... THERE'S NO BOTTLE. IT'S A COCKTAIL.
ARE YOU TRYING TO RUIN THIS FOR ME?
CAN I JUST GET A BEER, GRAHAM?

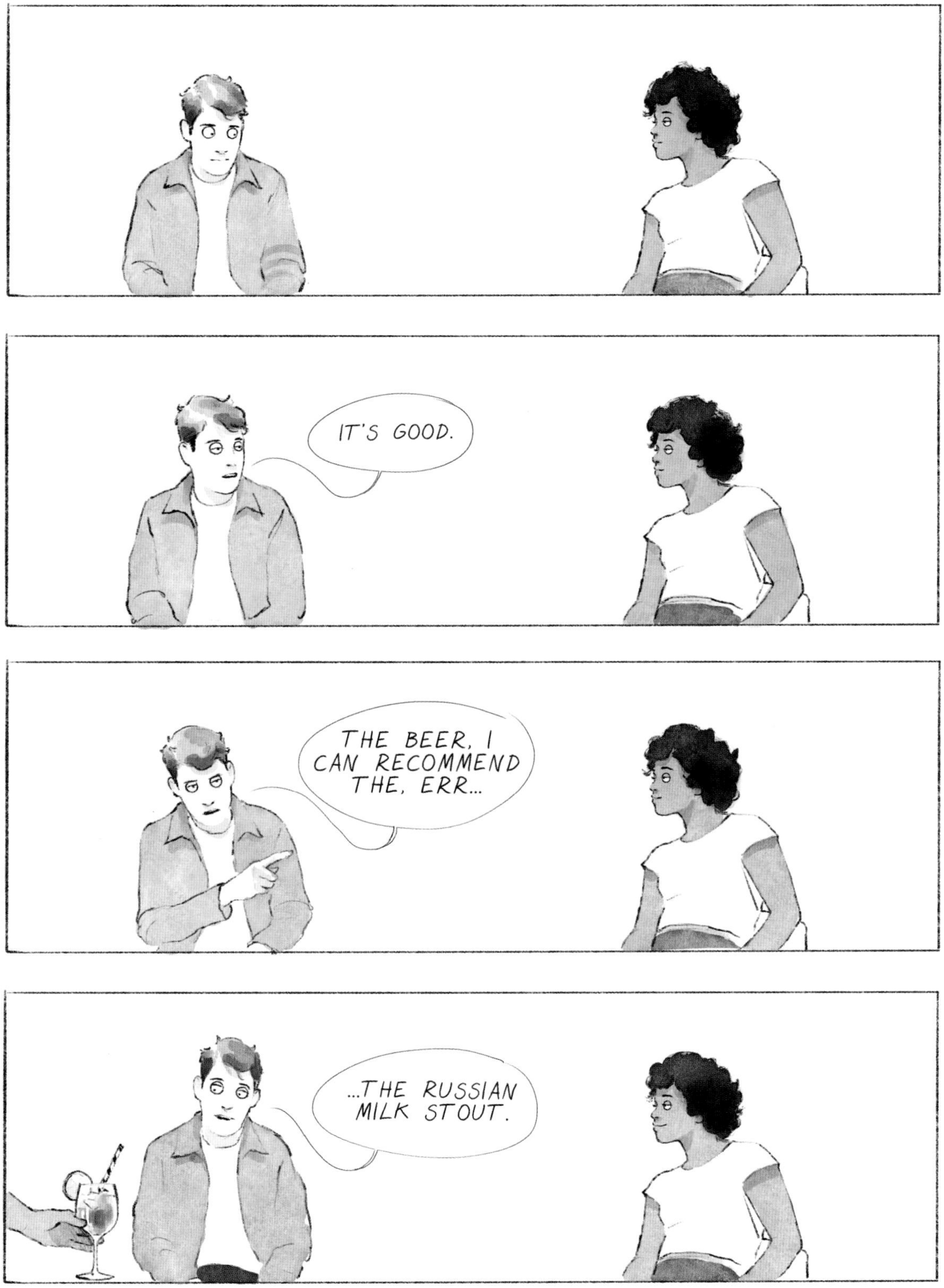
IT'S GOOD.
THE BEER. I CAN RECOMMEND THE, ERR...
...THE RUSSIAN MILK STOUT.

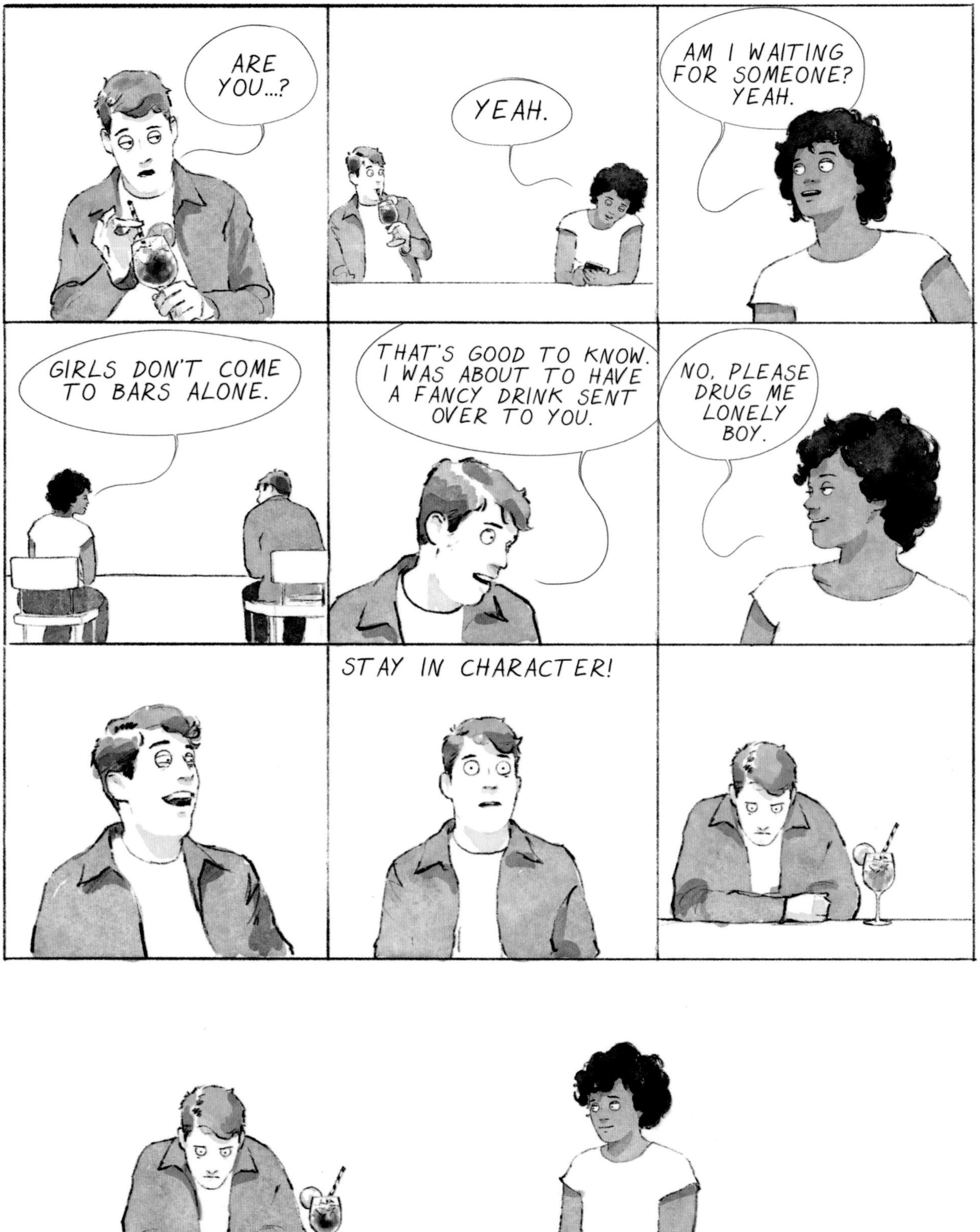
ARE YOU...?
YEAH.
AM I WAITING FOR SOMEONE? YEAH.
GIRLS DON'T COME TO BARS ALONE.
THAT'S GOOD TO KNOW. I WAS ABOUT TO HAVE A FANCY DRINK SENT OVER TO YOU.
NO, PLEASE DRUG ME LONELY BOY.
STAY IN CHARACTER!

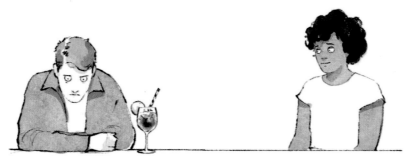

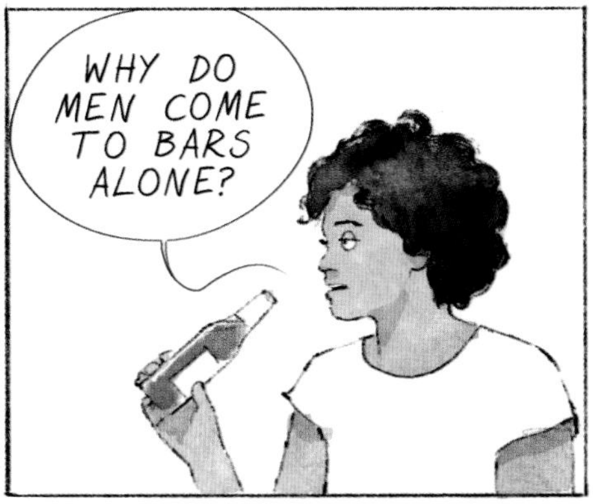
WHY DO MEN COME TO BARS ALONE?

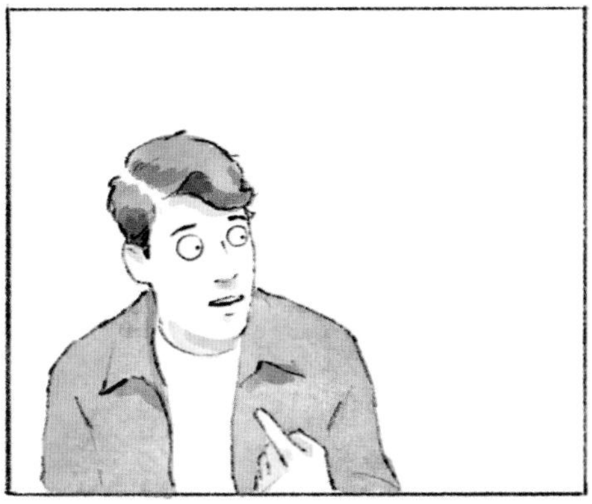

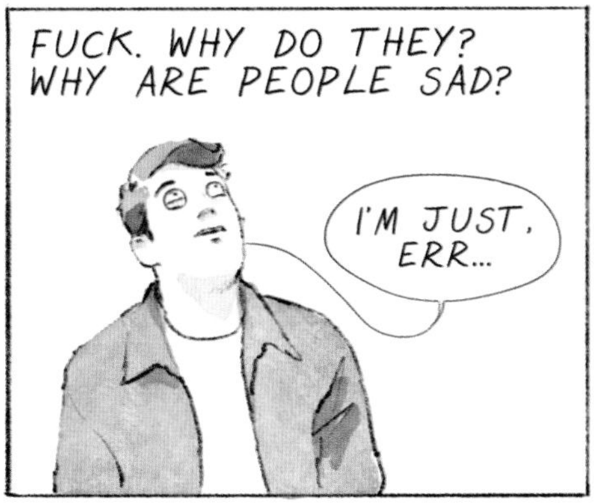
FUCK. WHY DO THEY? WHY ARE PEOPLE SAD?
I'M JUST, ERR...

CLIMATE CHANGE? SHELLFISH ALLERGIES?
IT'S JUST BEEN...
IT'S BEEN A ROUGH DAY AND I...
I MIXED UP MY BEARD OIL WITH MY CBD OIL LAST WEEK. IS THAT ANYTHING?
I DIDN'T EVEN NOTICE A DIFFERENCE.
I GUESS I'M...
YOU'RE NOT SAD.

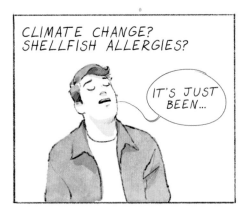

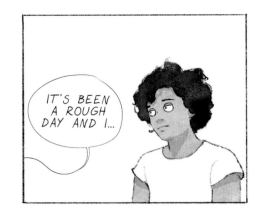

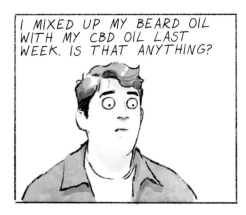

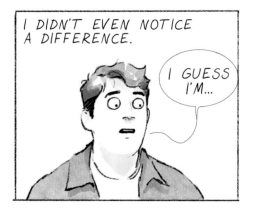

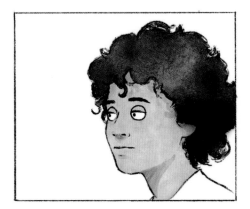

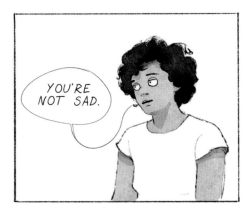

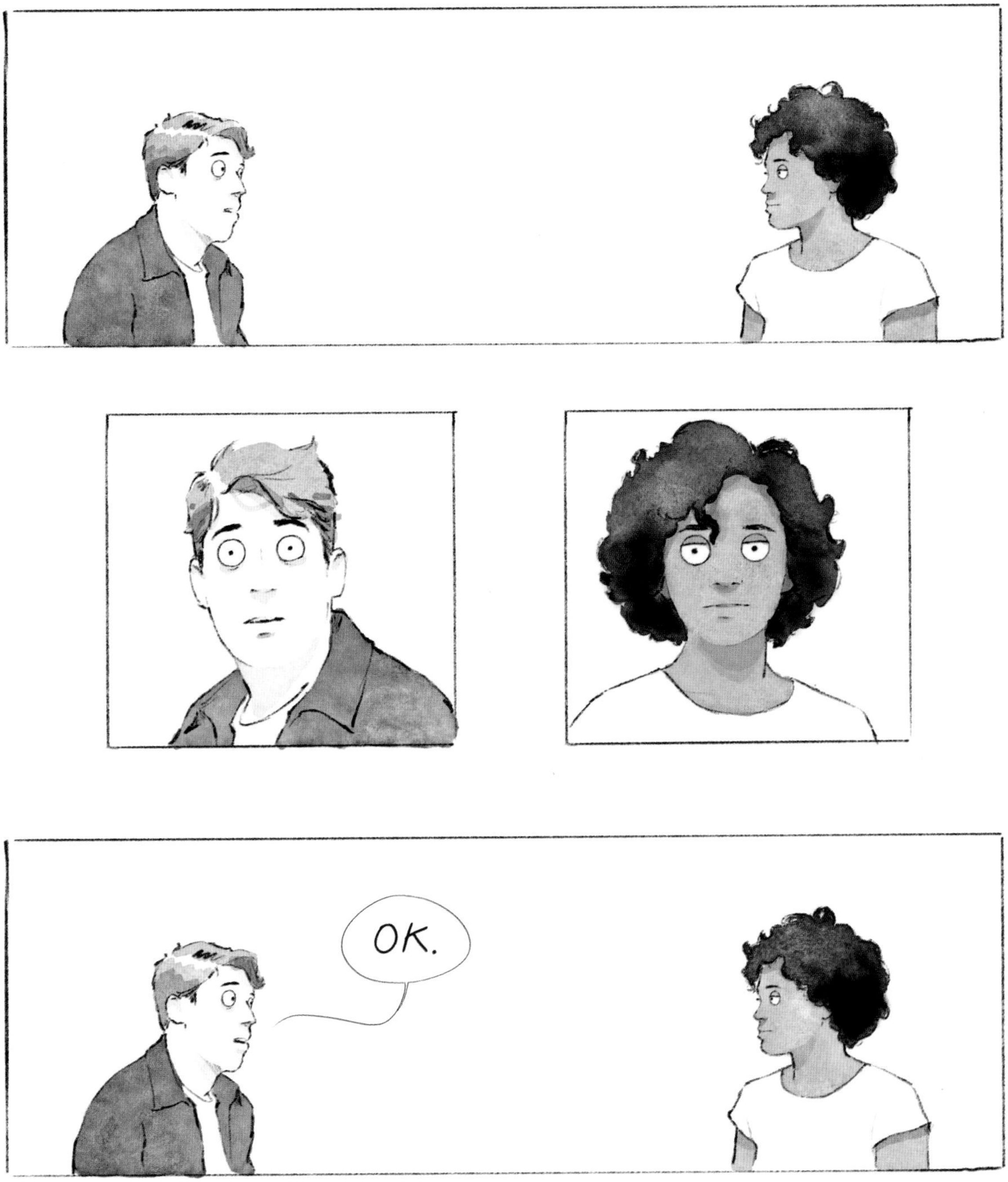
OK.

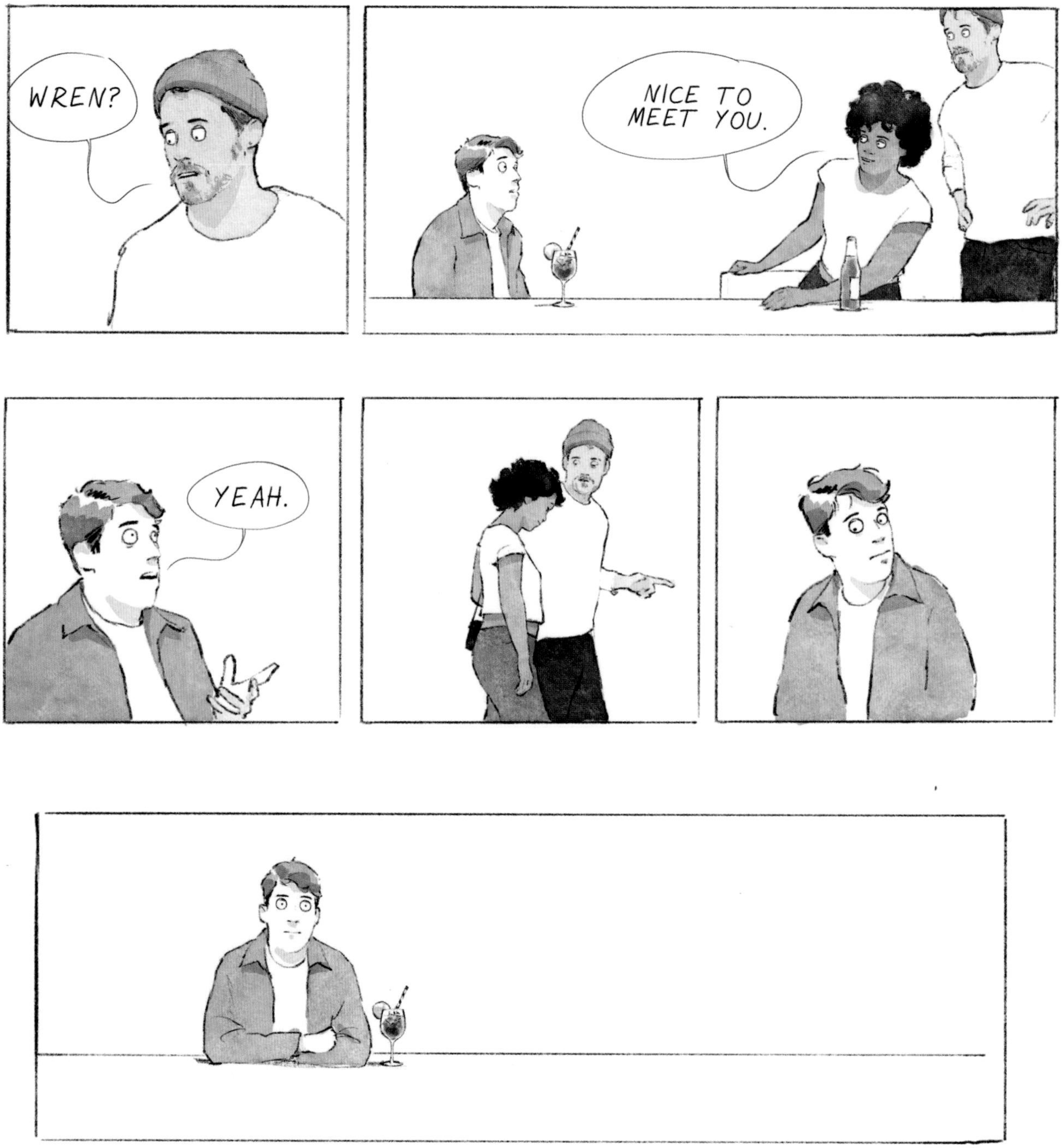
WREN?
NICE TO MEET YOU.
YEAH.

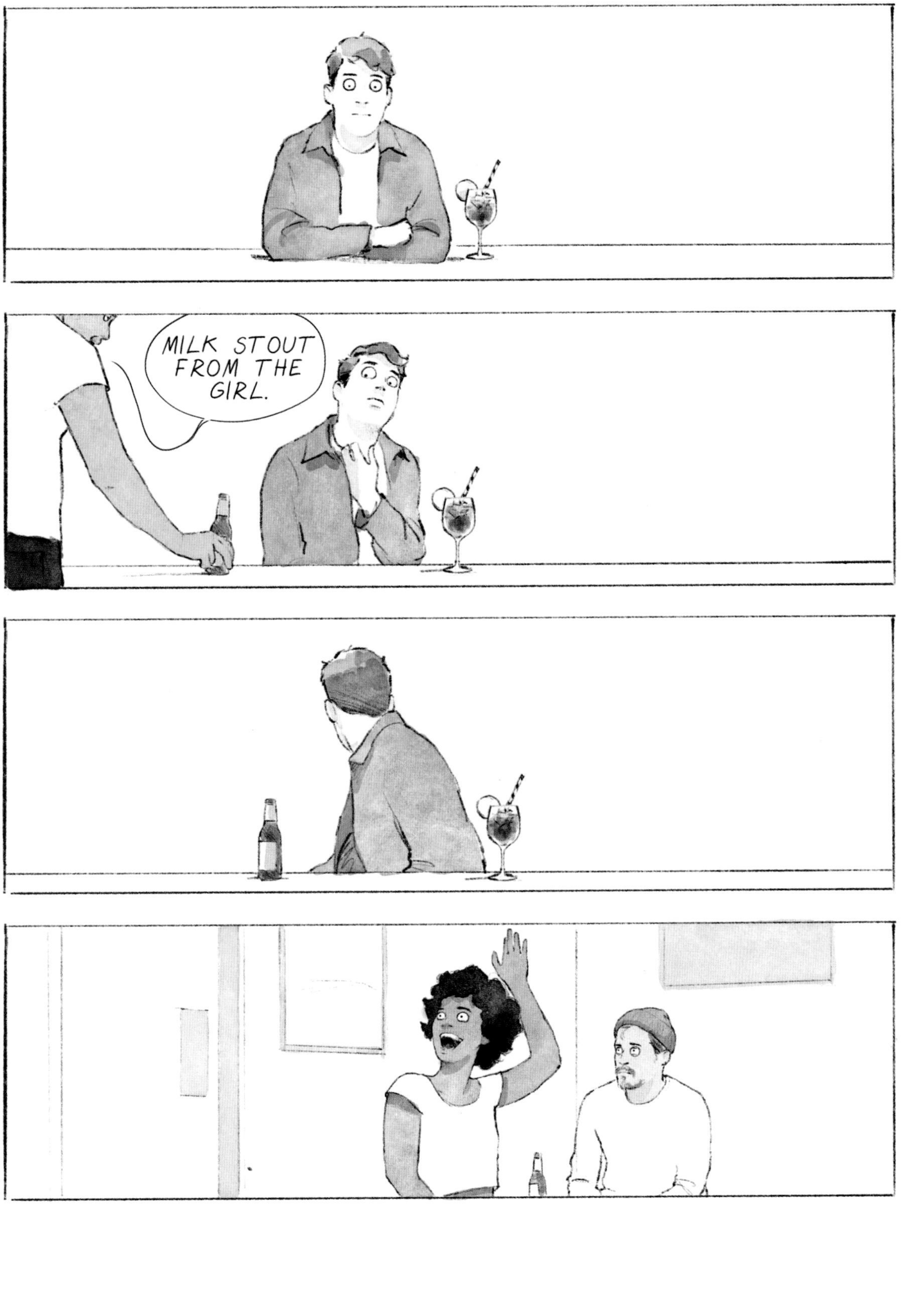
MILK STOUT FROM THE GIRL.

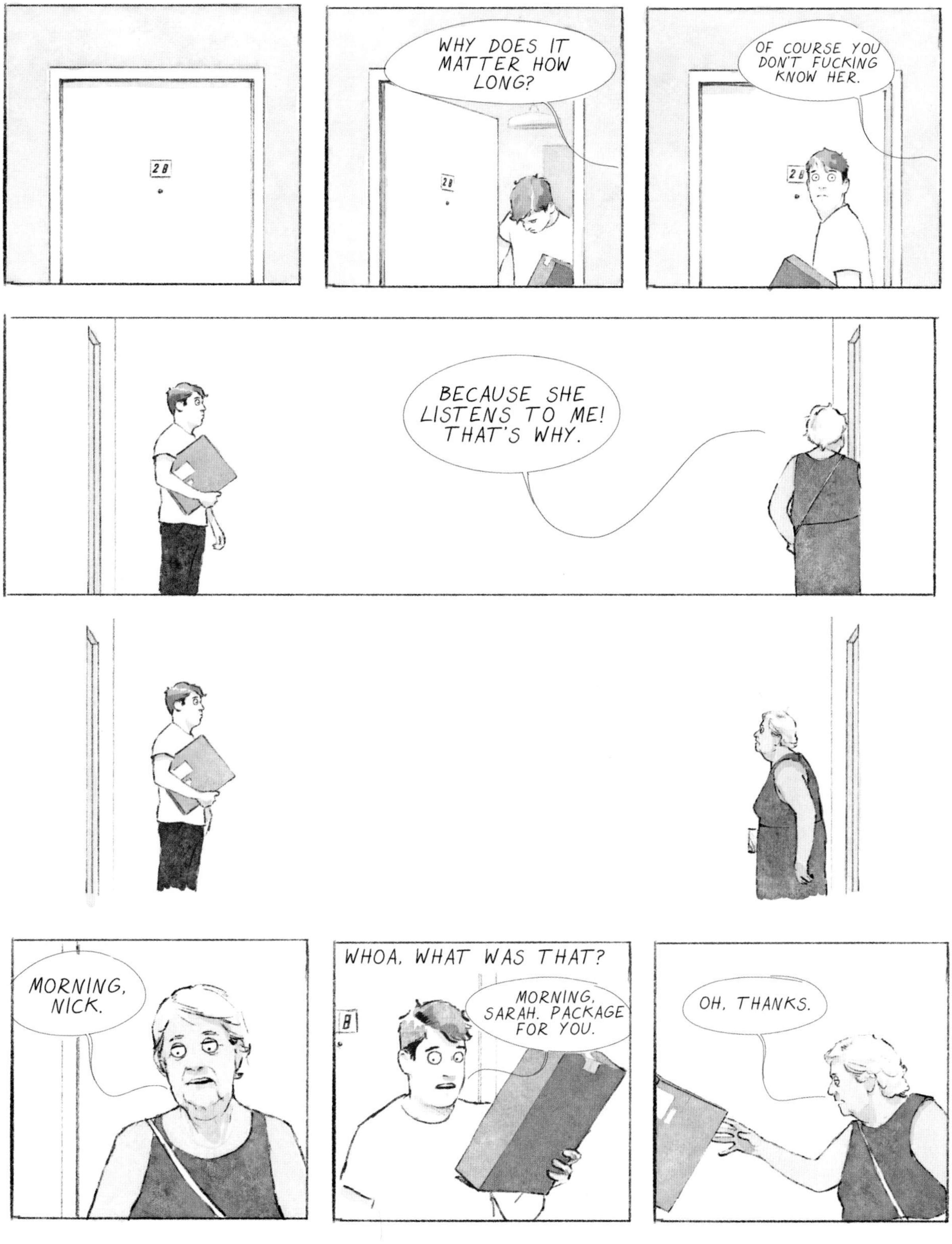

WHY DOES IT MATTER HOW LONG?
OF COURSE YOU DON'T FUCKING KNOW HER.
BECAUSE SHE LISTENS TO ME! THAT'S WHY.
MORNING, NICK.
WHOA, WHAT WAS THAT?
MORNING, SARAH. PACKAGE FOR YOU.
OH, THANKS.

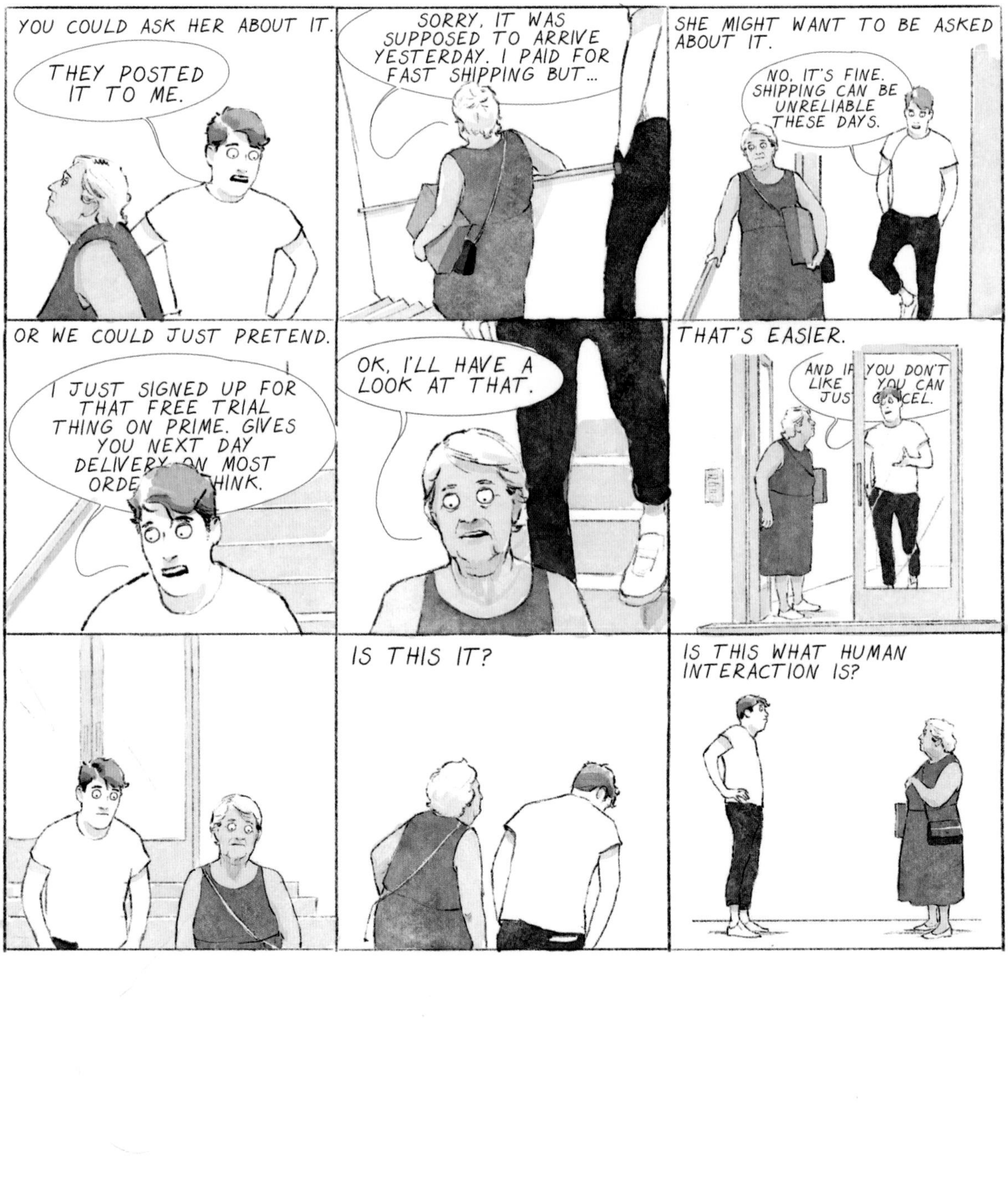
YOU COULD ASK HER ABOUT IT.
THEY POSTED IT TO ME.
SORRY, IT WAS SUPPOSED TO ARRIVE YESTERDAY. I PAID FOR FAST SHIPPING BUT...
SHE MIGHT WANT TO BE ASKED ABOUT IT.
NO, IT'S FINE. SHIPPING CAN BE UNRELIABLE THESE DAYS.
OR WE COULD JUST PRETEND.
I JUST SIGNED UP FOR THAT FREE TRIAL THING ON PRIME. GIVES YOU NEXT DAY DELIVERY ON MOST ORDERS I THINK.
OK, I'LL HAVE A LOOK AT THAT.
THAT'S EASIER.
AND IF YOU DON'T LIKE YOU CAN JUST CANCEL.
IS THIS IT?
IS THIS WHAT HUMAN INTERACTION IS?

SHE MIGHT BE WANT TO BE ASKED ABOUT IT.

SEE YER.

Exit

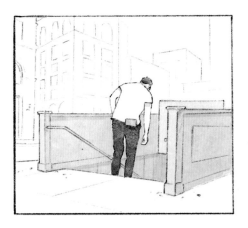

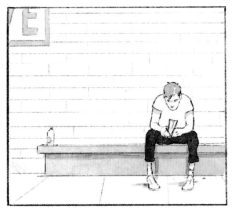

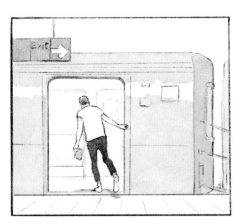

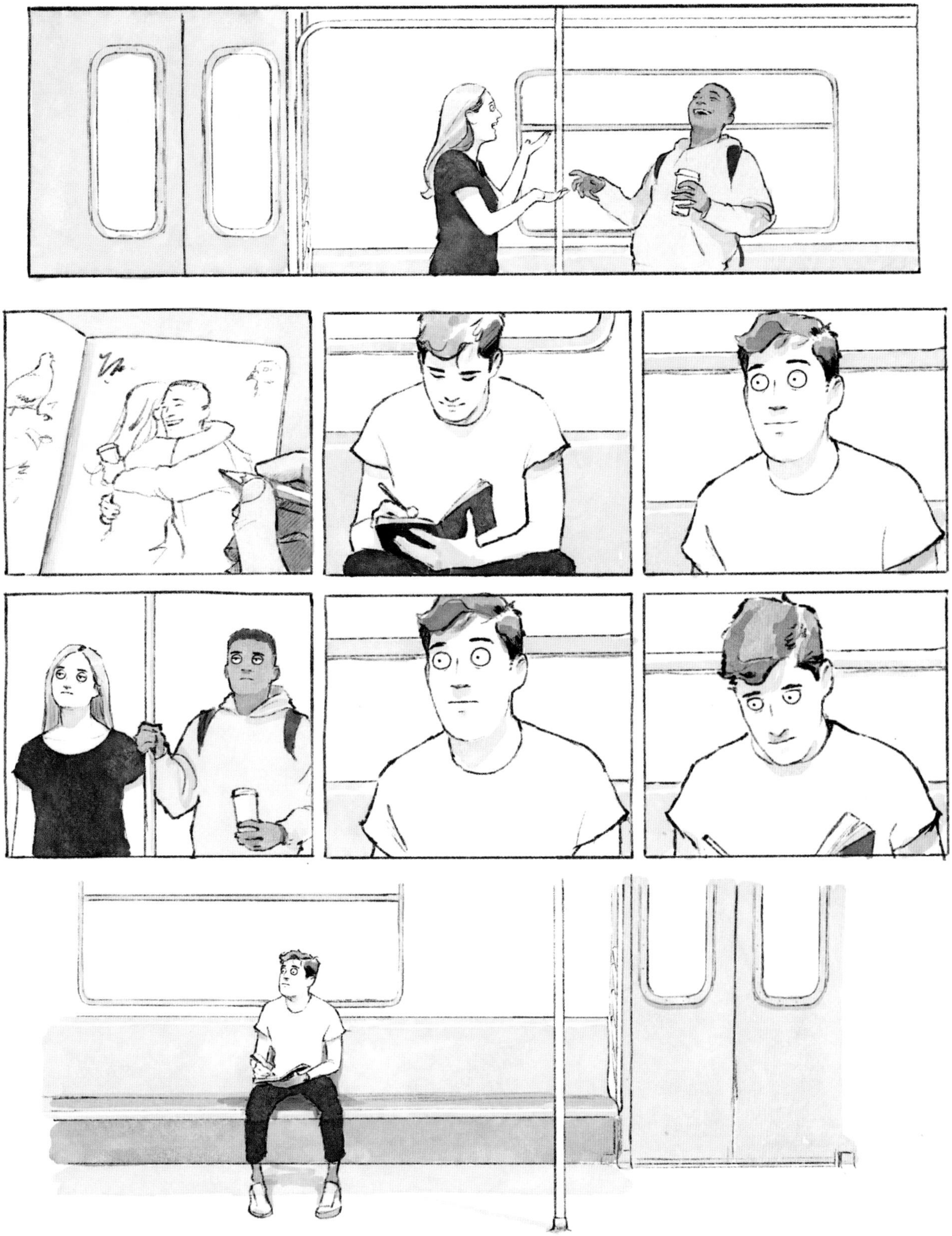

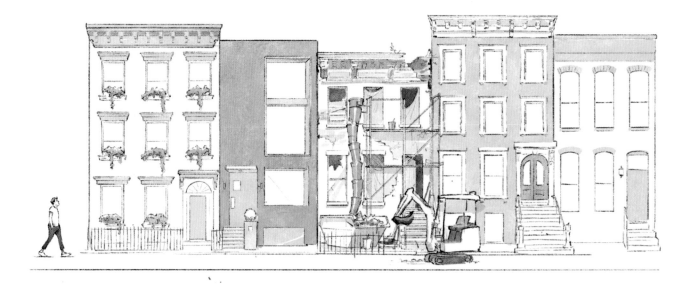

MUM?

WWHHEEEEEEEE

WWHHEEEEEEEE

EEEEEEEE

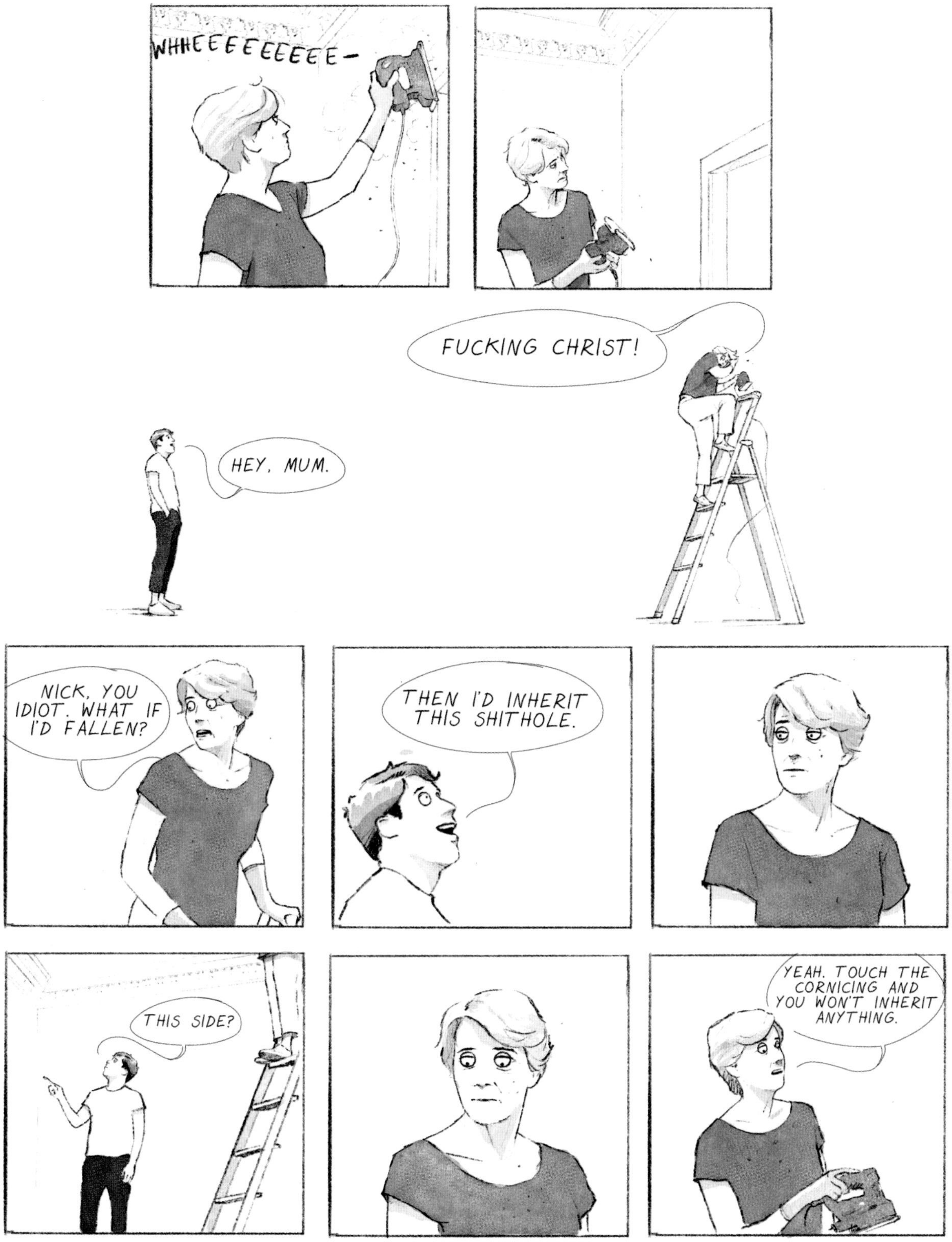
WHHEEEEEEEEE-
FUCKING CHRIST!
HEY, MUM.
NICK, YOU IDIOT. WHAT IF I'D FALLEN?
THEN I'D INHERIT THIS SHITHOLE.
THIS SIDE?
YEAH. TOUCH THE CORNICING AND YOU WON'T INHERIT ANYTHING.

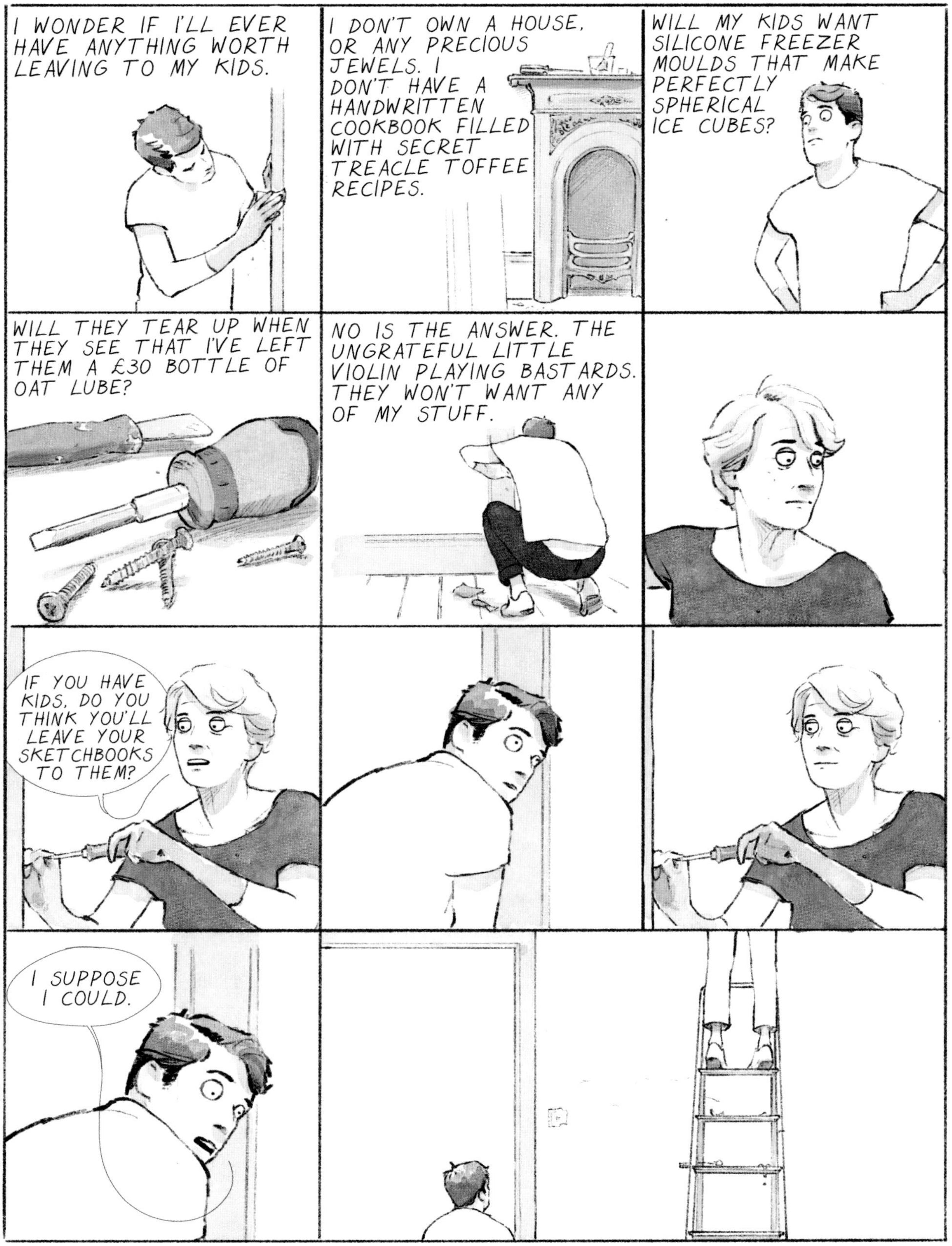
I WONDER IF I'LL EVER HAVE ANYTHING WORTH LEAVING TO MY KIDS.
I DON'T OWN A HOUSE, OR ANY PRECIOUS JEWELS. I DON'T HAVE A HANDWRITTEN COOKBOOK FILLED WITH SECRET TREACLE TOFFEE RECIPES.
WILL MY KIDS WANT SILICONE FREEZER MOULDS THAT MAKE PERFECTLY SPHERICAL ICE CUBES?
WILL THEY TEAR UP WHEN THEY SEE THAT I'VE LEFT THEM A £30 BOTTLE OF OAT LUBE?
NO IS THE ANSWER. THE UNGRATEFUL LITTLE VIOLIN PLAYING BASTARDS. THEY WON'T WANT ANY OF MY STUFF.
IF YOU HAVE KIDS, DO YOU THINK YOU'LL LEAVE YOUR SKETCHBOOKS TO THEM?
I SUPPOSE I COULD.

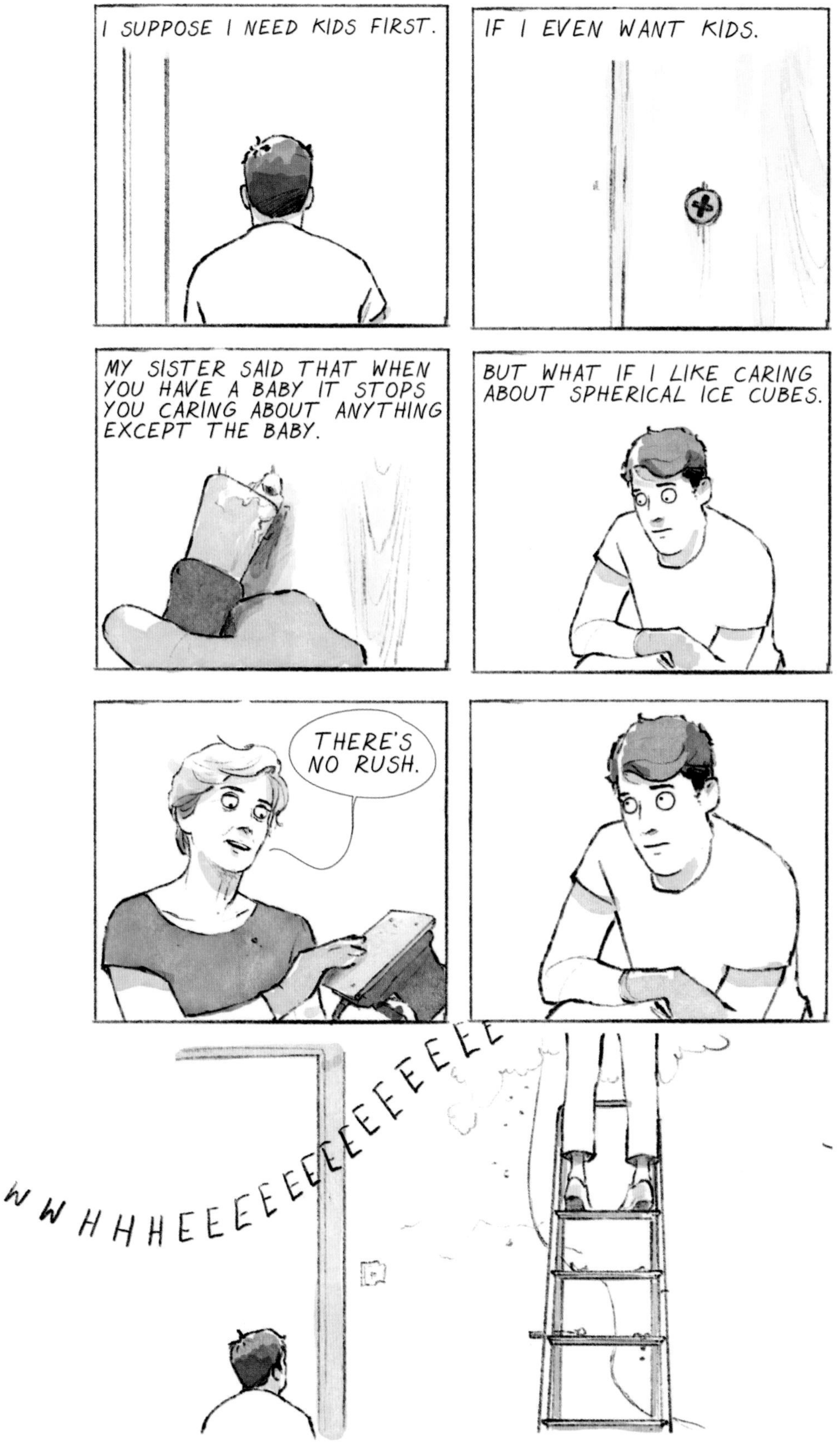
I SUPPOSE I NEED KIDS FIRST.
IF I EVEN WANT KIDS.
MY SISTER SAID THAT WHEN YOU HAVE A BABY IT STOPS YOU CARING ABOUT ANYTHING EXCEPT THE BABY.
BUT WHAT IF I LIKE CARING ABOUT SPHERICAL ICE CUBES.
THERE'S NO RUSH.
WWHHHEEEEEEEEEEEEEEEEE

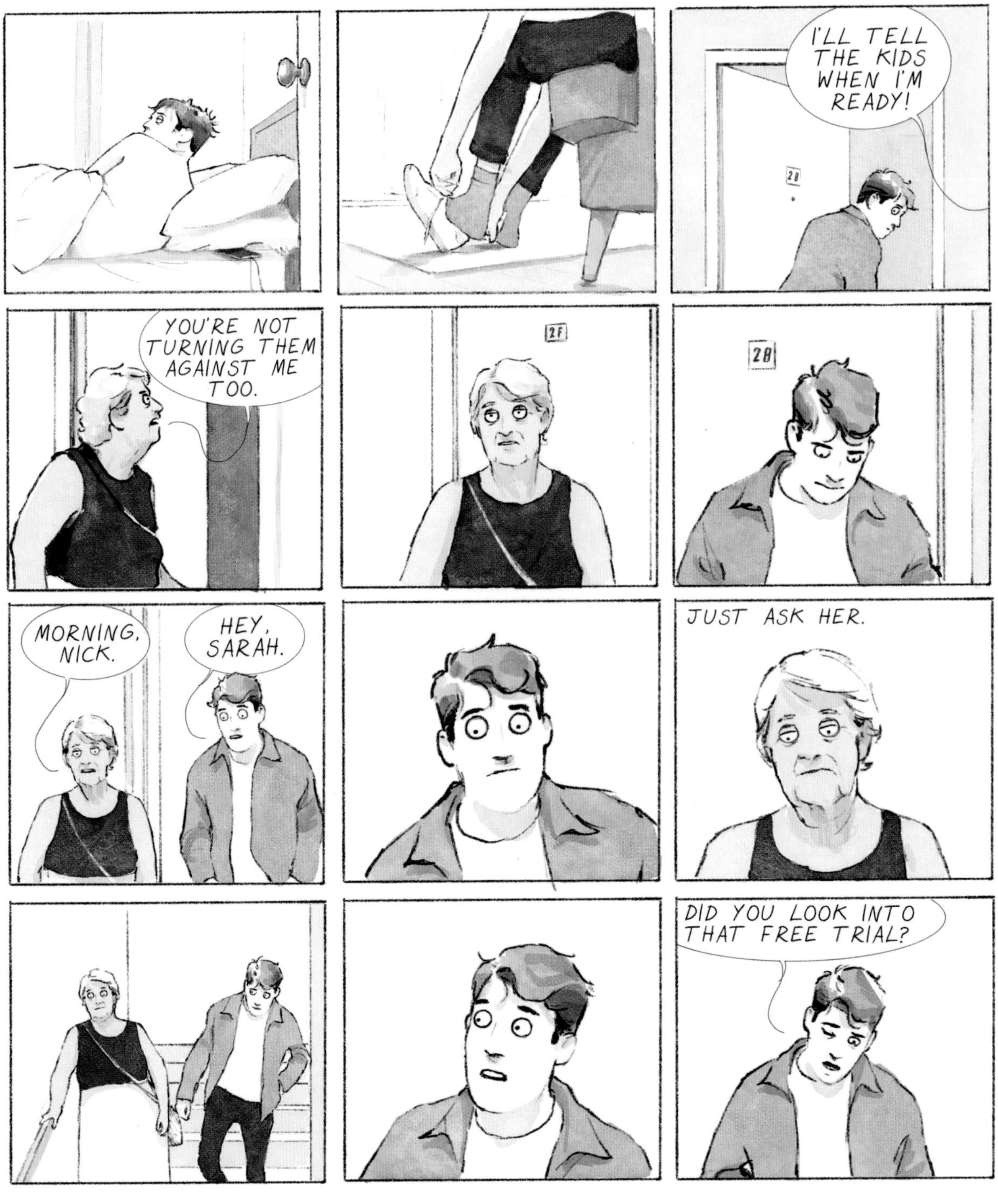
I'LL TELL THE KIDS WHEN I'M READY!
YOU'RE NOT TURNING THEM AGAINST ME TOO.
2F
2B
MORNING, NICK.
HEY, SARAH.
JUST ASK HER.
DID YOU LOOK INTO THAT FREE TRIAL?

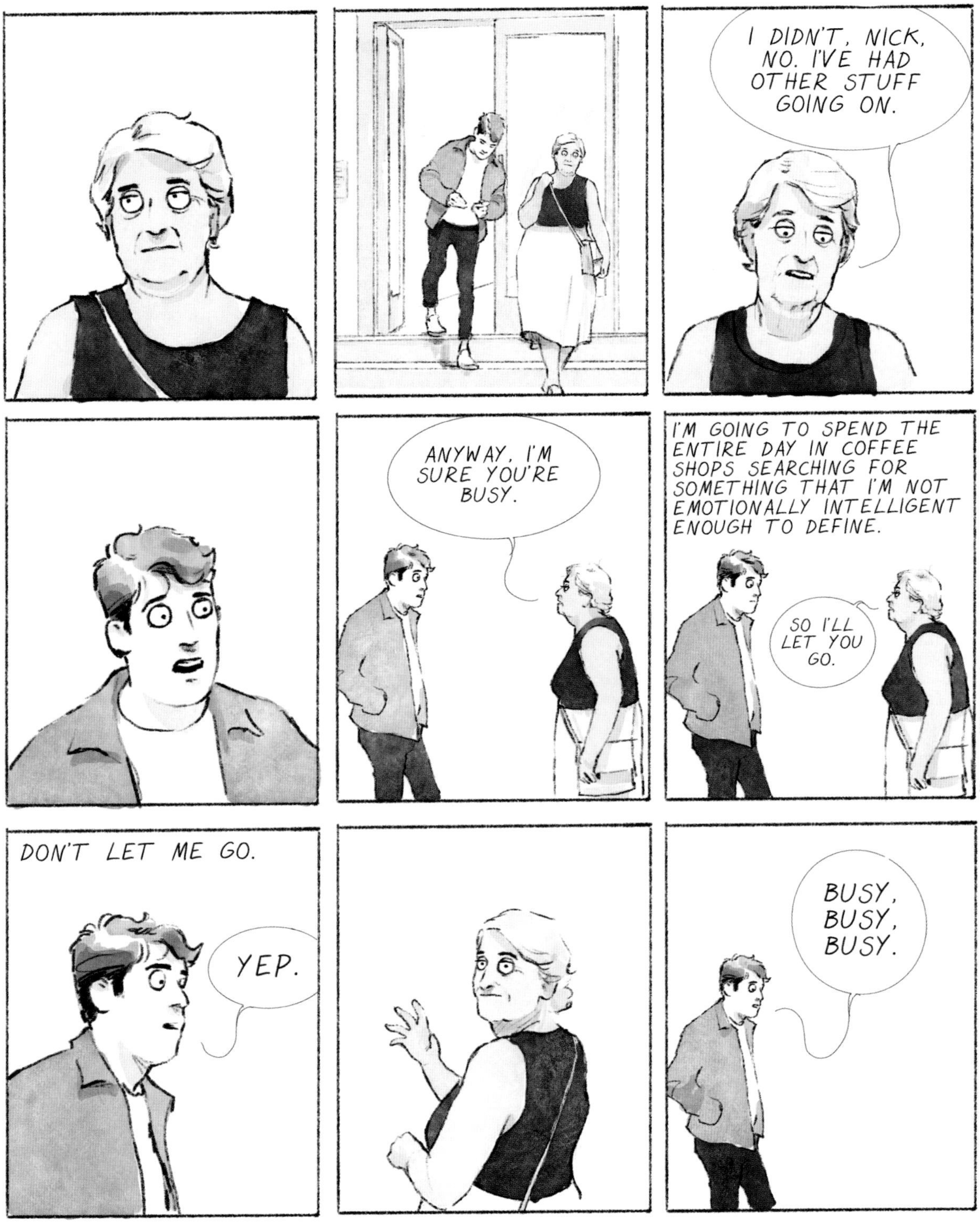
I DIDN'T, NICK, NO. I'VE HAD OTHER STUFF GOING ON.
ANYWAY, I'M SURE YOU'RE BUSY.
I'M GOING TO SPEND THE ENTIRE DAY IN COFFEE SHOPS SEARCHING FOR SOMETHING THAT I'M NOT EMOTIONALLY INTELLIGENT ENOUGH TO DEFINE.
SO I'LL LET YOU GO.
DON'T LET ME GO.
YEP.
BUSY, BUSY, BUSY.

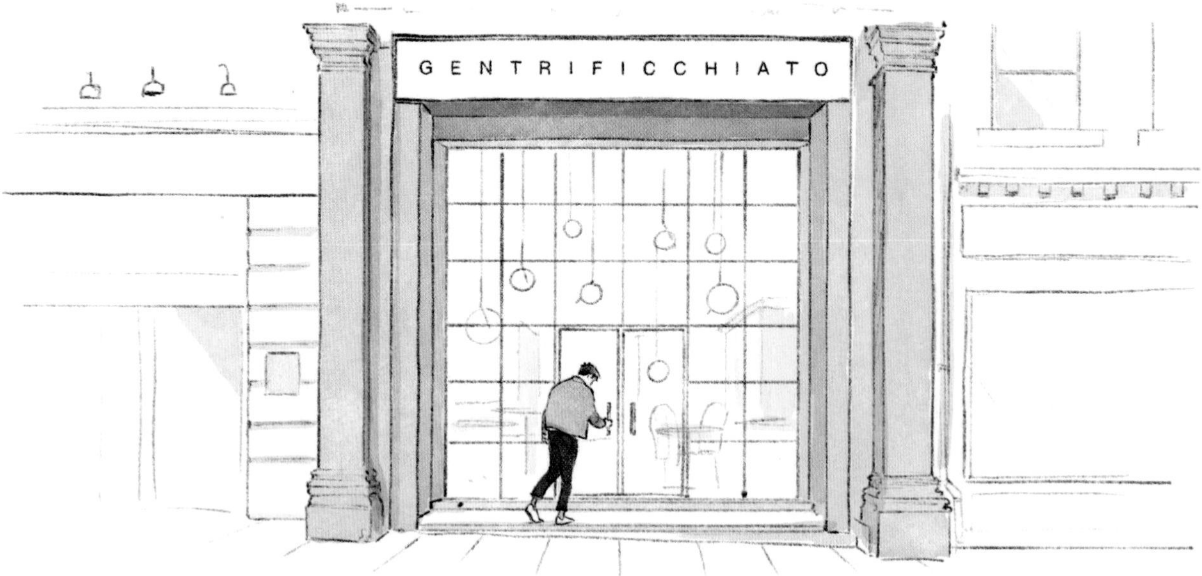
GENTRIFICCHIATO

'GENTRIFICCHIATO' OFFERS AN UNWELCOMING AMBIANCE AND TWELVE VARIETIES OF MILK, NARY ONE FROM AN UDDER. IT IS MANAGED/HAUNTED BY A COLLECTION OF TIMOTHEES CHALAMET WHO RECOMMEND CACTUS MILK AND THEN REFUSE TO BESMIRCH THE COFFEE WITH IT.

THE HOUSE BREW IS A MISCHIEVOUS BLEND WITH NOTES OF FERMENTED APRICOT AND POLISHED CONCRETE.

PRICE? HARROWING.

WIFI PASSWORD? EdisonBulbFilament

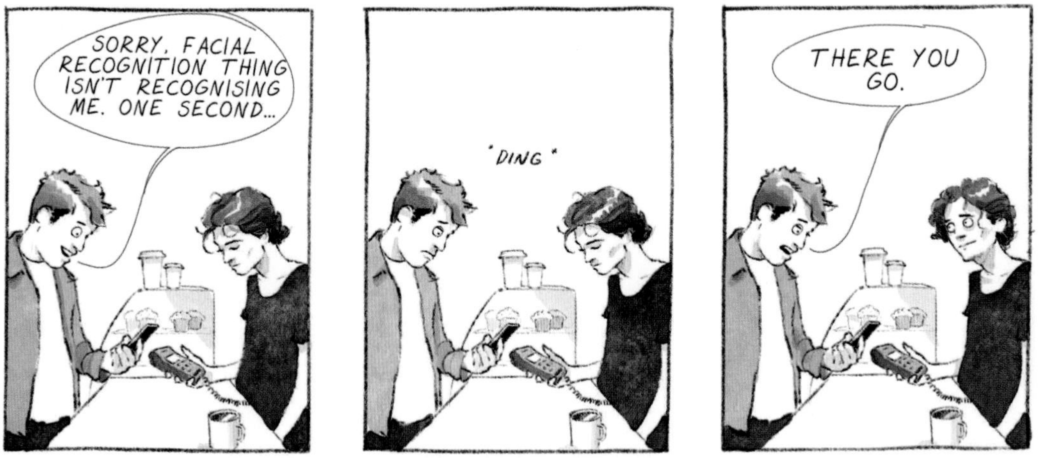
SORRY, FACIAL RECOGNITION THING ISN'T RECOGNISING ME. ONE SECOND...
DING
THERE YOU GO.

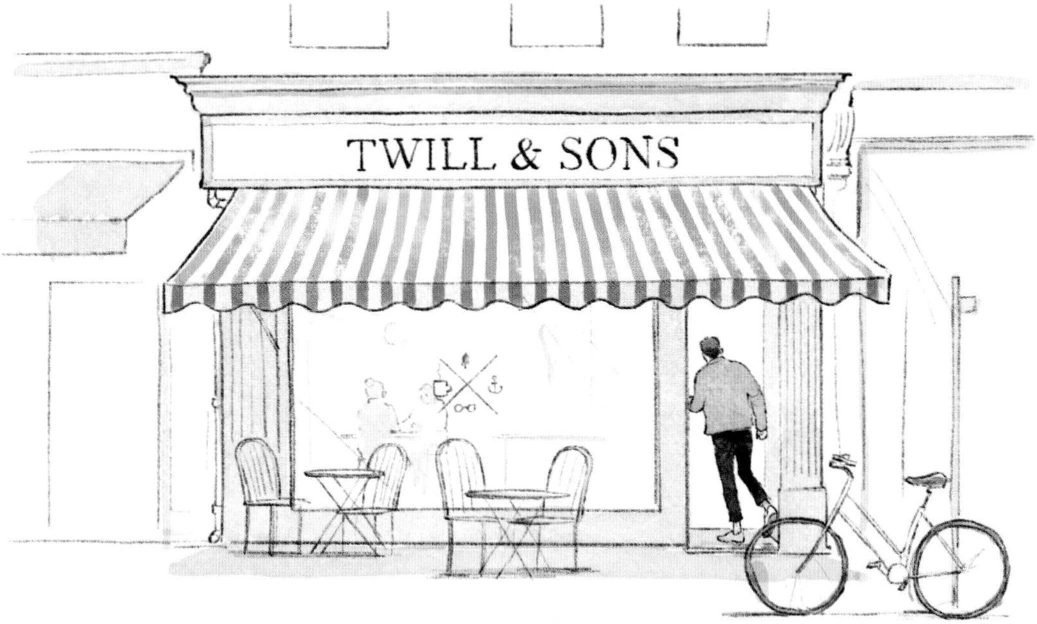
TWILL & SONS

NEXT UP IS 'TWILL & SONS'. EITHER A COFFEE SHOP OR A BARBERS. BUT IT COULD ALSO BE THE MOVIE 'DUNKIRK'. WHO IS TWILL? JE NE SAIS PAS. WHO ARE THE SONS? PERHAPS THEY ARE THE TRANSLUCENT STABLE BOYS BEHIND THE COUNTER WHO LEAK COLD BREW FROM CRYSTAL TANKS. THEIR HAIR IS WET AND LIKE NEW BORN FISH, THEIR TWITCHING ORGANS ARE CLEARLY VISIBLE THROUGH THEIR PAPER SKIN.

THE HOUSE BLEND IS AGED IN THE CAVITIES OF RECLAIMED STRING INSTRUMENTS AND THEIR CROISSANTS ASK NOT WHAT THEY CAN DO FOR YOU, BUT WHAT YOU CAN DO FOR THEM.

NO WIFI. WHICH IS FINE.

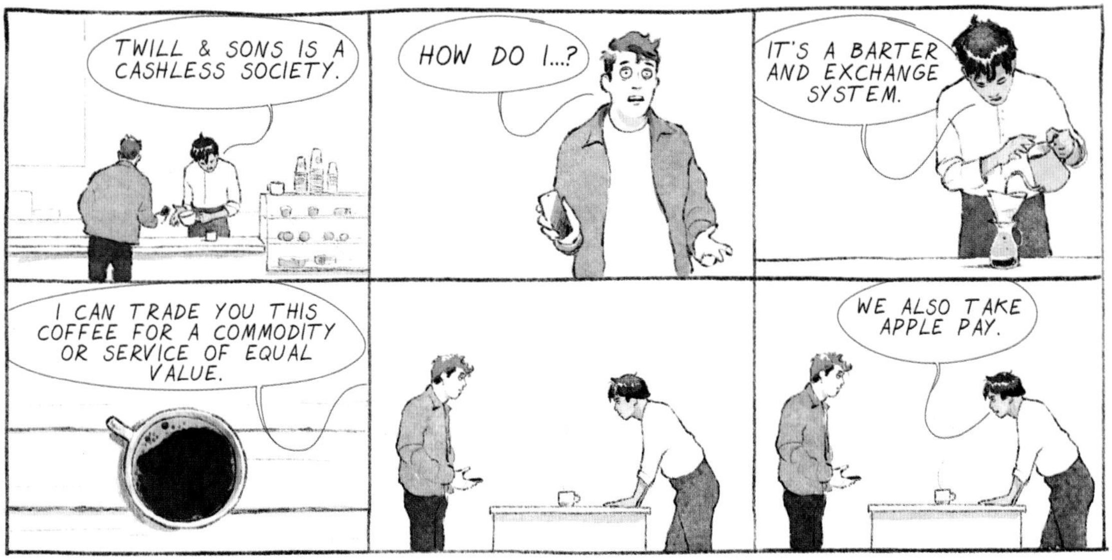
TWILL & SONS IS A CASHLESS SOCIETY.
HOW DO I...?
IT'S A BARTER AND EXCHANGE SYSTEM.
I CAN TRADE YOU THIS COFFEE FOR A COMMODITY OR SERVICE OF EQUAL VALUE.
WE ALSO TAKE APPLE PAY.

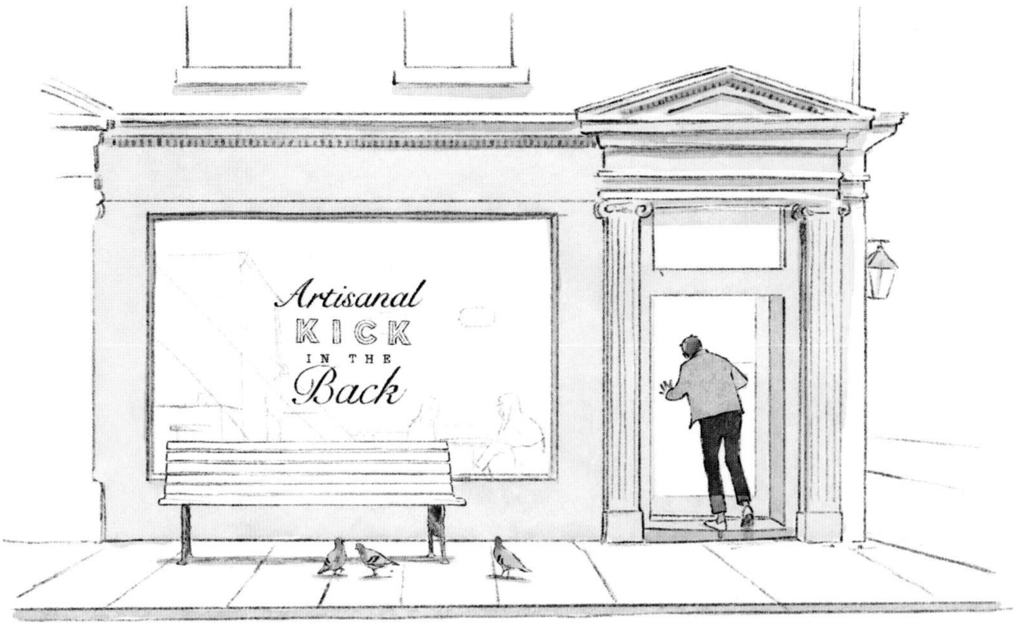
Artisanal
KICK
IN THE
Back

'ARTISANAL KICK IN THE BACK' HAS EXCEPTIONAL WIFI AND ONLY ONE POWER OUTLET: A TWISTED GAME DESIGNED BY THE OWNERS TO TURN DESPERATE WRITERS AGAINST EACH OTHER. THE COFFEE IS FREE AND INSTEAD THEY CHARGE BY THE NUMBER OF PAGES YOU WRITE FOR YOUR SCREENPLAY.

'ARTISANAL KICK IN THE BACK' OPERATES AT A STAGGERING LOSS.

WIFI PASSWORD: DialogueIsNotForExposition2007.

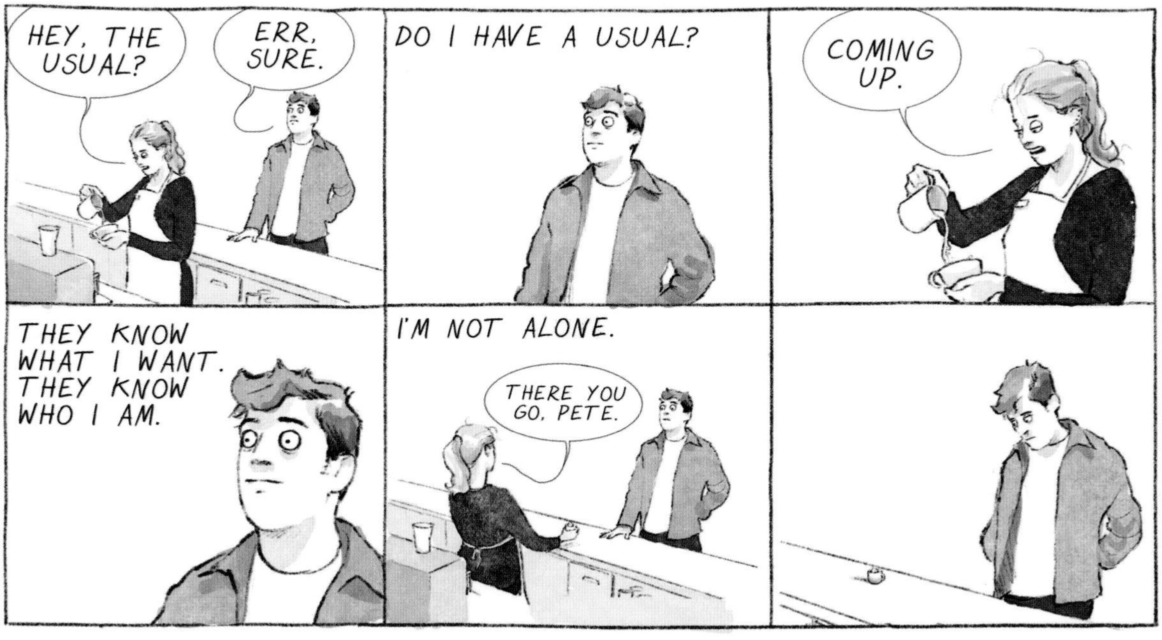
HEY, THE USUAL?
ERR, SURE.
DO I HAVE A USUAL?
COMING UP.
THEY KNOW WHAT I WANT. THEY KNOW WHO I AM.
I'M NOT ALONE.
THERE YOU GO, PETE.

I TEND TO WORK
IN PUBLIC PLACES.

PARTLY TO ESCAPE
THE PORN IN MY
APARTMENT.

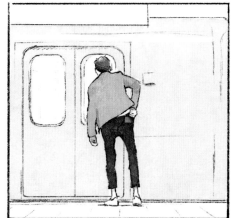

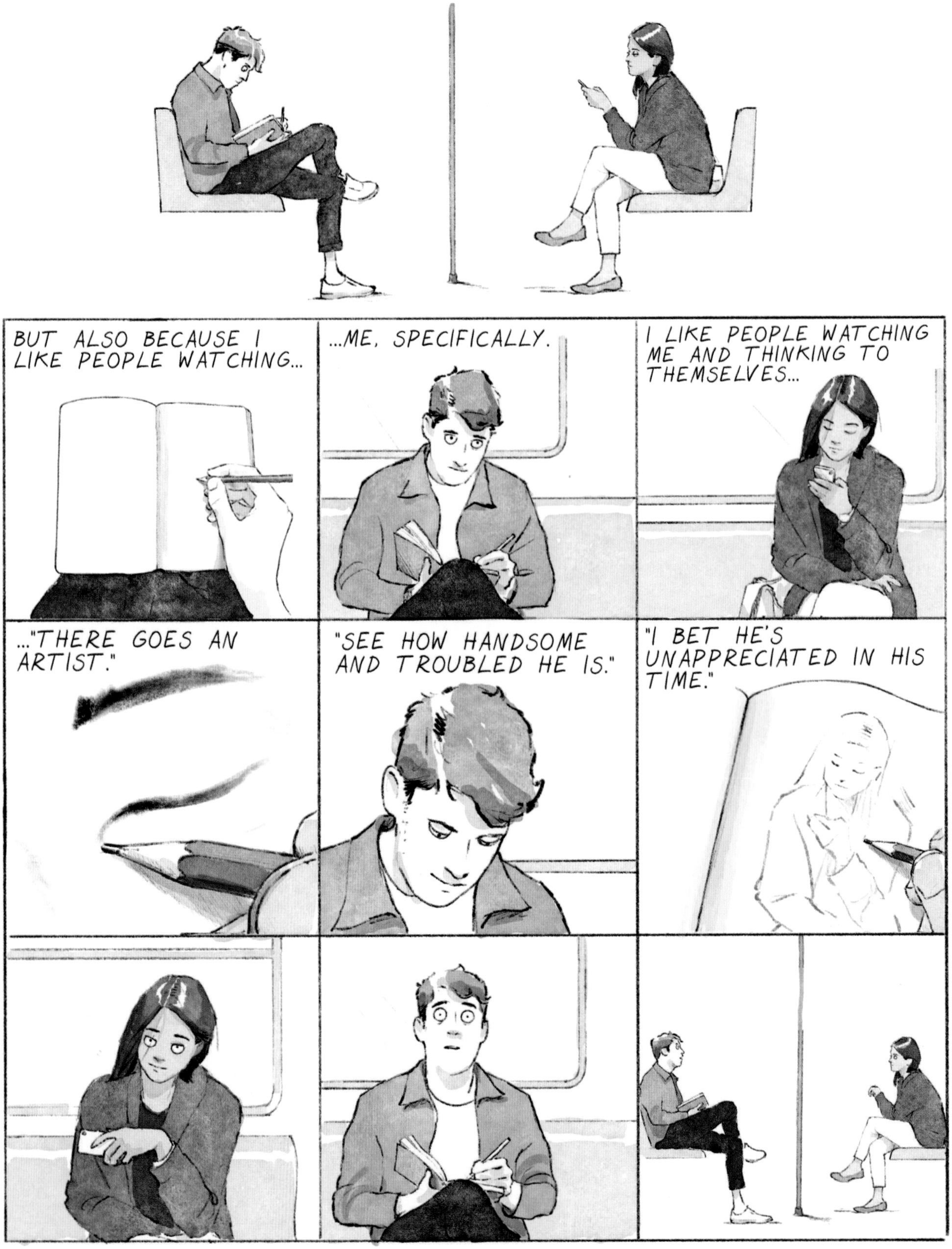
BUT ALSO BECAUSE I LIKE PEOPLE WATCHING...
...ME, SPECIFICALLY.
I LIKE PEOPLE WATCHING ME AND THINKING TO THEMSELVES...
..."THERE GOES AN ARTIST."
"SEE HOW HANDSOME AND TROUBLED HE IS."
"I BET HE'S UNAPPRECIATED IN HIS TIME."

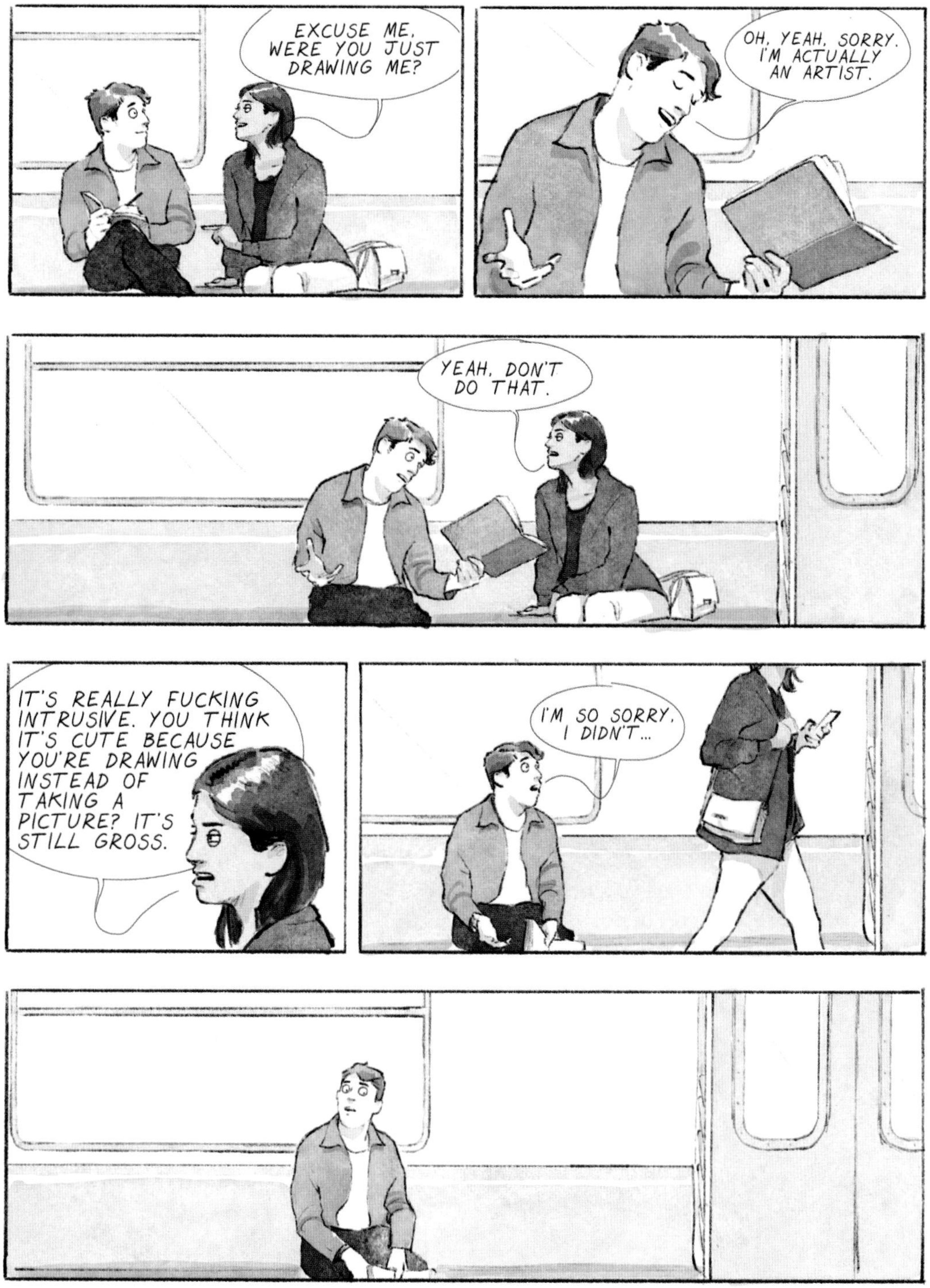
EXCUSE ME. WERE YOU JUST DRAWING ME?
OH, YEAH, SORRY. I'M ACTUALLY AN ARTIST.
YEAH, DON'T DO THAT.
IT'S REALLY FUCKING INTRUSIVE. YOU THINK IT'S CUTE BECAUSE YOU'RE DRAWING INSTEAD OF TAKING A PICTURE? IT'S STILL GROSS.
I'M SO SORRY, I DIDN'T...

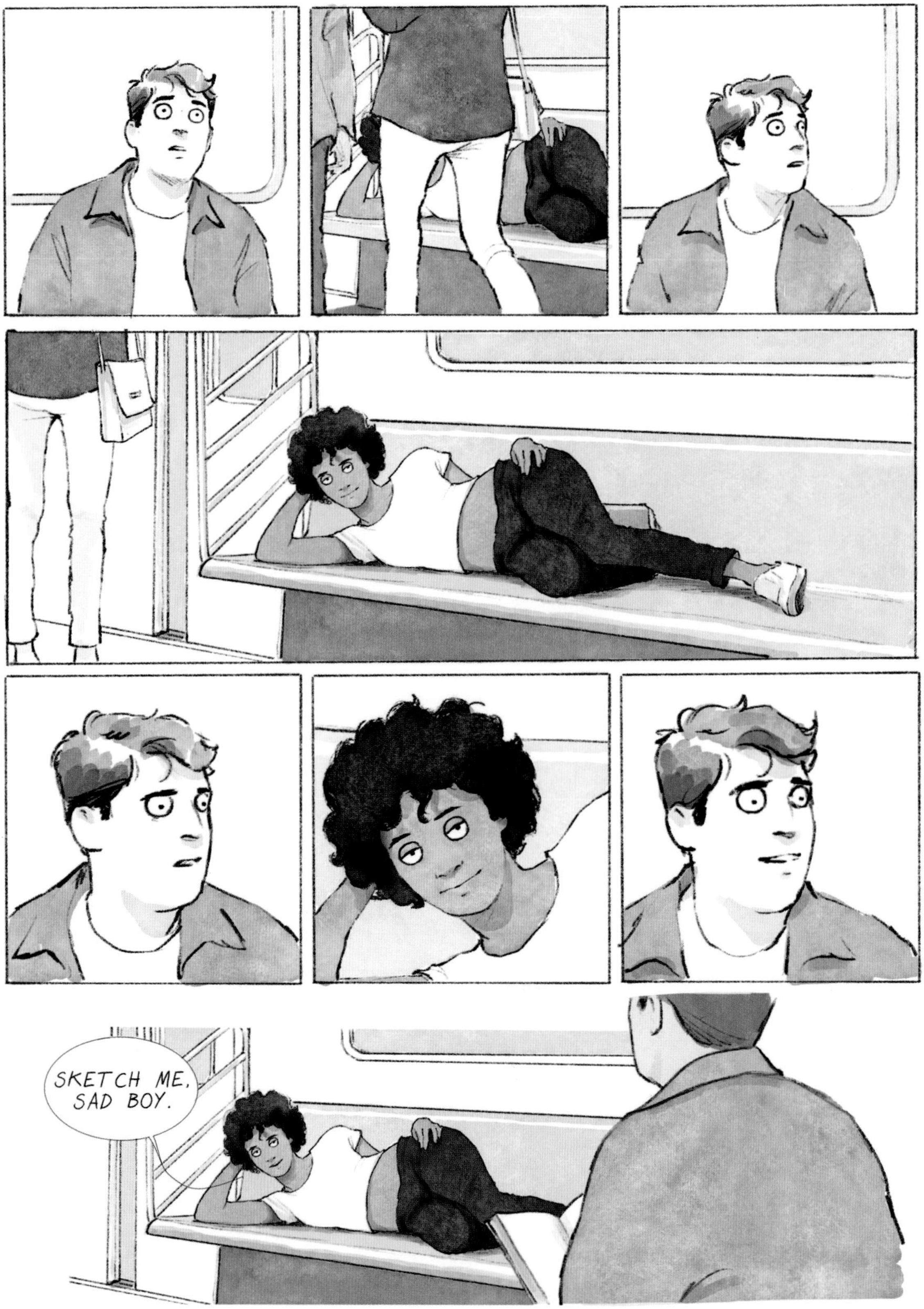
SKETCH ME, SAD BOY.

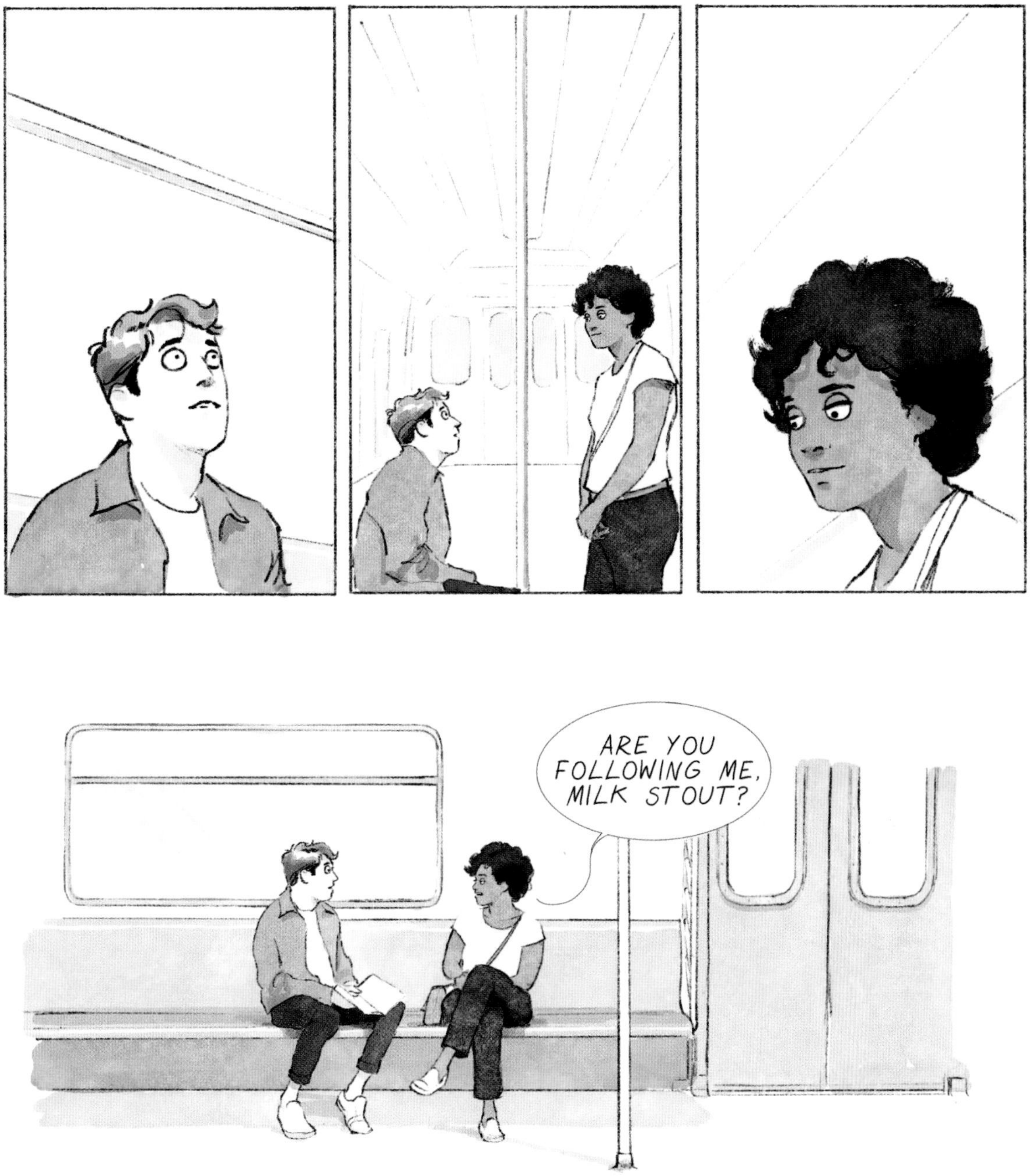
ARE YOU FOLLOWING ME, MILK STOUT?

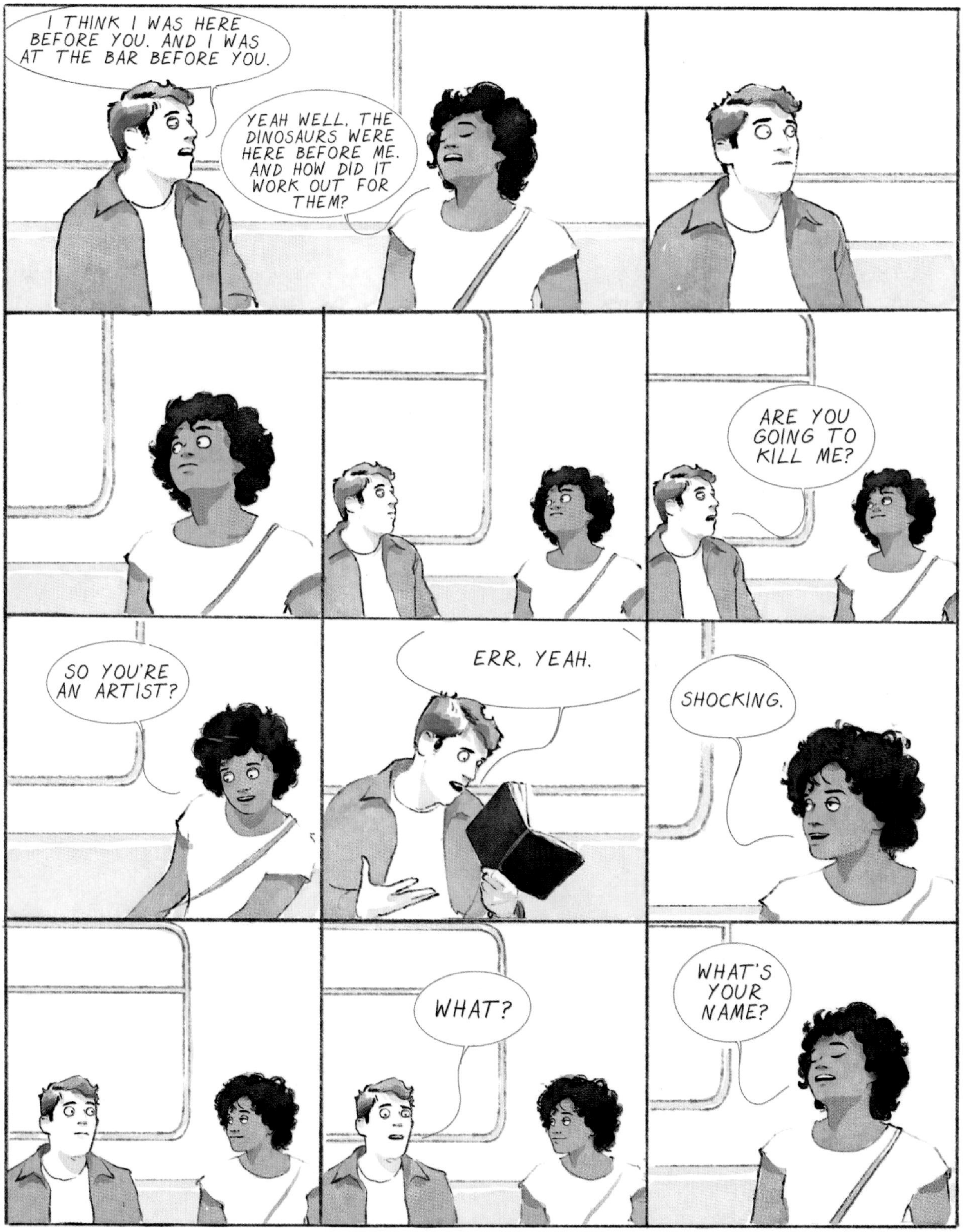
I THINK I WAS HERE BEFORE YOU. AND I WAS AT THE BAR BEFORE YOU.
YEAH WELL, THE DINOSAURS WERE HERE BEFORE ME. AND HOW DID IT WORK OUT FOR THEM?
ARE YOU GOING TO KILL ME?
SO YOU'RE AN ARTIST?
ERR, YEAH.
SHOCKING.
WHAT?
WHAT'S YOUR NAME?

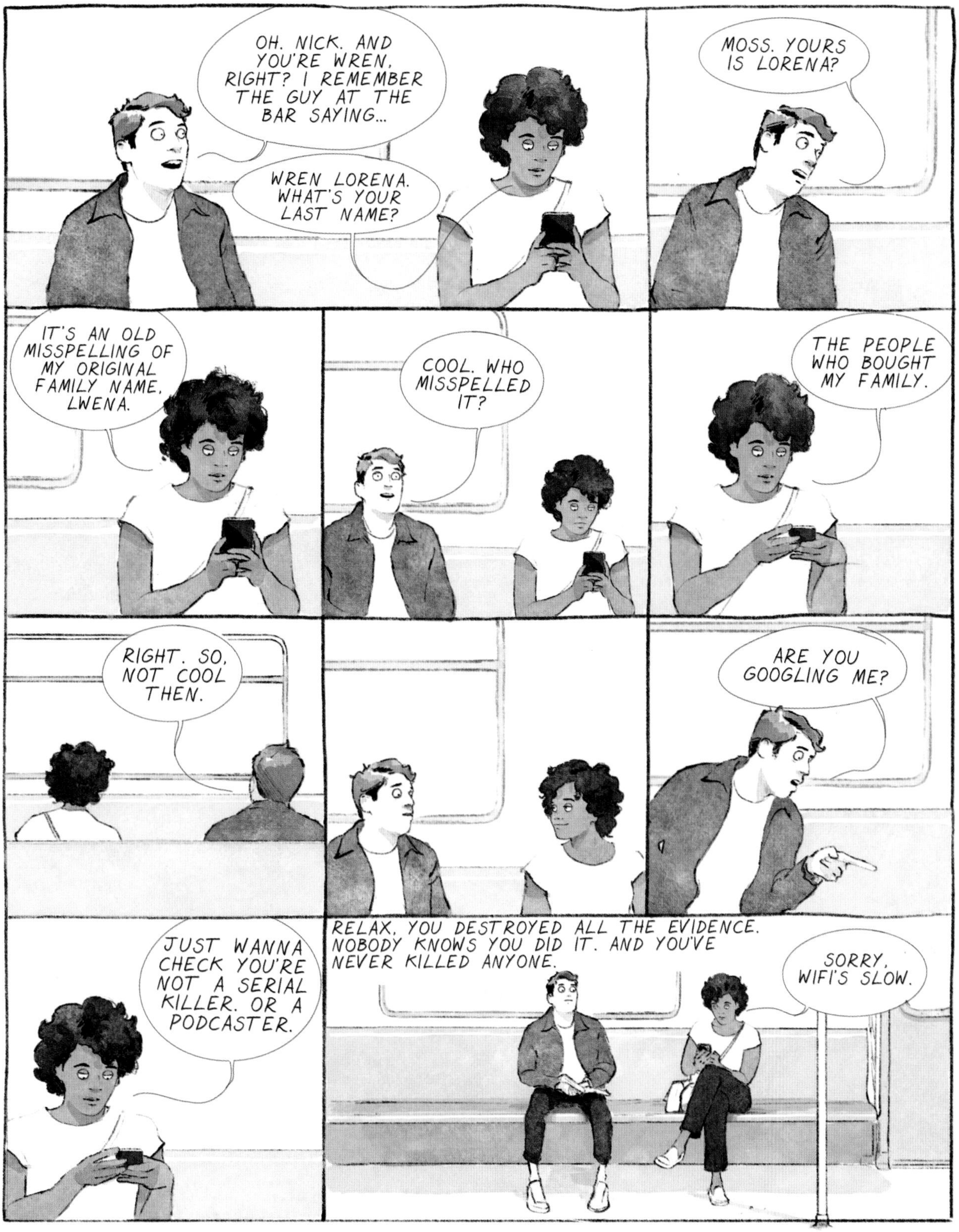
OH. NICK. AND YOU'RE WREN, RIGHT? I REMEMBER THE GUY AT THE BAR SAYING...
WREN LORENA. WHAT'S YOUR LAST NAME?
MOSS. YOURS IS LORENA?
IT'S AN OLD MISSPELLING OF MY ORIGINAL FAMILY NAME, LWENA.
COOL. WHO MISSPELLED IT?
THE PEOPLE WHO BOUGHT MY FAMILY.
RIGHT. SO, NOT COOL THEN.
ARE YOU GOOGLING ME?
JUST WANNA CHECK YOU'RE NOT A SERIAL KILLER. OR A PODCASTER.
RELAX. YOU DESTROYED ALL THE EVIDENCE. NOBODY KNOWS YOU DID IT. AND YOU'VE NEVER KILLED ANYONE.
SORRY, WIFI'S SLOW.

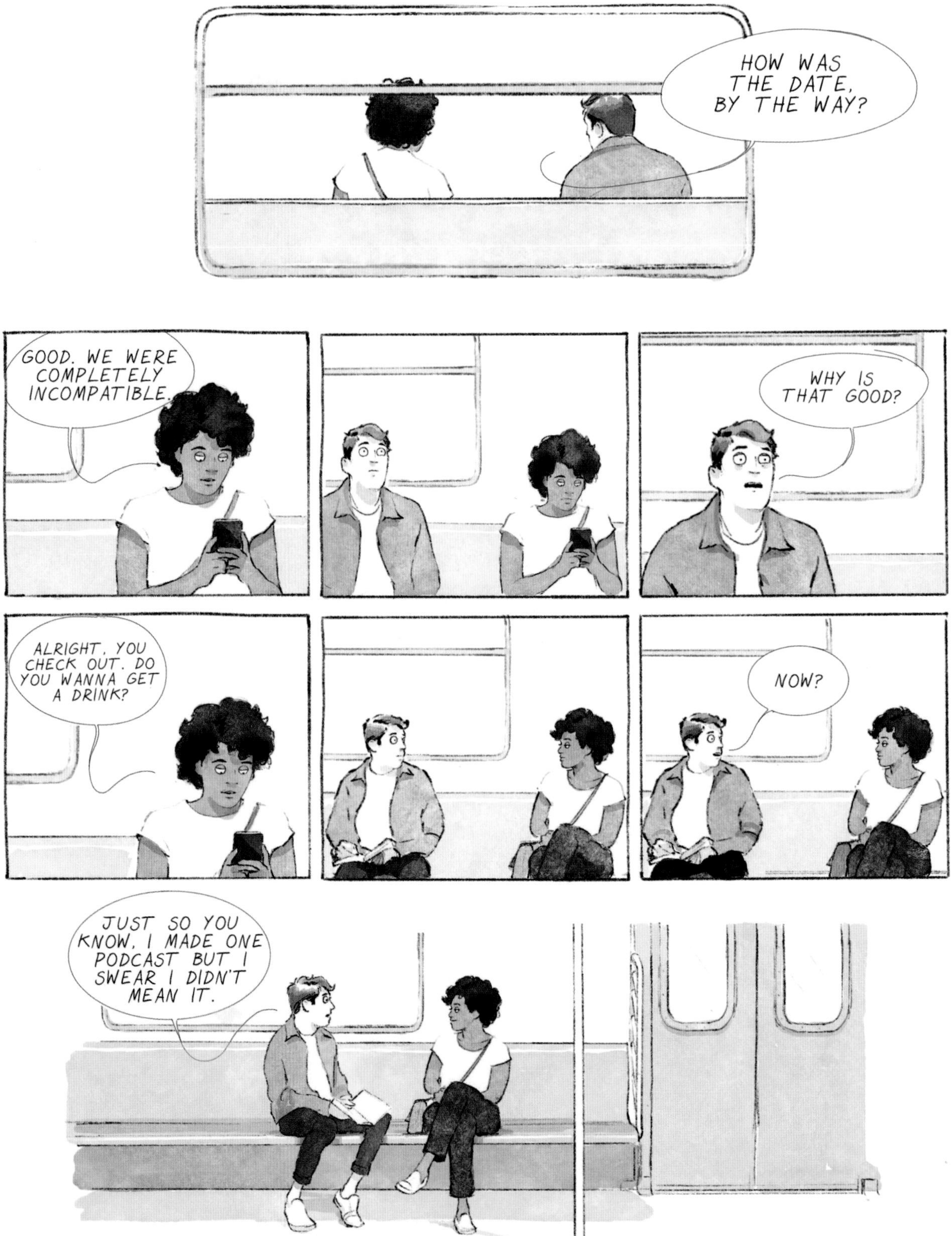
HOW WAS THE DATE, BY THE WAY?
GOOD. WE WERE COMPLETELY INCOMPATIBLE.
WHY IS THAT GOOD?
ALRIGHT, YOU CHECK OUT. DO YOU WANNA GET A DRINK?
NOW?
JUST SO YOU KNOW, I MADE ONE PODCAST BUT I SWEAR I DIDN'T MEAN IT.

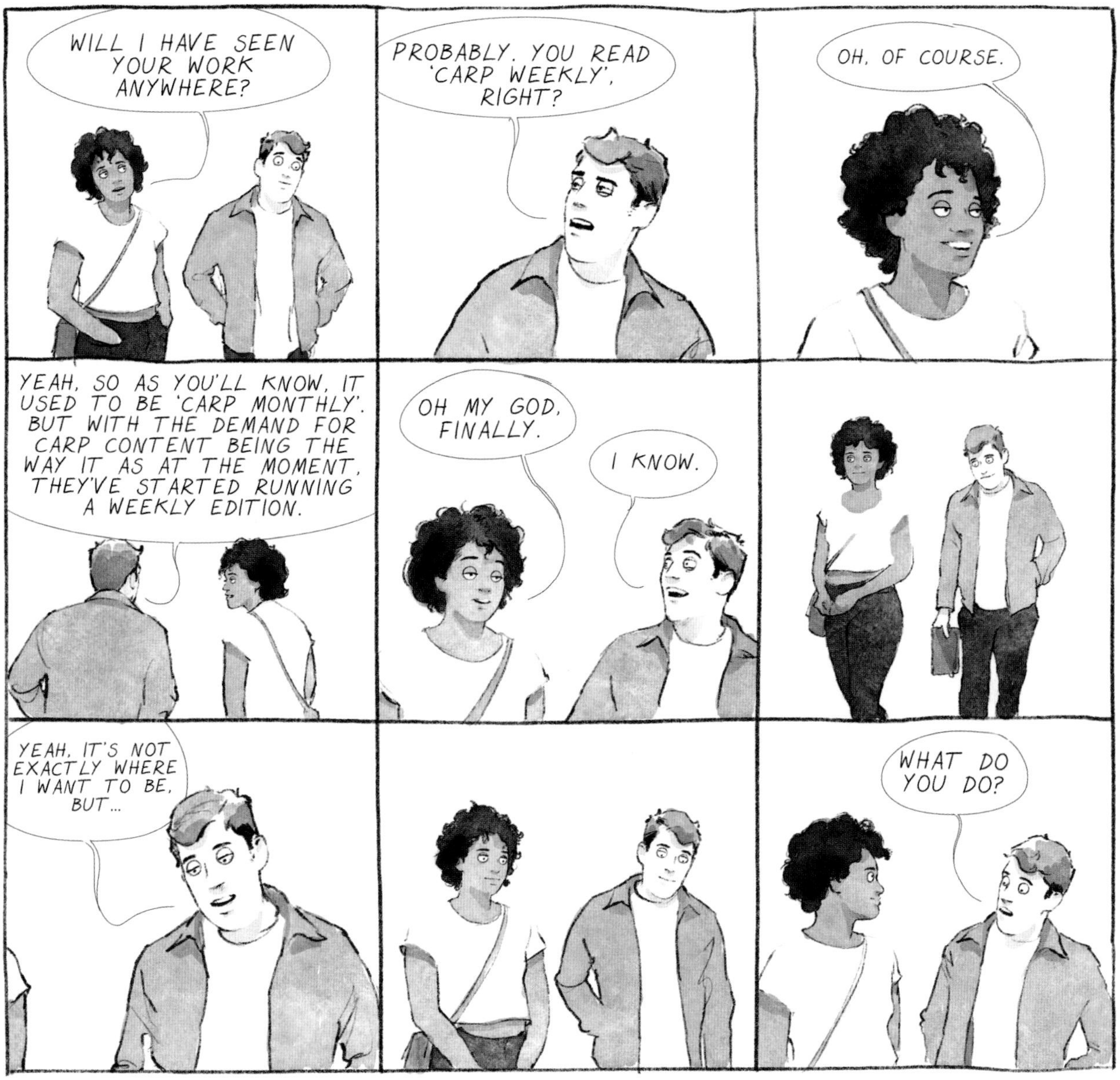
WILL I HAVE SEEN YOUR WORK ANYWHERE?
PROBABLY. YOU READ 'CARP WEEKLY', RIGHT?
OH, OF COURSE.
YEAH, SO AS YOU'LL KNOW, IT USED TO BE 'CARP MONTHLY'. BUT WITH THE DEMAND FOR CARP CONTENT BEING THE WAY IT AS AT THE MOMENT, THEY'VE STARTED RUNNING A WEEKLY EDITION.
OH MY GOD, FINALLY.
I KNOW.
YEAH, IT'S NOT EXACTLY WHERE I WANT TO BE, BUT...
WHAT DO YOU DO?

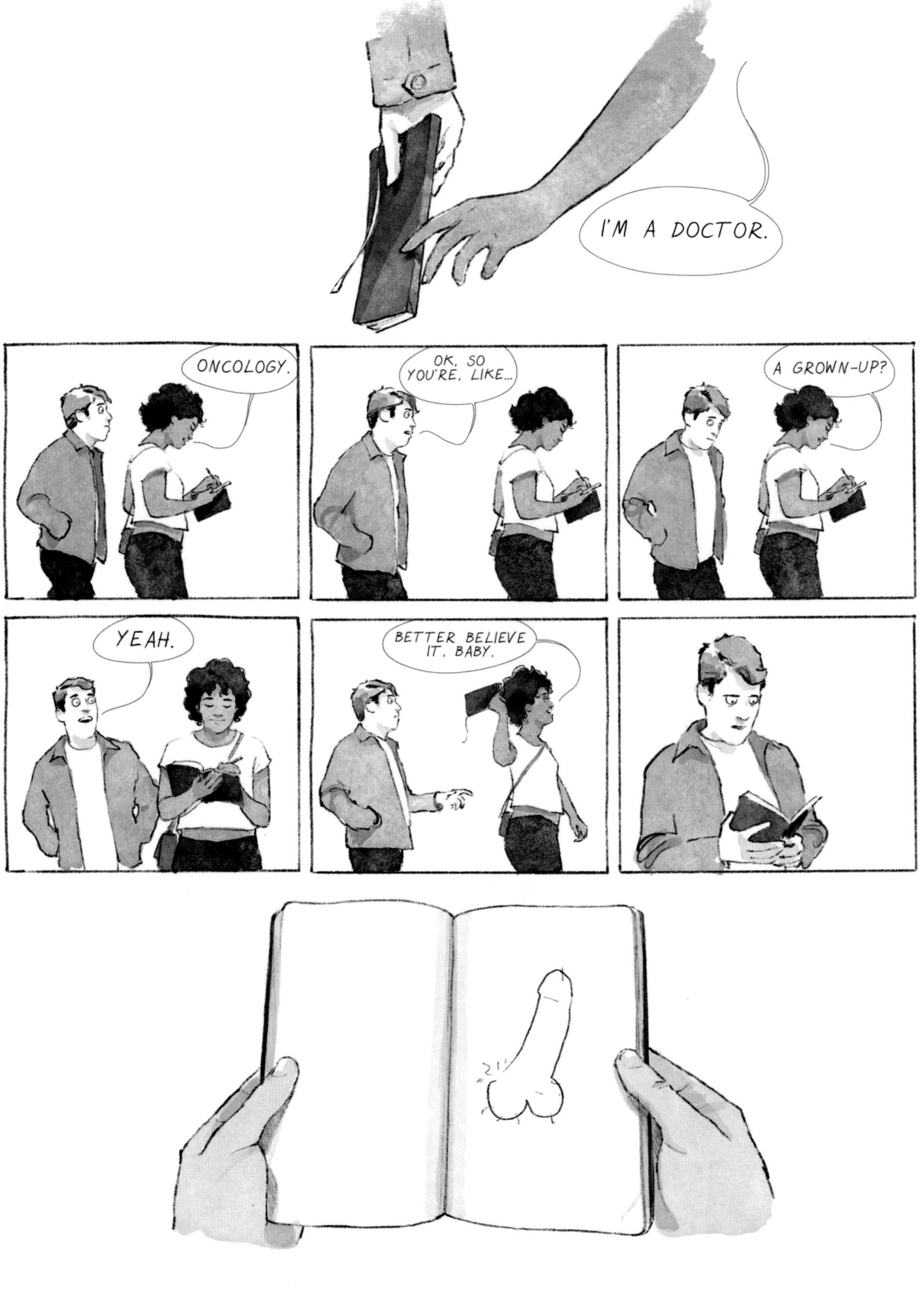
I'M A DOCTOR.
ONCOLOGY.
OK, SO YOU'RE, LIKE...
A GROWN-UP?
YEAH.
BETTER BELIEVE IT, BABY.

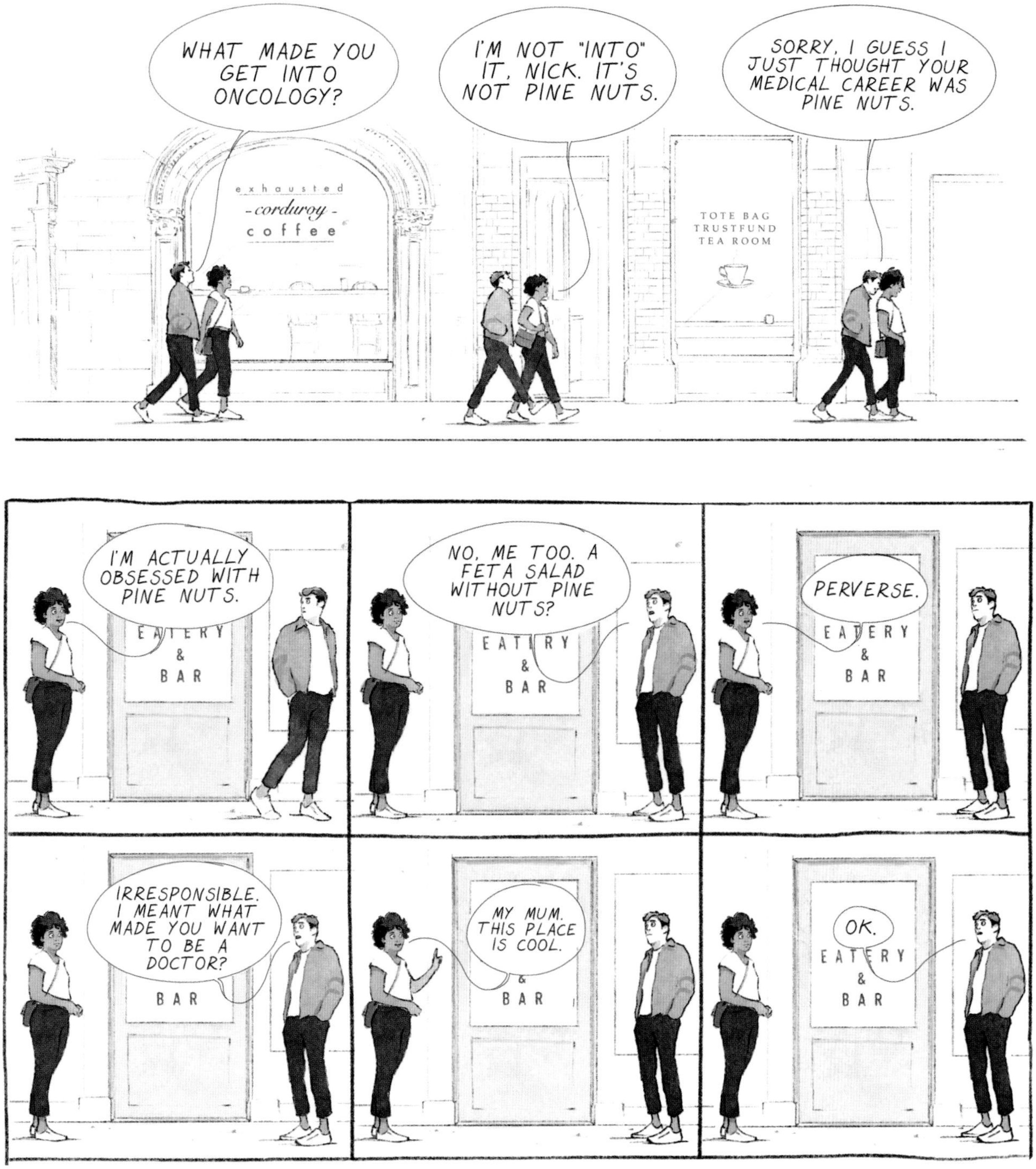
WHAT MADE YOU GET INTO ONCOLOGY?
exhausted -corduroy- coffee
I'M NOT "INTO" IT, NICK. IT'S NOT PINE NUTS.
TOTE BAG TRUSTFUND TEA ROOM
SORRY, I GUESS I JUST THOUGHT YOUR MEDICAL CAREER WAS PINE NUTS.
I'M ACTUALLY OBSESSED WITH PINE NUTS.
EATERY & BAR
NO, ME TOO. A FETA SALAD WITHOUT PINE NUTS?
PERVERSE.
IRRESPONSIBLE. I MEANT WHAT MADE YOU WANT TO BE A DOCTOR?
MY MUM. THIS PLACE IS COOL.
OK.

SHOWTIME.

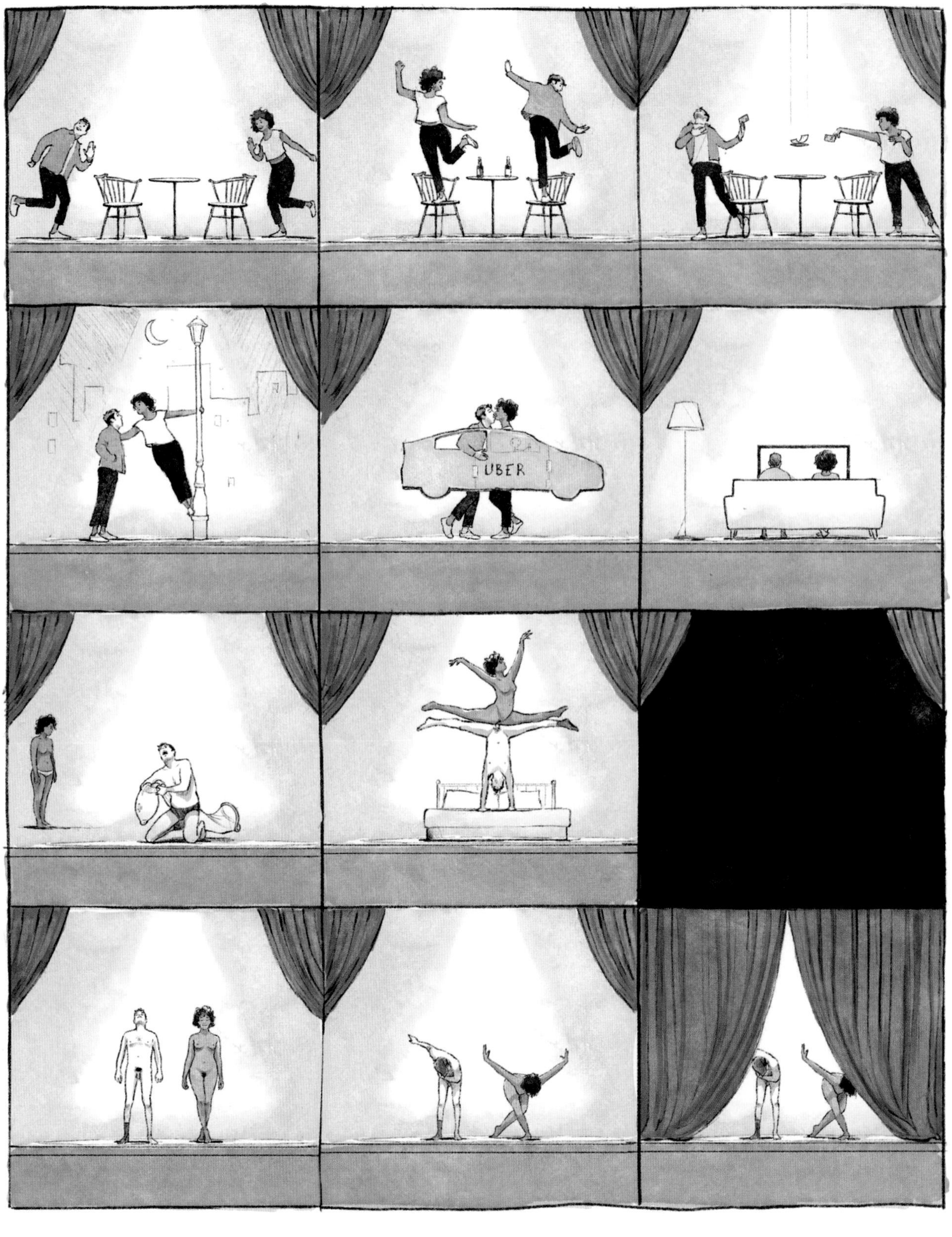
UBER

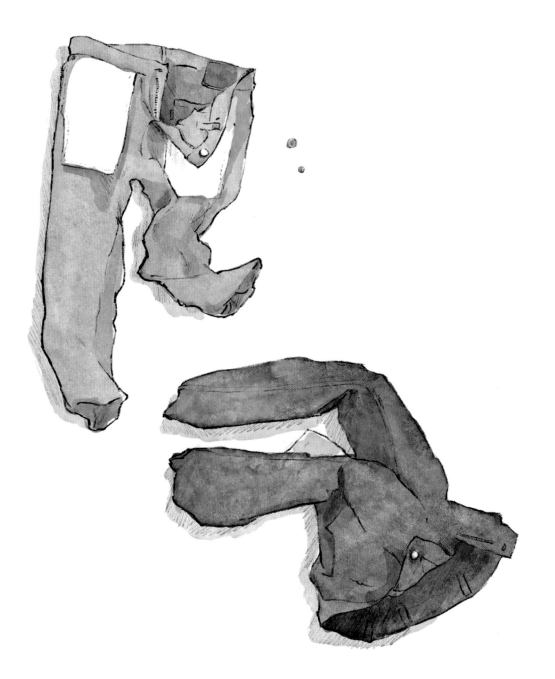

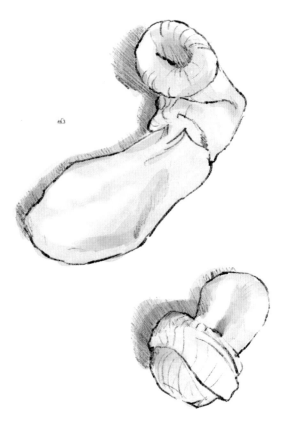

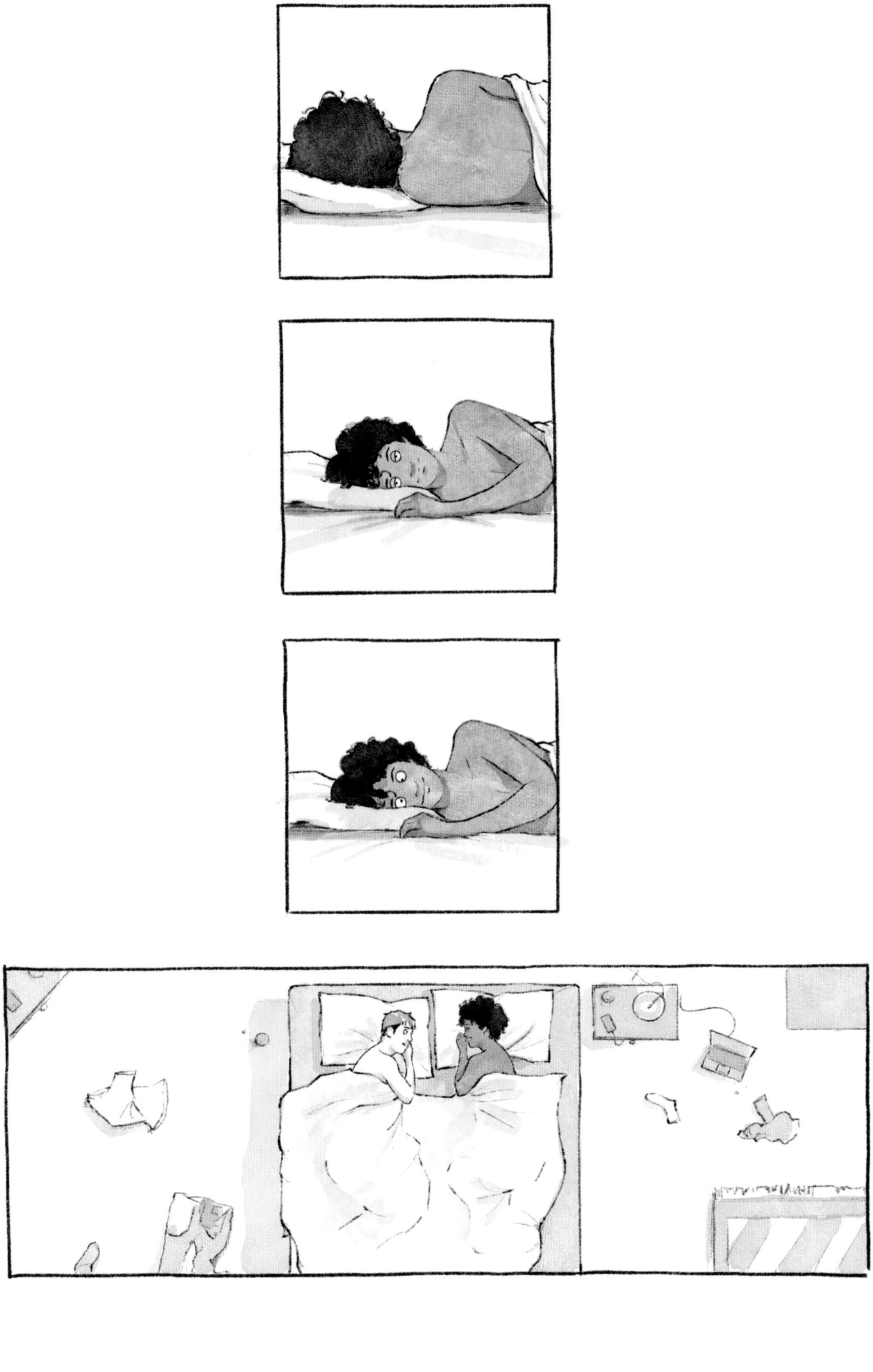

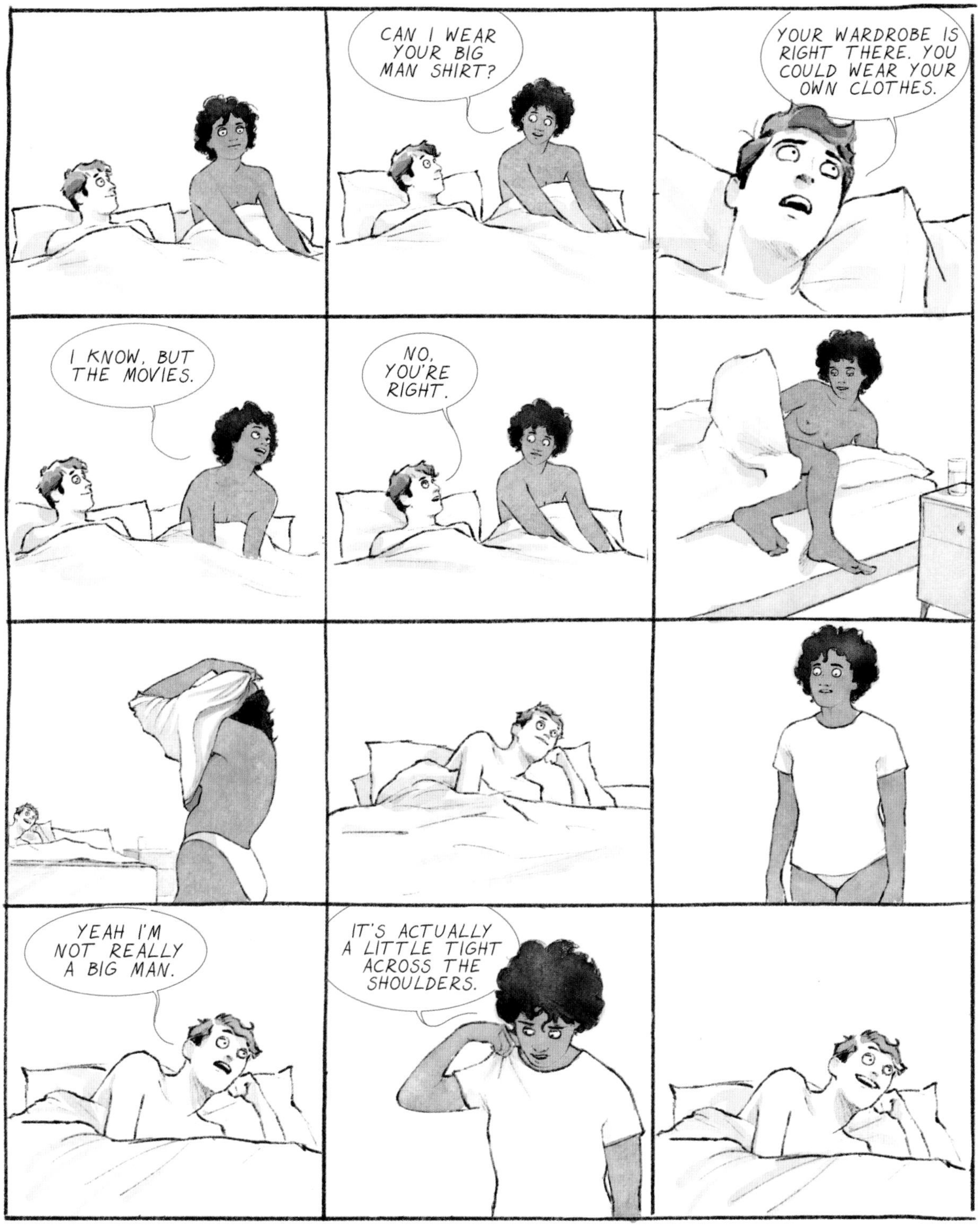
CAN I WEAR YOUR BIG MAN SHIRT?
YOUR WARDROBE IS RIGHT THERE. YOU COULD WEAR YOUR OWN CLOTHES.
I KNOW, BUT THE MOVIES.
NO, YOU'RE RIGHT.
YEAH I'M NOT REALLY A BIG MAN.
IT'S ACTUALLY A LITTLE TIGHT ACROSS THE SHOULDERS.

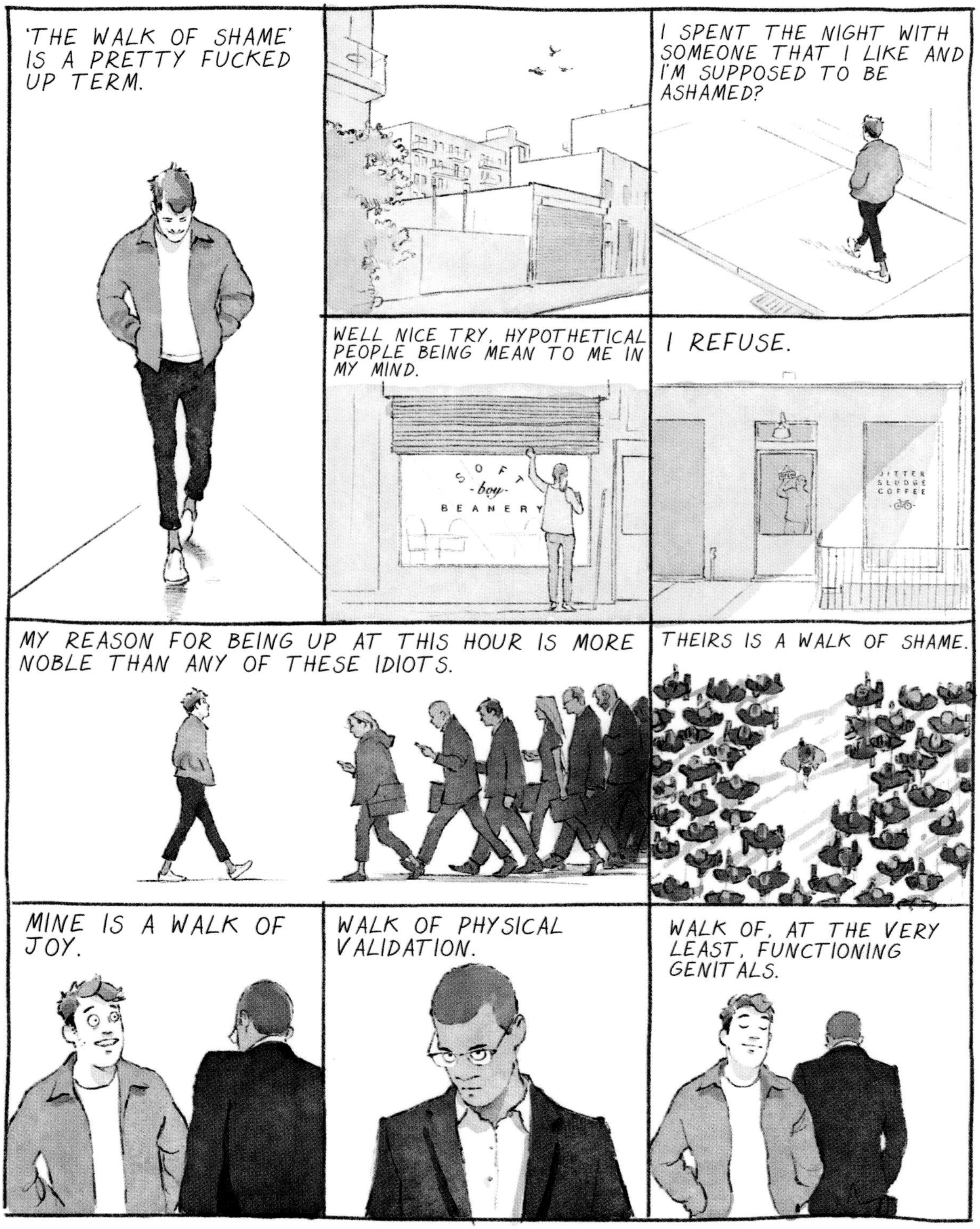
'THE WALK OF SHAME' IS A PRETTY FUCKED UP TERM.
I SPENT THE NIGHT WITH SOMEONE THAT I LIKE AND I'M SUPPOSED TO BE ASHAMED?
WELL NICE TRY, HYPOTHETICAL PEOPLE BEING MEAN TO ME IN MY MIND.
SOFT -boy- BEANERY
I REFUSE.
JITTER SLUDGE COFFEE
MY REASON FOR BEING UP AT THIS HOUR IS MORE NOBLE THAN ANY OF THESE IDIOTS.
THEIRS IS A WALK OF SHAME.
MINE IS A WALK OF JOY.
WALK OF PHYSICAL VALIDATION.
WALK OF, AT THE VERY LEAST, FUNCTIONING GENITALS.

ALSO, MY HAIR IS IN THAT CAREFREE SORT OF MESS THAT JUST BELLOWS "SEXUALLY ACTIVE".

EVERY JADED BUSINESSMAN THAT I PASS KNOWS EXACTLY WHAT I WAS DOING LAST NIGHT. MY HAIR TELLS THE WHOLE SEEDY STORY, BABY!

EXCEPT THAT PART WHERE I DIDN'T FEEL ANYTHING AND PERFORMED EVERY EMOTION.

BABY.

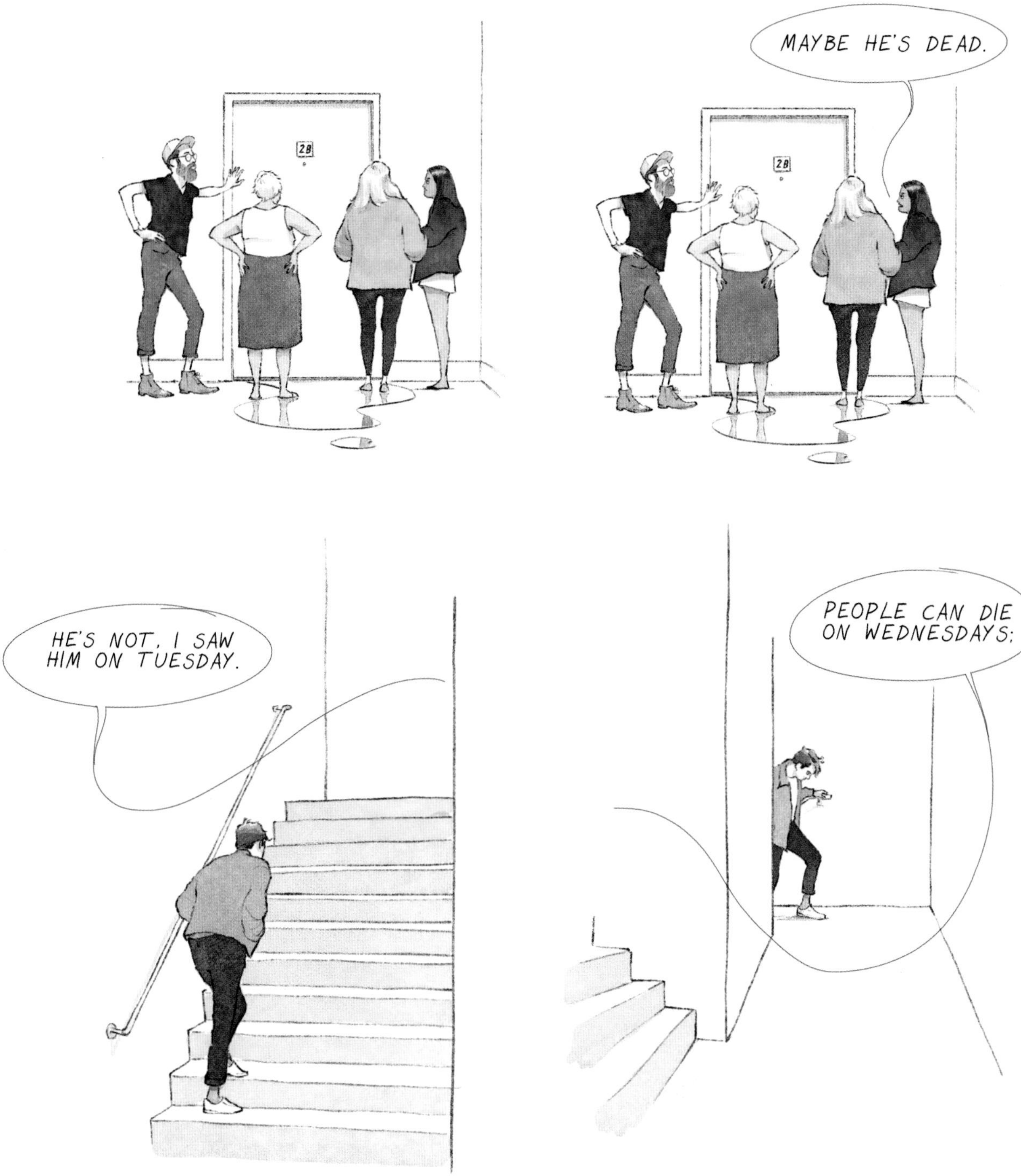
MAYBE HE'S DEAD.
HE'S NOT, I SAW HIM ON TUESDAY.
PEOPLE CAN DIE ON WEDNESDAYS.

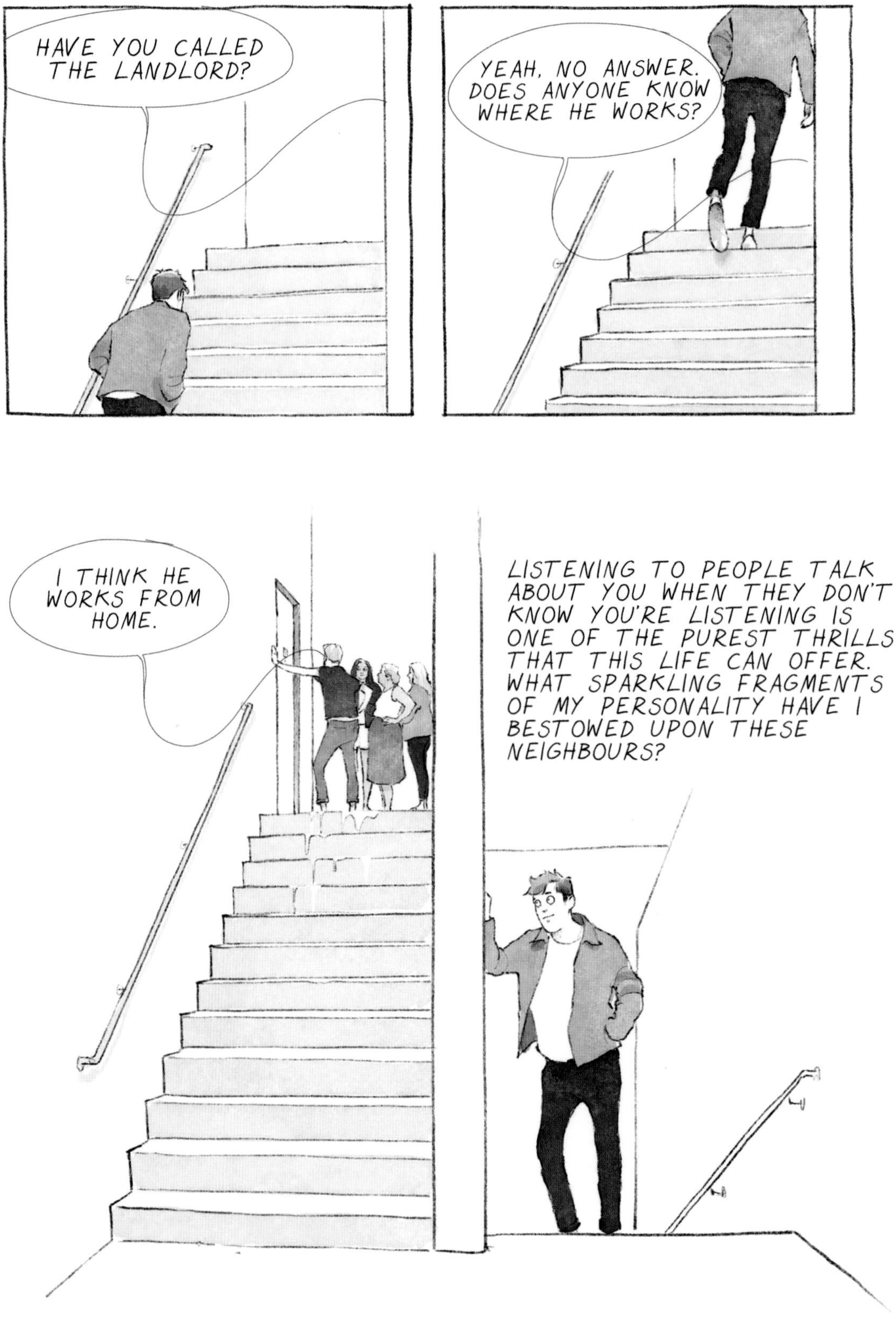
HAVE YOU CALLED THE LANDLORD?
YEAH, NO ANSWER. DOES ANYONE KNOW WHERE HE WORKS?
I THINK HE WORKS FROM HOME.
LISTENING TO PEOPLE TALK ABOUT YOU WHEN THEY DON'T KNOW YOU'RE LISTENING IS ONE OF THE PUREST THRILLS THAT THIS LIFE CAN OFFER. WHAT SPARKLING FRAGMENTS OF MY PERSONALITY HAVE I BESTOWED UPON THESE NEIGHBOURS?

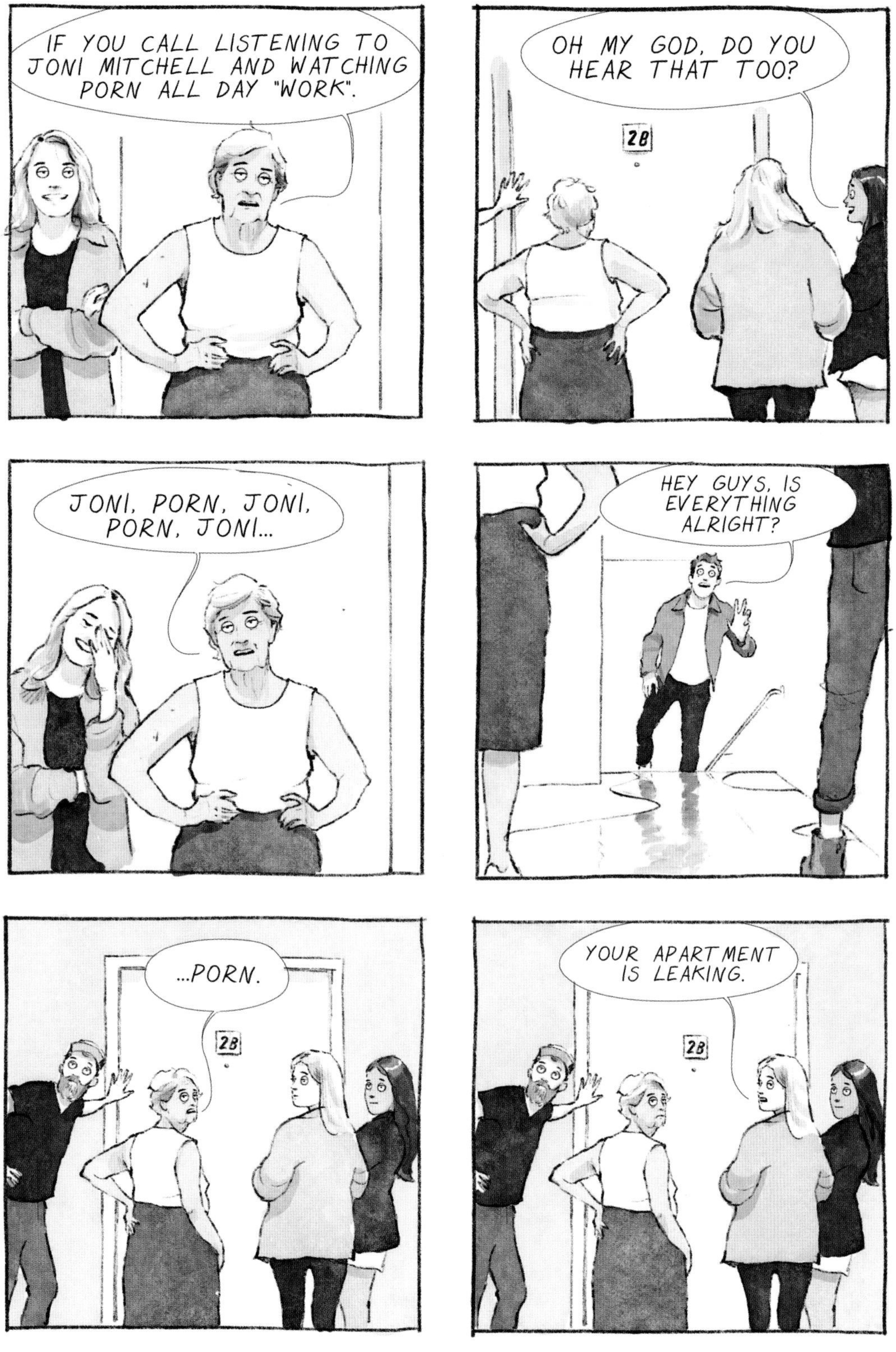
IF YOU CALL LISTENING TO JONI MITCHELL AND WATCHING PORN ALL DAY "WORK".
OH MY GOD, DO YOU HEAR THAT TOO?
2B
JONI, PORN, JONI, PORN, JONI...
HEY GUYS, IS EVERYTHING ALRIGHT?
...PORN.
2B
YOUR APARTMENT IS LEAKING.
2B

OH, SORRY.

THEY WERE RIGHT.

SOMETIMES I LISTEN TO JONI MITCHELL AFTER I MASTURBATE.

ALSO MY APARTMENT IS LEAKING.

BUT ONE PROBLEM AT A TIME.

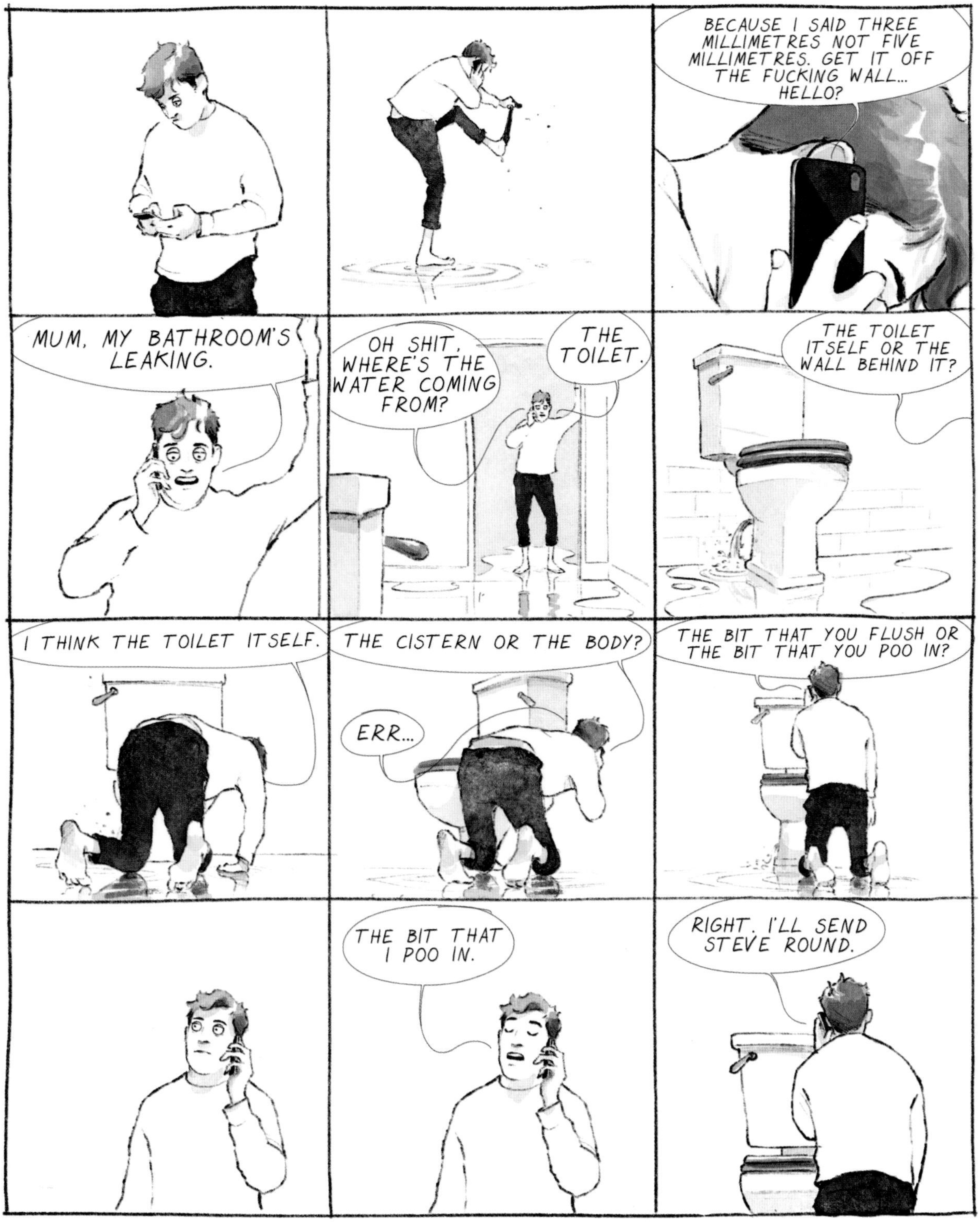
BECAUSE I SAID THREE MILLIMETRES NOT FIVE MILLIMETRES. GET IT OFF THE FUCKING WALL... HELLO?
MUM, MY BATHROOM'S LEAKING.
OH SHIT, WHERE'S THE WATER COMING FROM?
THE TOILET.
THE TOILET ITSELF OR THE WALL BEHIND IT?
I THINK THE TOILET ITSELF.
THE CISTERN OR THE BODY?
ERR...
THE BIT THAT YOU FLUSH OR THE BIT THAT YOU POO IN?
THE BIT THAT I POO IN.
RIGHT. I'LL SEND STEVE ROUND.

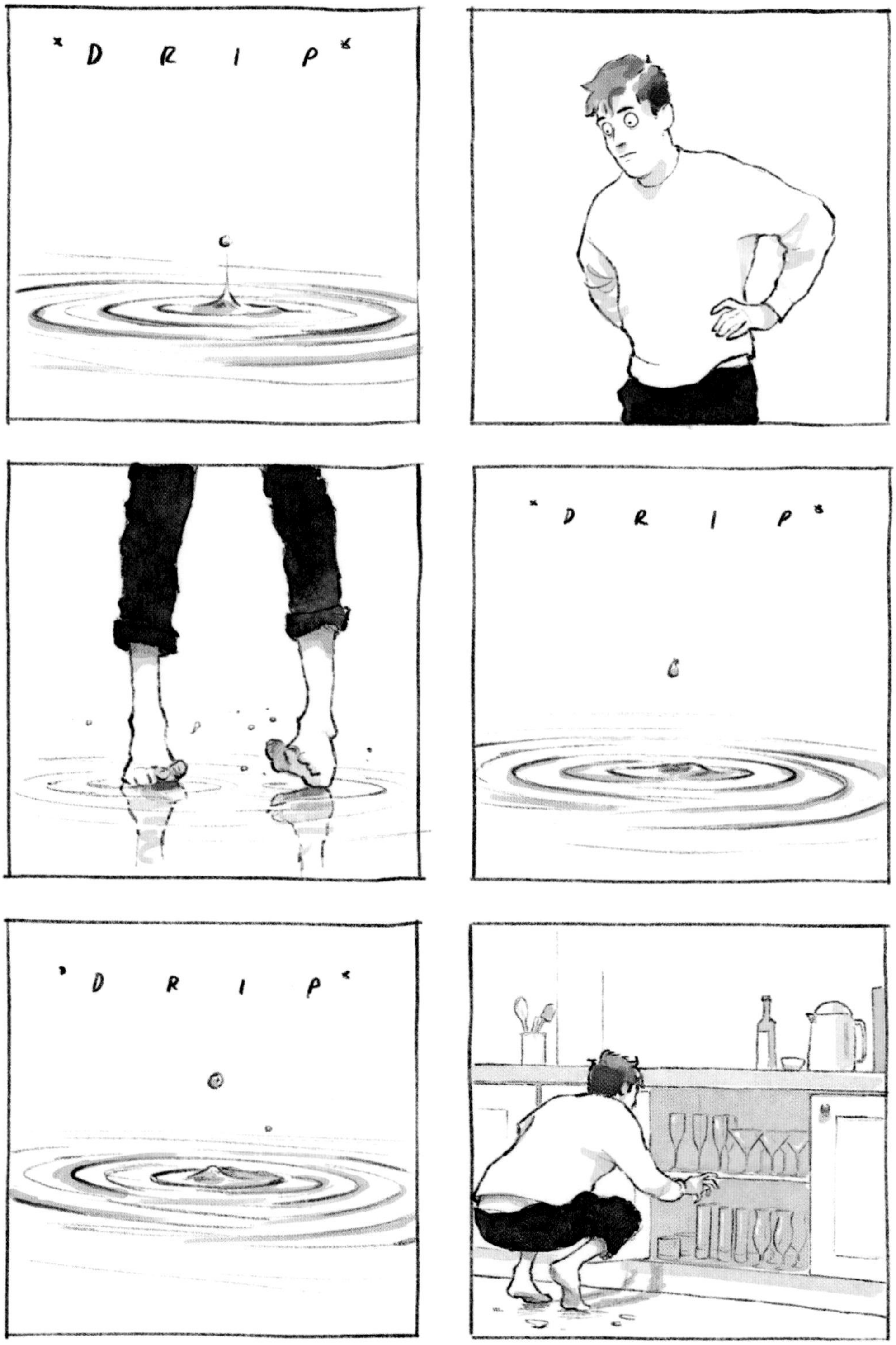
DRIP
DRIP
DRIP

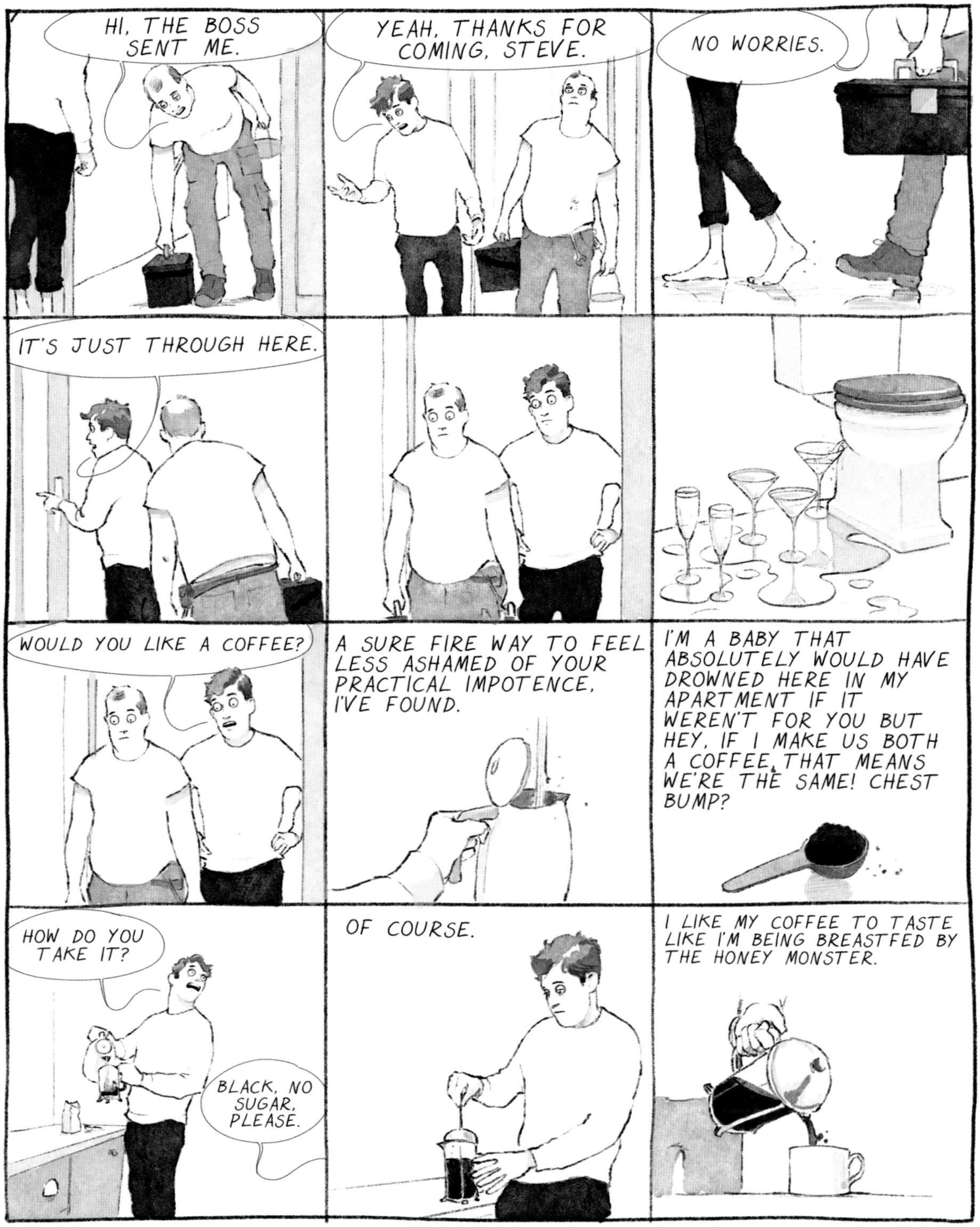
HI, THE BOSS SENT ME.
YEAH, THANKS FOR COMING, STEVE.
NO WORRIES.
IT'S JUST THROUGH HERE.
WOULD YOU LIKE A COFFEE?
A SURE FIRE WAY TO FEEL LESS ASHAMED OF YOUR PRACTICAL IMPOTENCE, I'VE FOUND.
I'M A BABY THAT ABSOLUTELY WOULD HAVE DROWNED HERE IN MY APARTMENT IF IT WEREN'T FOR YOU BUT HEY, IF I MAKE US BOTH A COFFEE, THAT MEANS WE'RE THE SAME! CHEST BUMP?
HOW DO YOU TAKE IT?
BLACK, NO SUGAR, PLEASE.
OF COURSE.
I LIKE MY COFFEE TO TASTE LIKE I'M BEING BREASTFED BY THE HONEY MONSTER.

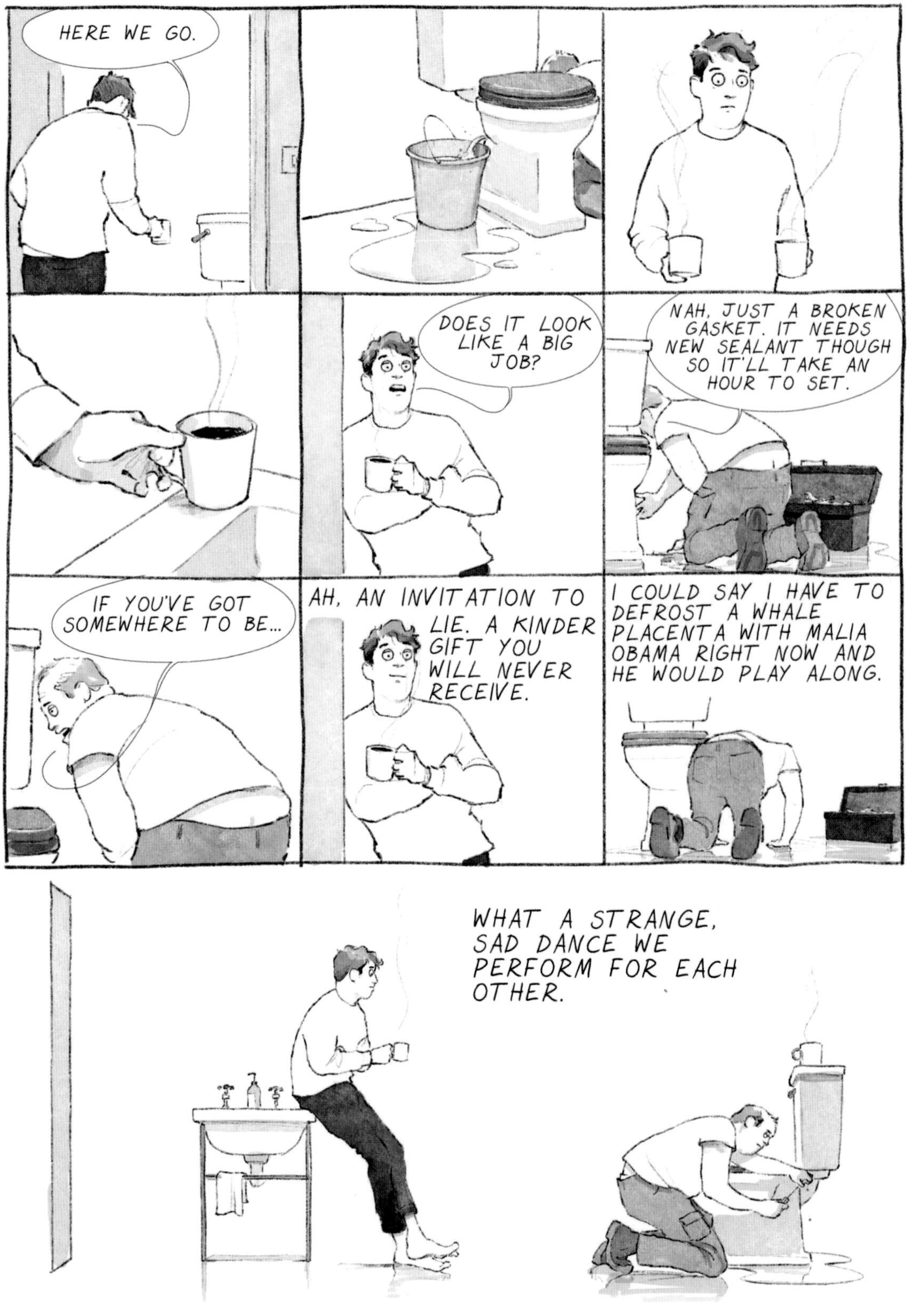
HERE WE GO.
DOES IT LOOK LIKE A BIG JOB?
NAH, JUST A BROKEN GASKET. IT NEEDS NEW SEALANT THOUGH SO IT'LL TAKE AN HOUR TO SET.
IF YOU'VE GOT SOMEWHERE TO BE...
AH, AN INVITATION TO LIE. A KINDER GIFT YOU WILL NEVER RECEIVE.
I COULD SAY I HAVE TO DEFROST A WHALE PLACENTA WITH MALIA OBAMA RIGHT NOW AND HE WOULD PLAY ALONG.
WHAT A STRANGE, SAD DANCE WE PERFORM FOR EACH OTHER.

ANY OTHER DAY AND I WOULD HAVE ACCEPTED THE PLUMBER'S GENEROUS OFFER AND GONE TO A COFFEE SHOP TO SEE IF AN ALMOND DUSTED CROISSANT MADE ME FEEL ANYTHING.

BUT FOR A REASON THAT I DON'T FULLY UNDERSTAND...

...TODAY I DON'T WANT TO.

I WANT TO MAKE A CONNECTION WITH THE MAN IN MY BATHROOM.

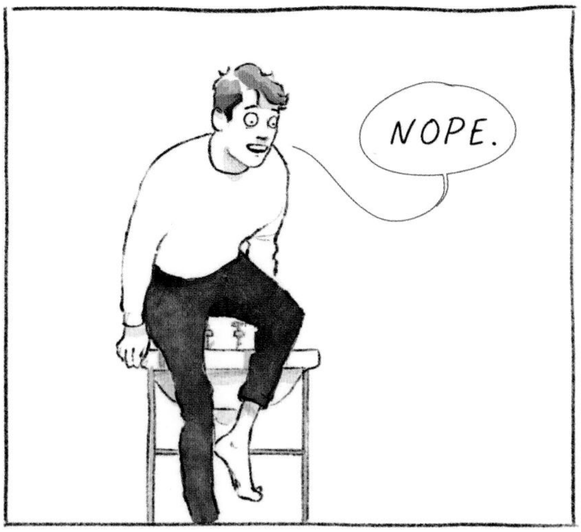
NOPE.

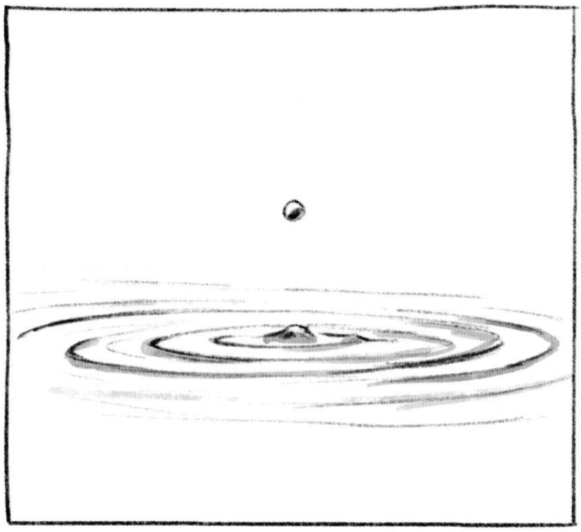

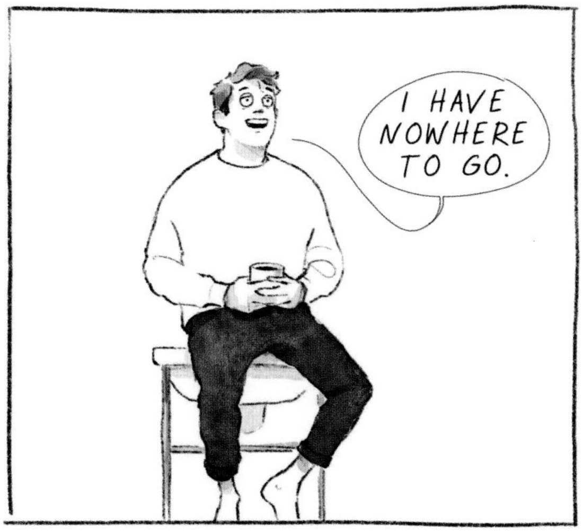
I HAVE NOWHERE TO GO.

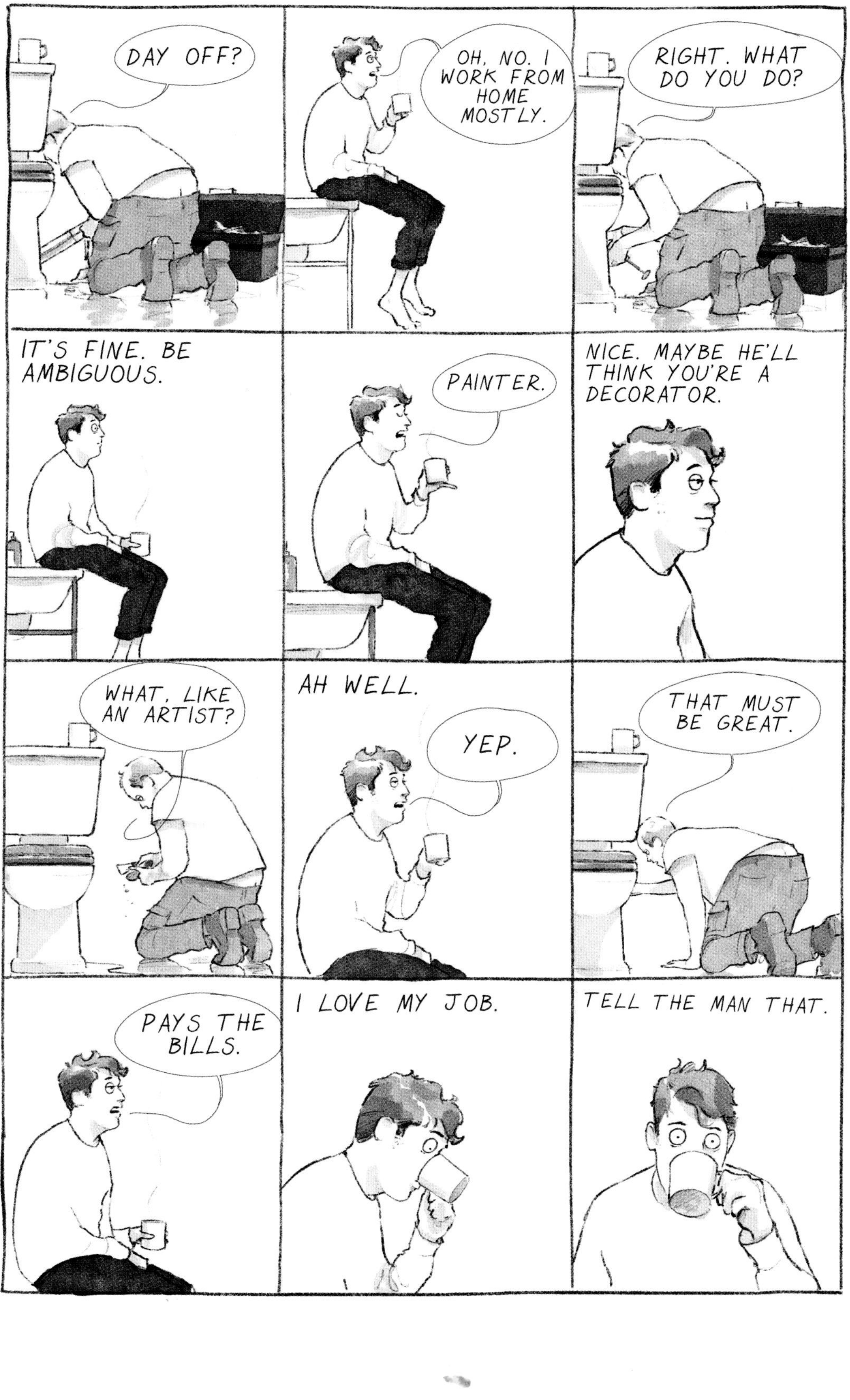
DAY OFF?
OH, NO. I WORK FROM HOME MOSTLY.
RIGHT. WHAT DO YOU DO?
IT'S FINE. BE AMBIGUOUS.
PAINTER.
NICE. MAYBE HE'LL THINK YOU'RE A DECORATOR.
WHAT, LIKE AN ARTIST?
AH WELL.
YEP.
THAT MUST BE GREAT.
PAYS THE BILLS.
I LOVE MY JOB.
TELL THE MAN THAT.

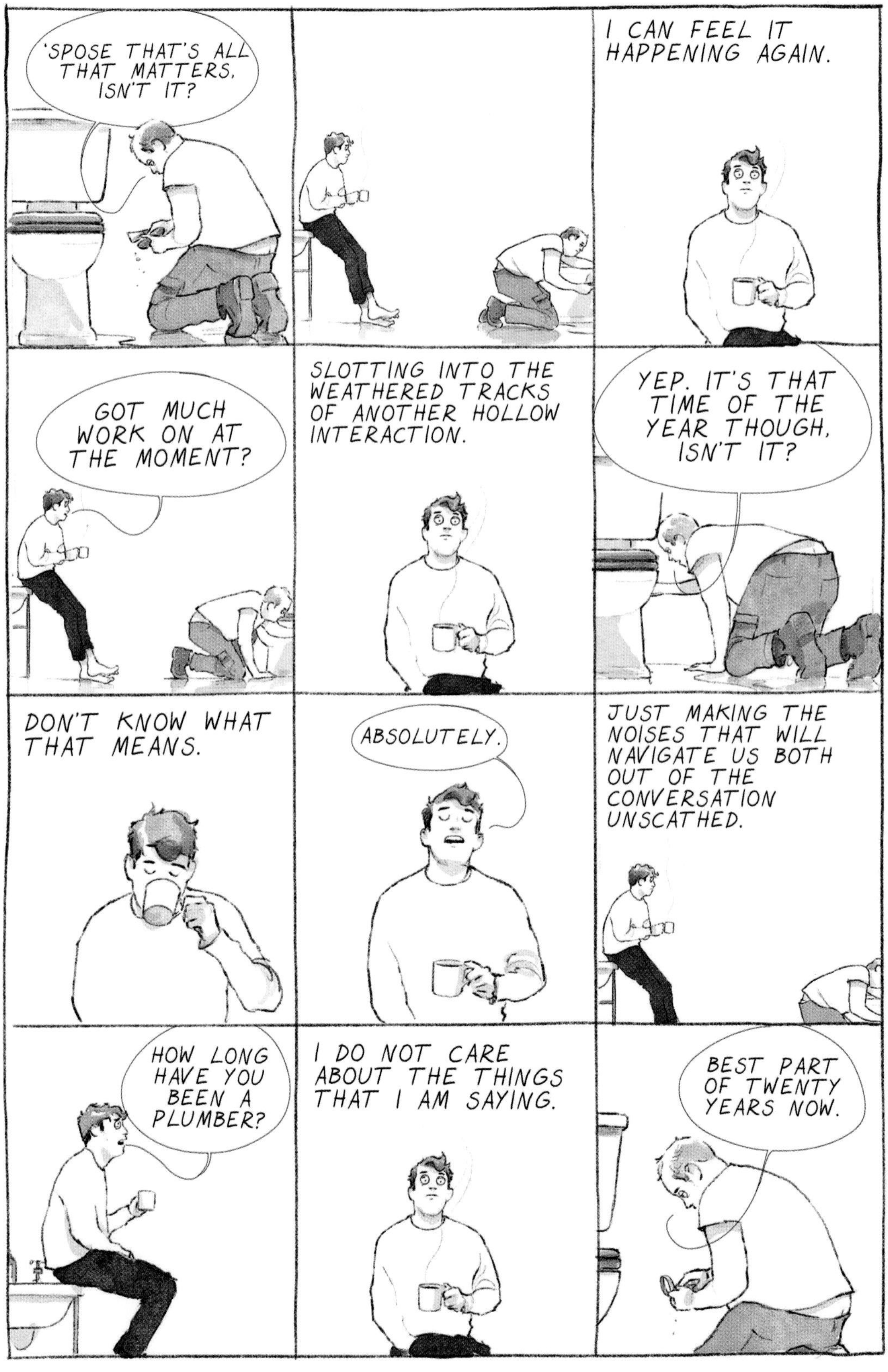
'SPOSE THAT'S ALL THAT MATTERS, ISN'T IT?
I CAN FEEL IT HAPPENING AGAIN.
GOT MUCH WORK ON AT THE MOMENT?
SLOTTING INTO THE WEATHERED TRACKS OF ANOTHER HOLLOW INTERACTION.
YEP. IT'S THAT TIME OF THE YEAR THOUGH, ISN'T IT?
DON'T KNOW WHAT THAT MEANS.
ABSOLUTELY.
JUST MAKING THE NOISES THAT WILL NAVIGATE US BOTH OUT OF THE CONVERSATION UNSCATHED.
HOW LONG HAVE YOU BEEN A PLUMBER?
I DO NOT CARE ABOUT THE THINGS THAT I AM SAYING.
BEST PART OF TWENTY YEARS NOW.

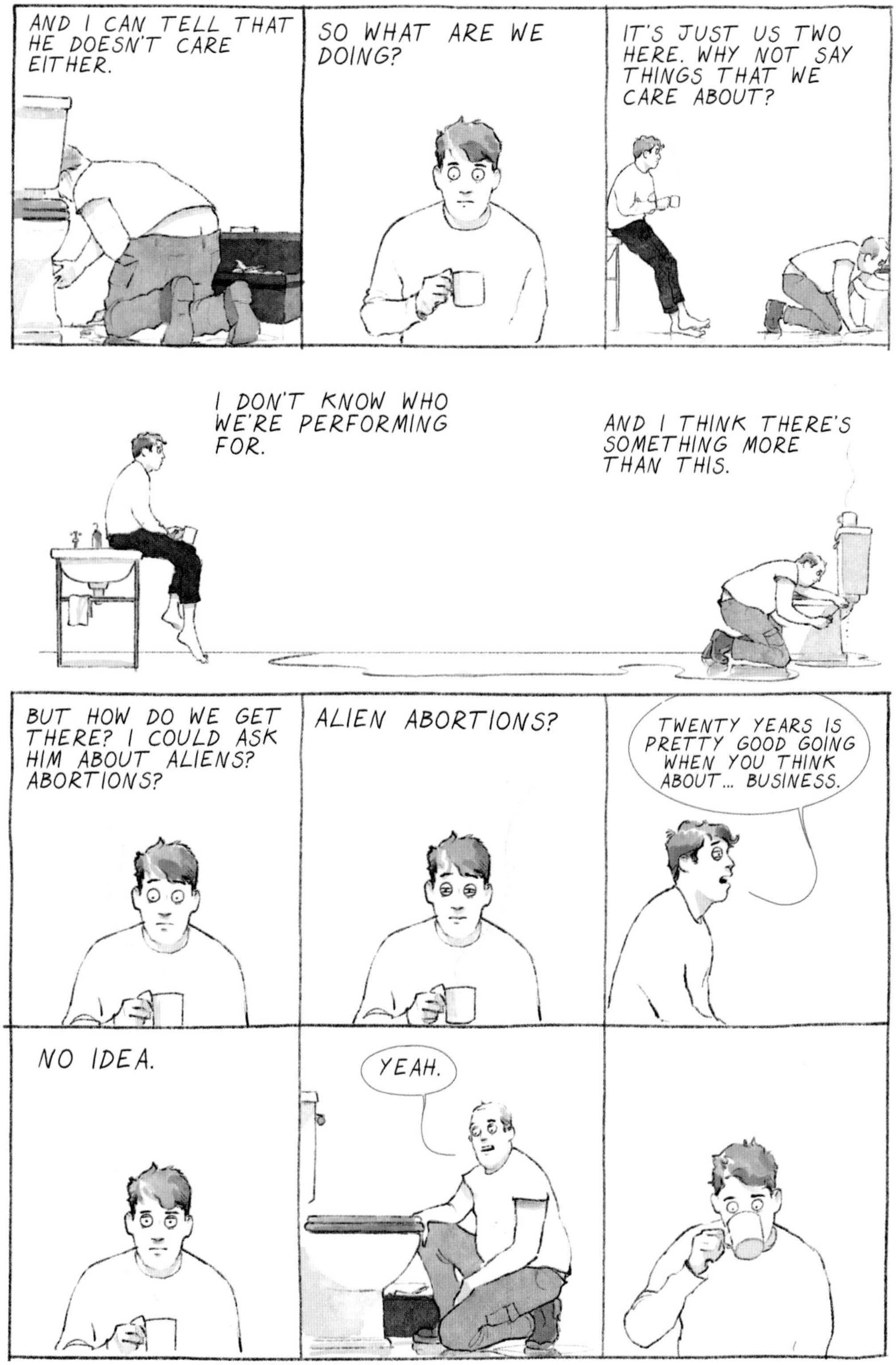
AND I CAN TELL THAT HE DOESN'T CARE EITHER.
SO WHAT ARE WE DOING?
IT'S JUST US TWO HERE. WHY NOT SAY THINGS THAT WE CARE ABOUT?
I DON'T KNOW WHO WE'RE PERFORMING FOR.
AND I THINK THERE'S SOMETHING MORE THAN THIS.
BUT HOW DO WE GET THERE? I COULD ASK HIM ABOUT ALIENS? ABORTIONS?
ALIEN ABORTIONS?
TWENTY YEARS IS PRETTY GOOD GOING WHEN YOU THINK ABOUT... BUSINESS.
NO IDEA.
YEAH.

WHAT BARRIER IS HOLDING US BACK?
HE'S RIGHT IN FRONT OF ME.
I COULD REACH OUT AND TOUCH HIM BUT I CAN'T ACCESS HIM.

THE REMOTENESS OF IT PANICS ME.

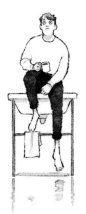

HE'S IN THERE, I JUST NEED TO FIND THE DOOR.

IT CAN ONLY BE WORDS.

WHEN BAD THINGS HAVE HAPPENED IN THE PAST, THERE HAS ALWAYS BEEN A SERIES OF LETTERS THAT, IF PUT IN THE RIGHT ORDER AND SAID IN THE RIGHT WAY...

...CAN CHANGE EVERYTHING. IT'S LIKE A SPELL. OR THE COMBINATION ON A LOCK, IF YOU'RE NOT INTO WITCHES. AND YOU ARE INTO LOCKS.

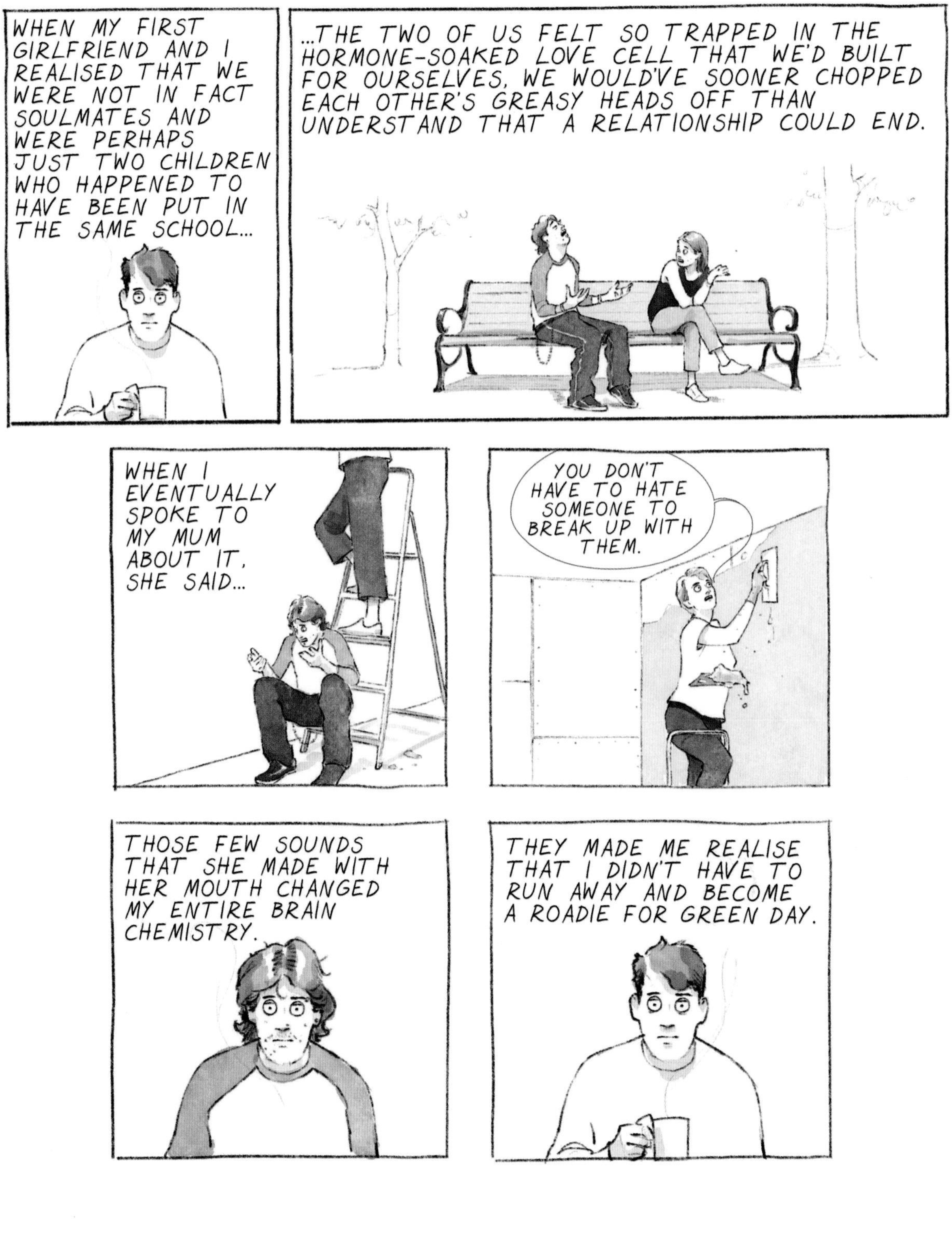
WHEN MY FIRST GIRLFRIEND AND I REALISED THAT WE WERE NOT IN FACT SOULMATES AND WERE PERHAPS JUST TWO CHILDREN WHO HAPPENED TO HAVE BEEN PUT IN THE SAME SCHOOL...
...THE TWO OF US FELT SO TRAPPED IN THE HORMONE-SOAKED LOVE CELL THAT WE'D BUILT FOR OURSELVES, WE WOULD'VE SOONER CHOPPED EACH OTHER'S GREASY HEADS OFF THAN UNDERSTAND THAT A RELATIONSHIP COULD END.
WHEN I EVENTUALLY SPOKE TO MY MUM ABOUT IT, SHE SAID...
YOU DON'T HAVE TO HATE SOMEONE TO BREAK UP WITH THEM.
THOSE FEW SOUNDS THAT SHE MADE WITH HER MOUTH CHANGED MY ENTIRE BRAIN CHEMISTRY.
THEY MADE ME REALISE THAT I DIDN'T HAVE TO RUN AWAY AND BECOME A ROADIE FOR GREEN DAY.

WORDS THAT MATTER.

THAT'S WHAT I
HAVE TO SAY TO
THE PLUMBER.

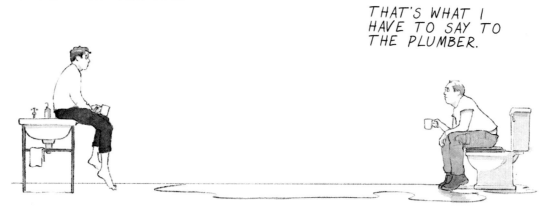

BECAUSE WHAT'S THE
ALTERNATIVE?

ANOTHER MEANINGLESS
ENCOUNTER.

I DON'T WANT THAT ANYMORE.

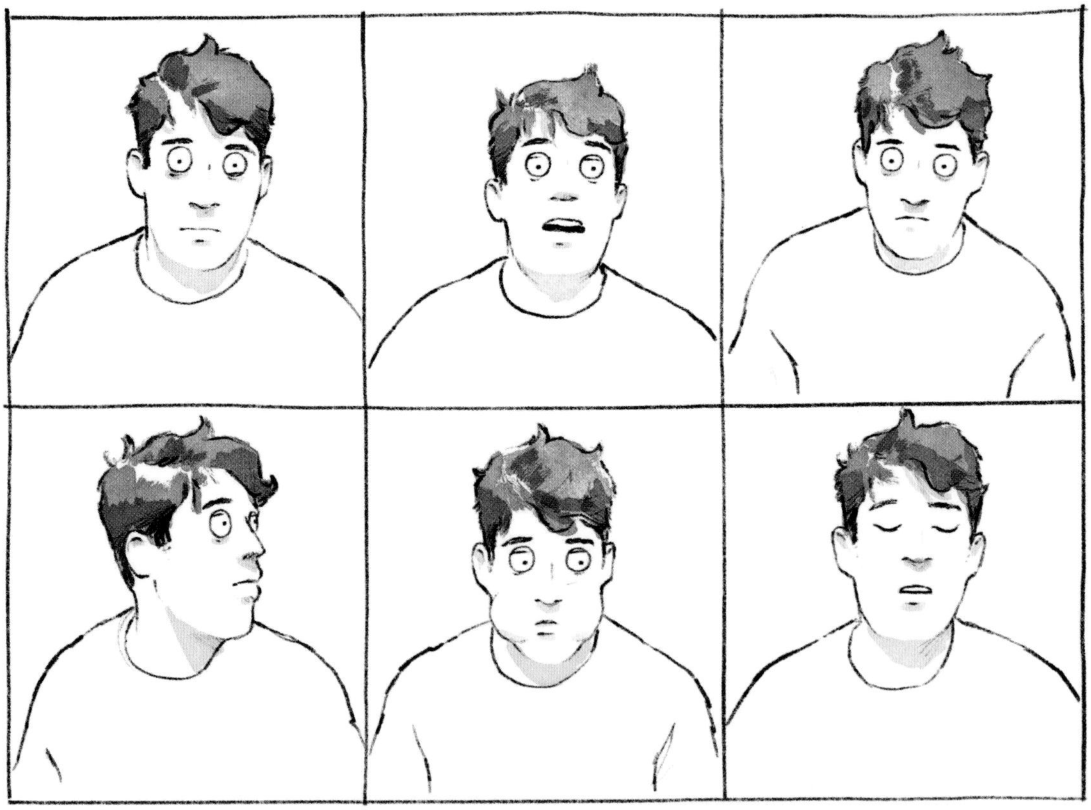

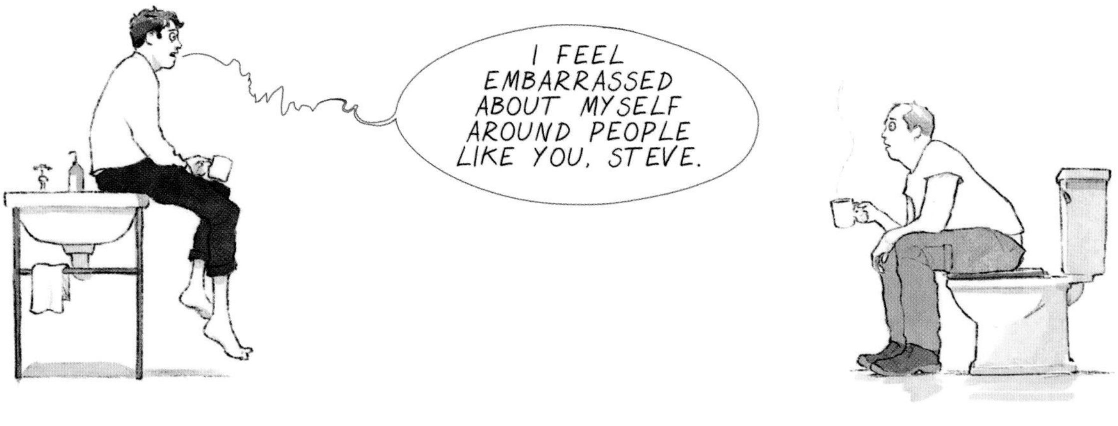
I FEEL EMBARRASSED ABOUT MYSELF AROUND PEOPLE LIKE YOU, STEVE.

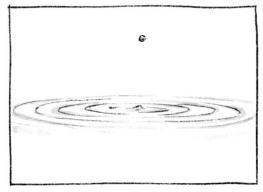

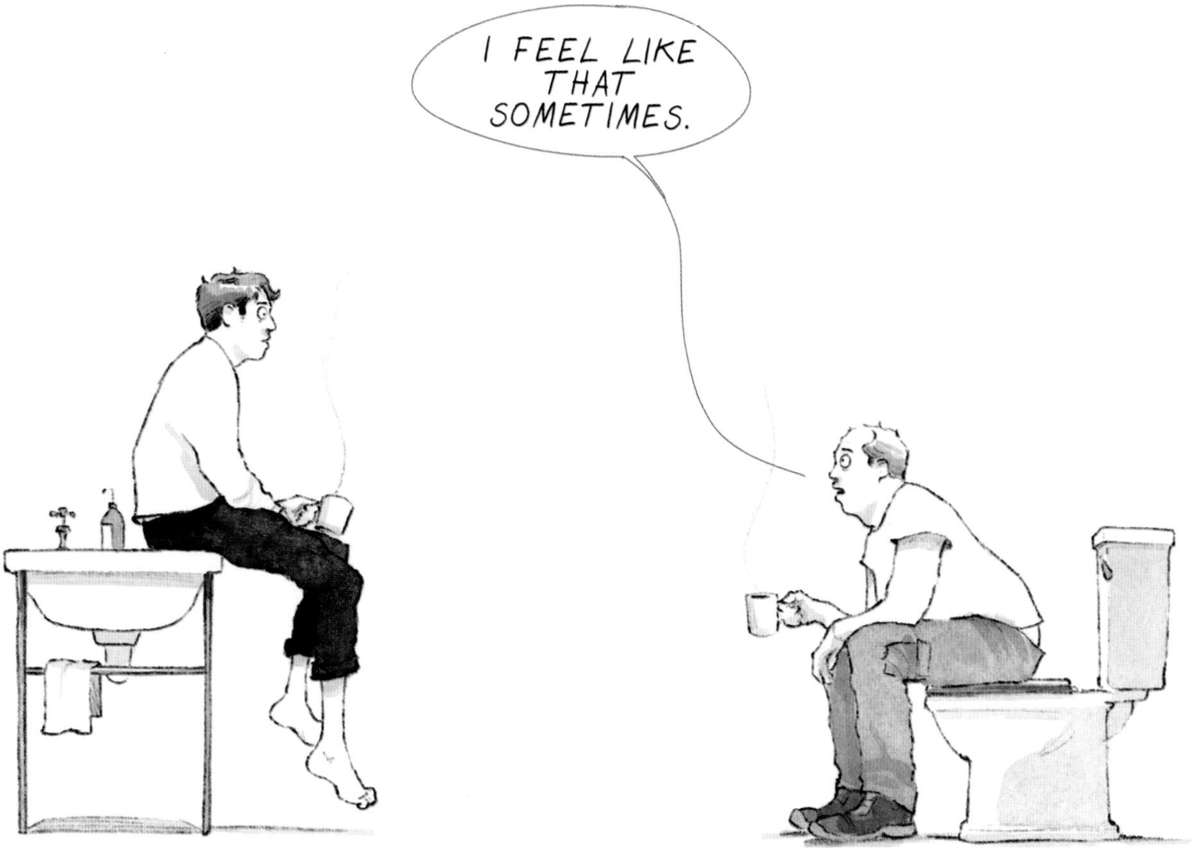
I FEEL LIKE THAT SOMETIMES.

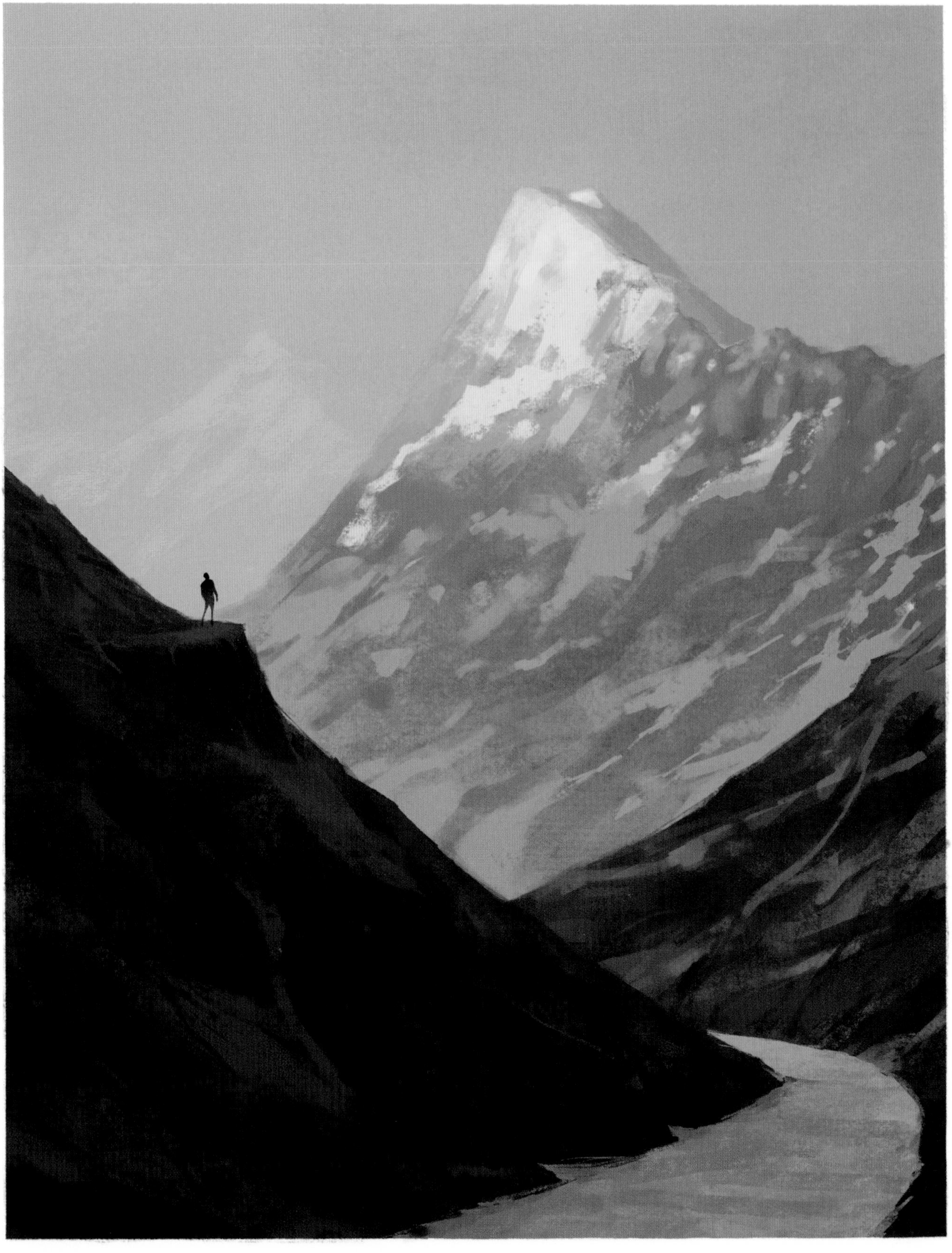

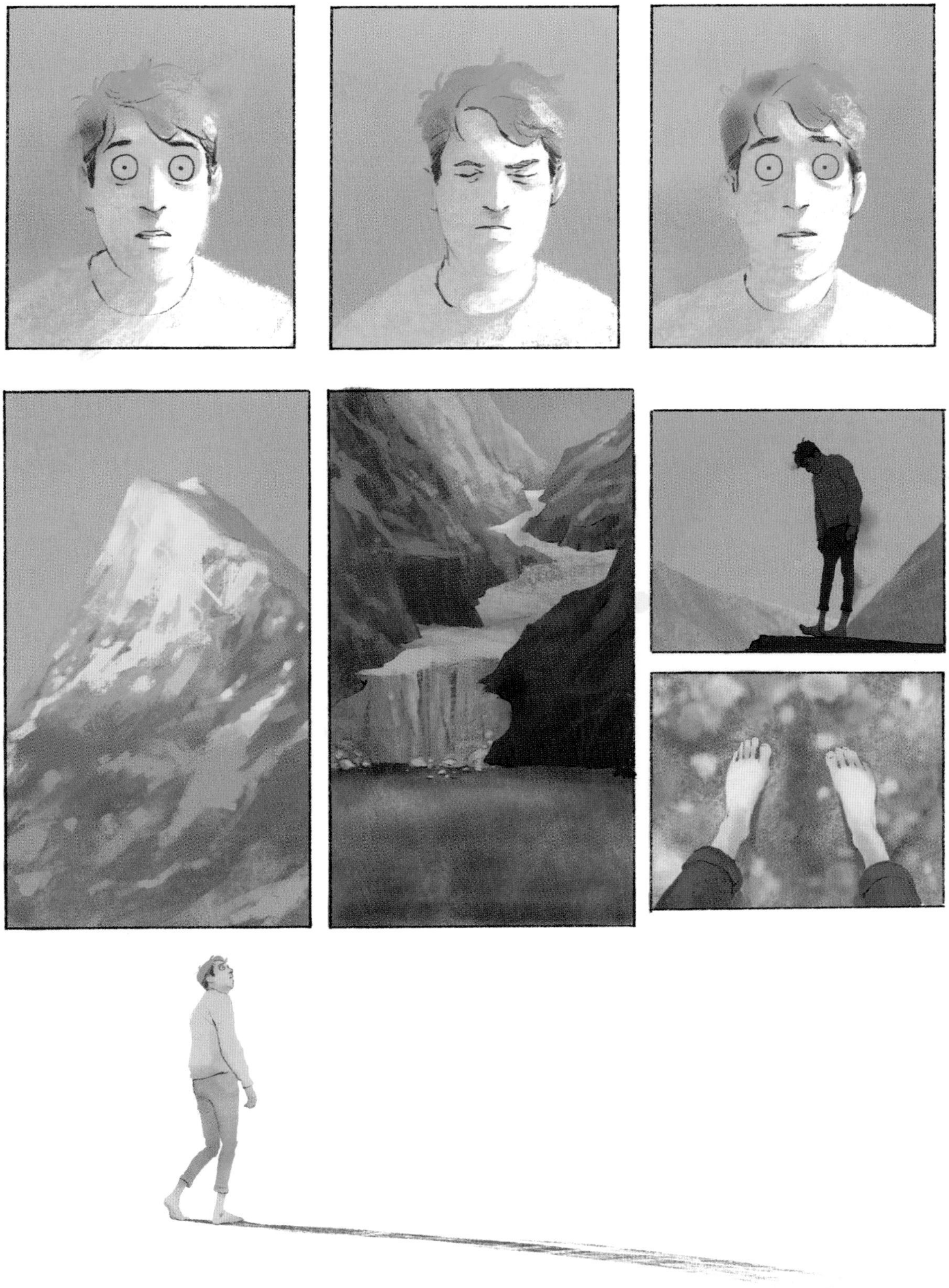

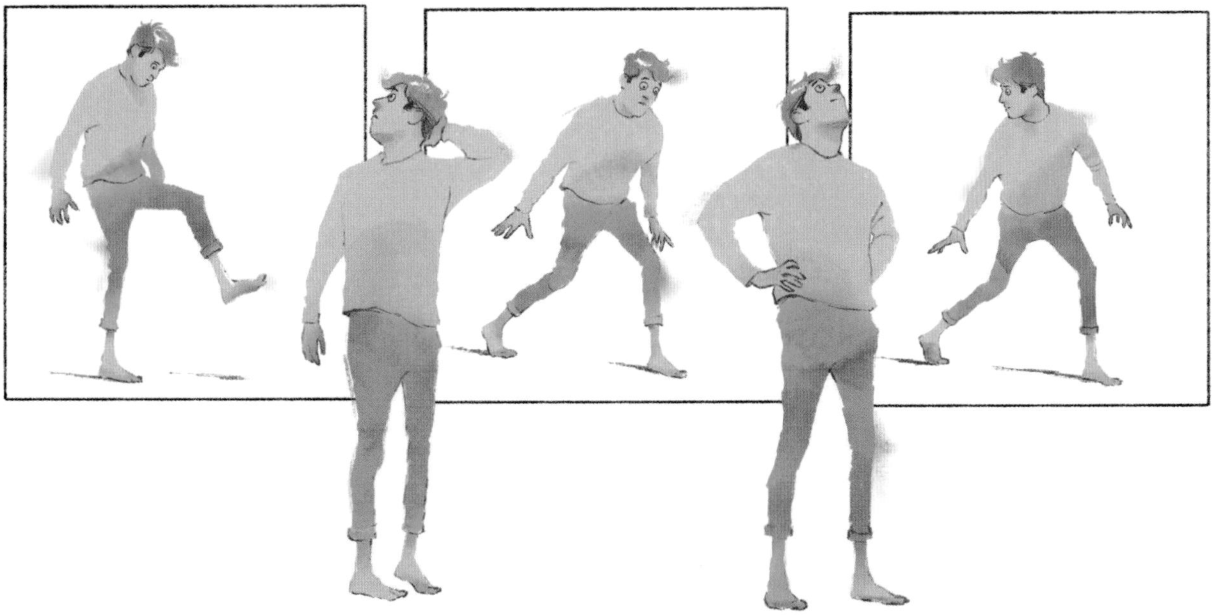

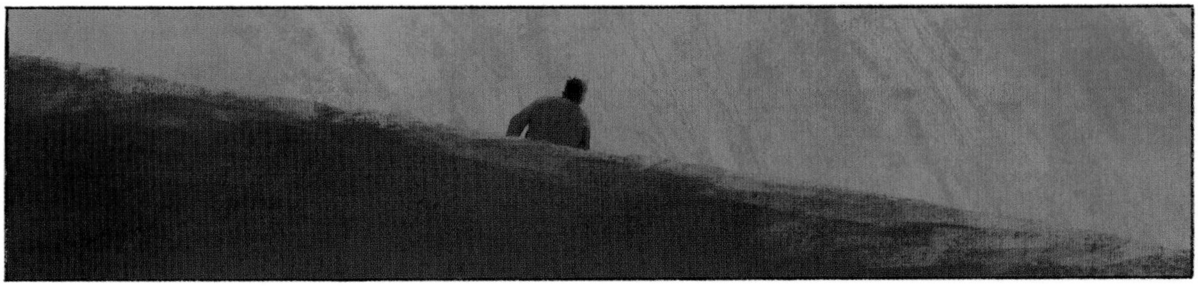

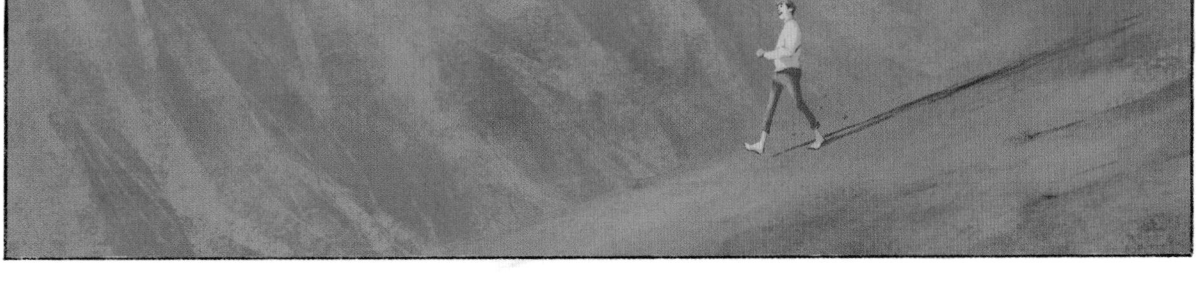

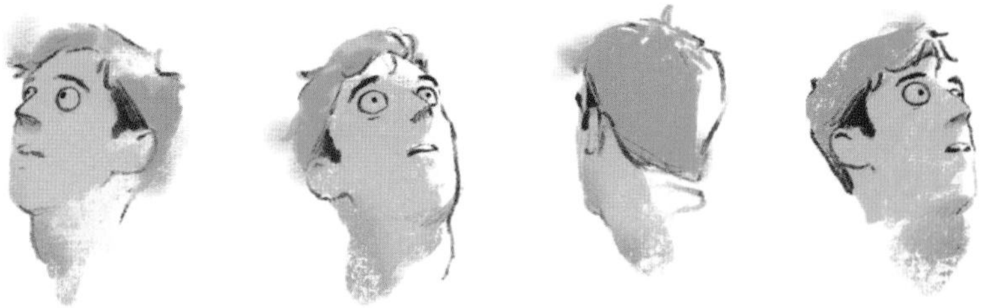
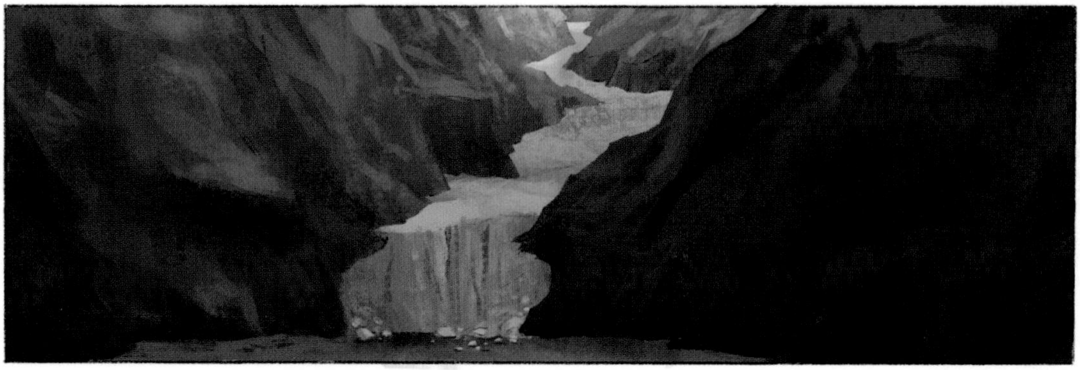
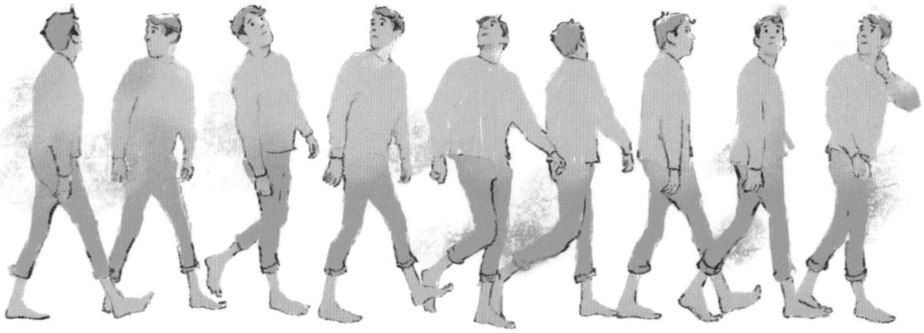
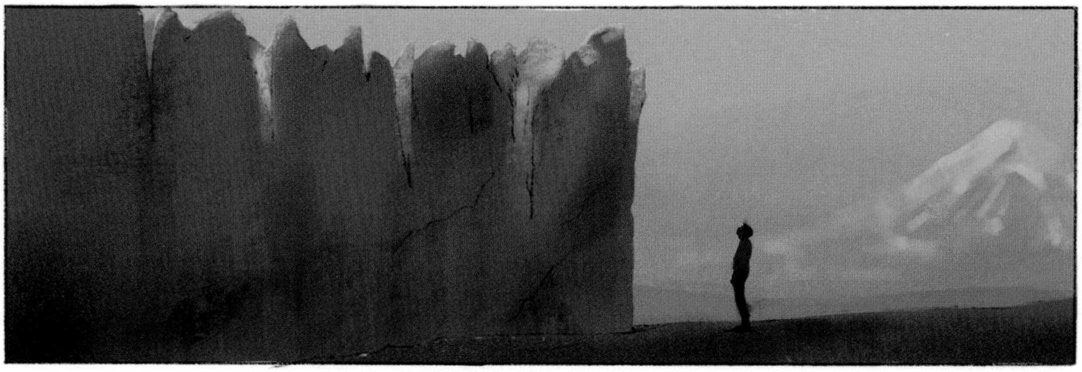

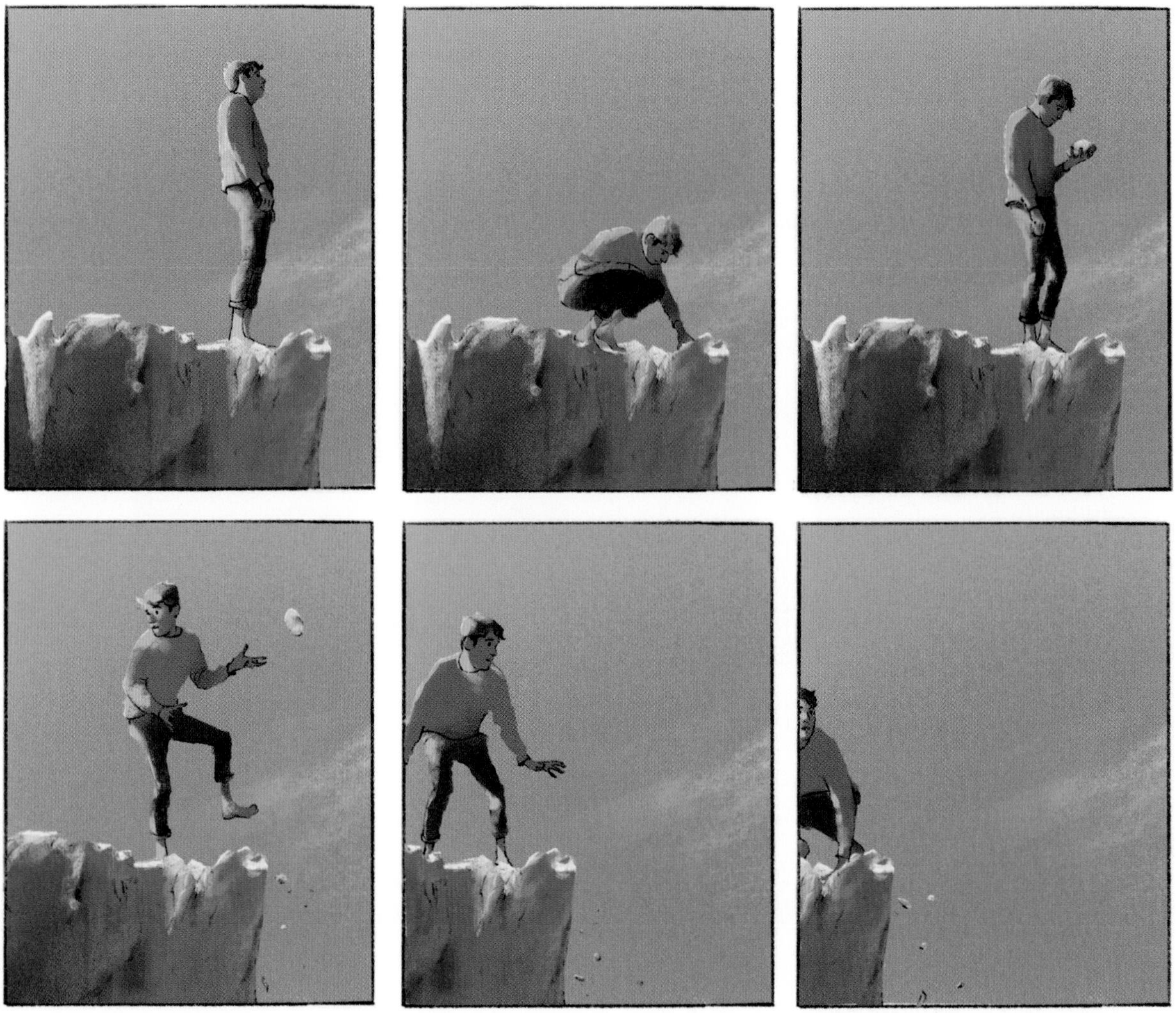

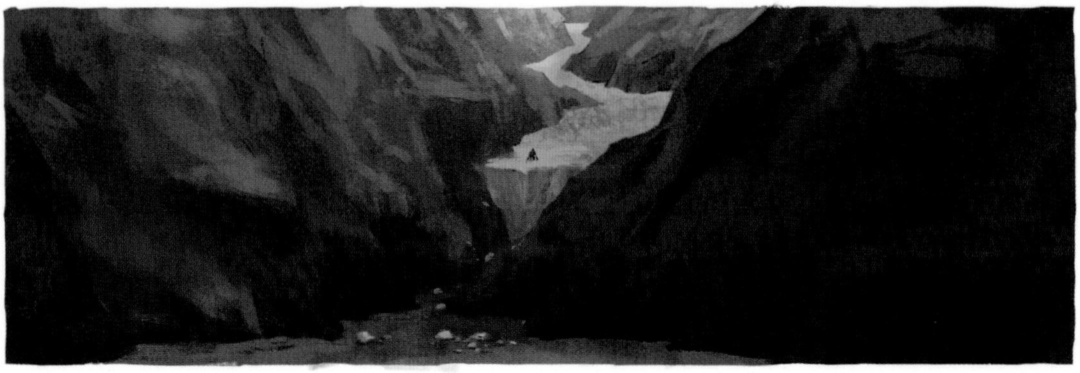

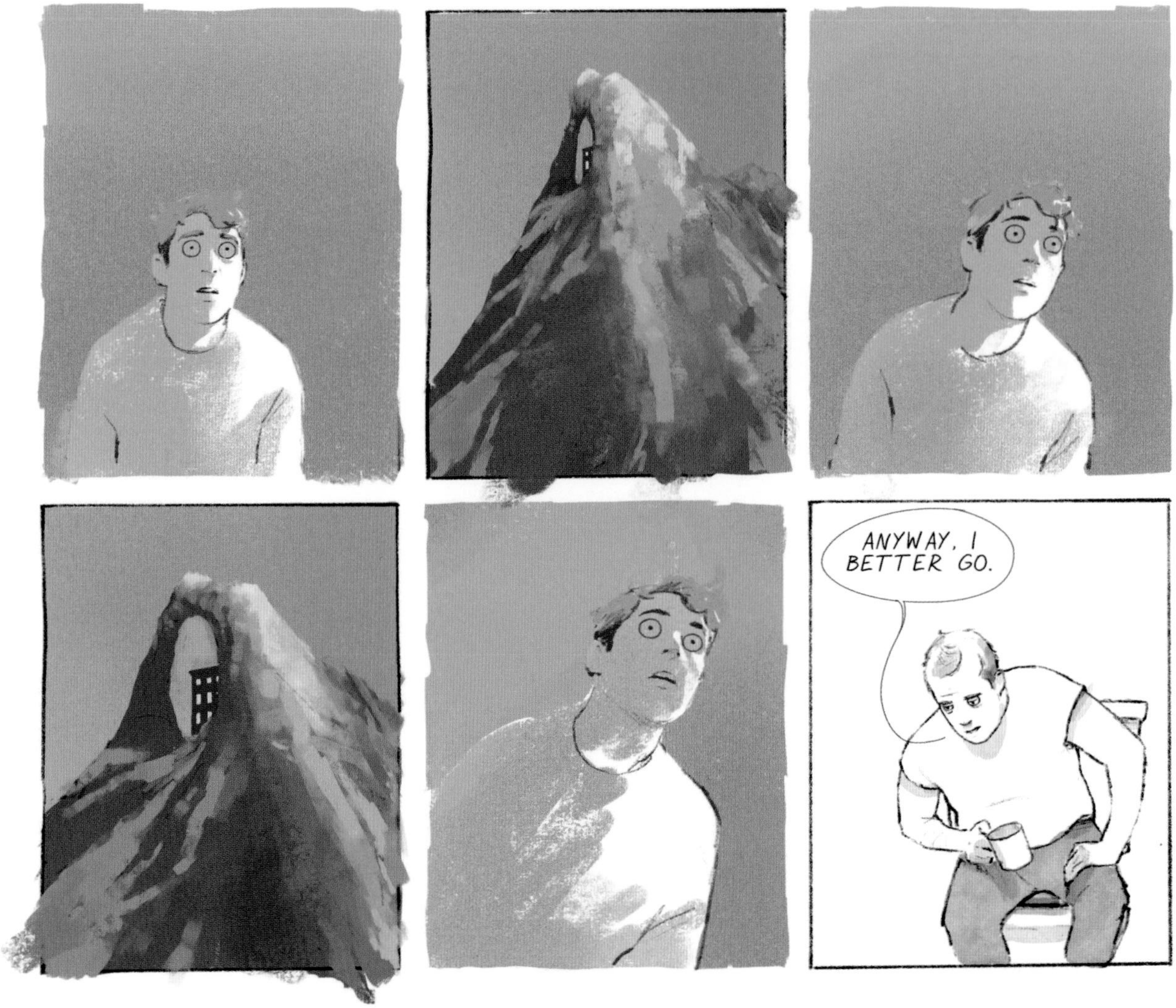
ANYWAY, I BETTER GO.

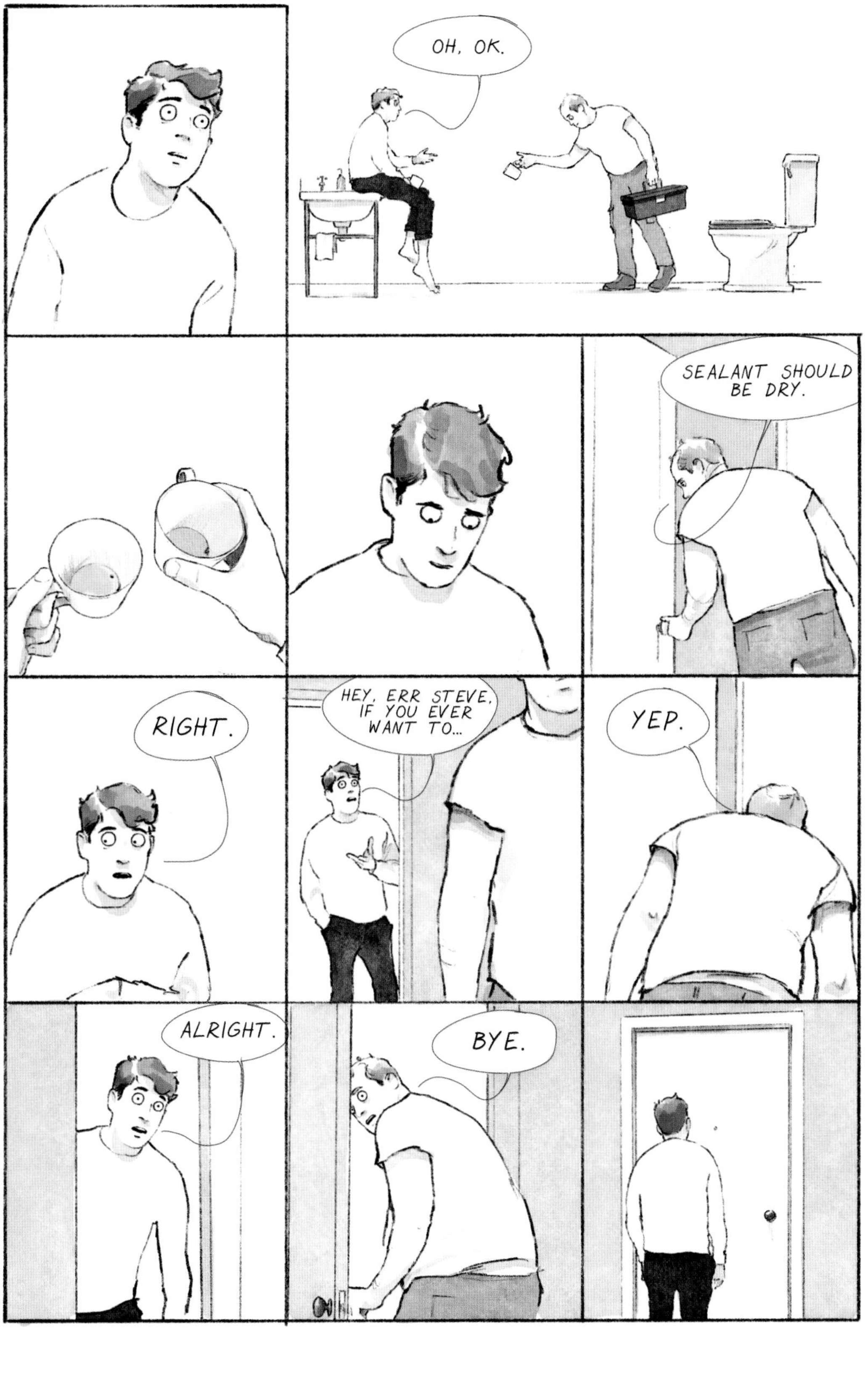
OH, OK.
SEALANT SHOULD BE DRY.
RIGHT.
HEY, ERR STEVE, IF YOU EVER WANT TO...
YEP.
ALRIGHT.
BYE.

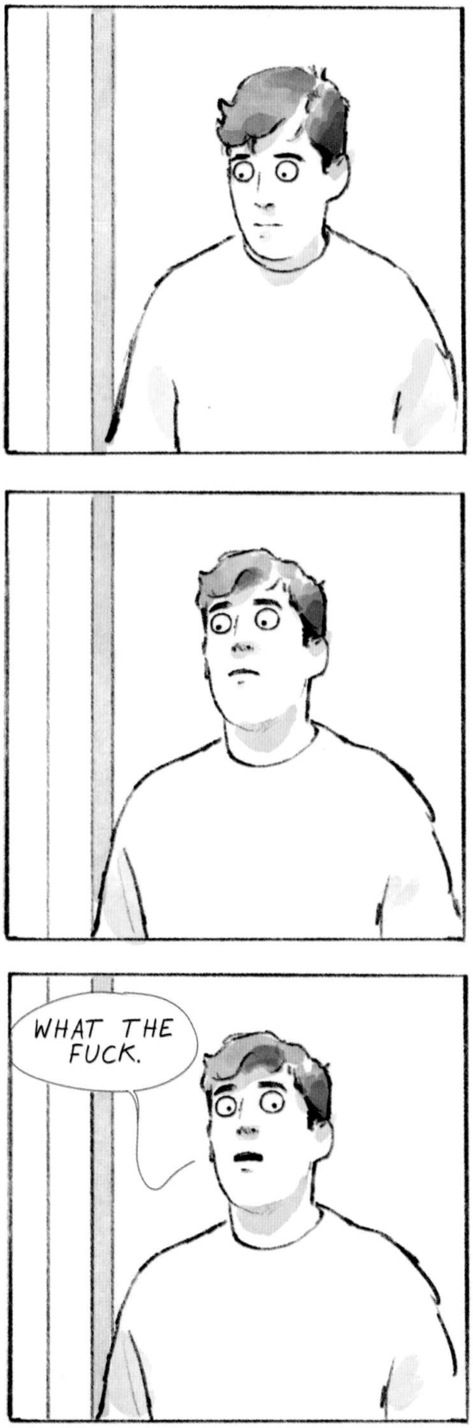
WHAT THE FUCK.

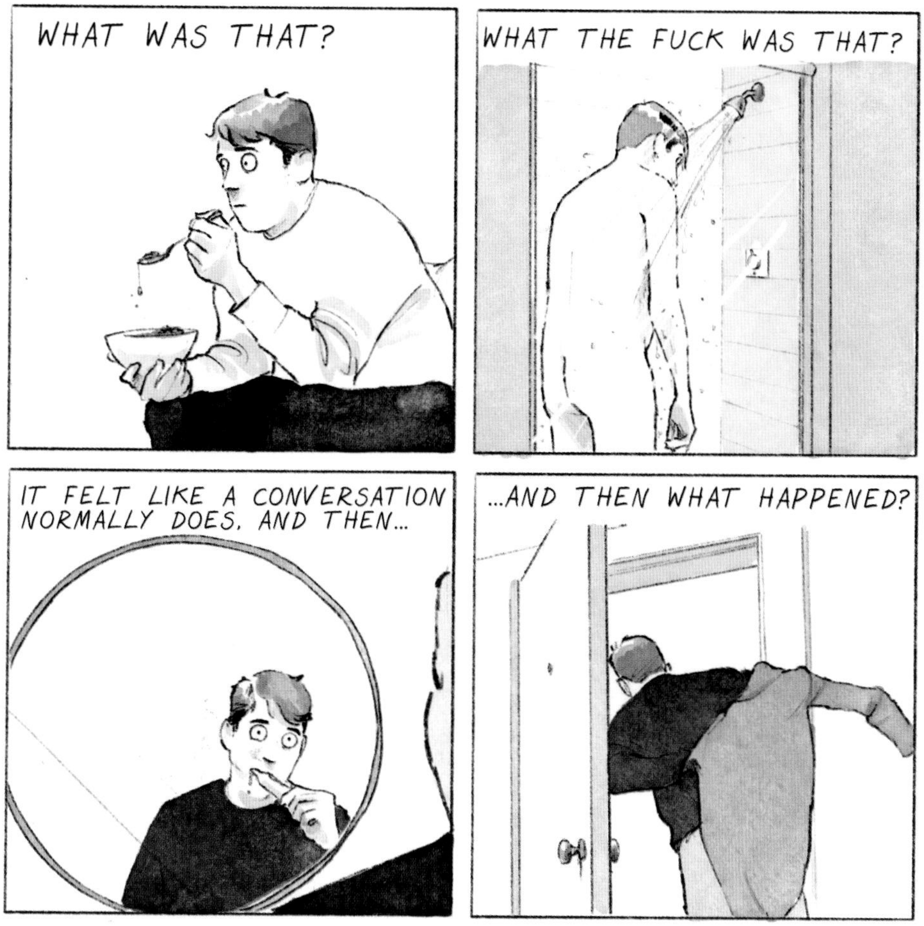
WHAT WAS THAT?
WHAT THE FUCK WAS THAT?
IT FELT LIKE A CONVERSATION NORMALLY DOES, AND THEN...
...AND THEN WHAT HAPPENED?

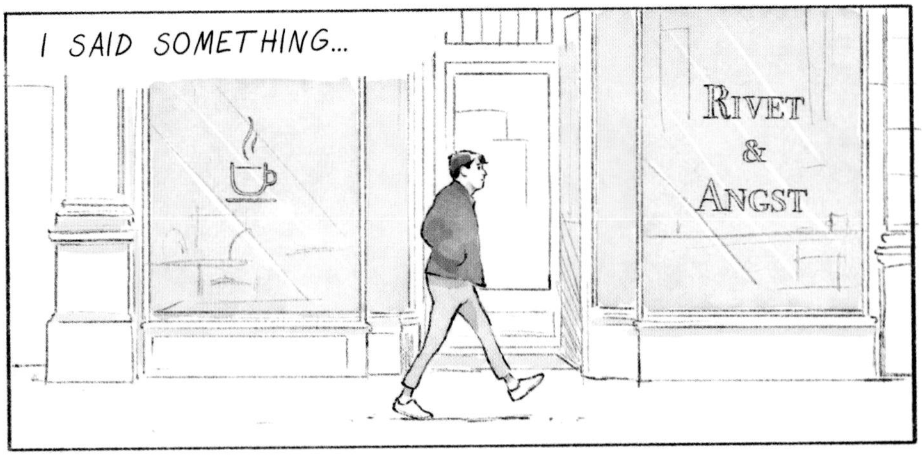
I SAID SOMETHING...
RIVET & ANGST

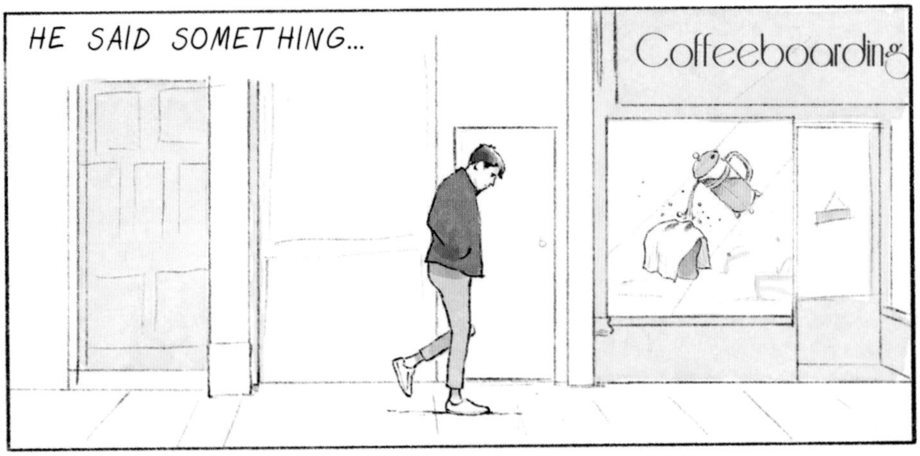
HE SAID SOMETHING...
Coffeeboarding

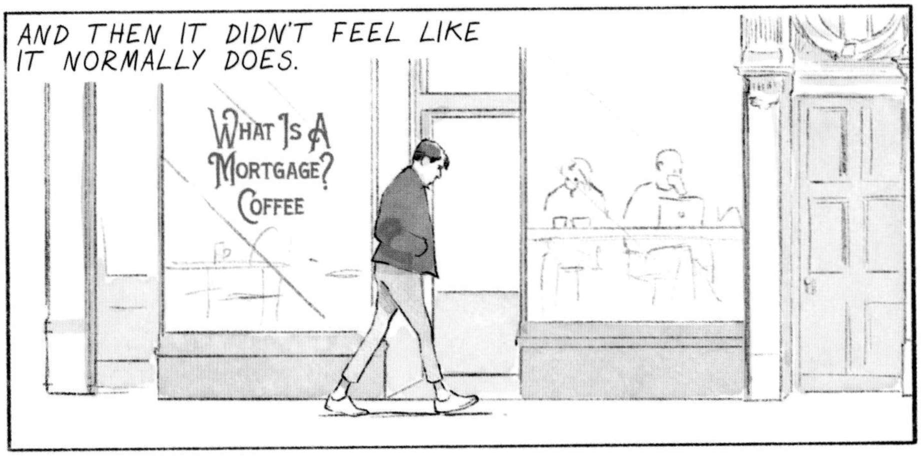
AND THEN IT DIDN'T FEEL LIKE IT NORMALLY DOES.
WHAT IS A MORTGAGE? COFFEE

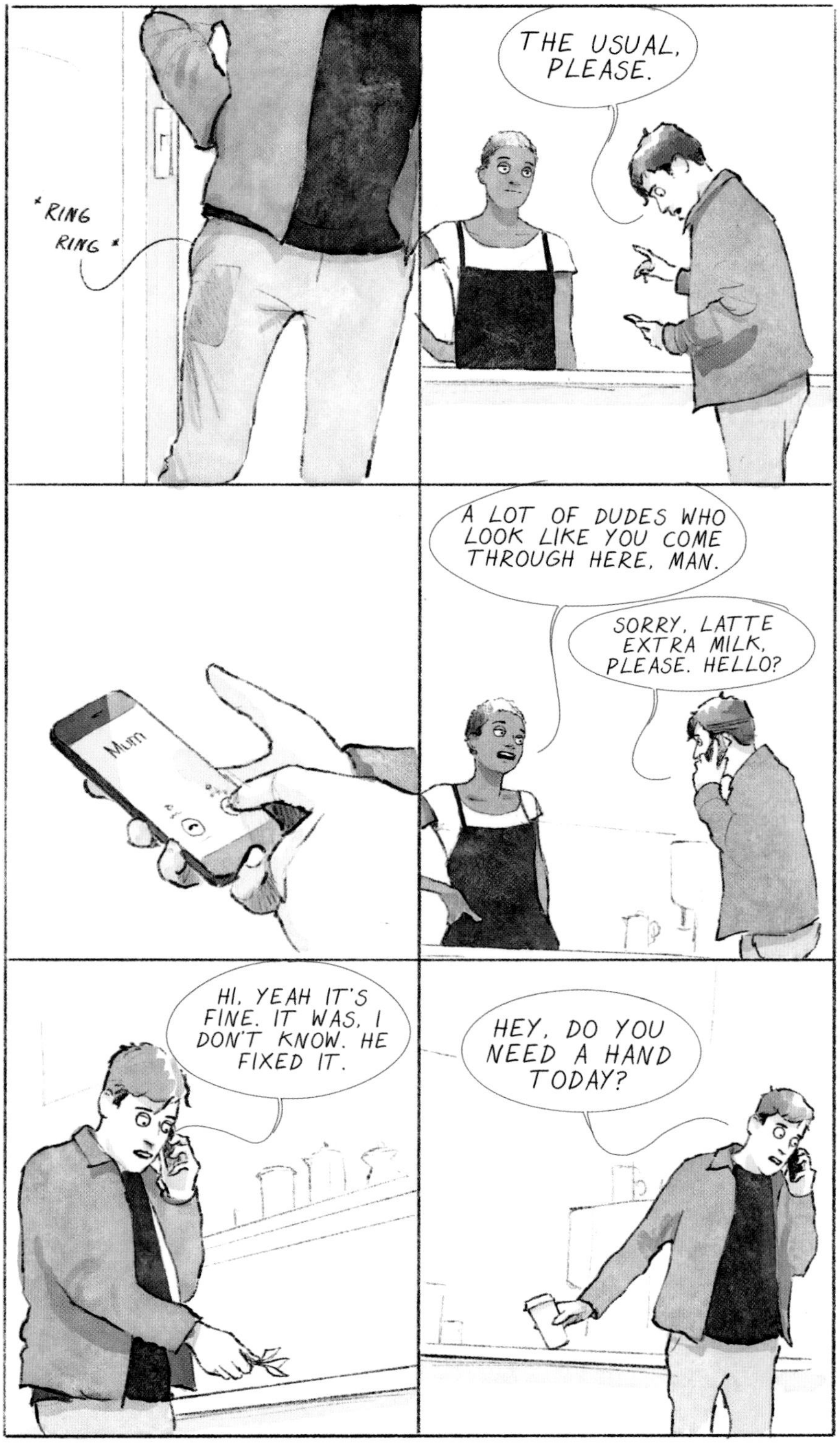
RING RING
THE USUAL, PLEASE.
Mum
A LOT OF DUDES WHO LOOK LIKE YOU COME THROUGH HERE, MAN.
SORRY, LATTE EXTRA MILK, PLEASE. HELLO?
HI. YEAH IT'S FINE. IT WAS, I DON'T KNOW. HE FIXED IT.
HEY, DO YOU NEED A HAND TODAY?

I SAID SOMETHING...
...HE SAID SOMETHING...
...AND THEN IT HAPPENED.

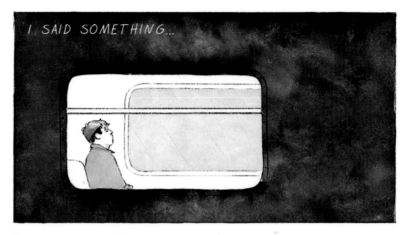

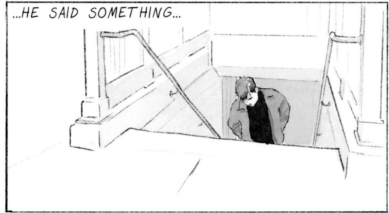

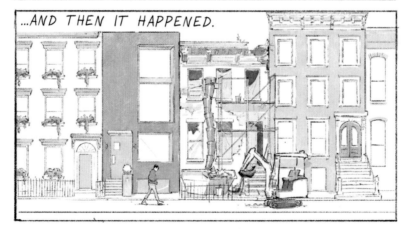

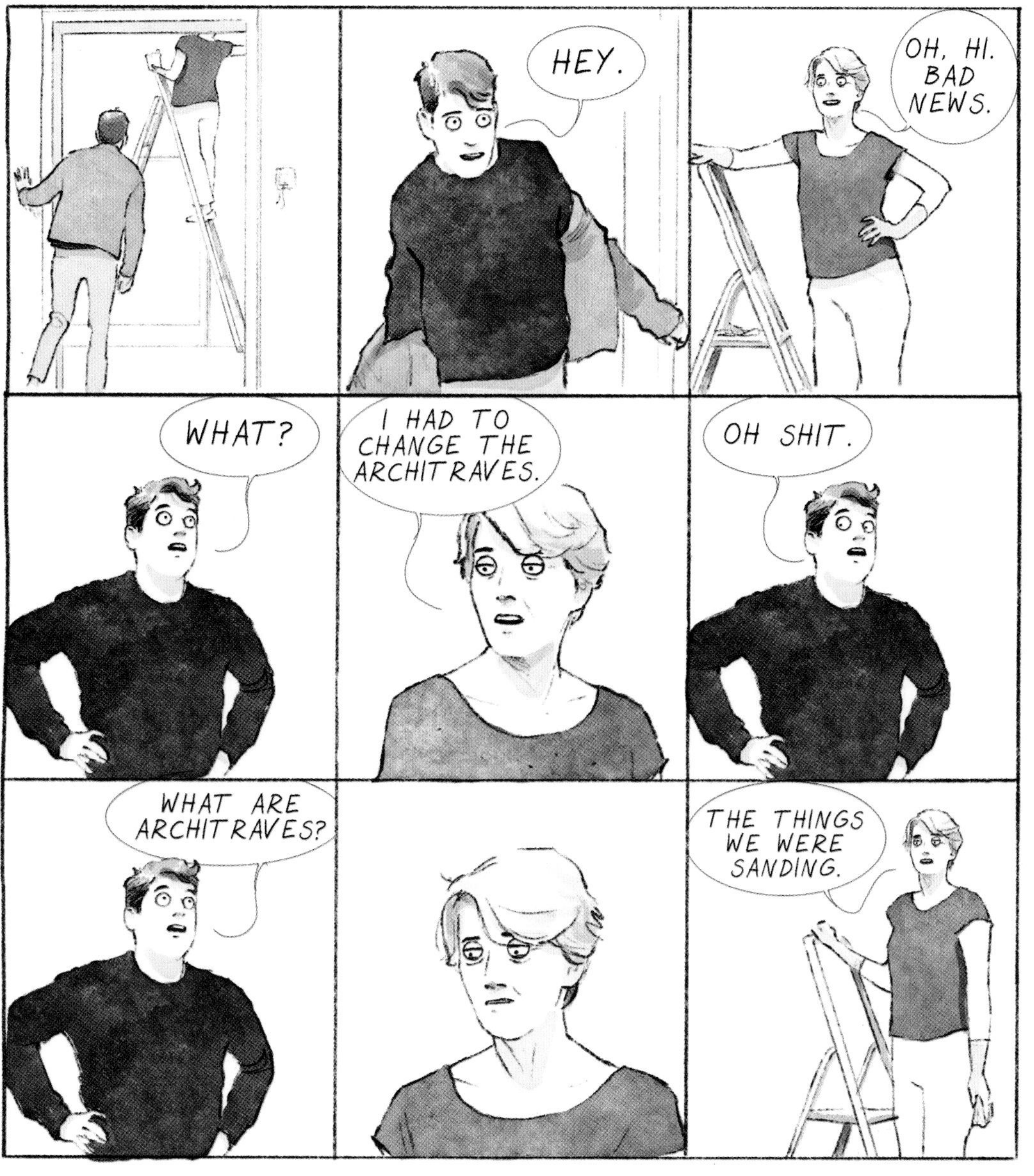
HEY.
OH, HI. BAD NEWS.
WHAT?
I HAD TO CHANGE THE ARCHITRAVES.
OH SHIT.
WHAT ARE ARCHITRAVES?
THE THINGS WE WERE SANDING.

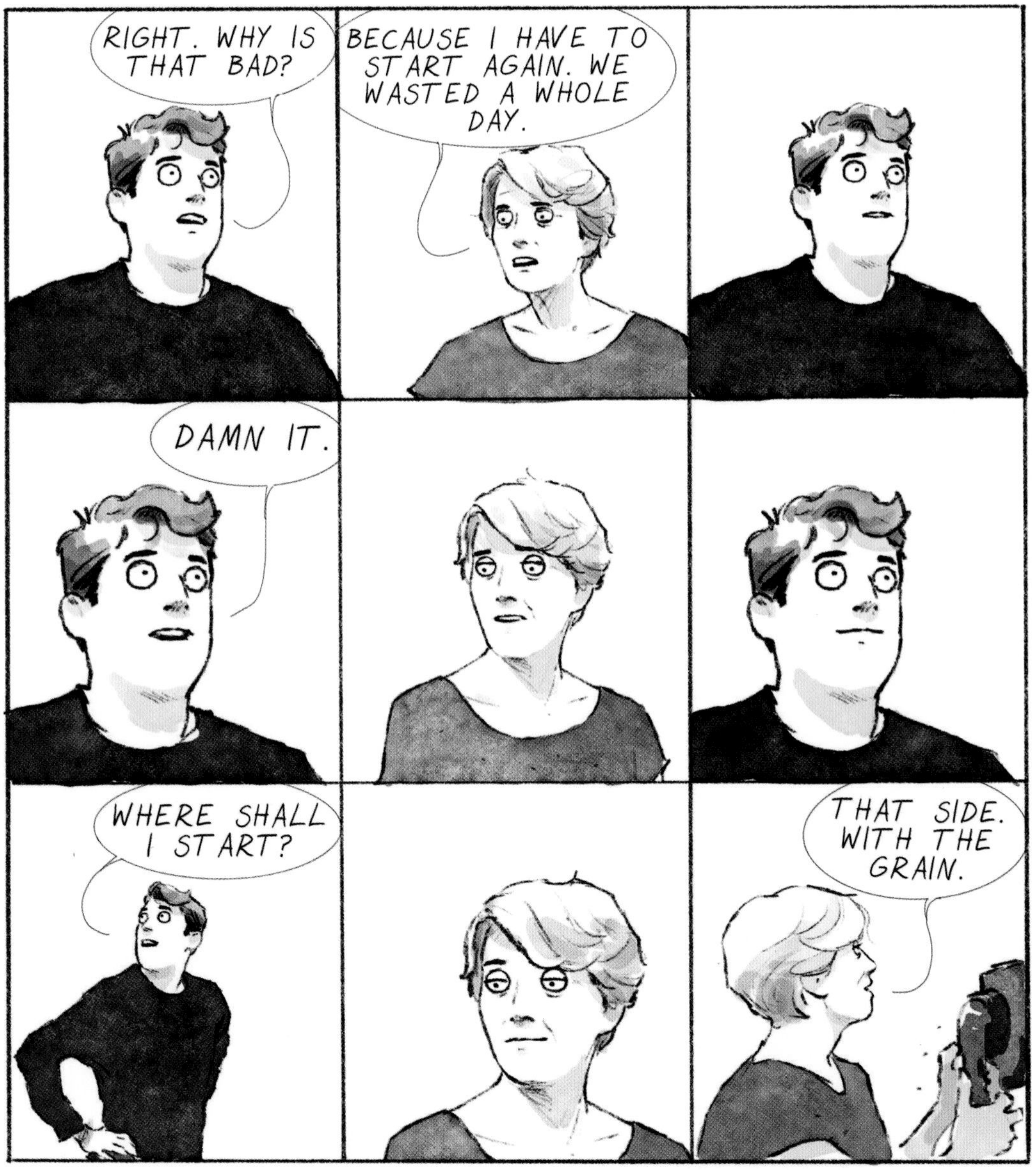
RIGHT. WHY IS THAT BAD?
BECAUSE I HAVE TO START AGAIN. WE WASTED A WHOLE DAY.
DAMN IT.
WHERE SHALL I START?
THAT SIDE. WITH THE GRAIN.

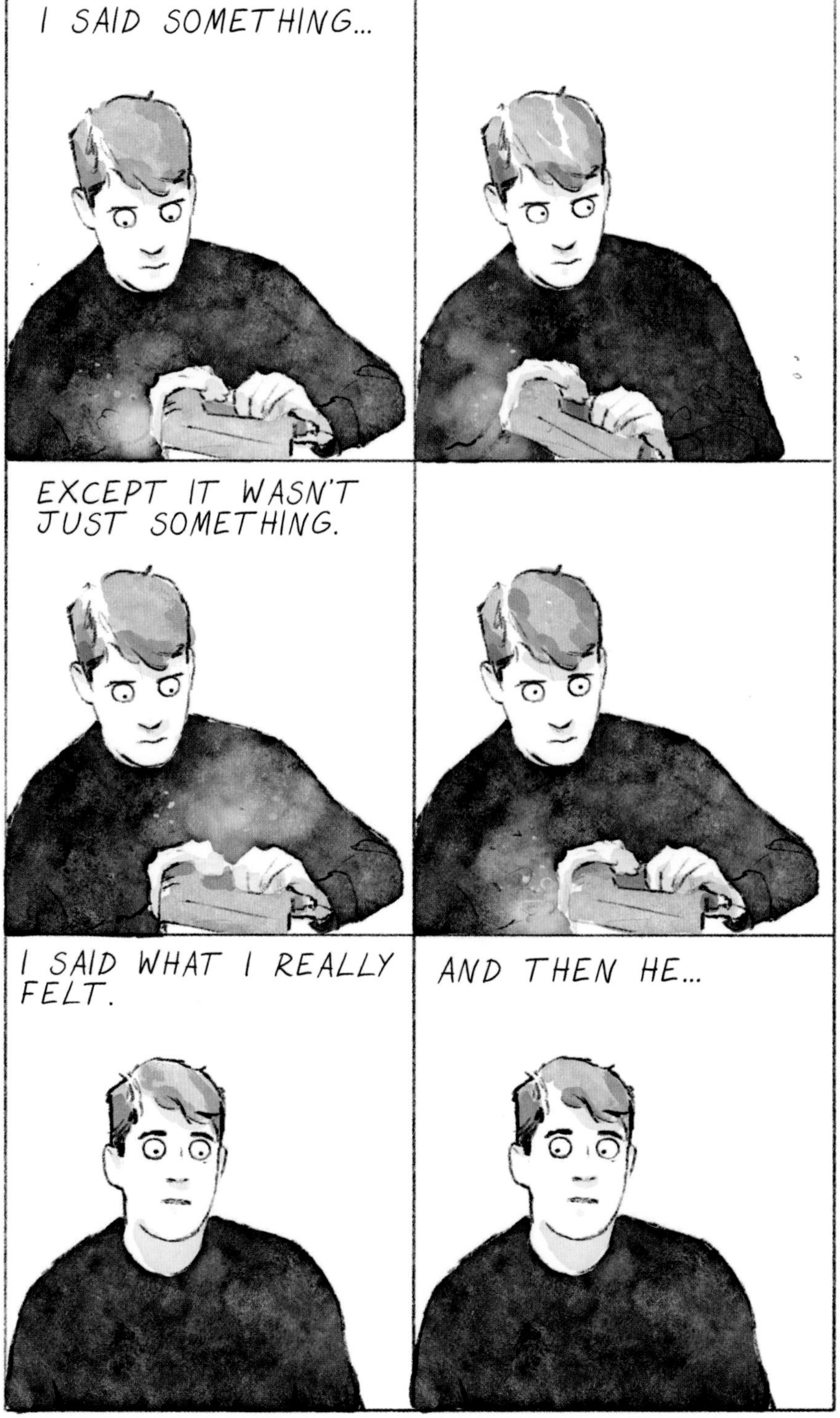
I SAID SOMETHING...
EXCEPT IT WASN'T JUST SOMETHING.
I SAID WHAT I REALLY FELT.
AND THEN HE...

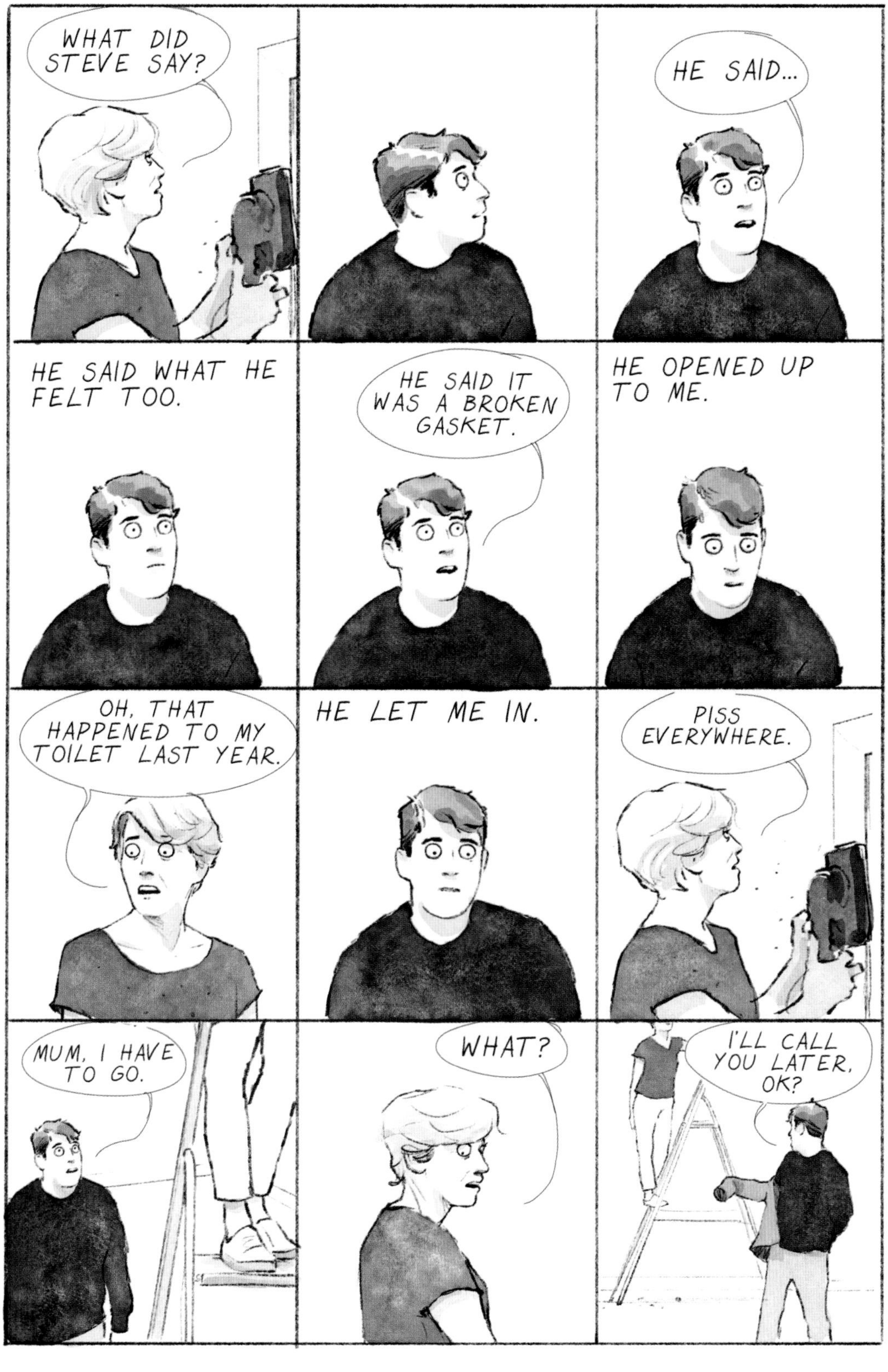
WHAT DID STEVE SAY?
HE SAID...
HE SAID WHAT HE FELT TOO.
HE SAID IT WAS A BROKEN GASKET.
HE OPENED UP TO ME.
OH, THAT HAPPENED TO MY TOILET LAST YEAR.
HE LET ME IN.
PISS EVERYWHERE.
MUM, I HAVE TO GO.
WHAT?
I'LL CALL YOU LATER, OK?

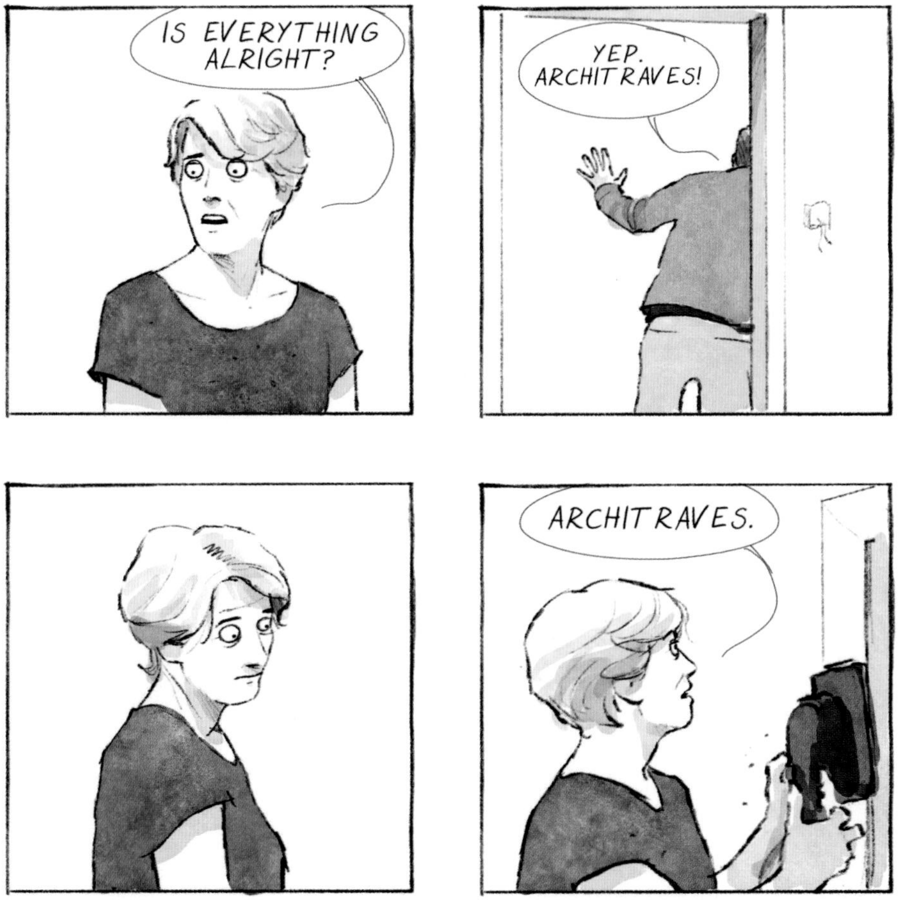
IS EVERYTHING ALRIGHT?
YEP. ARCHITRAVES!
ARCHITRAVES.

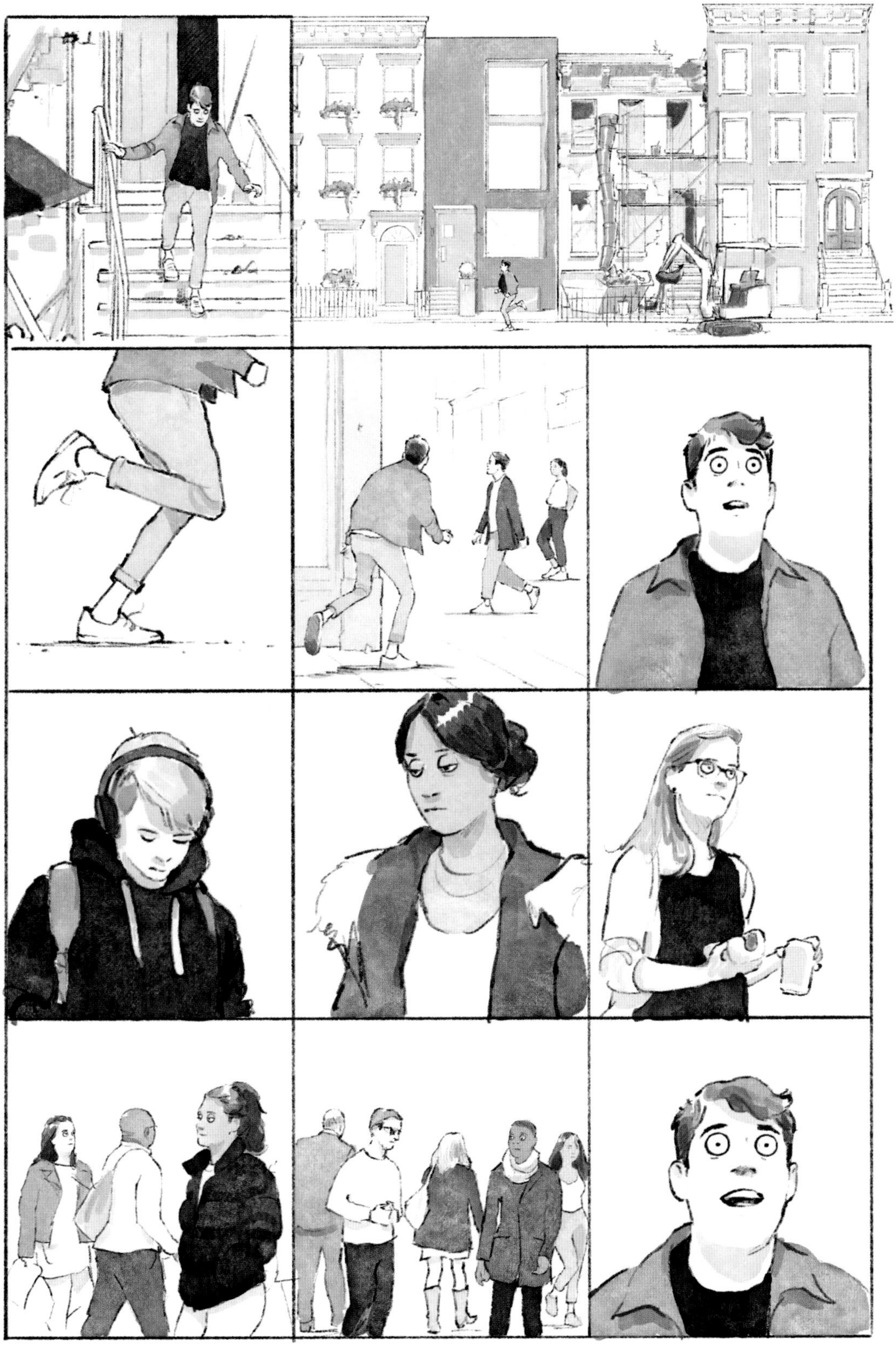

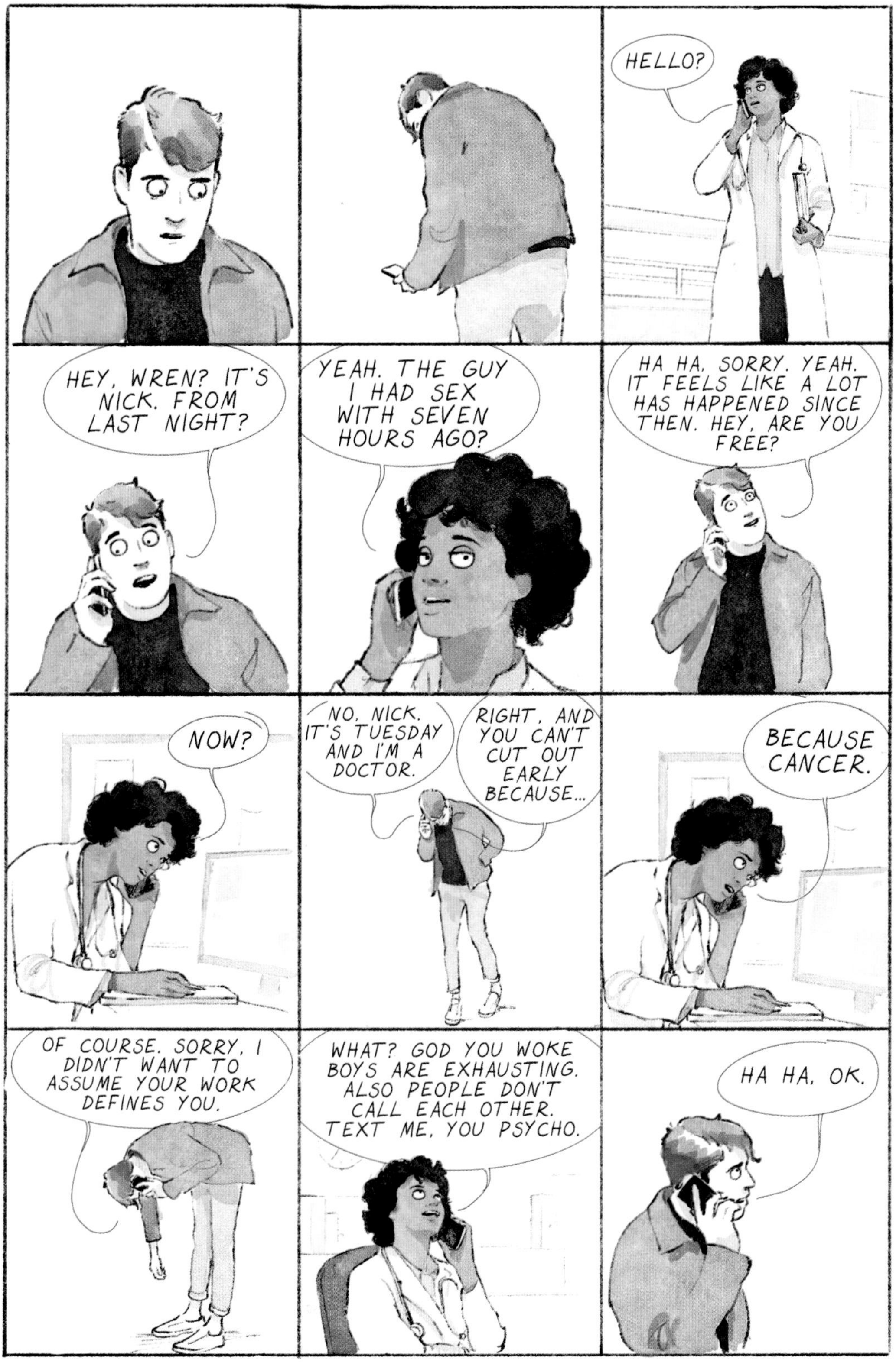
HELLO?
HEY, WREN? IT'S NICK. FROM LAST NIGHT?
YEAH. THE GUY I HAD SEX WITH SEVEN HOURS AGO?
HA HA, SORRY. YEAH. IT FEELS LIKE A LOT HAS HAPPENED SINCE THEN. HEY, ARE YOU FREE?
NOW?
NO, NICK. IT'S TUESDAY AND I'M A DOCTOR.
RIGHT, AND YOU CAN'T CUT OUT EARLY BECAUSE...
BECAUSE CANCER.
OF COURSE. SORRY, I DIDN'T WANT TO ASSUME YOUR WORK DEFINES YOU.
WHAT? GOD YOU WOKE BOYS ARE EXHAUSTING. ALSO PEOPLE DON'T CALL EACH OTHER. TEXT ME, YOU PSYCHO.
HA HA, OK.

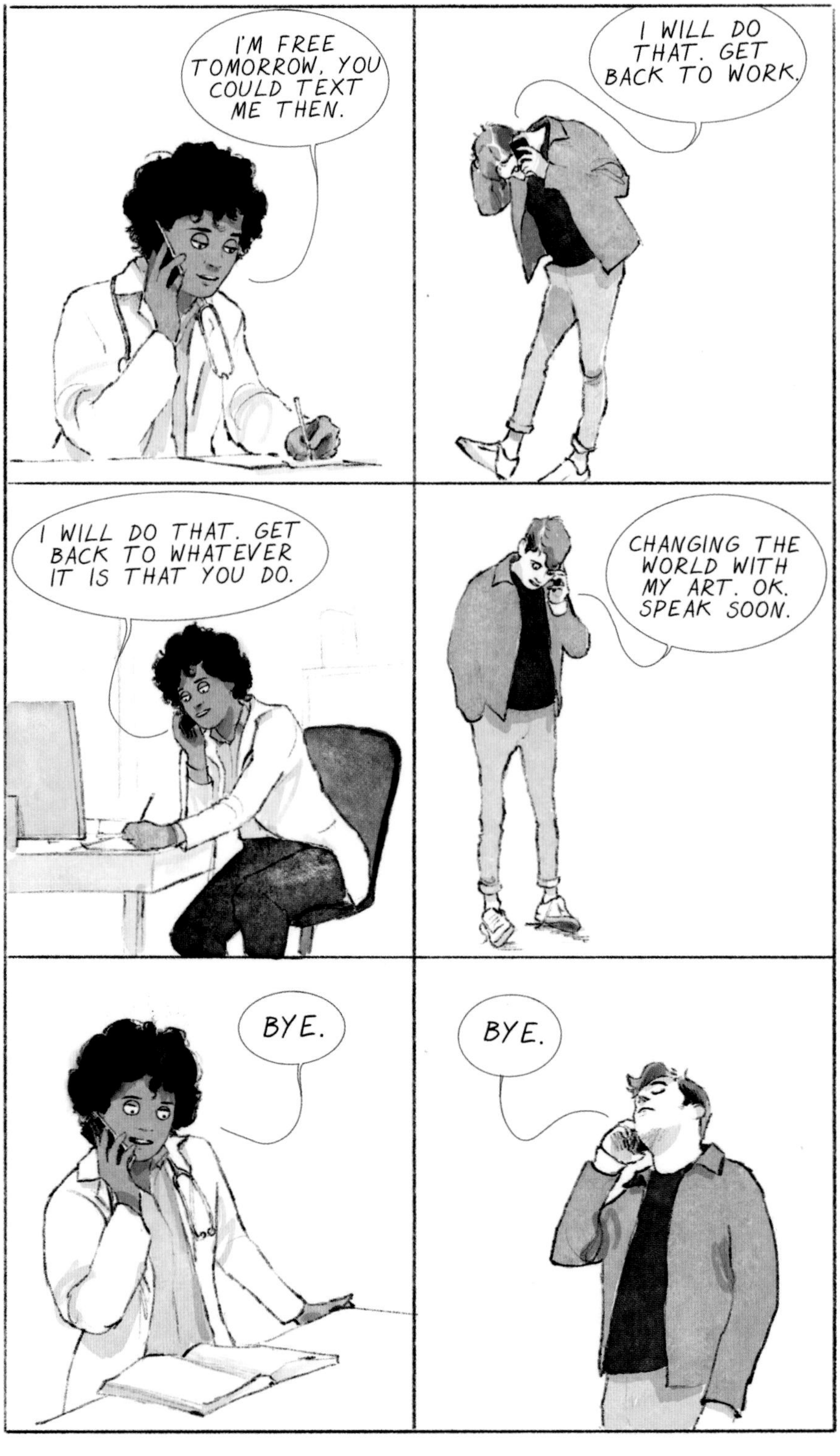
I'M FREE TOMORROW, YOU COULD TEXT ME THEN.
I WILL DO THAT. GET BACK TO WORK.
I WILL DO THAT. GET BACK TO WHATEVER IT IS THAT YOU DO.
CHANGING THE WORLD WITH MY ART. OK. SPEAK SOON.
BYE.
BYE.

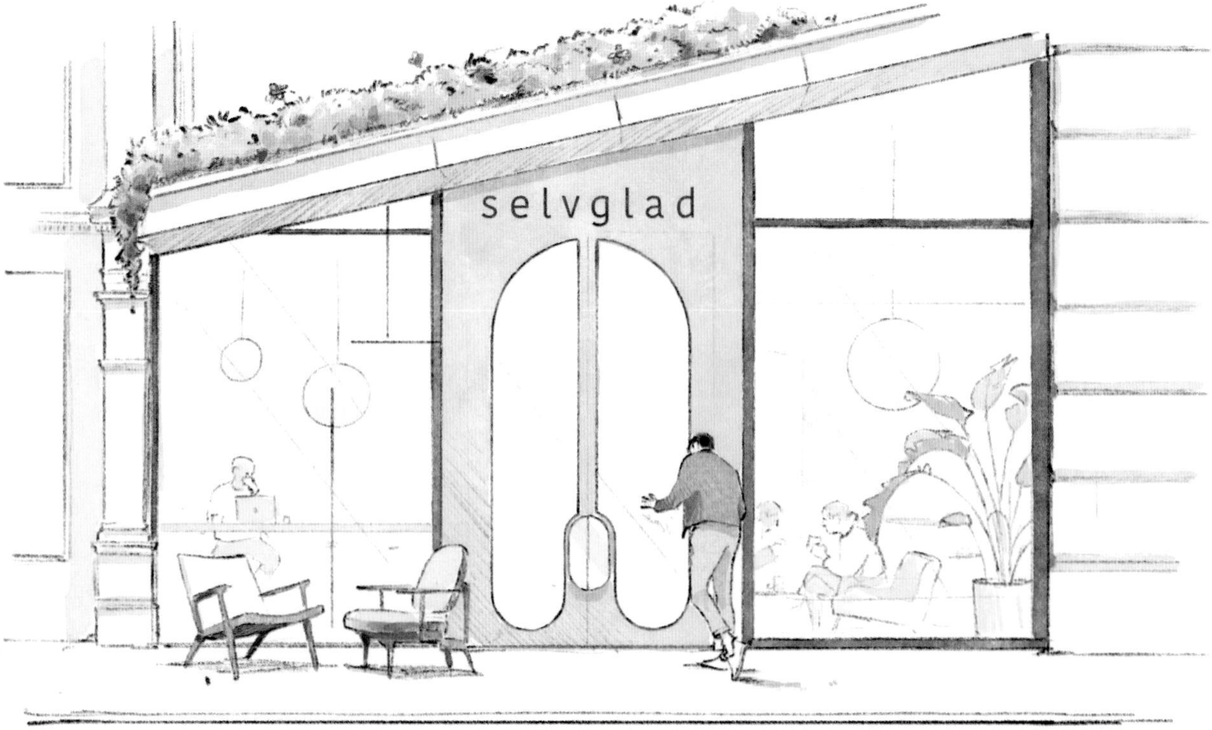
selvglad

SELVGLAD (THE DANISH CONCEPT OF SMUGNESS). NOT SO MUCH A COFFEE SHOP AS IT IS A VISION OF WHAT YOUR LIFE WOULD BE IF YOU WERE HAPPY. THEIR SPECIALTY TEA IS MADE OF PINE NEEDLES THAT HAVE BEEN THROUGH THE DIGESTIVE SYSTEM OF A VOLE THAT HAS BEEN THROUGH THE DIGESTIVE SYSTEM OF AN OWL THAT HAS BEEN THROUGH THE DIGESTIVE SYSTEM OF A BEAUTIFUL DANISH WIDOW, AND...

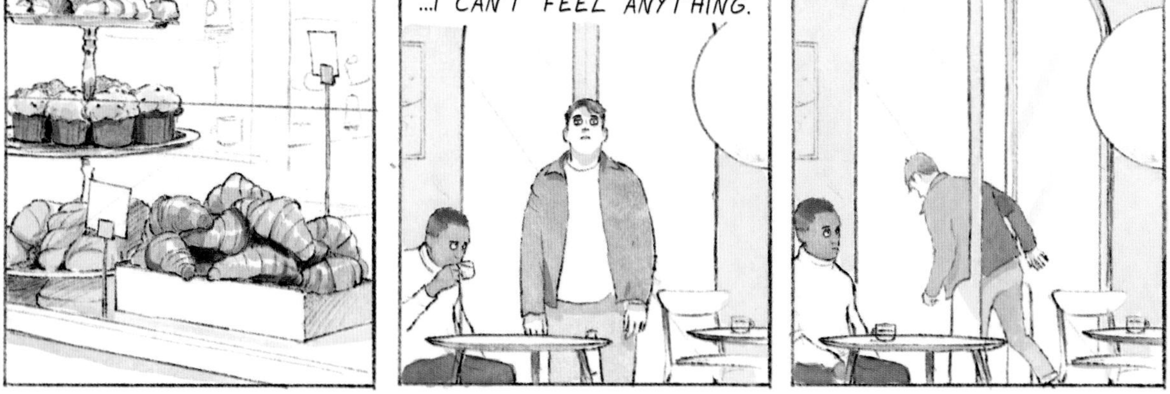
...I CAN'T FEEL ANYTHING.

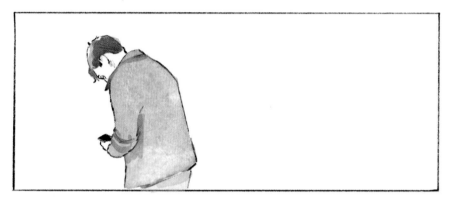

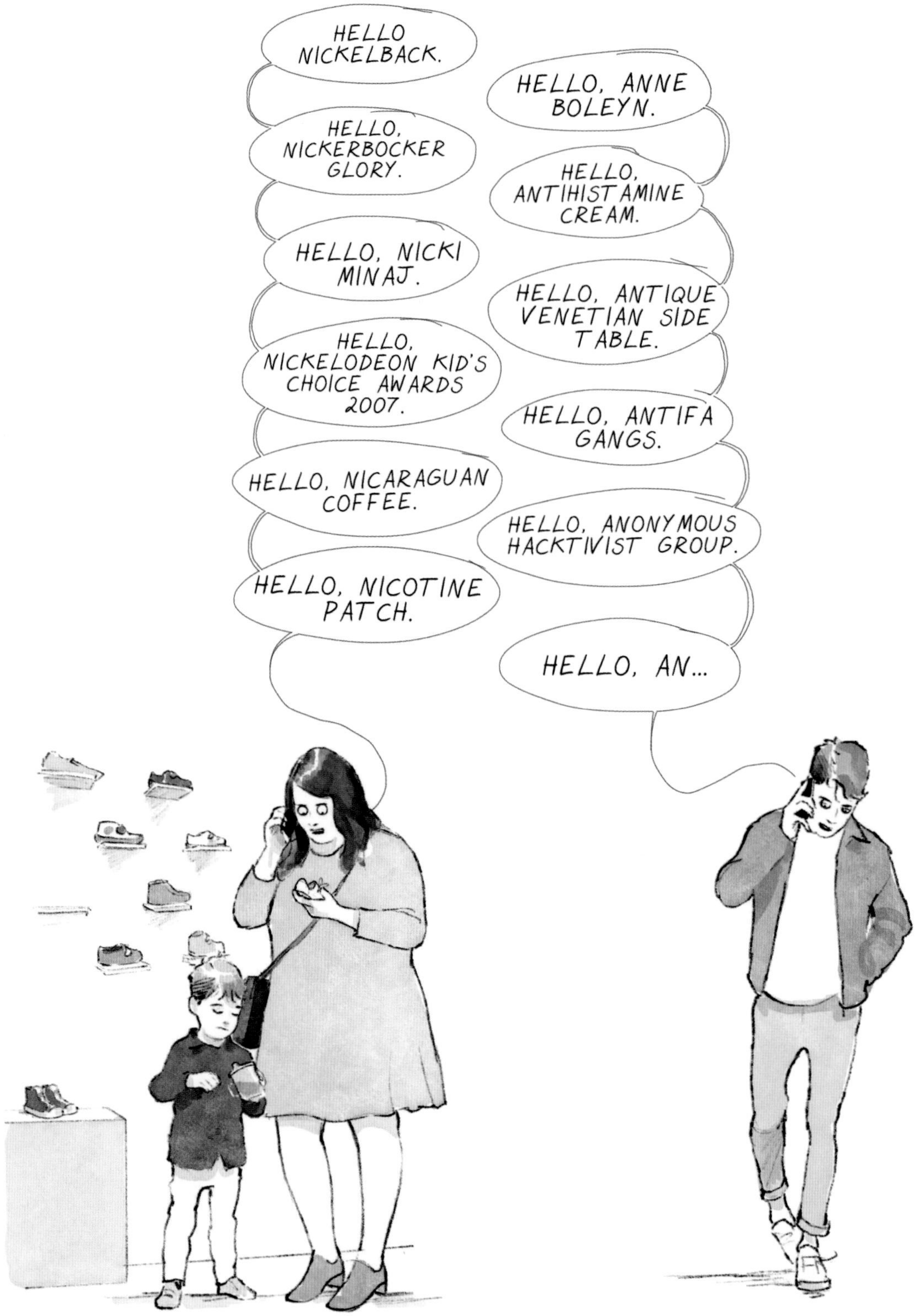
HELLO NICKELBACK.
HELLO, NICKERBOCKER GLORY.
HELLO, NICKI MINAJ.
HELLO, NICKELODEON KID'S CHOICE AWARDS 2007.
HELLO, NICARAGUAN COFFEE.
HELLO, NICOTINE PATCH.
HELLO, ANNE BOLEYN.
HELLO, ANTIHISTAMINE CREAM.
HELLO, ANTIQUE VENETIAN SIDE TABLE.
HELLO, ANTIFA GANGS.
HELLO, ANONYMOUS HACKTIVIST GROUP.
HELLO, AN...

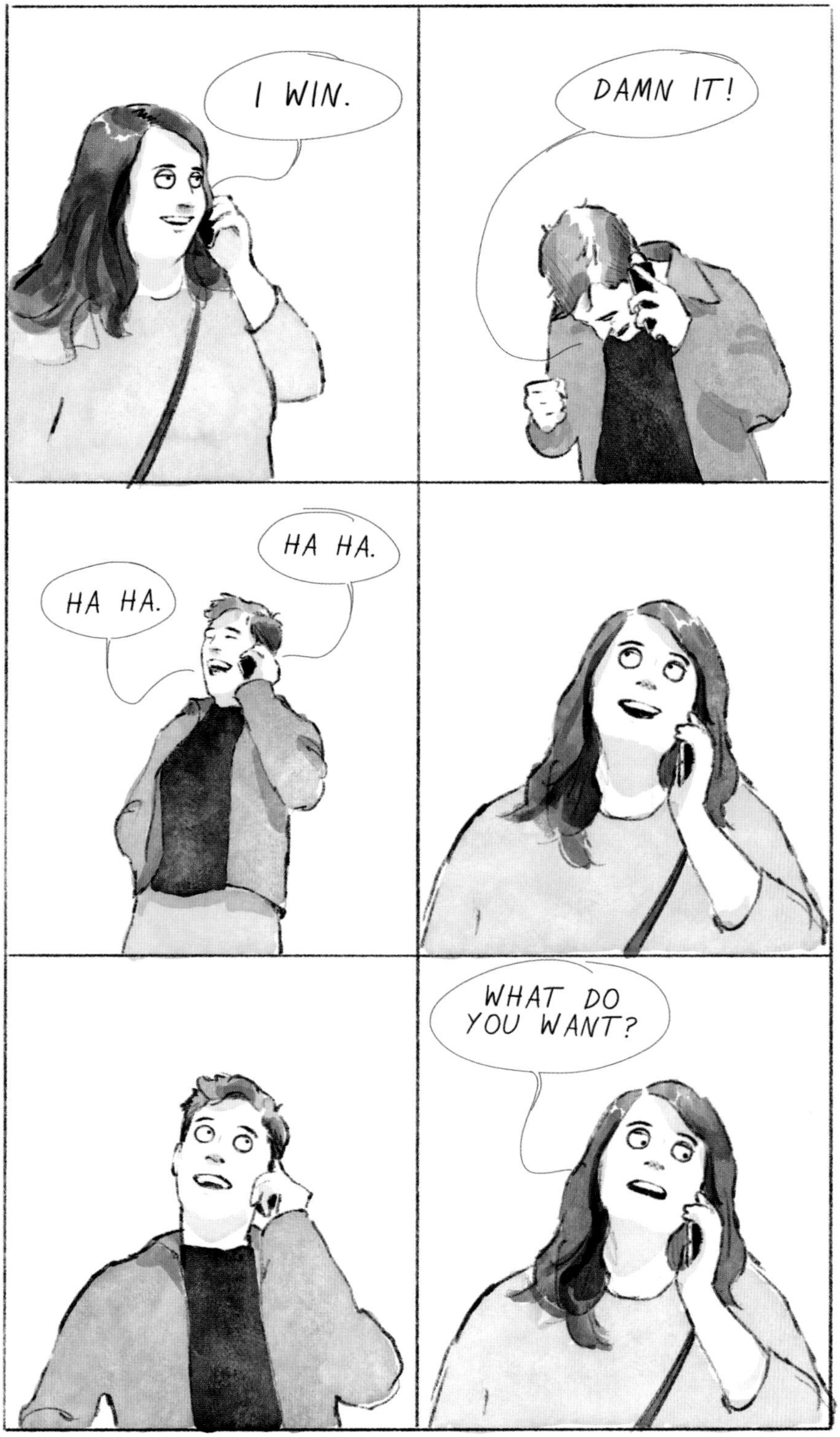
I WIN.
DAMN IT!
HA HA.
HA HA.
WHAT DO YOU WANT?

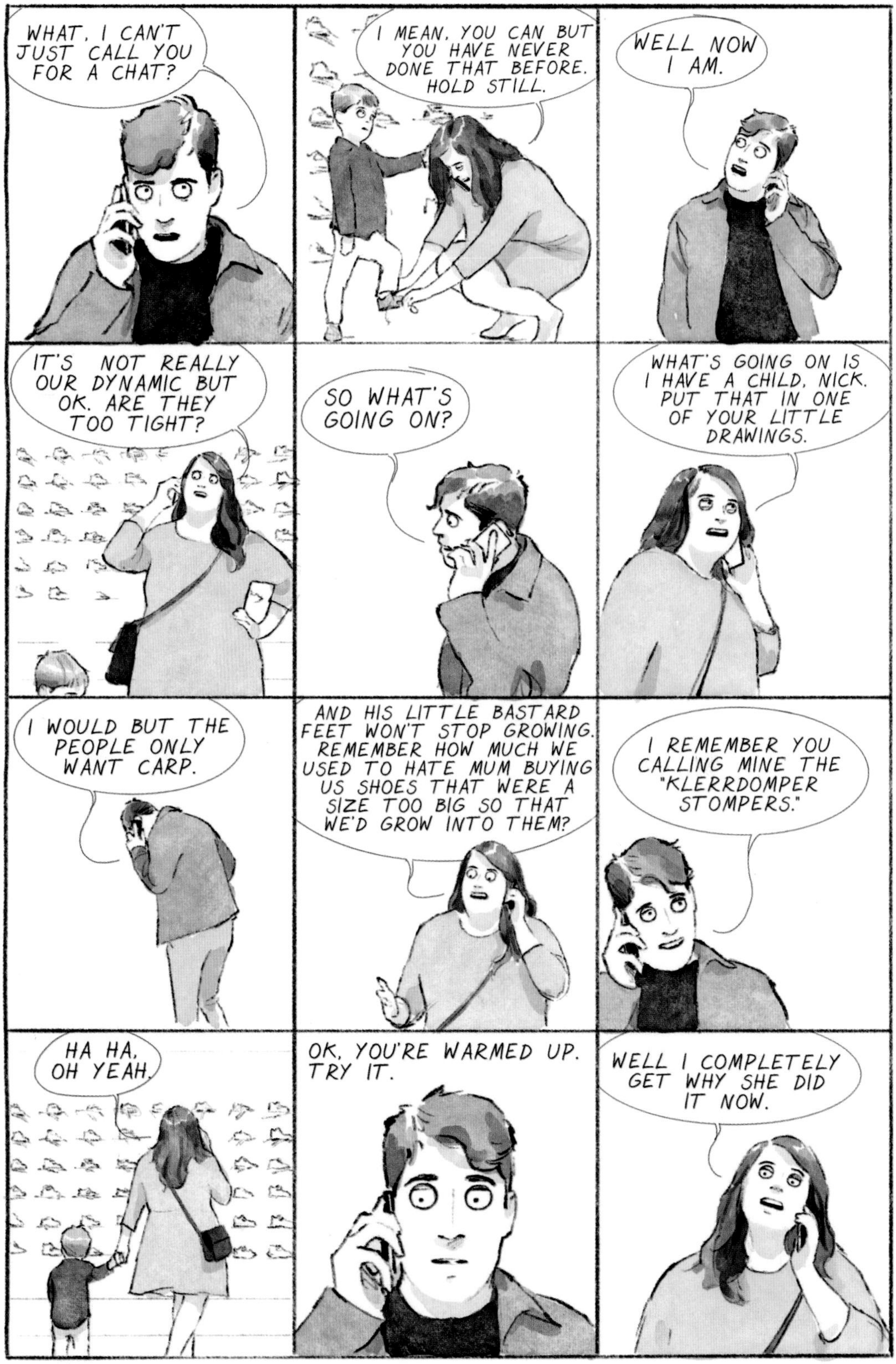
WHAT, I CAN'T JUST CALL YOU FOR A CHAT?
I MEAN, YOU CAN BUT YOU HAVE NEVER DONE THAT BEFORE. HOLD STILL.
WELL NOW I AM.
IT'S NOT REALLY OUR DYNAMIC BUT OK. ARE THEY TOO TIGHT?
SO WHAT'S GOING ON?
WHAT'S GOING ON IS I HAVE A CHILD, NICK. PUT THAT IN ONE OF YOUR LITTLE DRAWINGS.
I WOULD BUT THE PEOPLE ONLY WANT CARP.
AND HIS LITTLE BASTARD FEET WON'T STOP GROWING. REMEMBER HOW MUCH WE USED TO HATE MUM BUYING US SHOES THAT WERE A SIZE TOO BIG SO THAT WE'D GROW INTO THEM?
I REMEMBER YOU CALLING MINE THE "KLERRDOMPER STOMPERS."
HA HA, OH YEAH.
OK, YOU'RE WARMED UP. TRY IT.
WELL I COMPLETELY GET WHY SHE DID IT NOW.

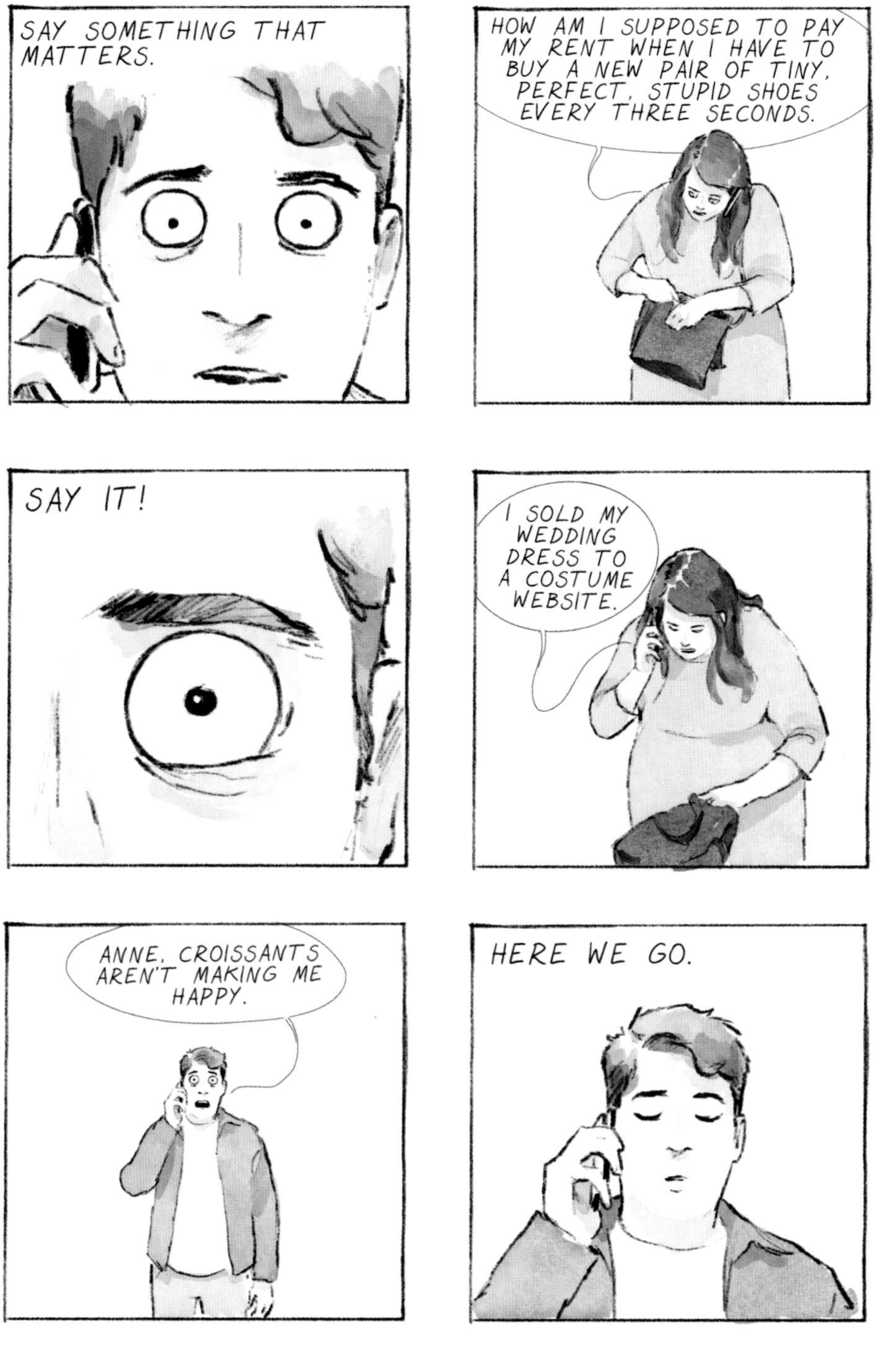
SAY SOMETHING THAT MATTERS.
HOW AM I SUPPOSED TO PAY MY RENT WHEN I HAVE TO BUY A NEW PAIR OF TINY, PERFECT, STUPID SHOES EVERY THREE SECONDS.
SAY IT!
I SOLD MY WEDDING DRESS TO A COSTUME WEBSITE.
ANNE, CROISSANTS AREN'T MAKING ME HAPPY.
HERE WE GO.

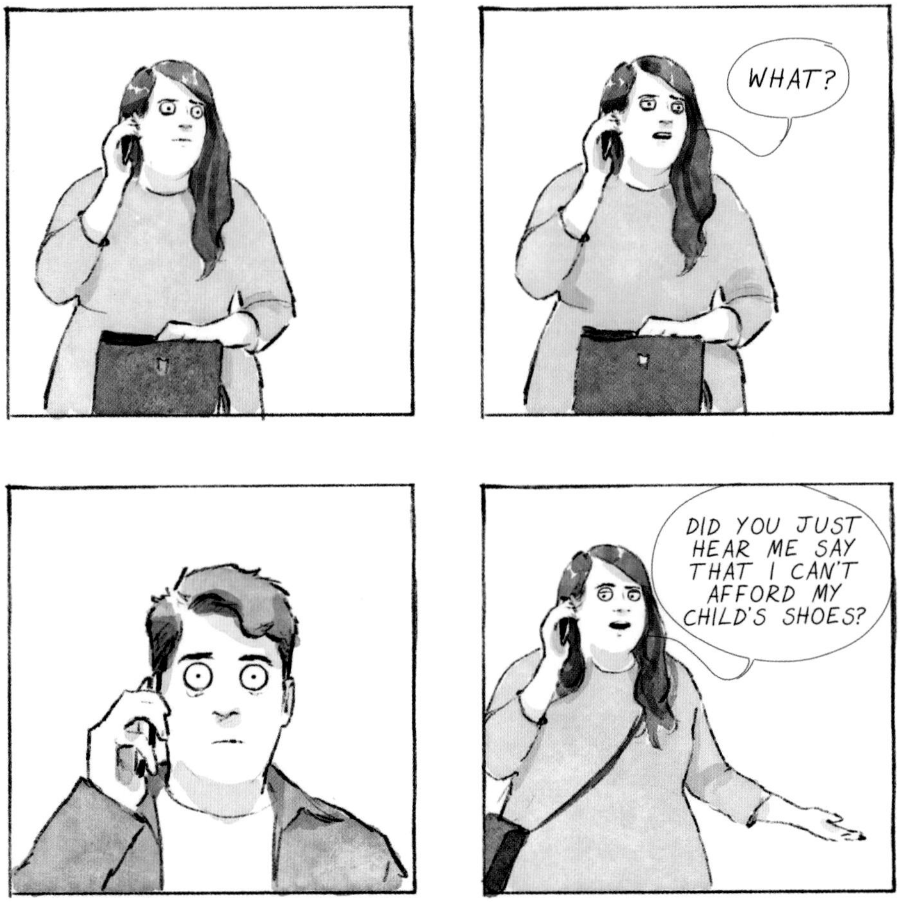
WHAT?
DID YOU JUST HEAR ME SAY THAT I CAN'T AFFORD MY CHILD'S SHOES?

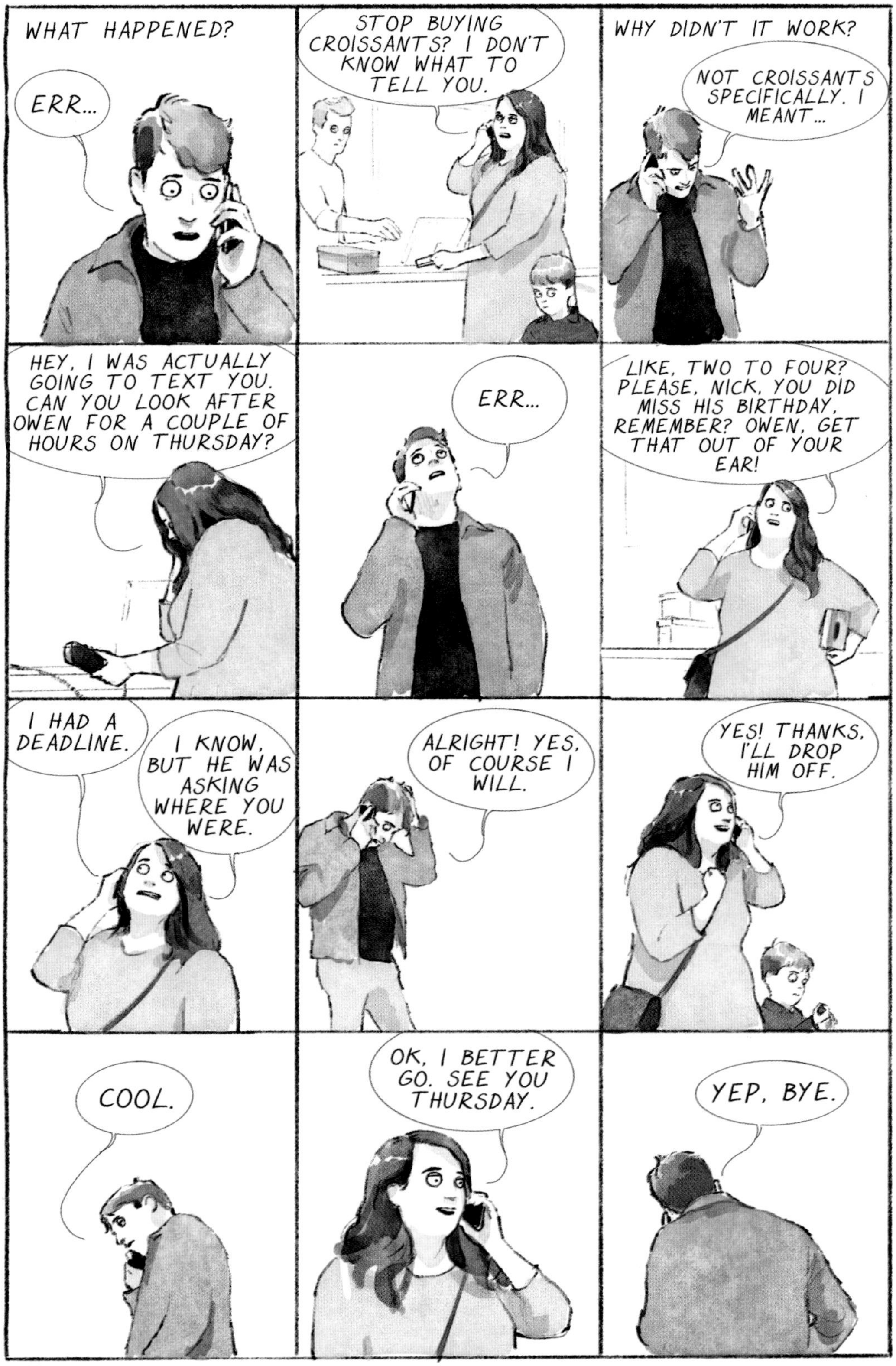
WHAT HAPPENED?
ERR...
STOP BUYING CROISSANTS? I DON'T KNOW WHAT TO TELL YOU.
WHY DIDN'T IT WORK?
NOT CROISSANTS SPECIFICALLY. I MEANT...
HEY, I WAS ACTUALLY GOING TO TEXT YOU. CAN YOU LOOK AFTER OWEN FOR A COUPLE OF HOURS ON THURSDAY?
ERR...
LIKE, TWO TO FOUR? PLEASE, NICK, YOU DID MISS HIS BIRTHDAY, REMEMBER? OWEN, GET THAT OUT OF YOUR EAR!
I HAD A DEADLINE.
I KNOW, BUT HE WAS ASKING WHERE YOU WERE.
ALRIGHT! YES, OF COURSE I WILL.
YES! THANKS, I'LL DROP HIM OFF.
COOL.
OK, I BETTER GO. SEE YOU THURSDAY.
YEP, BYE.

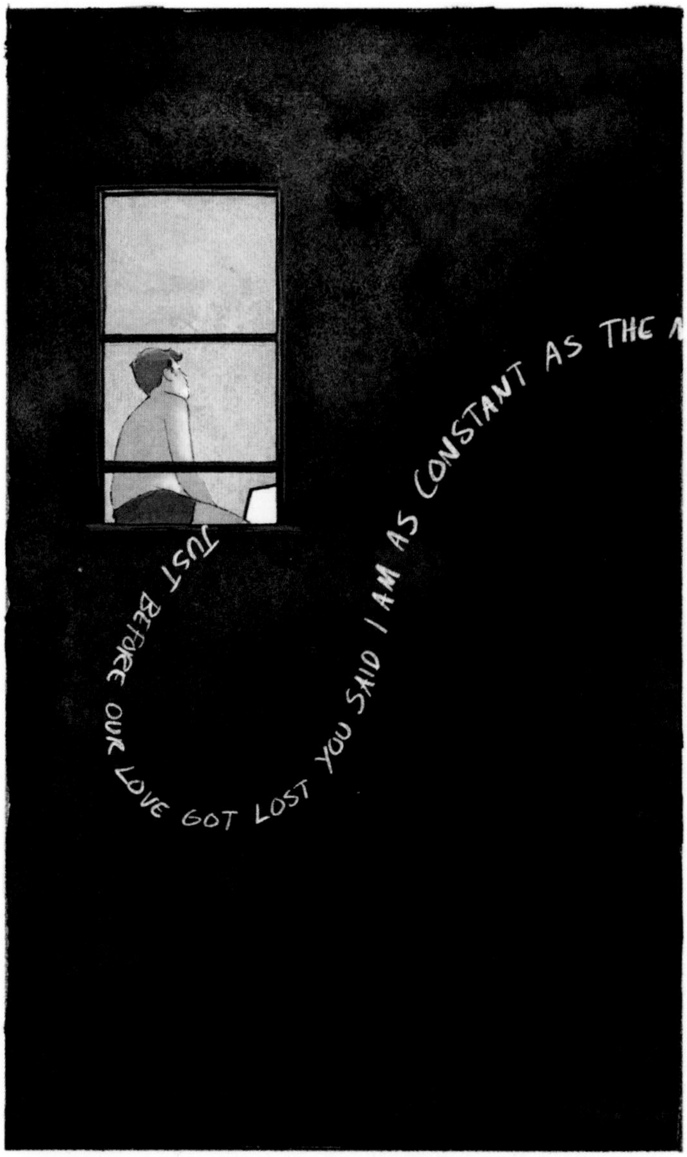
JUST BEFORE OUR LOVE GOT LOST YOU SAID I AM AS CONSTANT AS THE

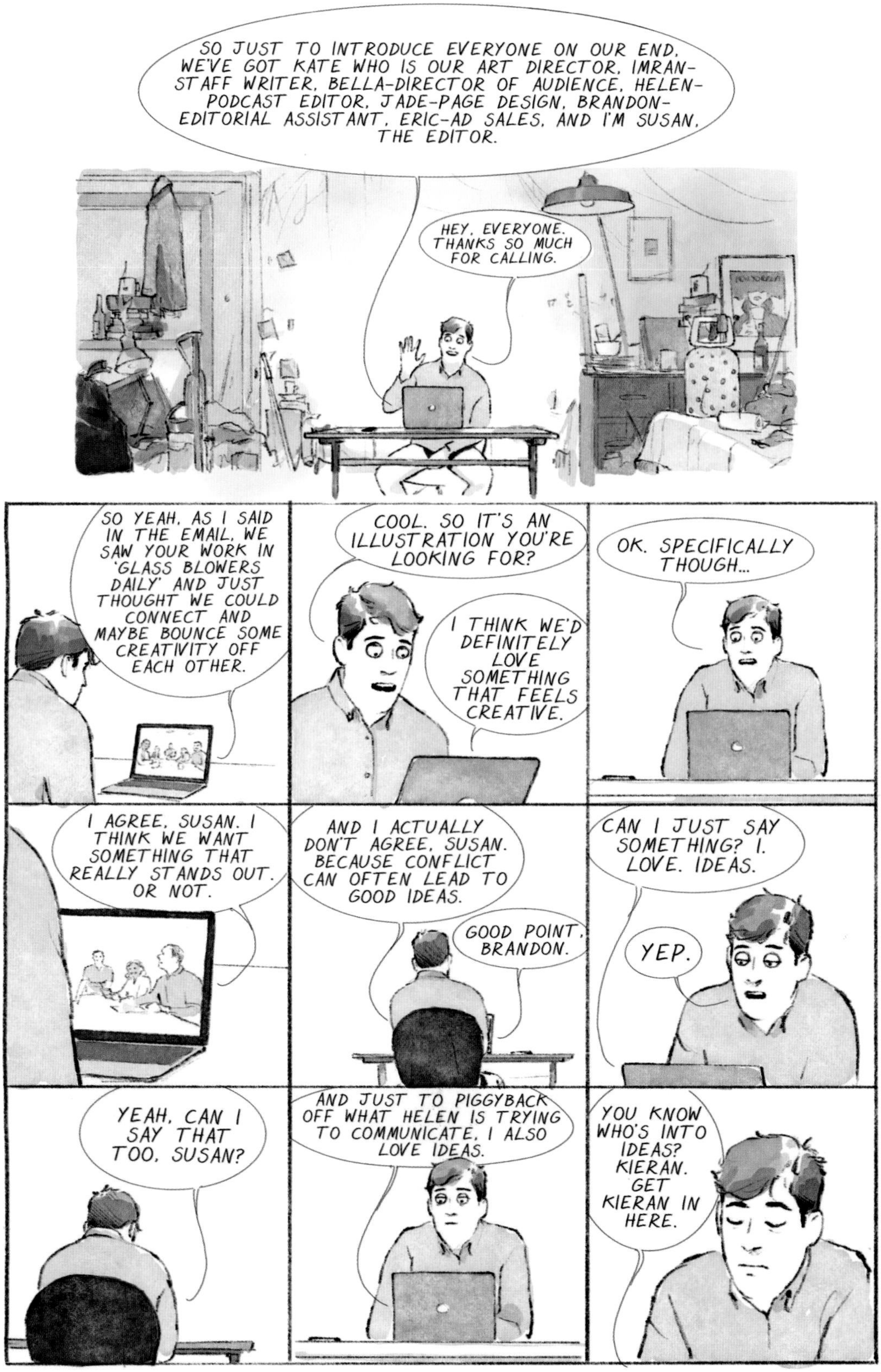
SO JUST TO INTRODUCE EVERYONE ON OUR END, WE'VE GOT KATE WHO IS OUR ART DIRECTOR, IMRAN-STAFF WRITER, BELLA-DIRECTOR OF AUDIENCE, HELEN-PODCAST EDITOR, JADE-PAGE DESIGN, BRANDON-EDITORIAL ASSISTANT, ERIC-AD SALES, AND I'M SUSAN, THE EDITOR.
HEY, EVERYONE. THANKS SO MUCH FOR CALLING.
SO YEAH, AS I SAID IN THE EMAIL, WE SAW YOUR WORK IN 'GLASS BLOWERS DAILY' AND JUST THOUGHT WE COULD CONNECT AND MAYBE BOUNCE SOME CREATIVITY OFF EACH OTHER.
COOL. SO IT'S AN ILLUSTRATION YOU'RE LOOKING FOR?
I THINK WE'D DEFINITELY LOVE SOMETHING THAT FEELS CREATIVE.
OK. SPECIFICALLY THOUGH...
I AGREE, SUSAN. I THINK WE WANT SOMETHING THAT REALLY STANDS OUT. OR NOT.
AND I ACTUALLY DON'T AGREE, SUSAN. BECAUSE CONFLICT CAN OFTEN LEAD TO GOOD IDEAS.
GOOD POINT, BRANDON.
CAN I JUST SAY SOMETHING? I. LOVE. IDEAS.
YEP.
YEAH, CAN I SAY THAT TOO, SUSAN?
AND JUST TO PIGGYBACK OFF WHAT HELEN IS TRYING TO COMMUNICATE, I ALSO LOVE IDEAS.
YOU KNOW WHO'S INTO IDEAS? KIERAN. GET KIERAN IN HERE.

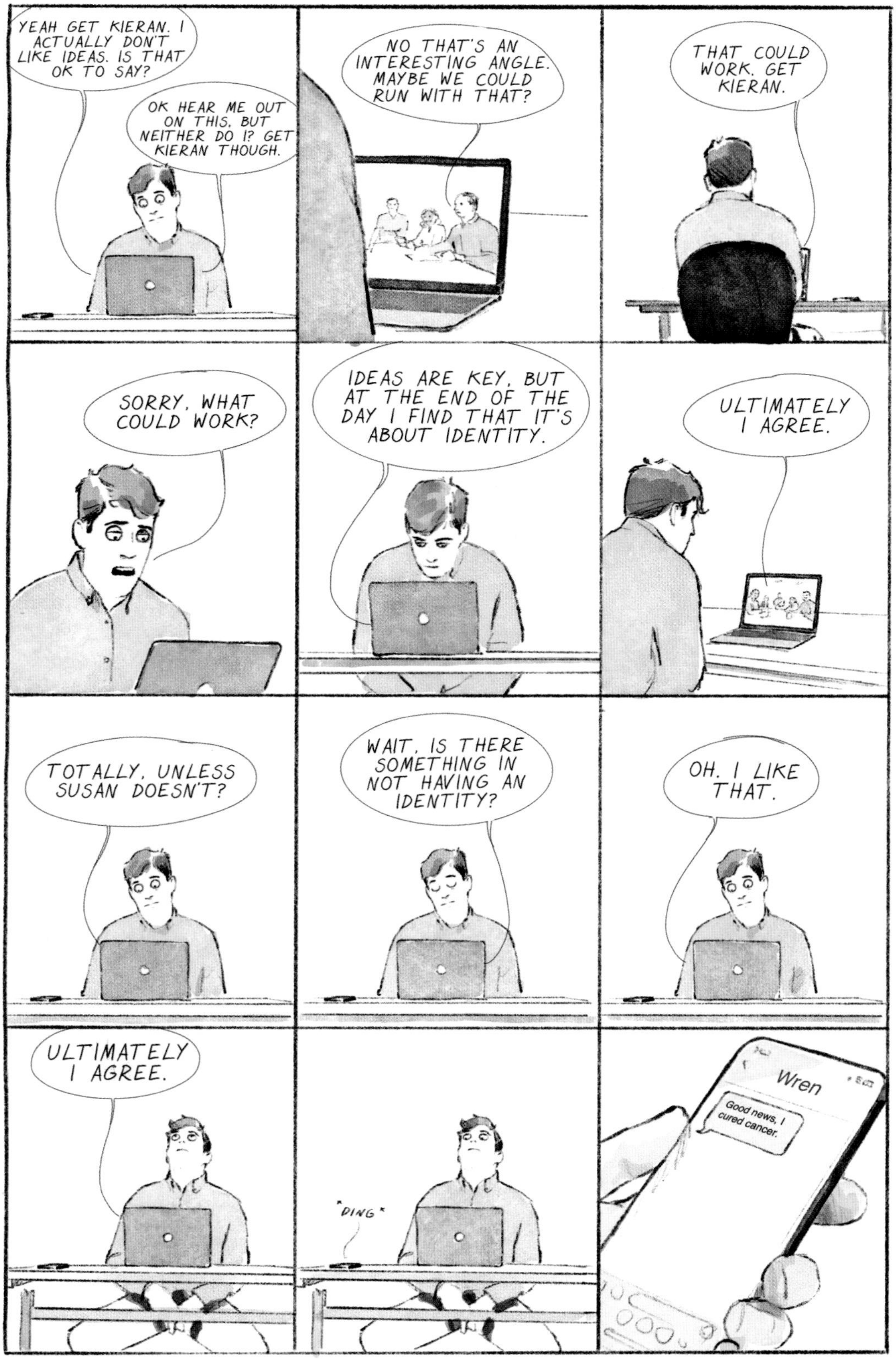
YEAH GET KIERAN. I ACTUALLY DON'T LIKE IDEAS. IS THAT OK TO SAY?
OK HEAR ME OUT ON THIS, BUT NEITHER DO I? GET KIERAN THOUGH.
NO THAT'S AN INTERESTING ANGLE. MAYBE WE COULD RUN WITH THAT?
THAT COULD WORK. GET KIERAN.
SORRY, WHAT COULD WORK?
IDEAS ARE KEY, BUT AT THE END OF THE DAY I FIND THAT IT'S ABOUT IDENTITY.
ULTIMATELY I AGREE.
TOTALLY, UNLESS SUSAN DOESN'T?
WAIT, IS THERE SOMETHING IN NOT HAVING AN IDENTITY?
OH. I LIKE THAT.
ULTIMATELY I AGREE.
DING
Wren
Good news, I cured cancer.

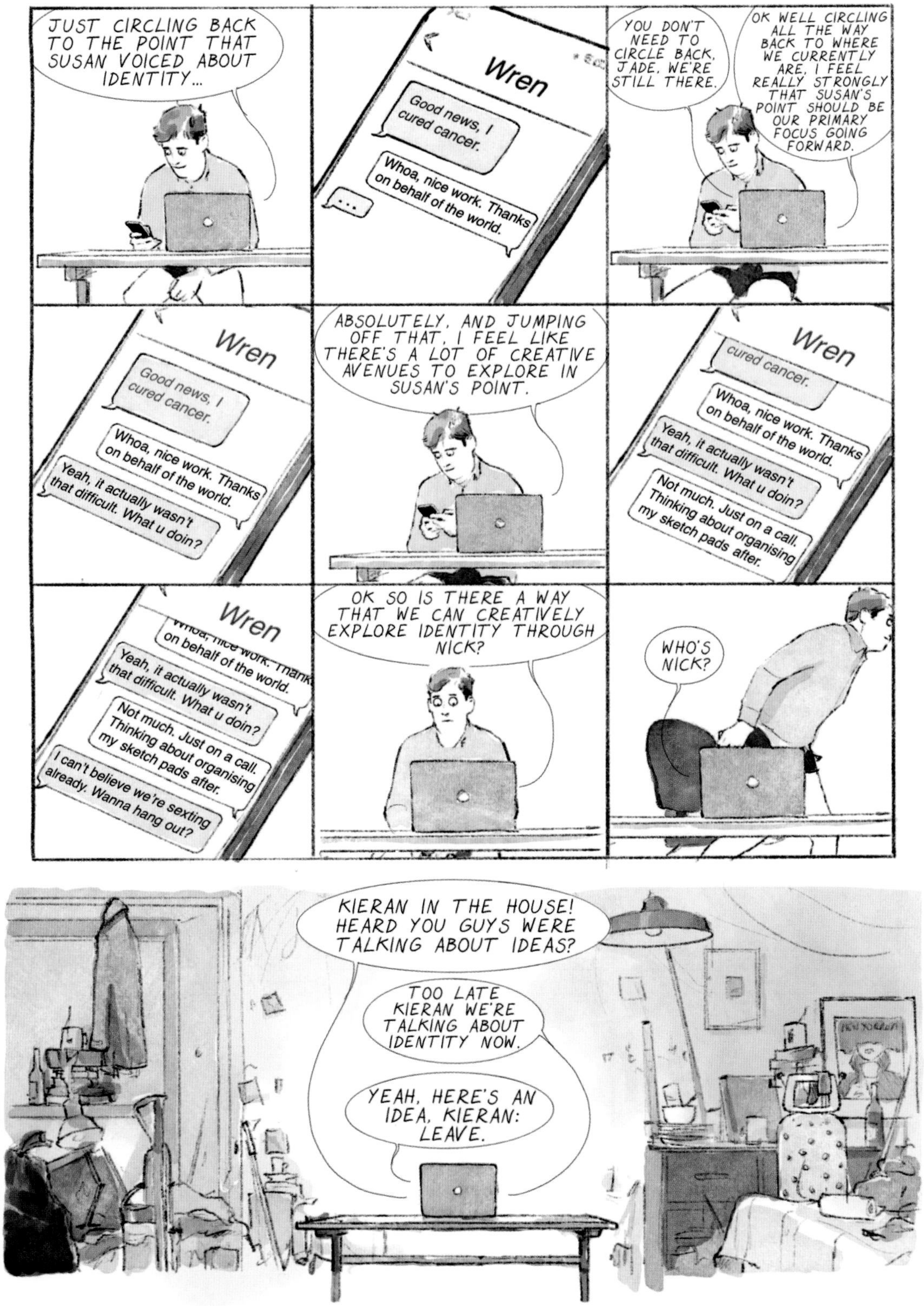
JUST CIRCLING BACK TO THE POINT THAT SUSAN VOICED ABOUT IDENTITY...
Wren
Good news, I cured cancer.
Whoa, nice work. Thanks on behalf of the world.
YOU DON'T NEED TO CIRCLE BACK, JADE. WE'RE STILL THERE.
OK WELL CIRCLING ALL THE WAY BACK TO WHERE WE CURRENTLY ARE, I FEEL REALLY STRONGLY THAT SUSAN'S POINT SHOULD BE OUR PRIMARY FOCUS GOING FORWARD.
Wren
Good news, I cured cancer.
Whoa, nice work. Thanks on behalf of the world.
Yeah, it actually wasn't that difficult. What u doin?
ABSOLUTELY, AND JUMPING OFF THAT, I FEEL LIKE THERE'S A LOT OF CREATIVE AVENUES TO EXPLORE IN SUSAN'S POINT.
Wren
cured cancer.
Whoa, nice work. Thanks on behalf of the world.
Yeah, it actually wasn't that difficult. What u doin?
Not much. Just on a call. Thinking about organising my sketch pads after.
Wren
on behalf of the world.
Yeah, it actually wasn't that difficult. What u doin?
Not much. Just on a call. Thinking about organising my sketch pads after.
I can't believe we're sexting already. Wanna hang out?
OK SO IS THERE A WAY THAT WE CAN CREATIVELY EXPLORE IDENTITY THROUGH NICK?
WHO'S NICK?
KIERAN IN THE HOUSE! HEARD YOU GUYS WERE TALKING ABOUT IDEAS?
TOO LATE KIERAN WE'RE TALKING ABOUT IDENTITY NOW.
YEAH, HERE'S AN IDEA, KIERAN: LEAVE.

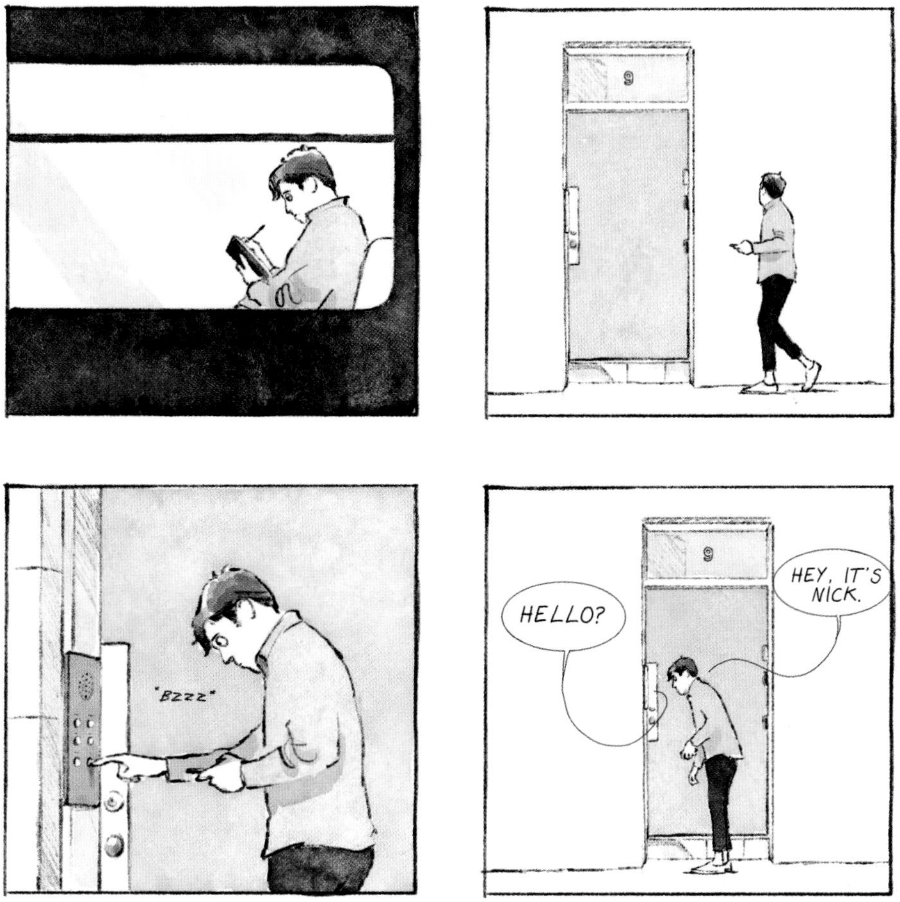
"BZZZ"
HELLO?
HEY, IT'S NICK.

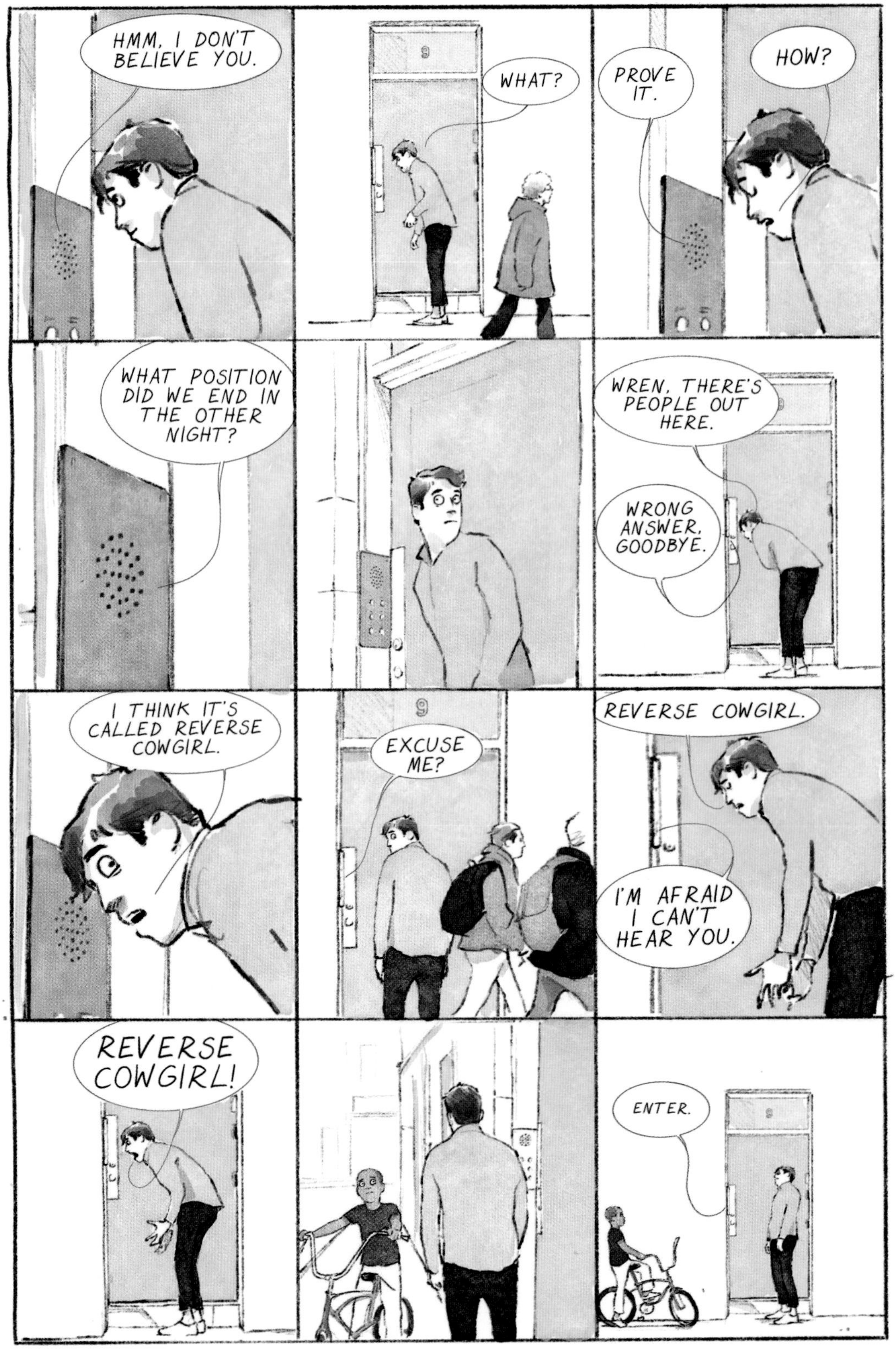
HMM, I DON'T BELIEVE YOU.
WHAT?
PROVE IT.
HOW?
WHAT POSITION DID WE END IN THE OTHER NIGHT?
WREN, THERE'S PEOPLE OUT HERE.
WRONG ANSWER, GOODBYE.
I THINK IT'S CALLED REVERSE COWGIRL.
EXCUSE ME?
REVERSE COWGIRL.
I'M AFRAID I CAN'T HEAR YOU.
REVERSE COWGIRL!
ENTER.

I GUESS THAT MAKES ME THE COW? EXCEPT COWGIRLS DON'T RIDE THE COW.
THEY RIDE THE HORSE.
I'M THE HORSE.
I'M HER REVERSE HORSE BOY.
NEIGH. I MEAN... HEY.

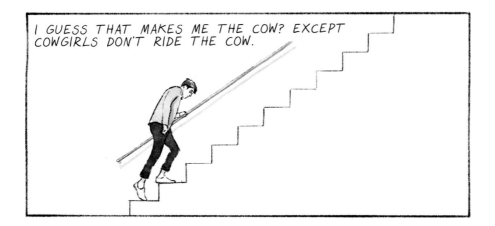

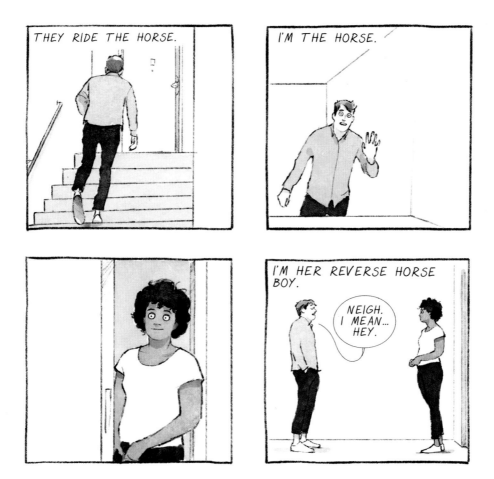

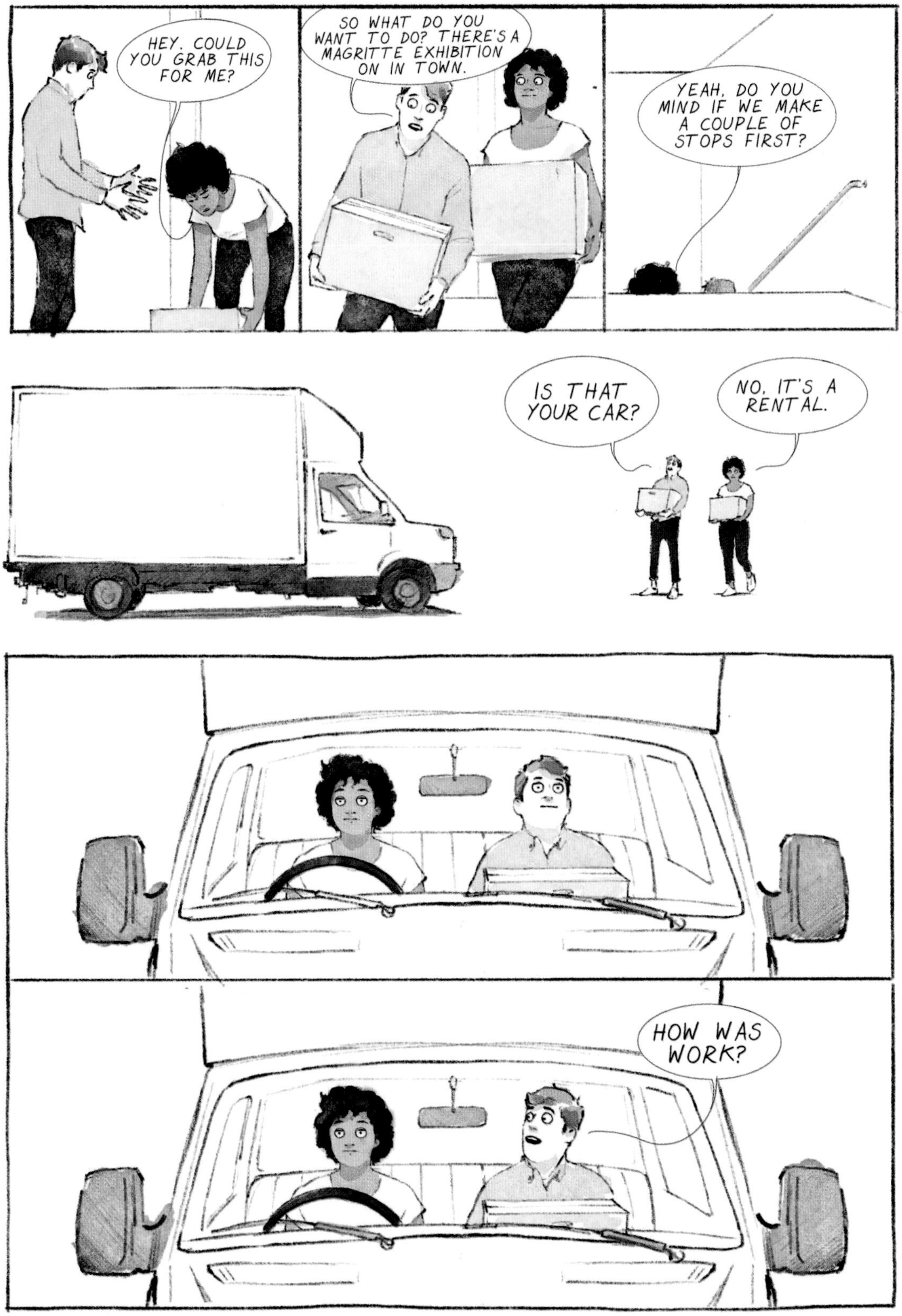
HEY. COULD YOU GRAB THIS FOR ME?
SO WHAT DO YOU WANT TO DO? THERE'S A MAGRITTE EXHIBITION ON IN TOWN.
YEAH, DO YOU MIND IF WE MAKE A COUPLE OF STOPS FIRST?
IS THAT YOUR CAR?
NO, IT'S A RENTAL.
HOW WAS WORK?

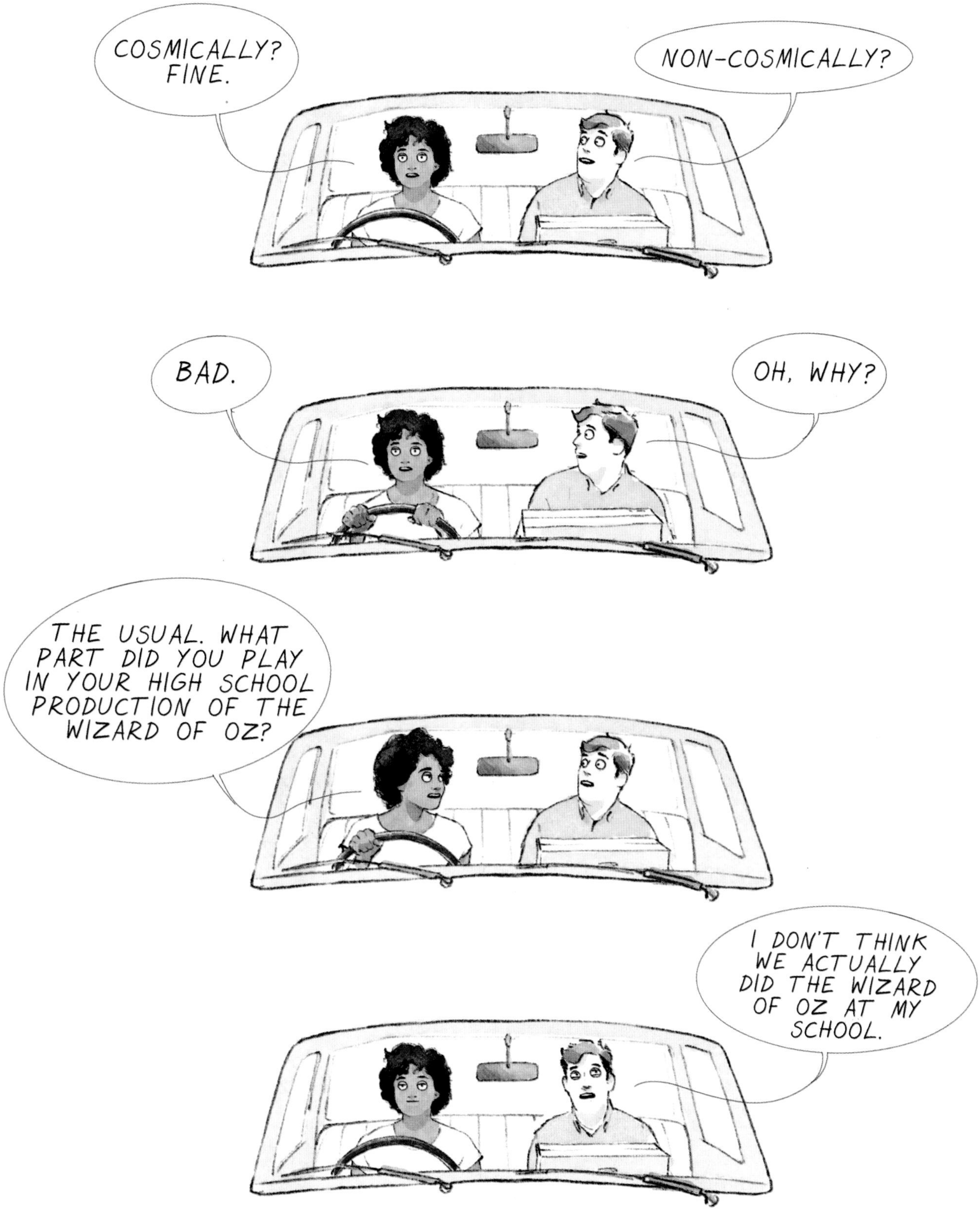
COSMICALLY? FINE.
NON-COSMICALLY?
BAD.
OH, WHY?
THE USUAL. WHAT PART DID YOU PLAY IN YOUR HIGH SCHOOL PRODUCTION OF THE WIZARD OF OZ?
I DON'T THINK WE ACTUALLY DID THE WIZARD OF OZ AT MY SCHOOL.

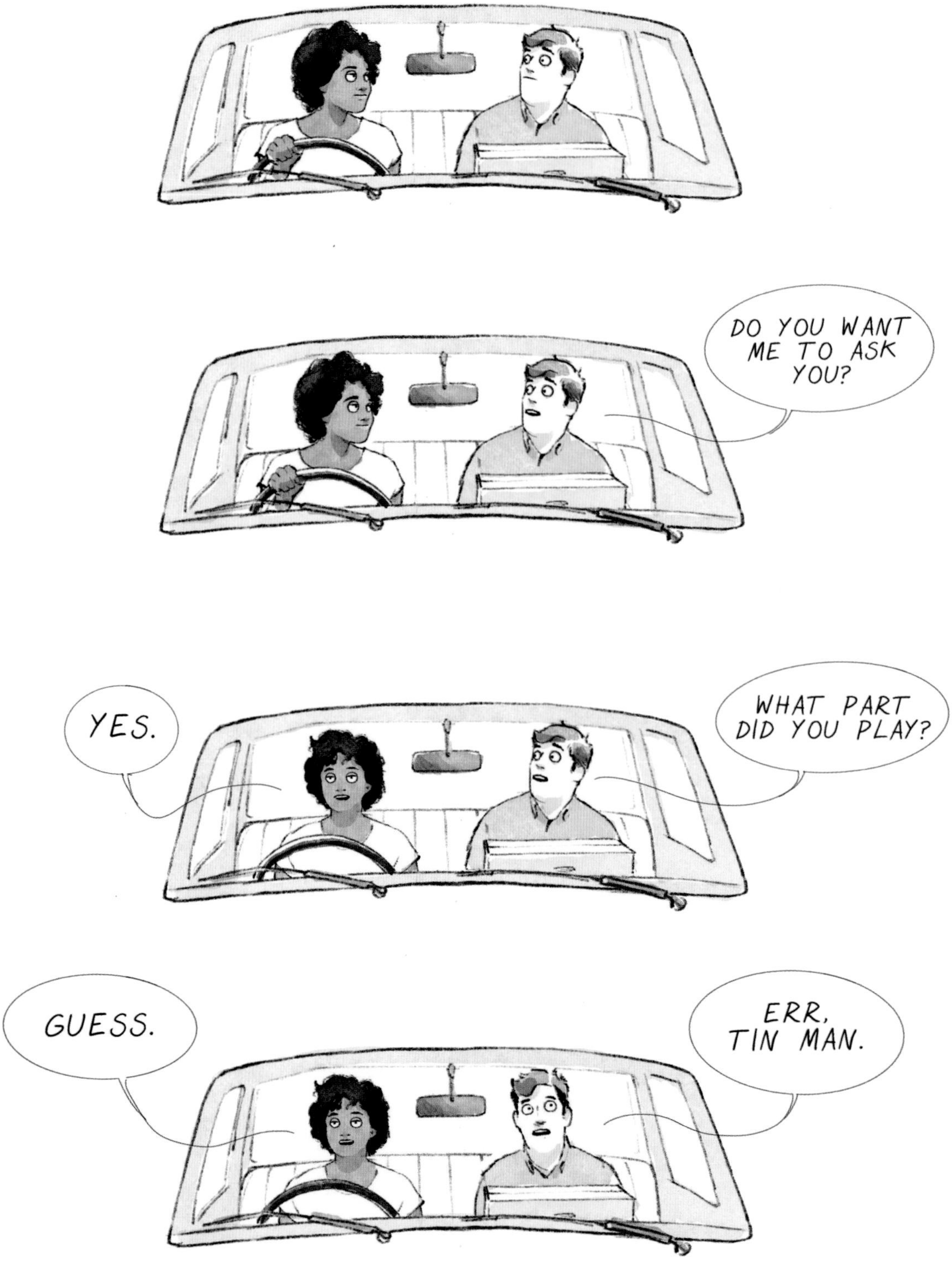
DO YOU WANT ME TO ASK YOU?
YES.
WHAT PART DID YOU PLAY?
GUESS.
ERR, TIN MAN.

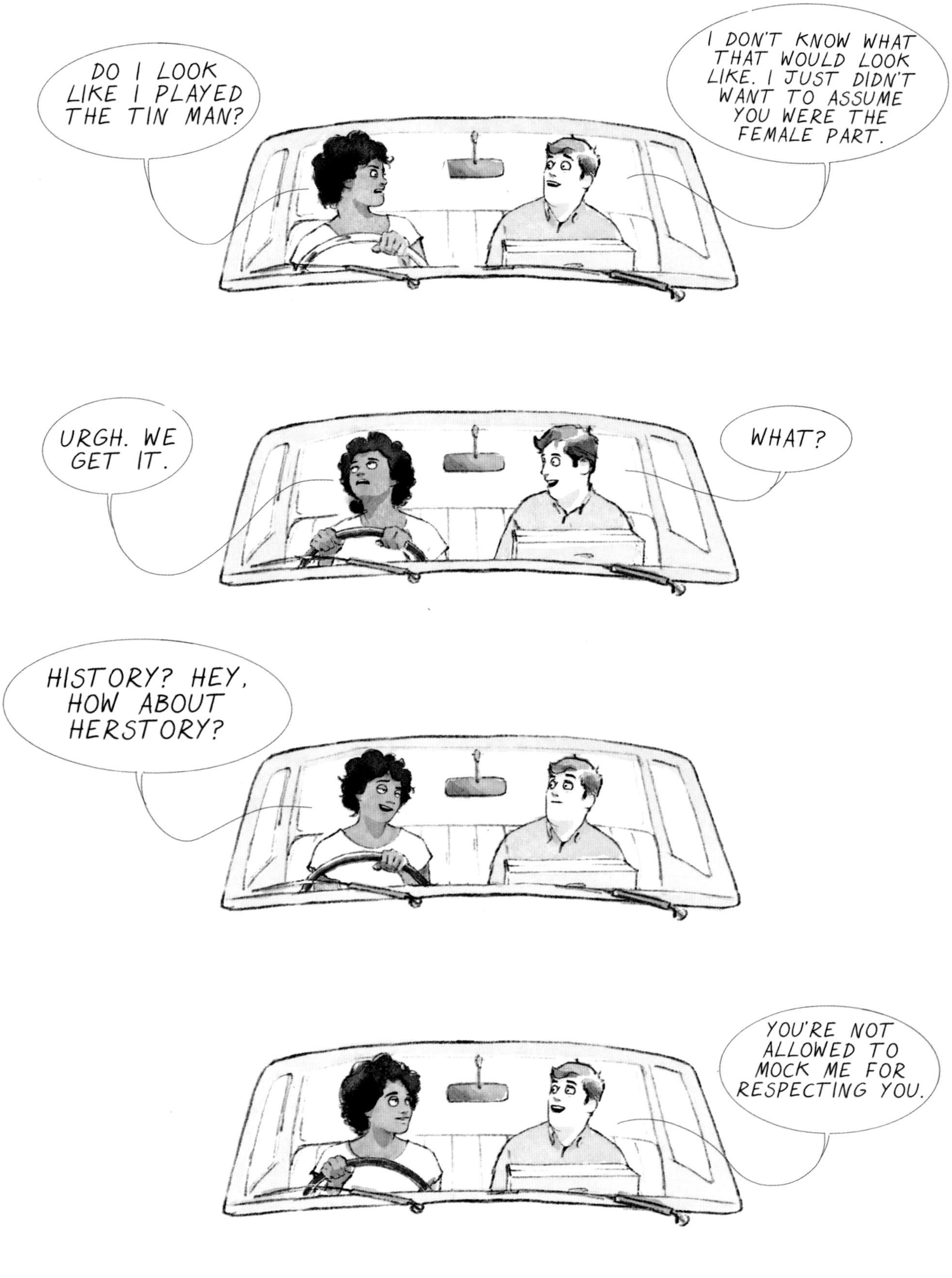
DO I LOOK LIKE I PLAYED THE TIN MAN?
I DON'T KNOW WHAT THAT WOULD LOOK LIKE. I JUST DIDN'T WANT TO ASSUME YOU WERE THE FEMALE PART.
URGH. WE GET IT.
WHAT?
HISTORY? HEY, HOW ABOUT HERSTORY?
YOU'RE NOT ALLOWED TO MOCK ME FOR RESPECTING YOU.

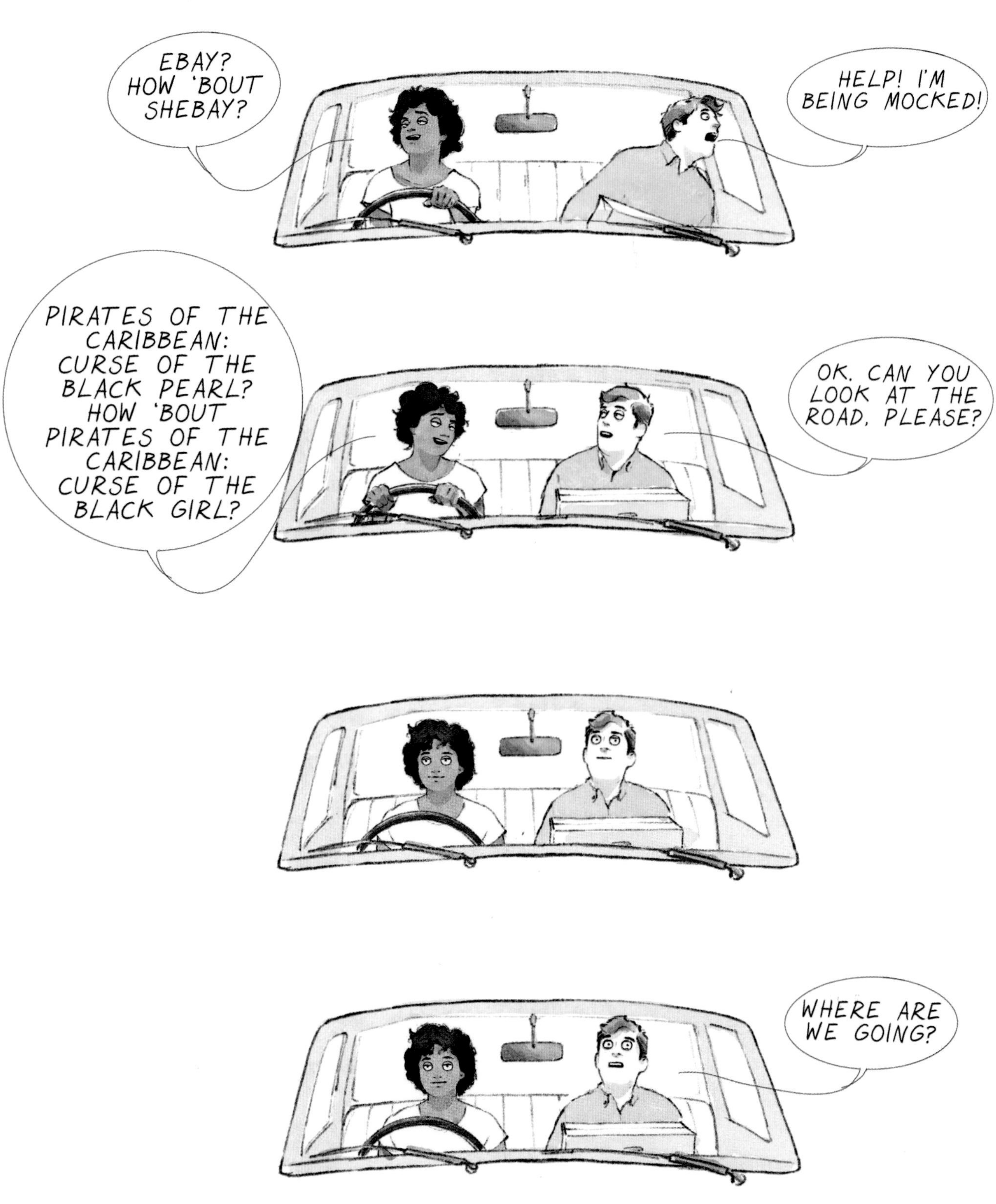
EBAY? HOW 'BOUT SHEBAY?
HELP! I'M BEING MOCKED!
PIRATES OF THE CARIBBEAN: CURSE OF THE BLACK PEARL? HOW 'BOUT PIRATES OF THE CARIBBEAN: CURSE OF THE BLACK GIRL?
OK. CAN YOU LOOK AT THE ROAD, PLEASE?
WHERE ARE WE GOING?

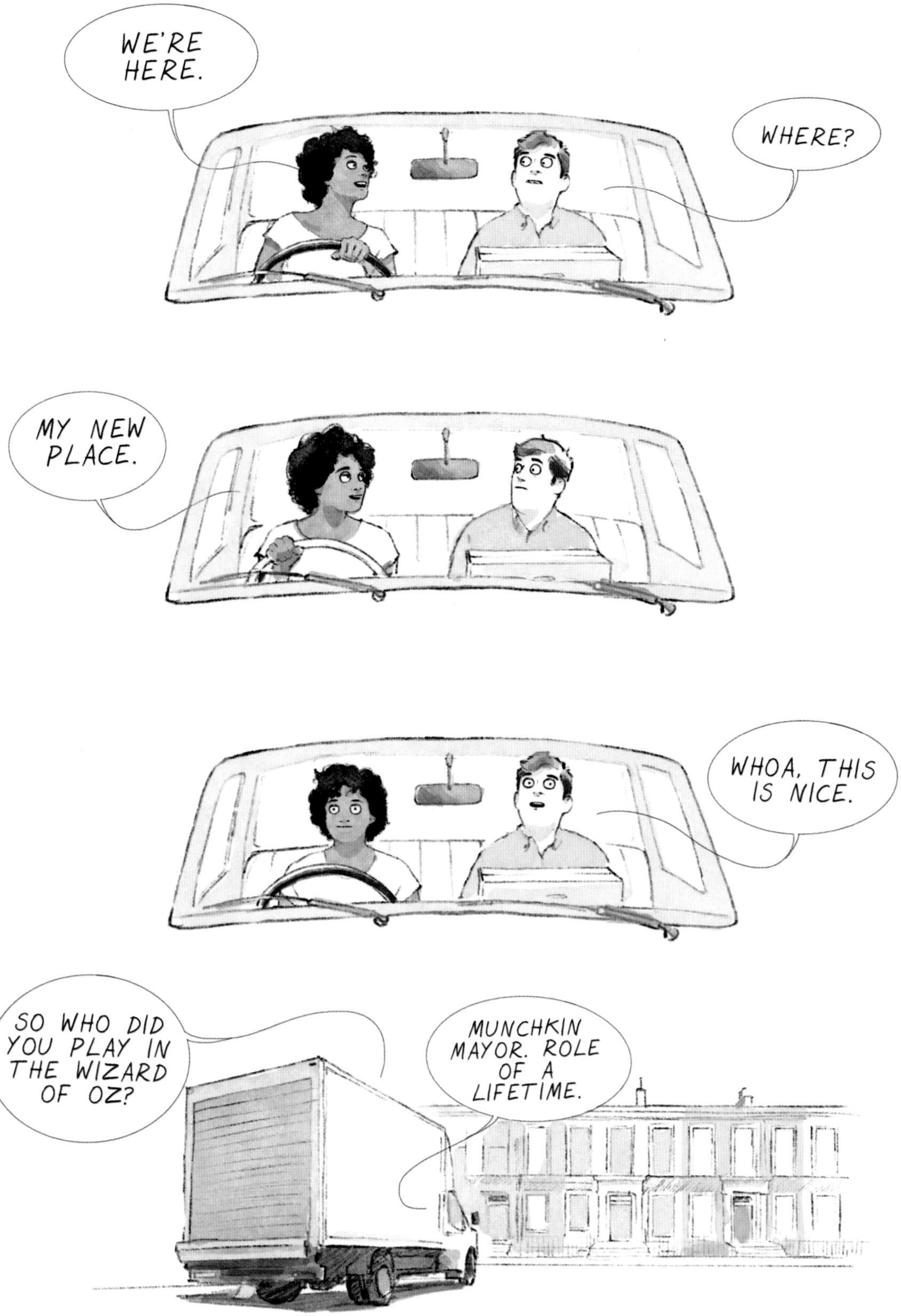
WE'RE HERE.
WHERE?
MY NEW PLACE.
WHOA, THIS IS NICE.
SO WHO DID YOU PLAY IN THE WIZARD OF OZ?
MUNCHKIN MAYOR. ROLE OF A LIFETIME.

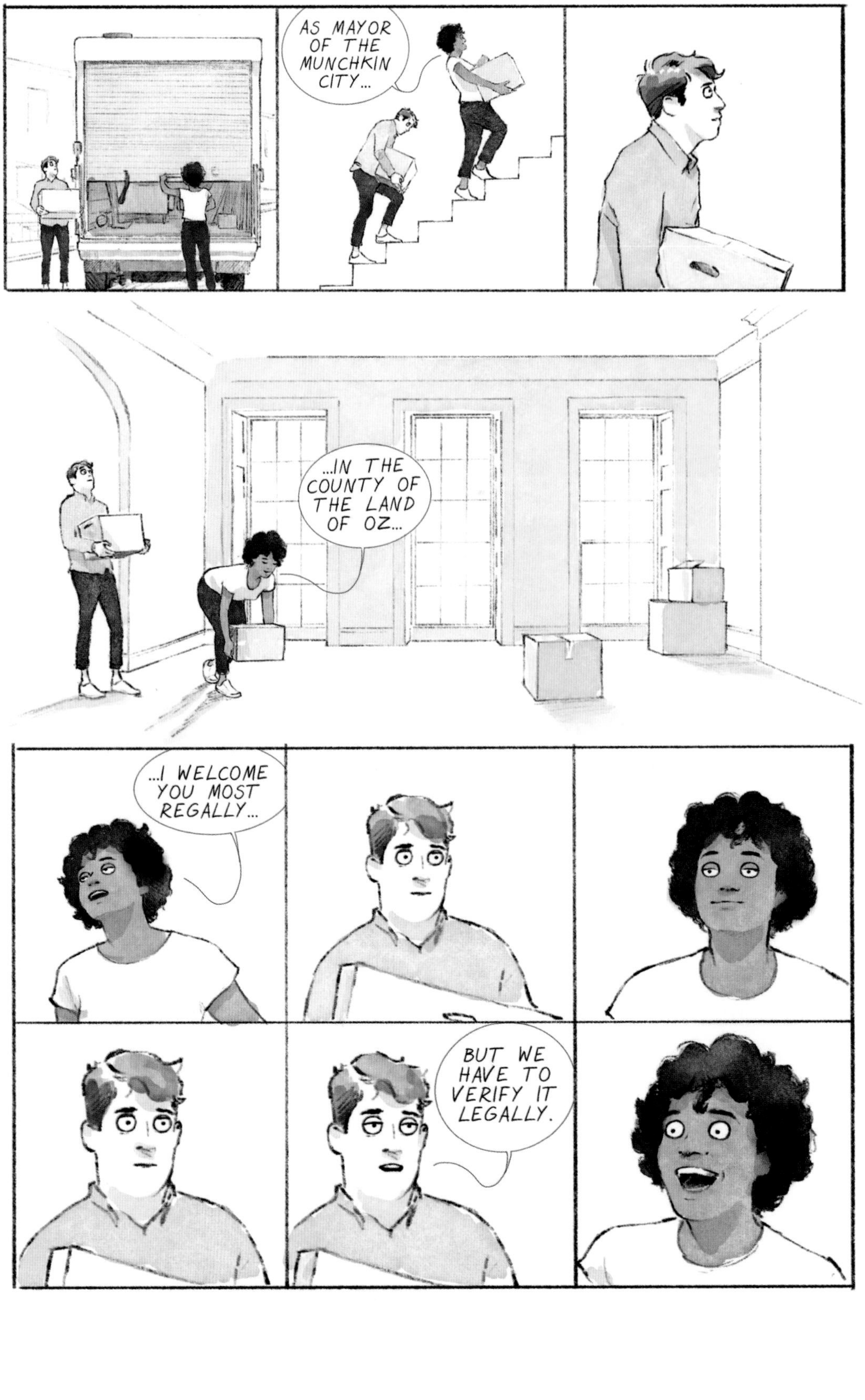
AS MAYOR OF THE MUNCHKIN CITY...
...IN THE COUNTY OF THE LAND OF OZ...
...I WELCOME YOU MOST REGALLY...
BUT WE HAVE TO VERIFY IT LEGALLY.

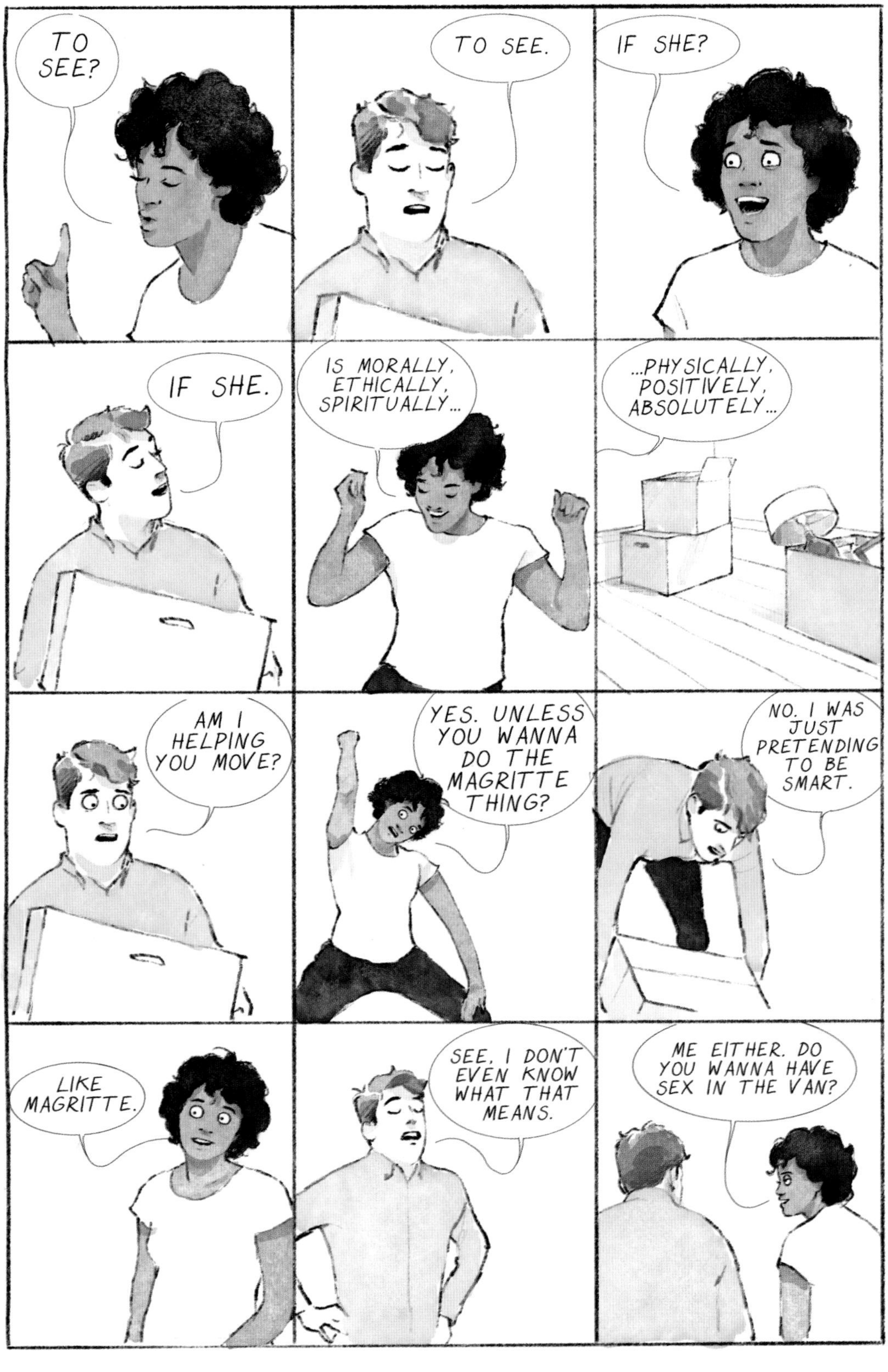
TO SEE?
TO SEE.
IF SHE?
IF SHE.
IS MORALLY, ETHICALLY, SPIRITUALLY...
...PHYSICALLY, POSITIVELY, ABSOLUTELY...
AM I HELPING YOU MOVE?
YES. UNLESS YOU WANNA DO THE MAGRITTE THING?
NO. I WAS JUST PRETENDING TO BE SMART.
LIKE MAGRITTE.
SEE, I DON'T EVEN KNOW WHAT THAT MEANS.
ME EITHER. DO YOU WANNA HAVE SEX IN THE VAN?

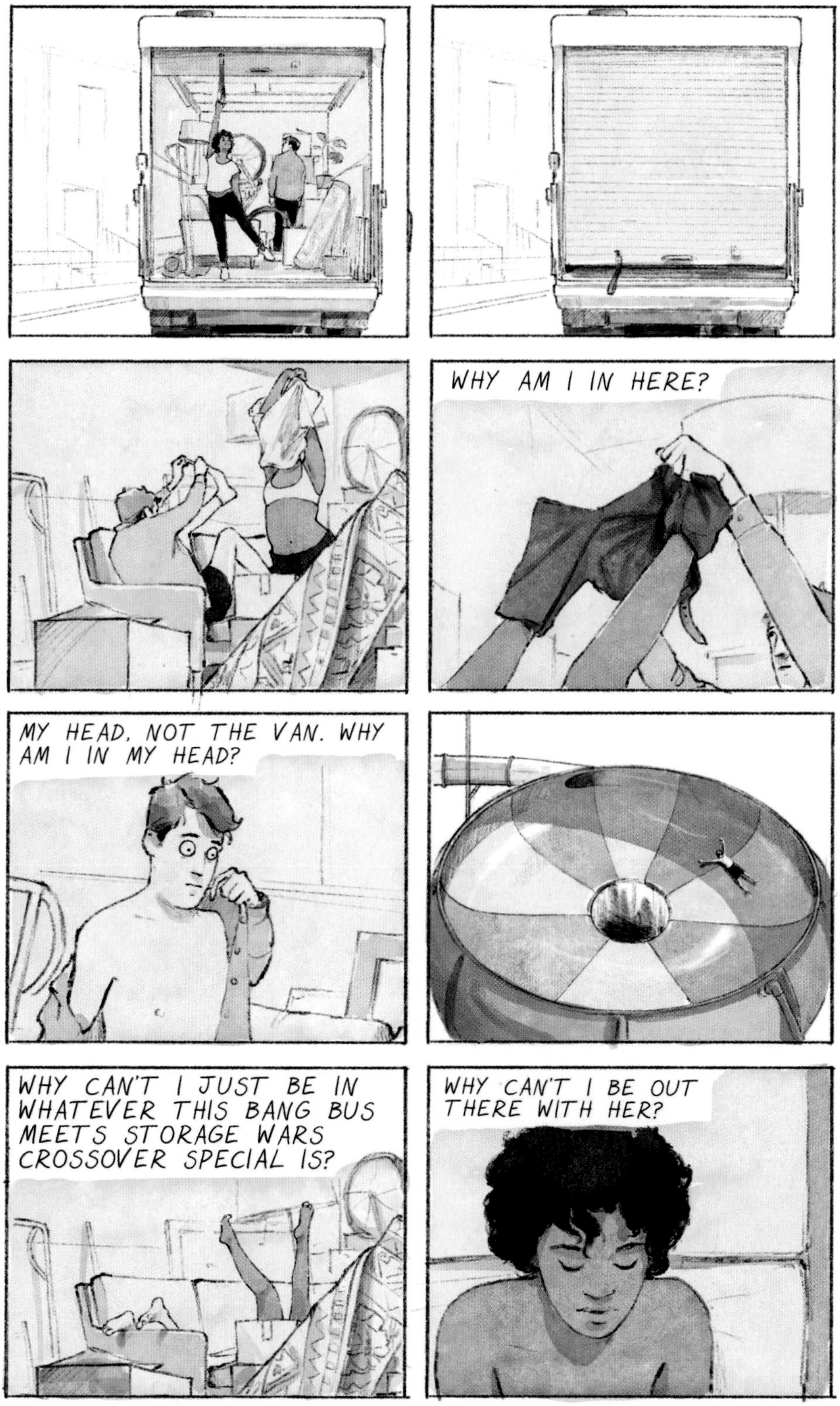
WHY AM I IN HERE?
MY HEAD, NOT THE VAN. WHY AM I IN MY HEAD?
WHY CAN'T I JUST BE IN WHATEVER THIS BANG BUS MEETS STORAGE WARS CROSSOVER SPECIAL IS?
WHY CAN'T I BE OUT THERE WITH HER?

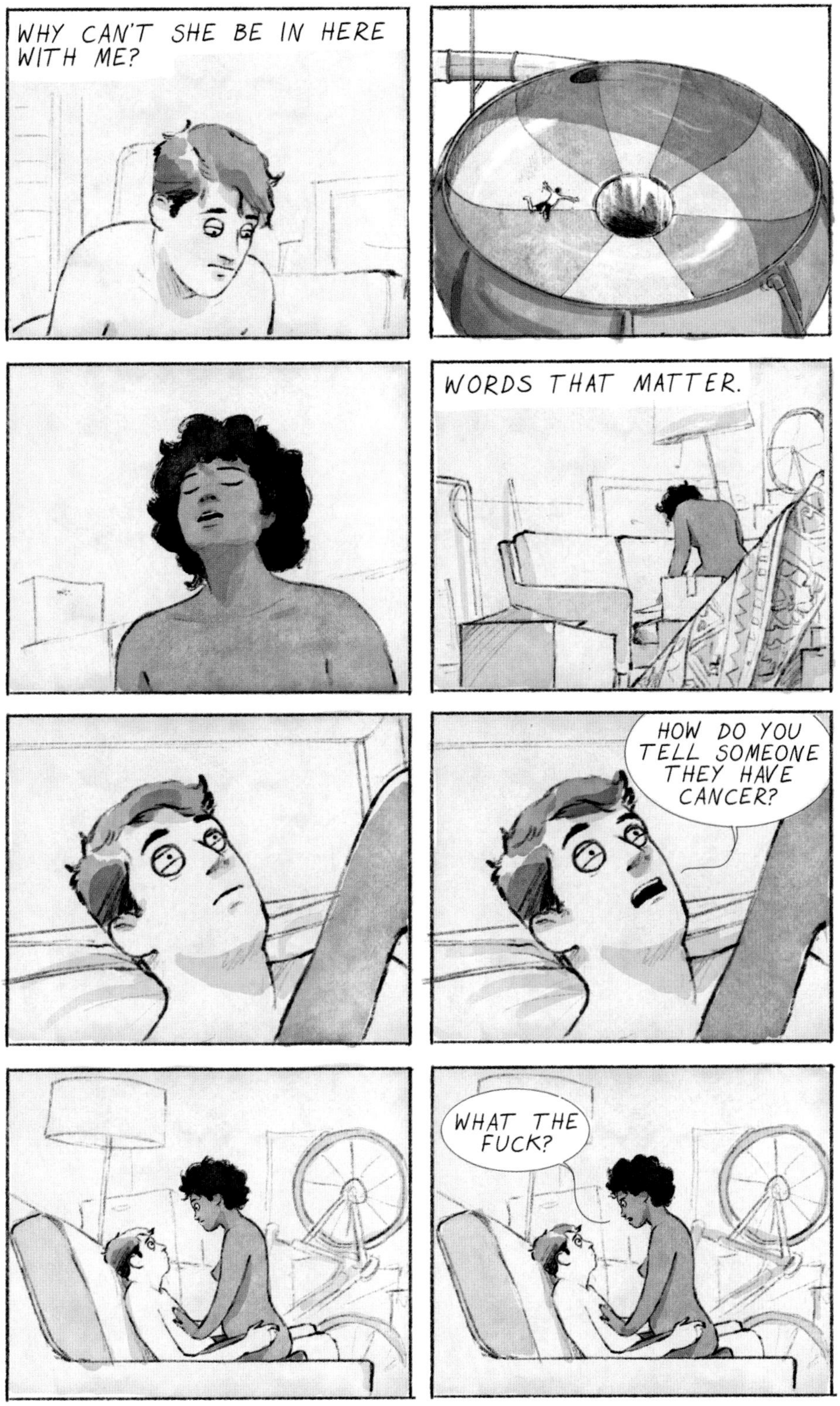
WHY CAN'T SHE BE IN HERE WITH ME?
WORDS THAT MATTER.
HOW DO YOU TELL SOMEONE THEY HAVE CANCER?
WHAT THE FUCK?

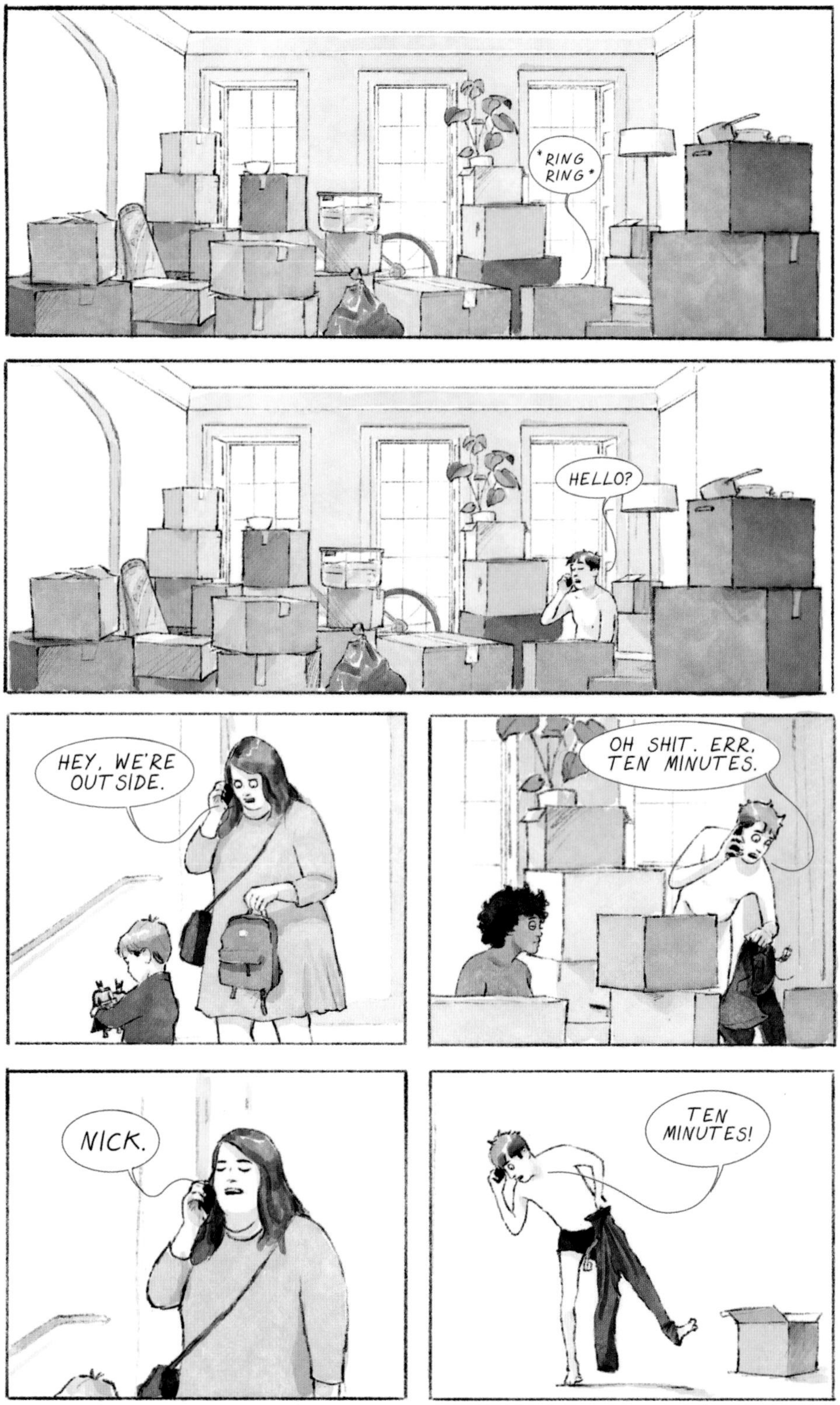
RING RING
HELLO?
HEY, WE'RE OUTSIDE.
OH SHIT. ERR. TEN MINUTES.
NICK.
TEN MINUTES!

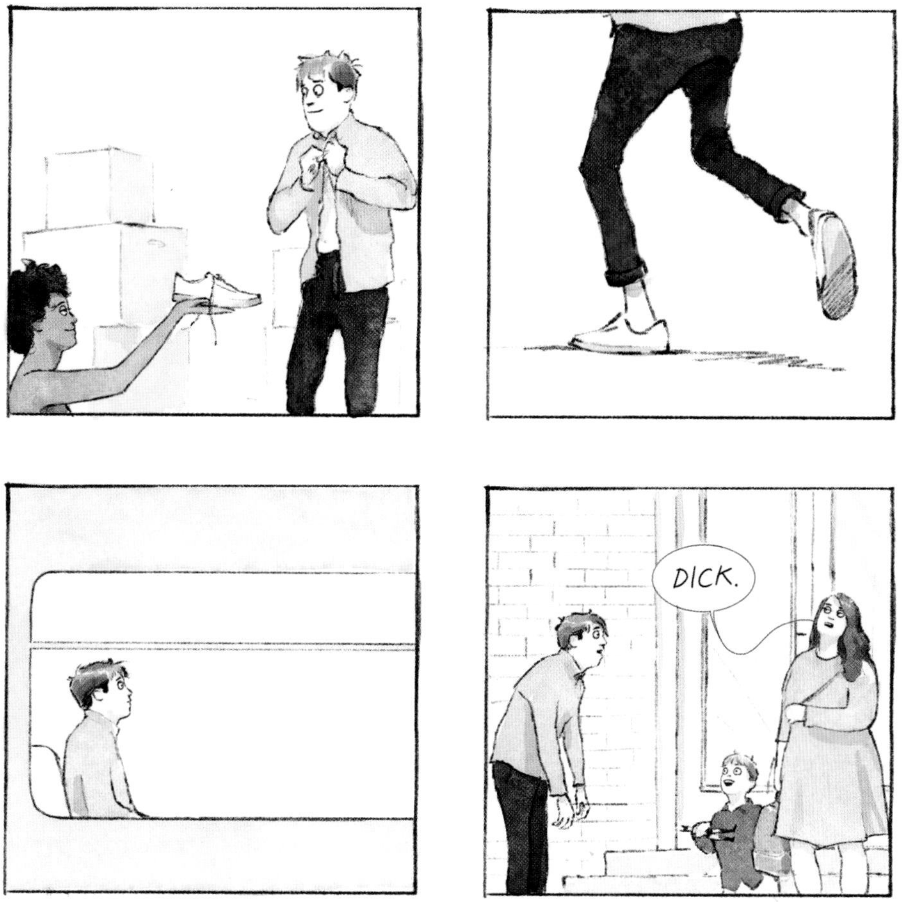
DICK.

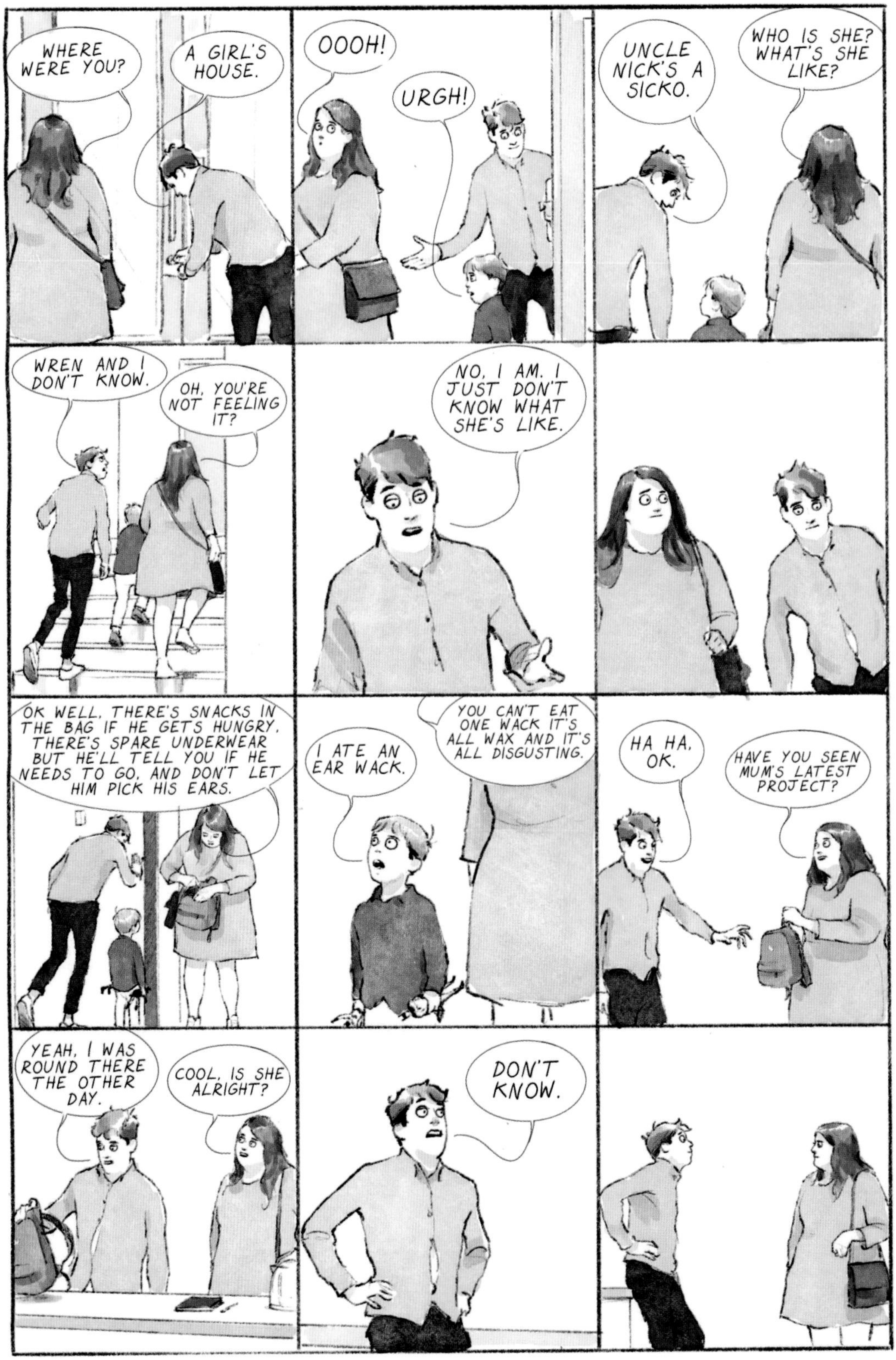
WHERE WERE YOU?
A GIRL'S HOUSE.
OOOH!
URGH!
UNCLE NICK'S A SICKO.
WHO IS SHE? WHAT'S SHE LIKE?
WREN AND I DON'T KNOW.
OH, YOU'RE NOT FEELING IT?
NO, I AM. I JUST DON'T KNOW WHAT SHE'S LIKE.
OK WELL, THERE'S SNACKS IN THE BAG IF HE GETS HUNGRY, THERE'S SPARE UNDERWEAR BUT HE'LL TELL YOU IF HE NEEDS TO GO, AND DON'T LET HIM PICK HIS EARS.
I ATE AN EAR WACK.
YOU CAN'T EAT ONE WACK IT'S ALL WAX AND IT'S ALL DISGUSTING.
HA HA, OK.
HAVE YOU SEEN MUM'S LATEST PROJECT?
YEAH, I WAS ROUND THERE THE OTHER DAY.
COOL, IS SHE ALRIGHT?
DON'T KNOW.

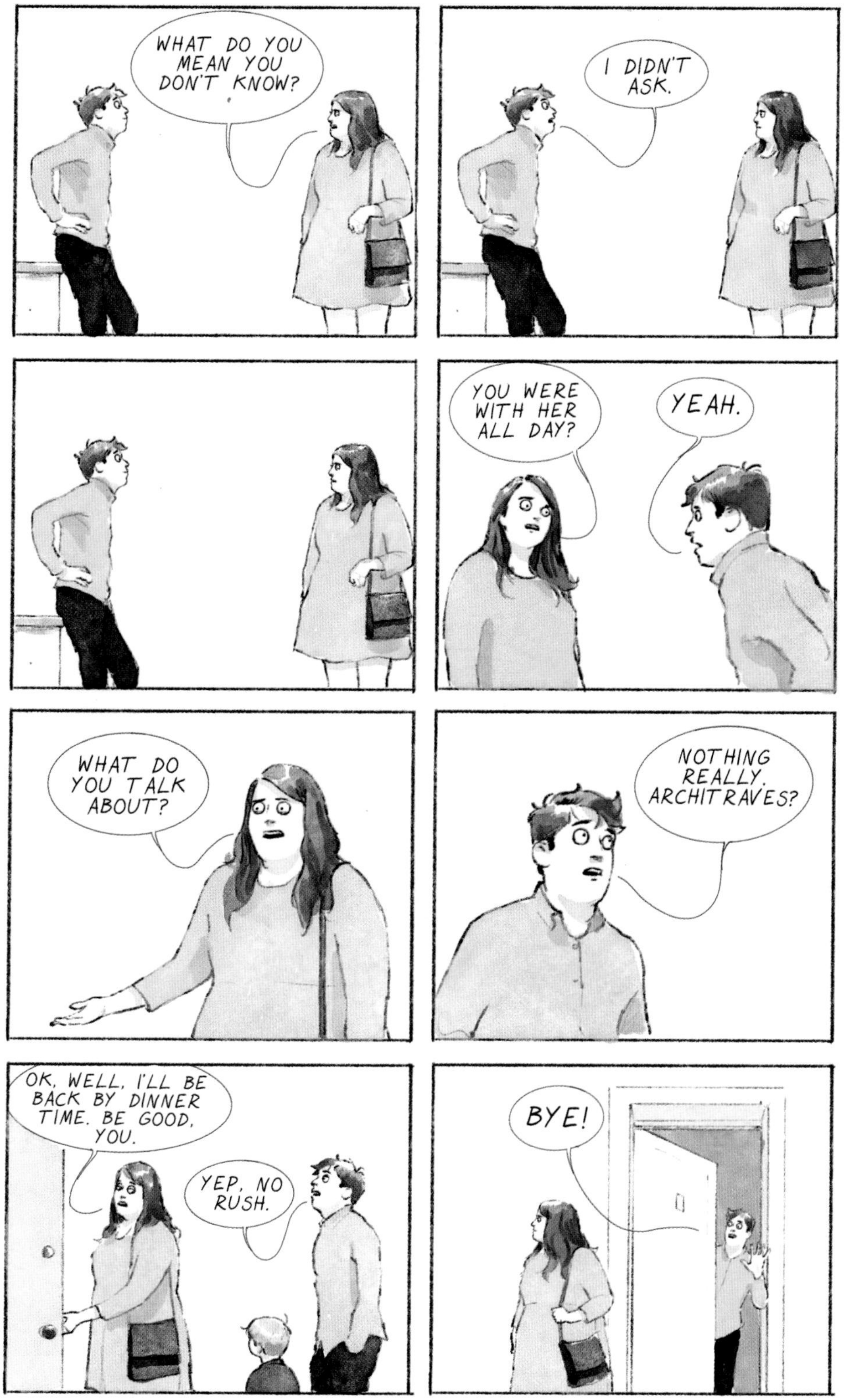
WHAT DO YOU MEAN YOU DON'T KNOW?
I DIDN'T ASK.
YOU WERE WITH HER ALL DAY?
YEAH.
WHAT DO YOU TALK ABOUT?
NOTHING REALLY. ARCHITRAVES?
OK, WELL, I'LL BE BACK BY DINNER TIME. BE GOOD, YOU.
YEP, NO RUSH.
BYE!

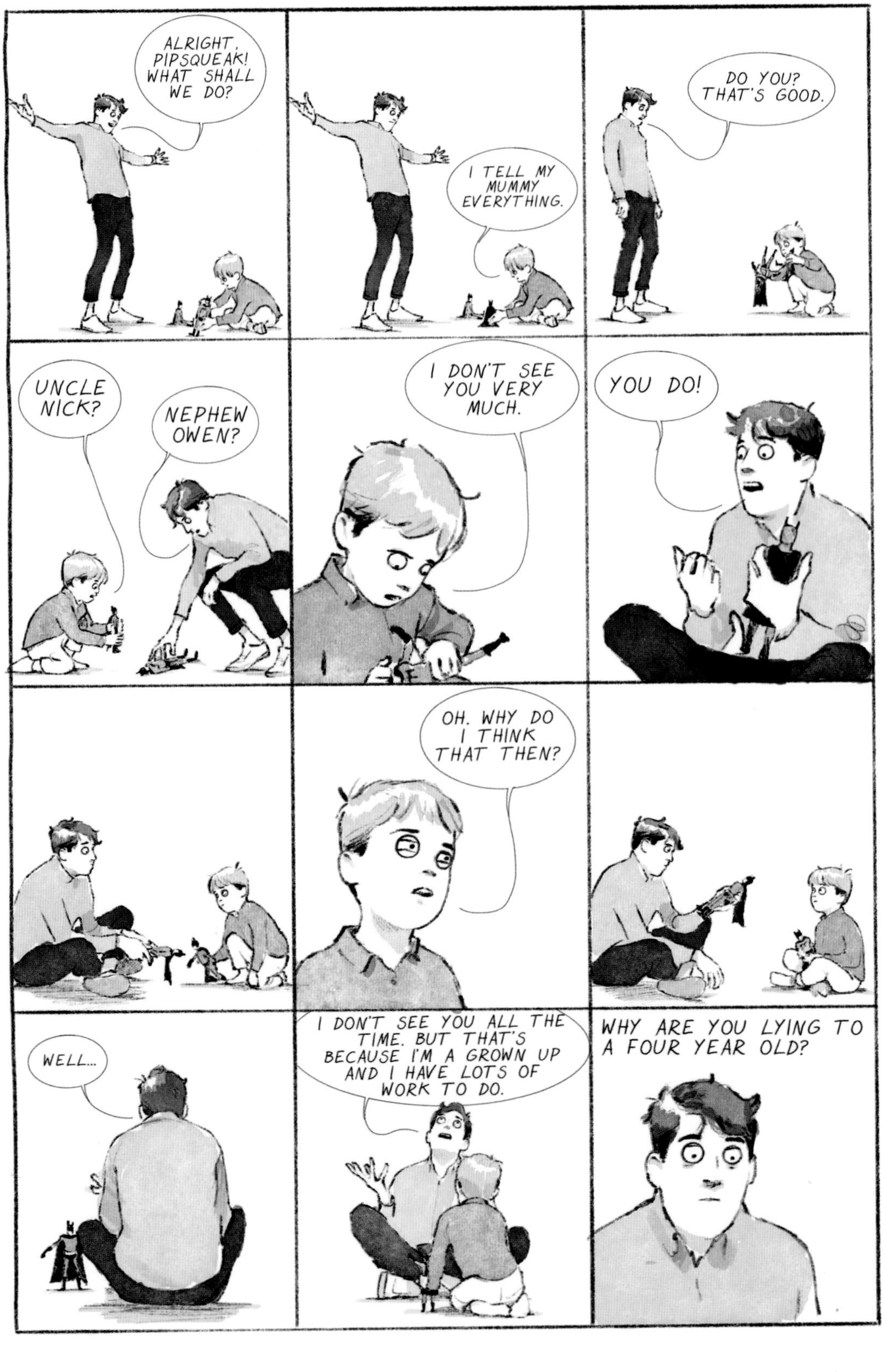
ALRIGHT, PIPSQUEAK! WHAT SHALL WE DO?
I TELL MY MUMMY EVERYTHING.
DO YOU? THAT'S GOOD.
UNCLE NICK?
NEPHEW OWEN?
I DON'T SEE YOU VERY MUCH.
YOU DO!
OH. WHY DO I THINK THAT THEN?
WELL...
I DON'T SEE YOU ALL THE TIME. BUT THAT'S BECAUSE I'M A GROWN UP AND I HAVE LOTS OF WORK TO DO.
WHY ARE YOU LYING TO A FOUR YEAR OLD?

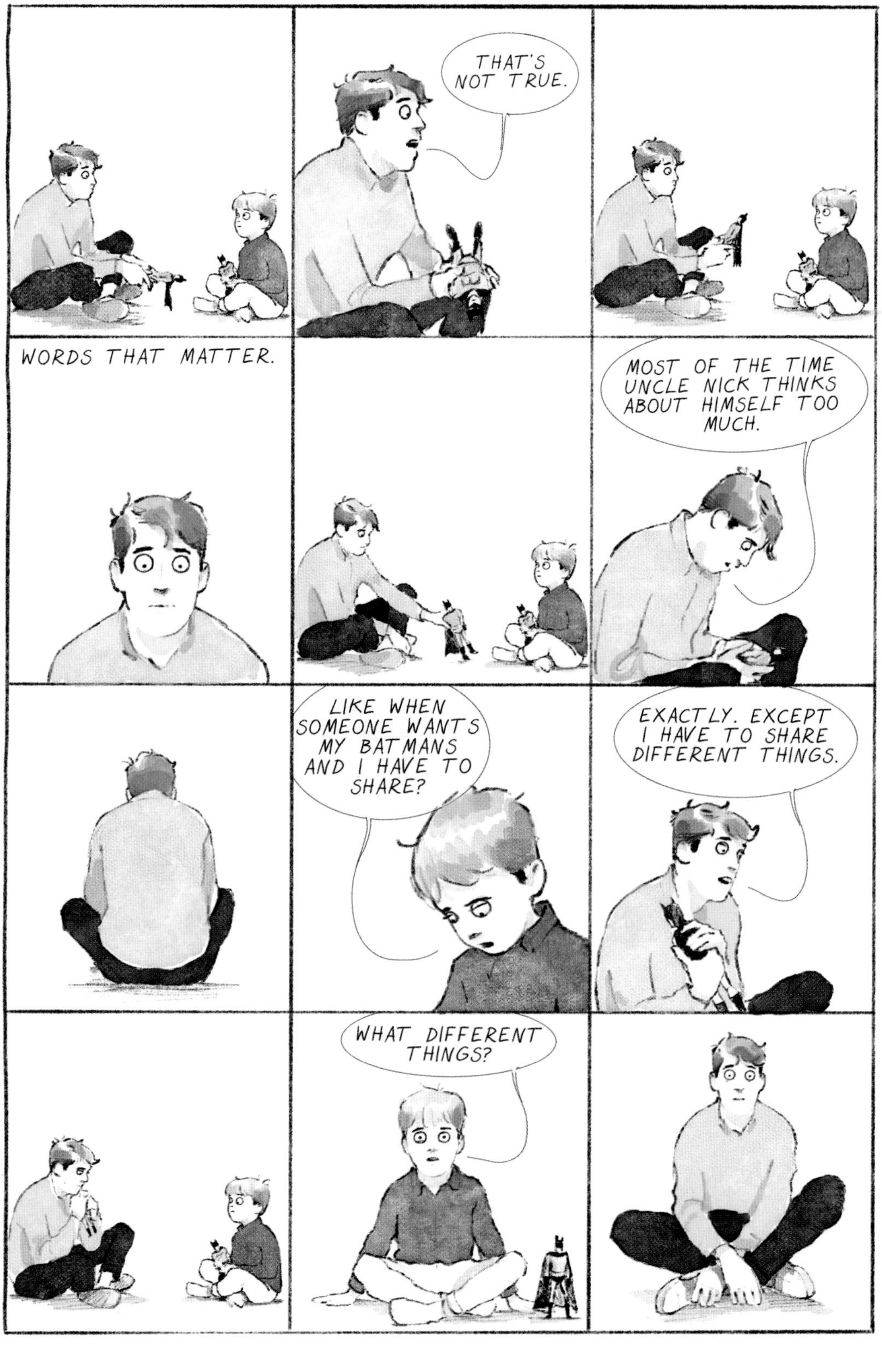
THAT'S NOT TRUE.
WORDS THAT MATTER.
MOST OF THE TIME UNCLE NICK THINKS ABOUT HIMSELF TOO MUCH.
LIKE WHEN SOMEONE WANTS MY BATMANS AND I HAVE TO SHARE?
EXACTLY. EXCEPT I HAVE TO SHARE DIFFERENT THINGS.
WHAT DIFFERENT THINGS?

WELL, YOU DON'T WANT MY BATMANS DO YOU?
NO.

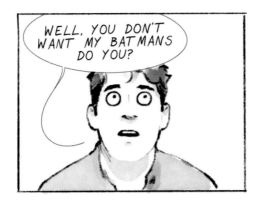

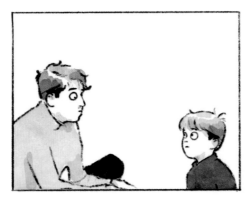

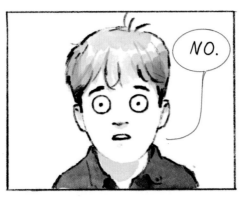

WHAT DO YOU WANT?
YOU.

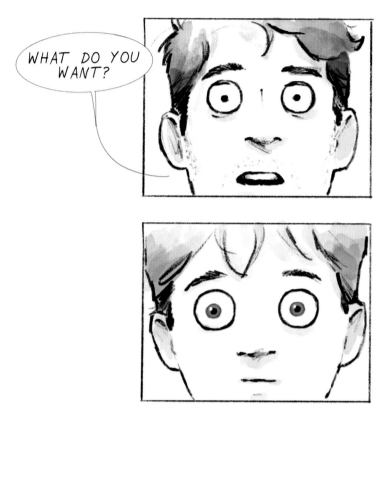

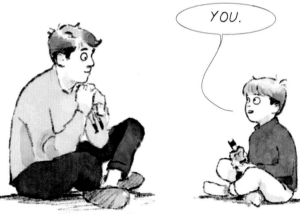

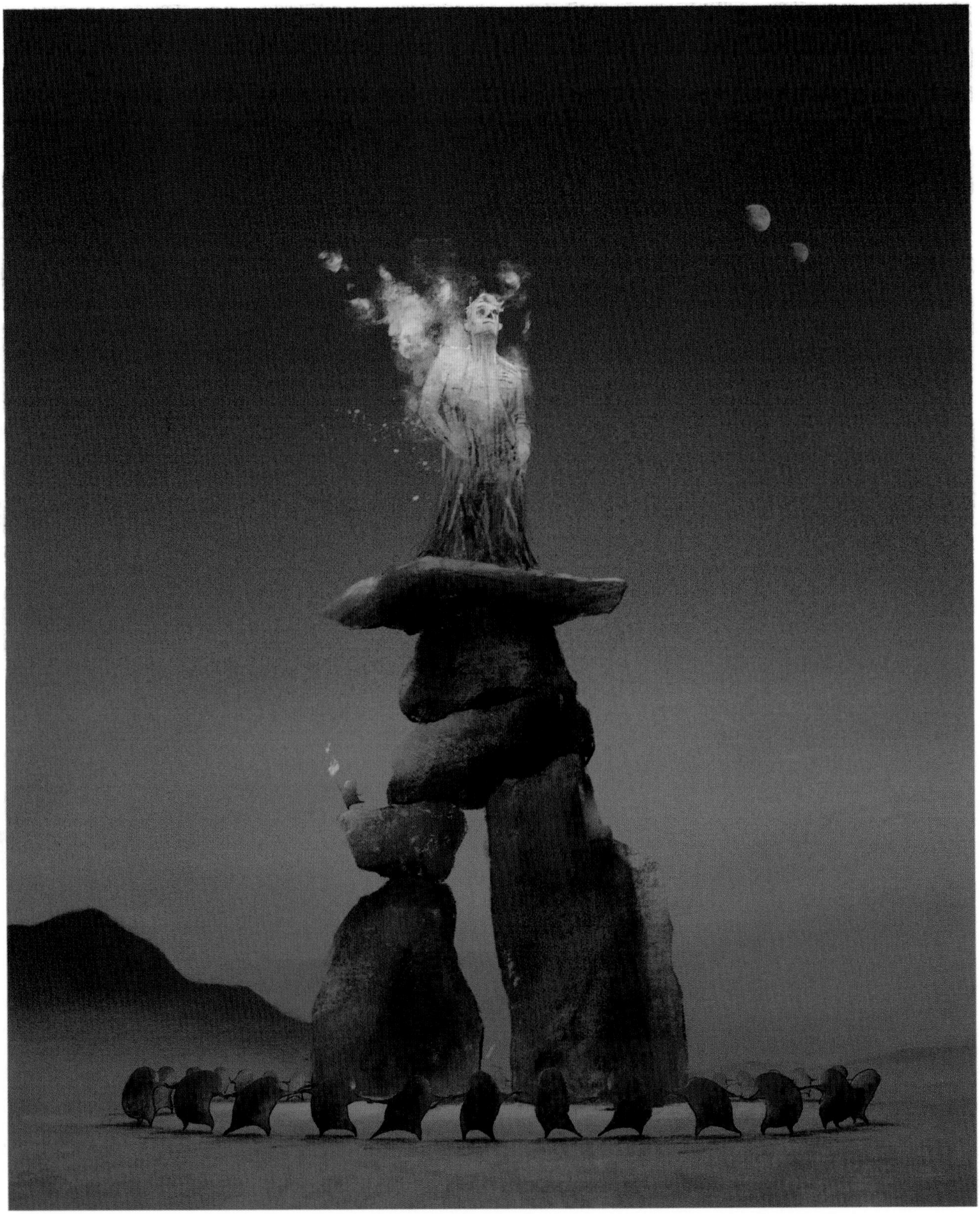

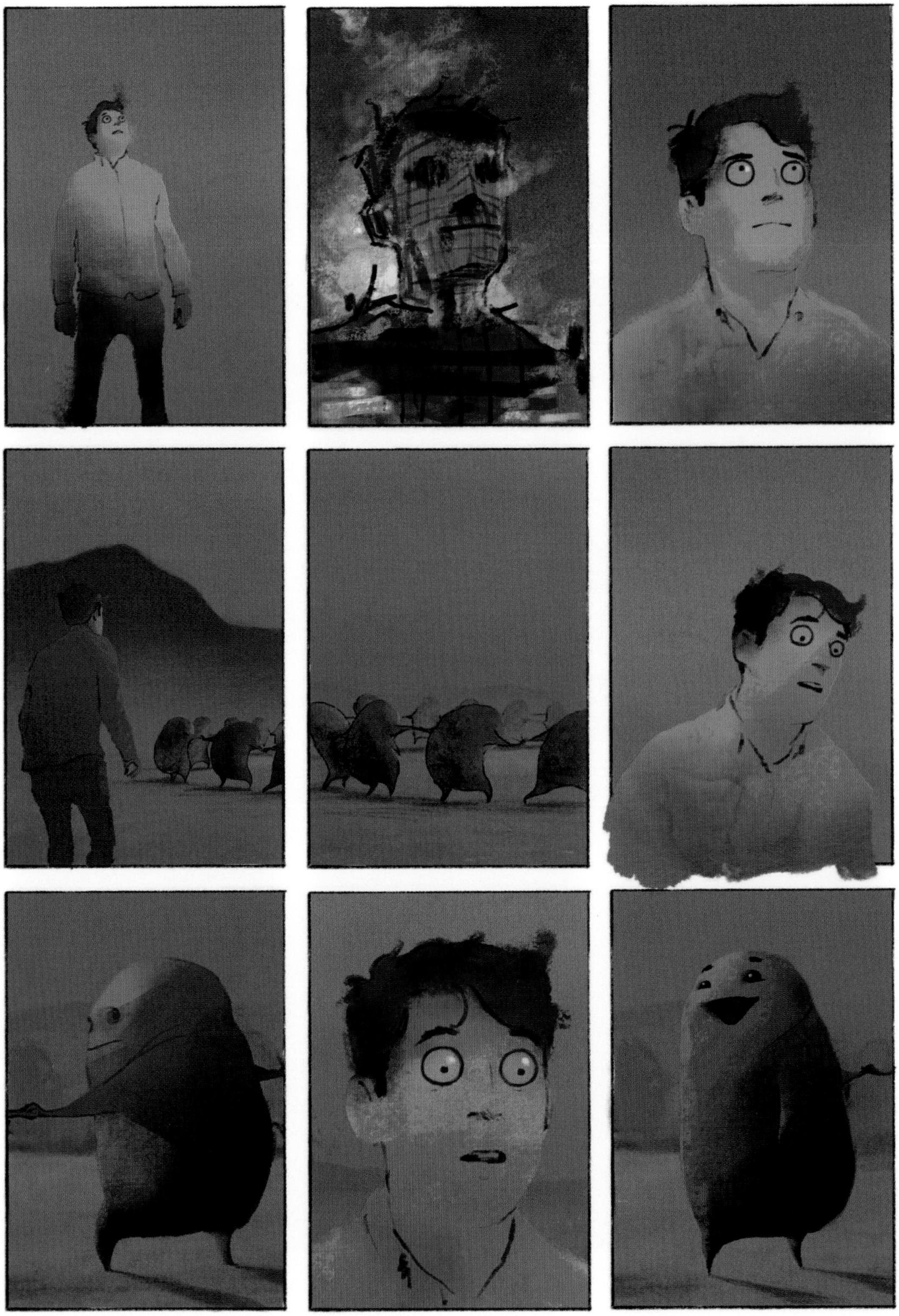

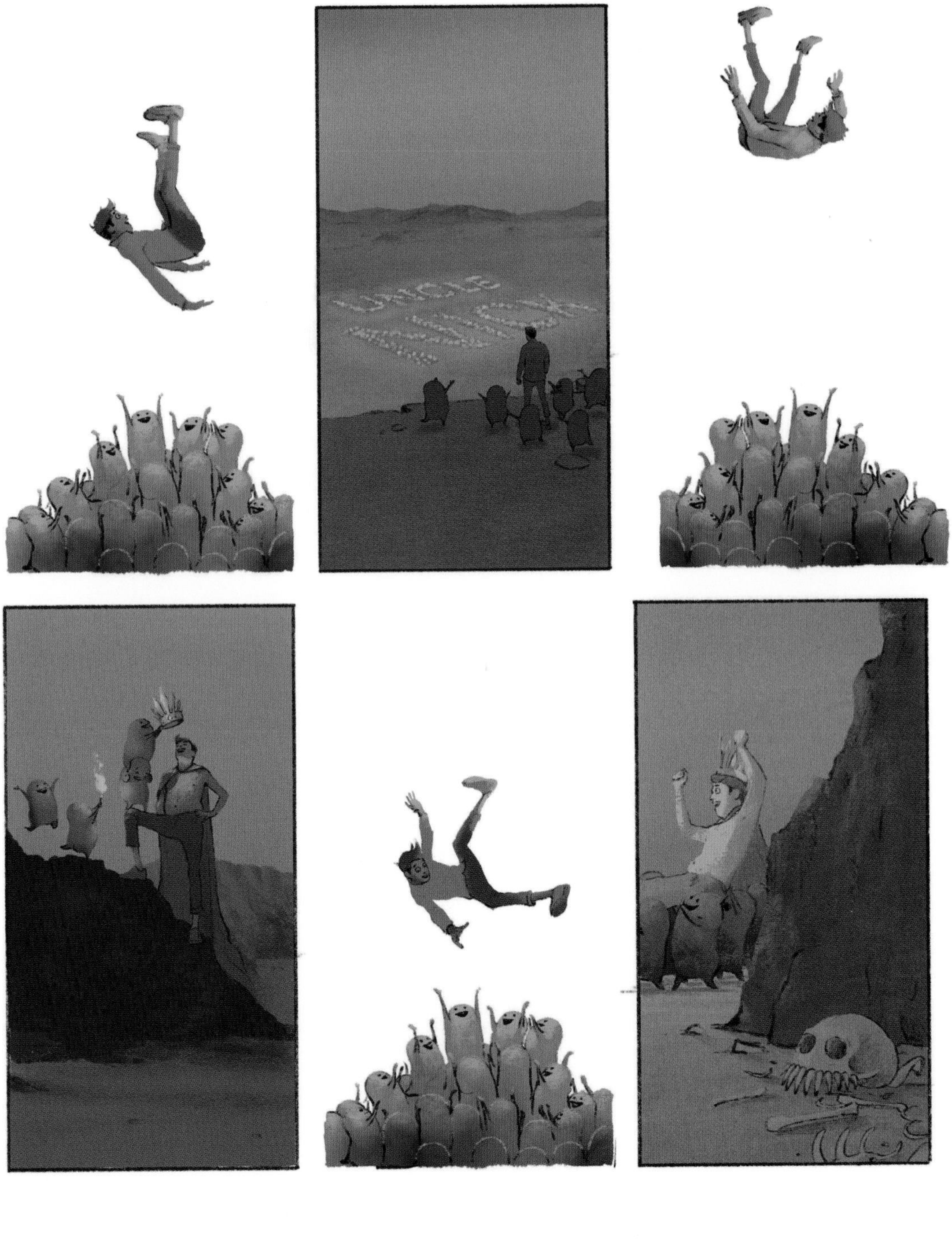
UNCLE

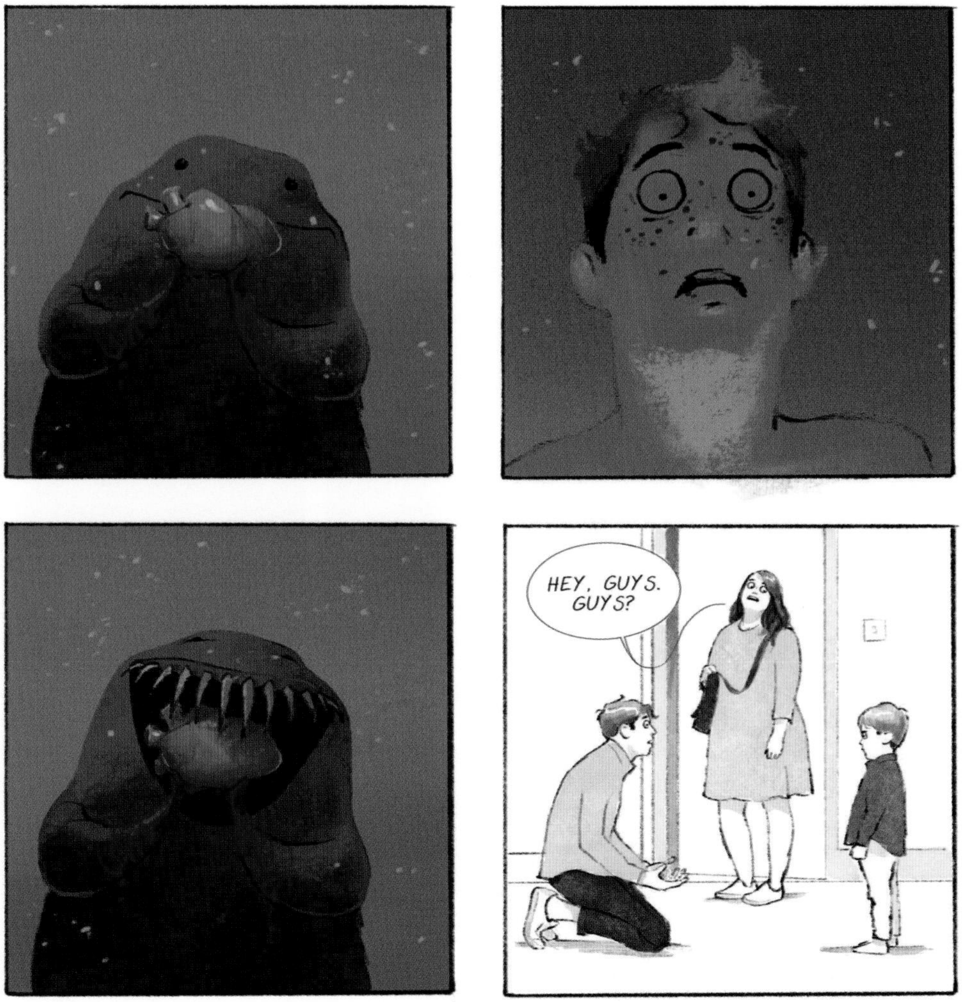
HEY, GUYS. GUYS?

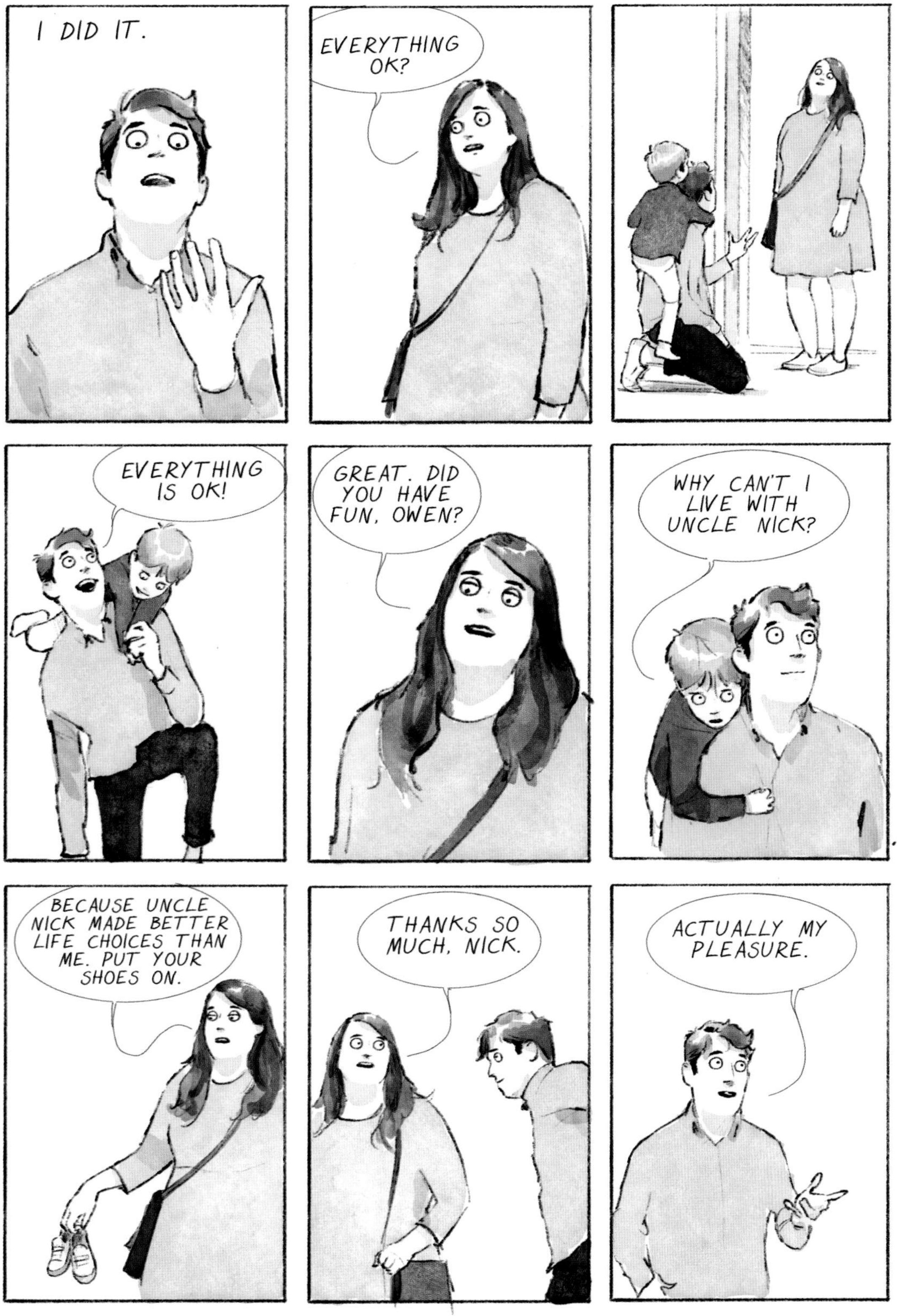
I DID IT.
EVERYTHING OK?
EVERYTHING IS OK!
GREAT. DID YOU HAVE FUN, OWEN?
WHY CAN'T I LIVE WITH UNCLE NICK?
BECAUSE UNCLE NICK MADE BETTER LIFE CHOICES THAN ME. PUT YOUR SHOES ON.
THANKS SO MUCH, NICK.
ACTUALLY MY PLEASURE.

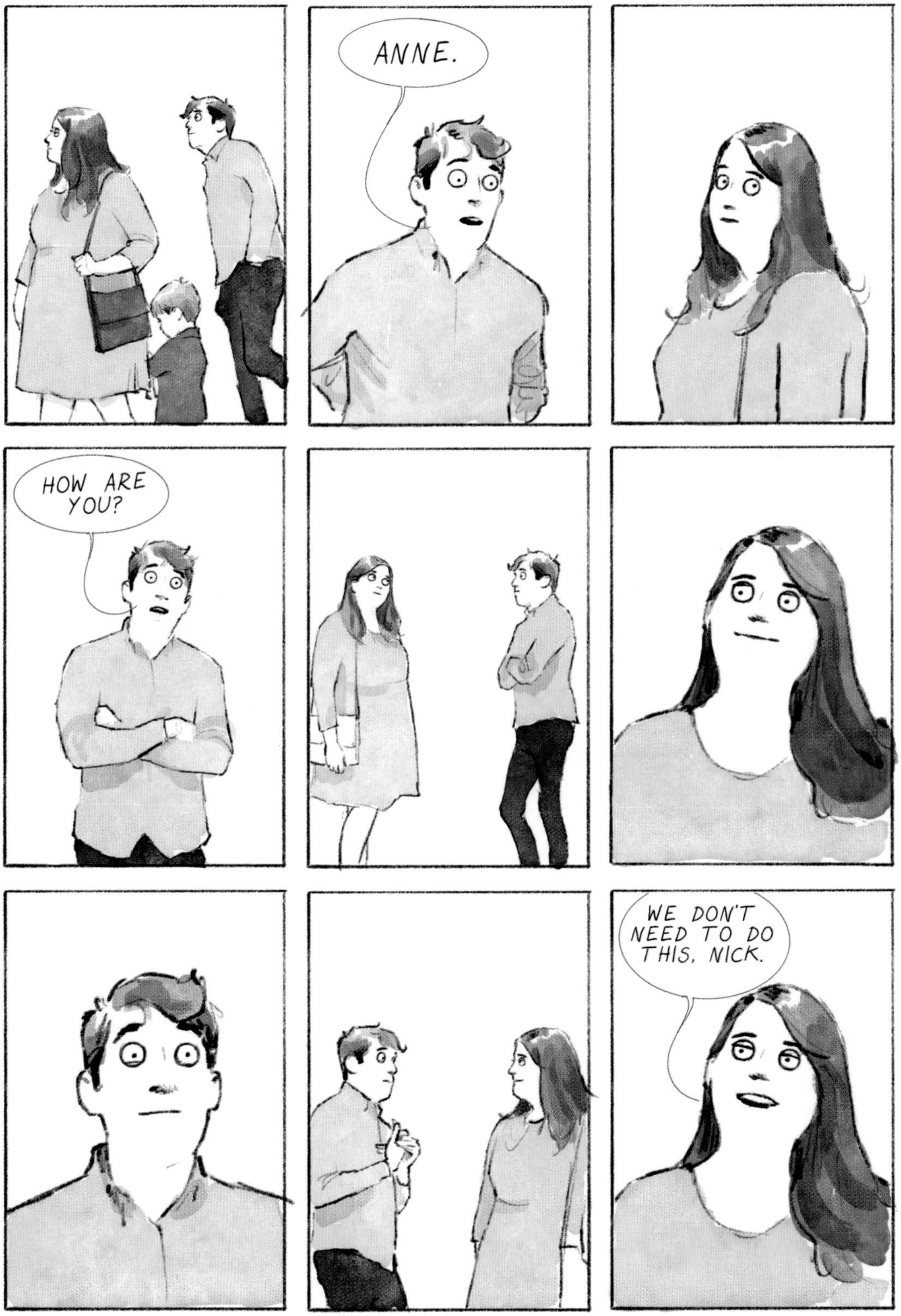
ANNE.
HOW ARE YOU?
WE DON'T NEED TO DO THIS, NICK.

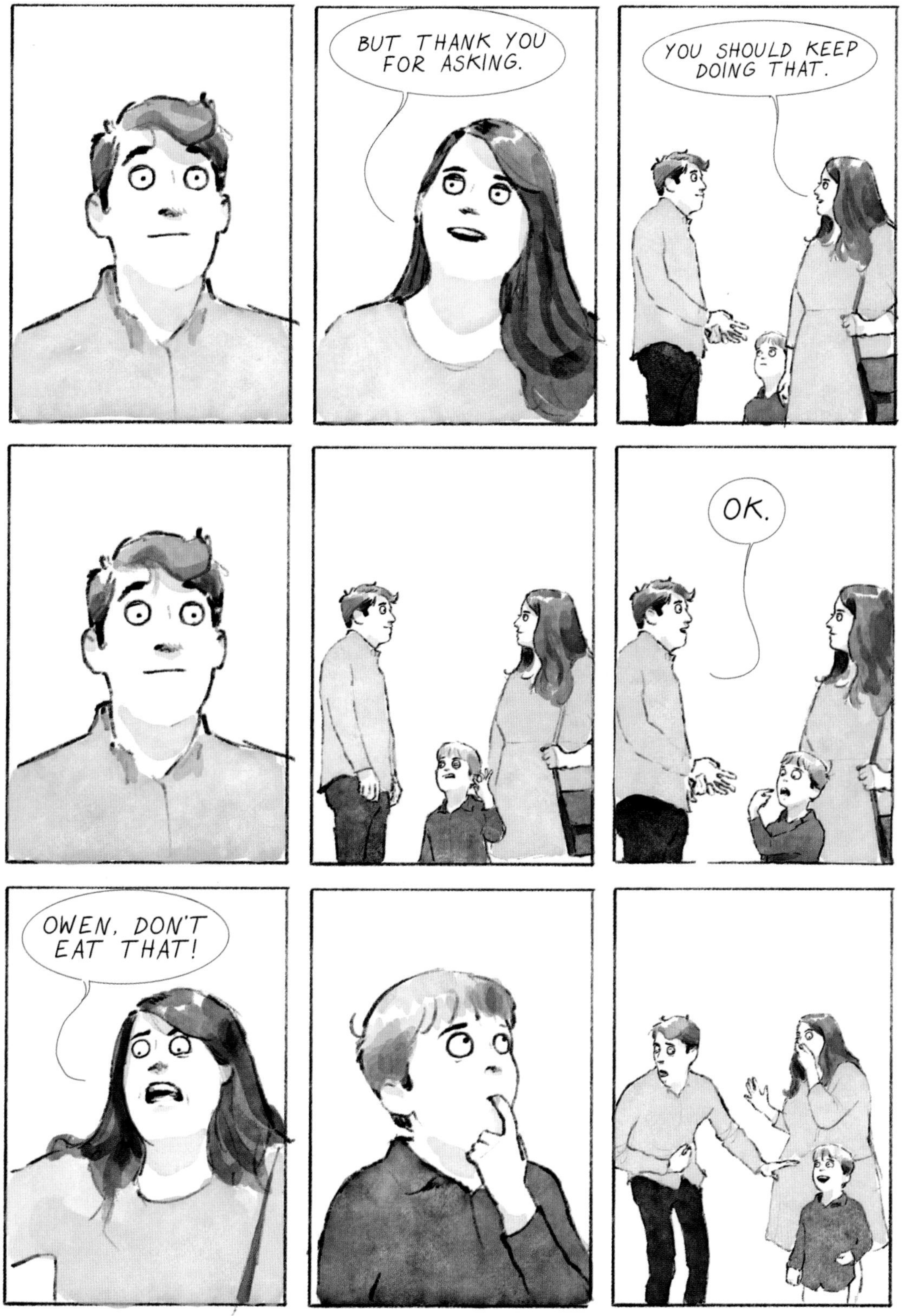
BUT THANK YOU FOR ASKING.
YOU SHOULD KEEP DOING THAT.
OK.
OWEN, DON'T EAT THAT!

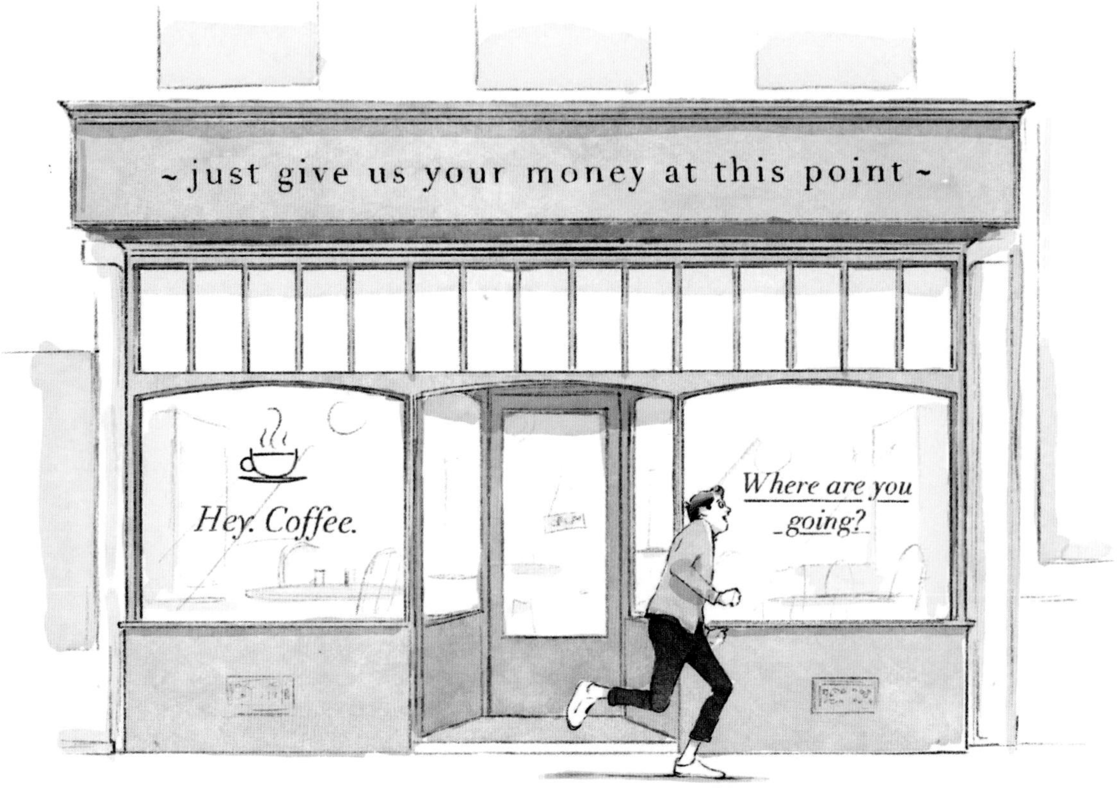
~ just give us your money at this point ~
Hey. Coffee.
Where are you going?

I WENT DOWN ON CATHERINE FROM BOOK CLUB.

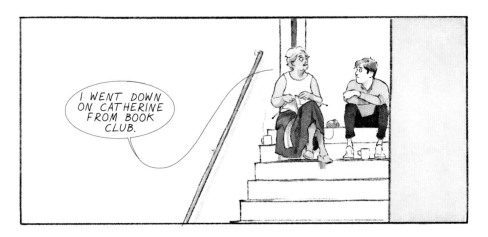

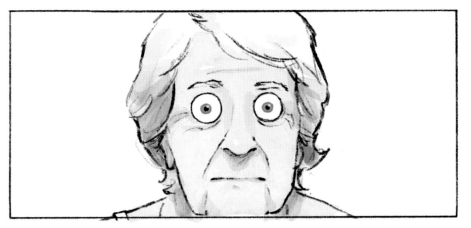

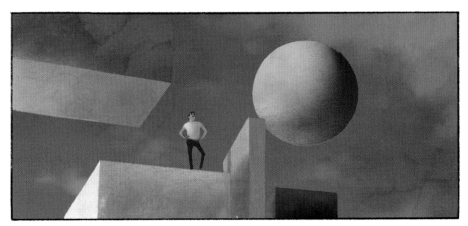

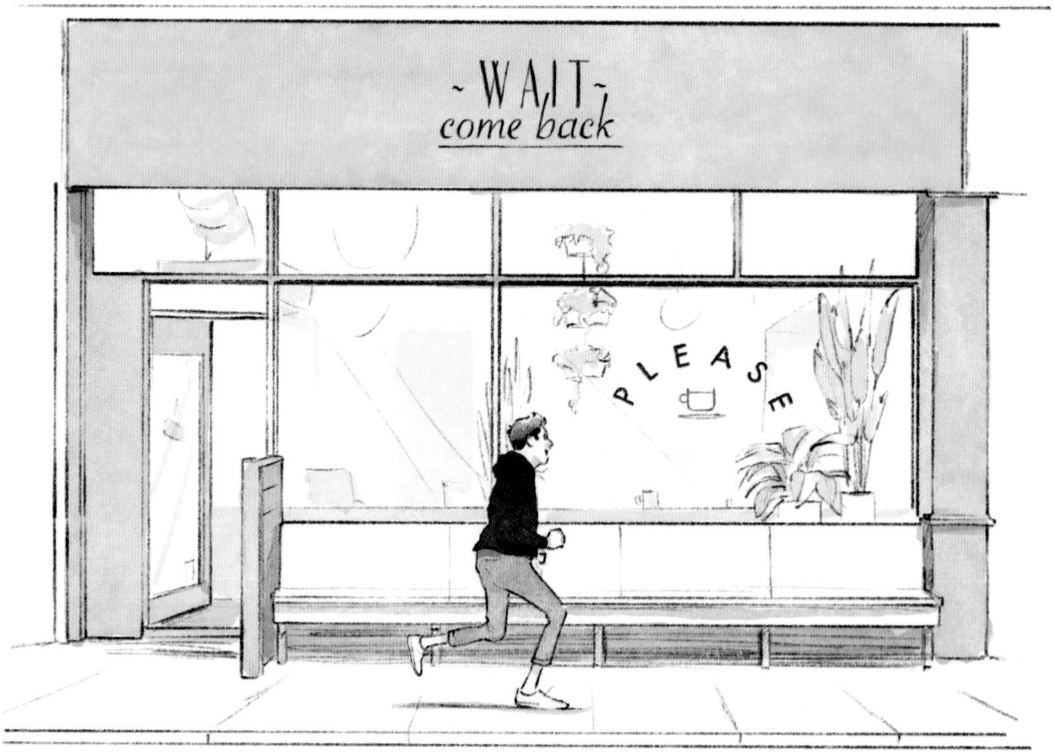
~WAIT~
come back
PLEASE

I KNOW IT'S A SHITTY BAR, BUT WHEN YOU'VE TIED YOUR IDENTITY TO SOMETHING, IT'S HARD TO CHANGE IT.

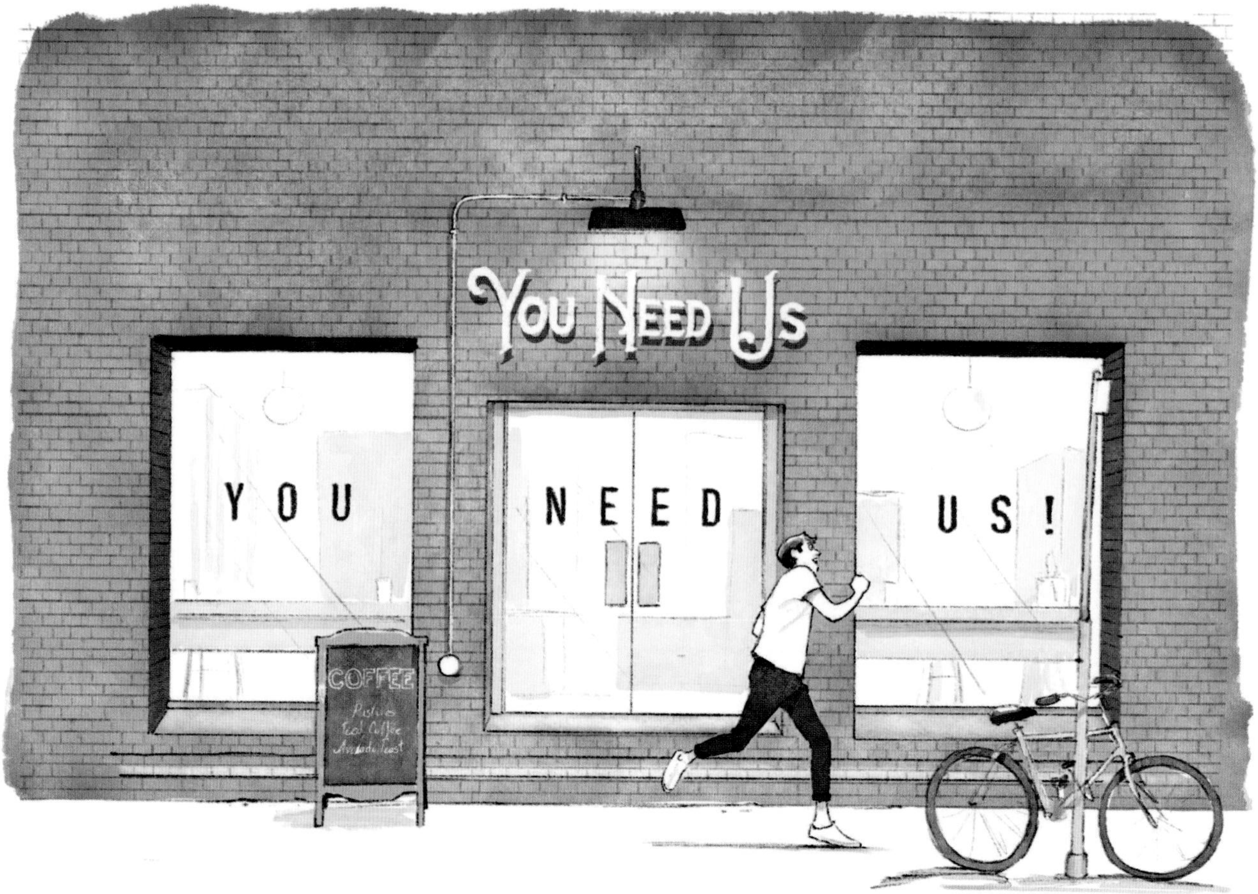
YOU NEED US
YOU
NEED
US!
COFFEE

I SAW THEM TOO! THE CHILDREN OF THE BOWL.

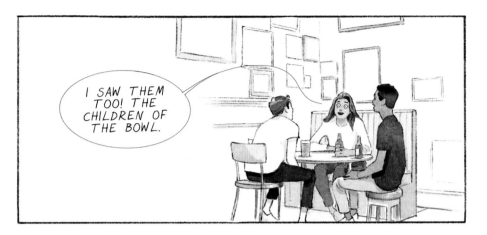

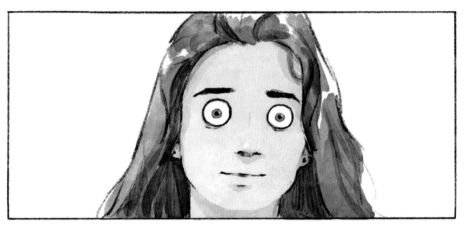

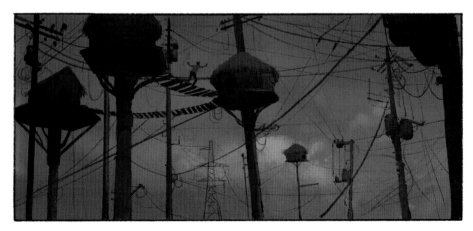

MUM?

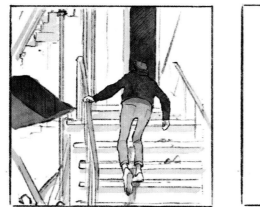

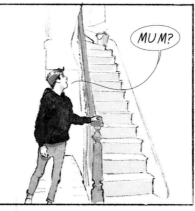

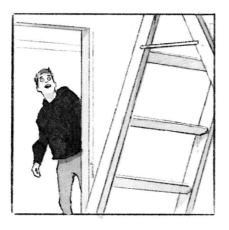

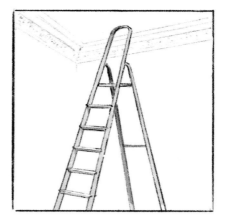

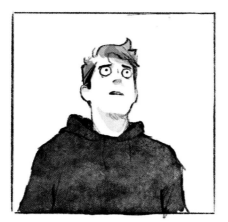

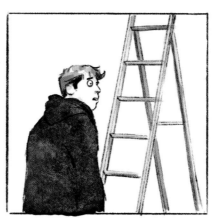

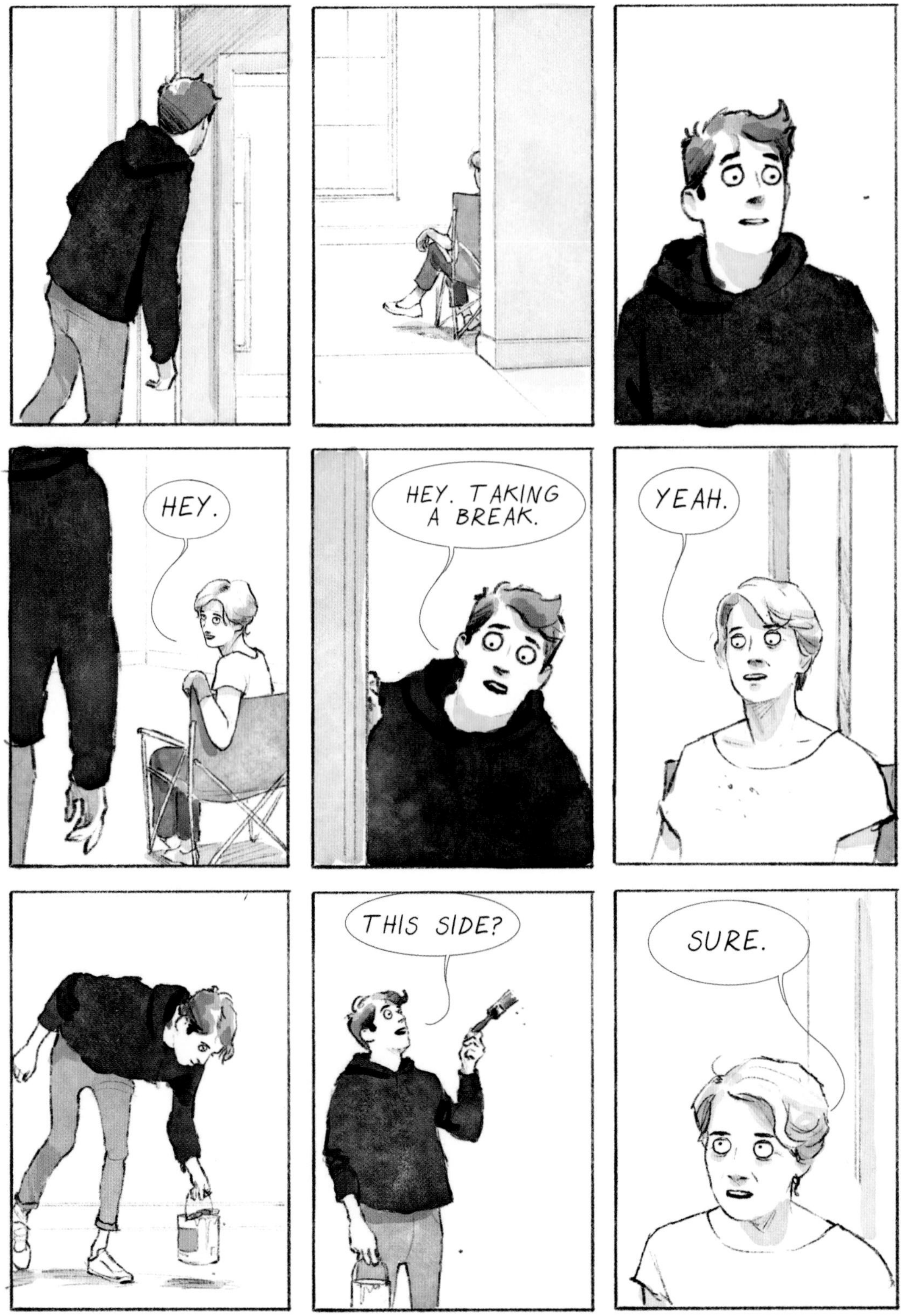
HEY.
HEY. TAKING A BREAK.
YEAH.
THIS SIDE?
SURE.

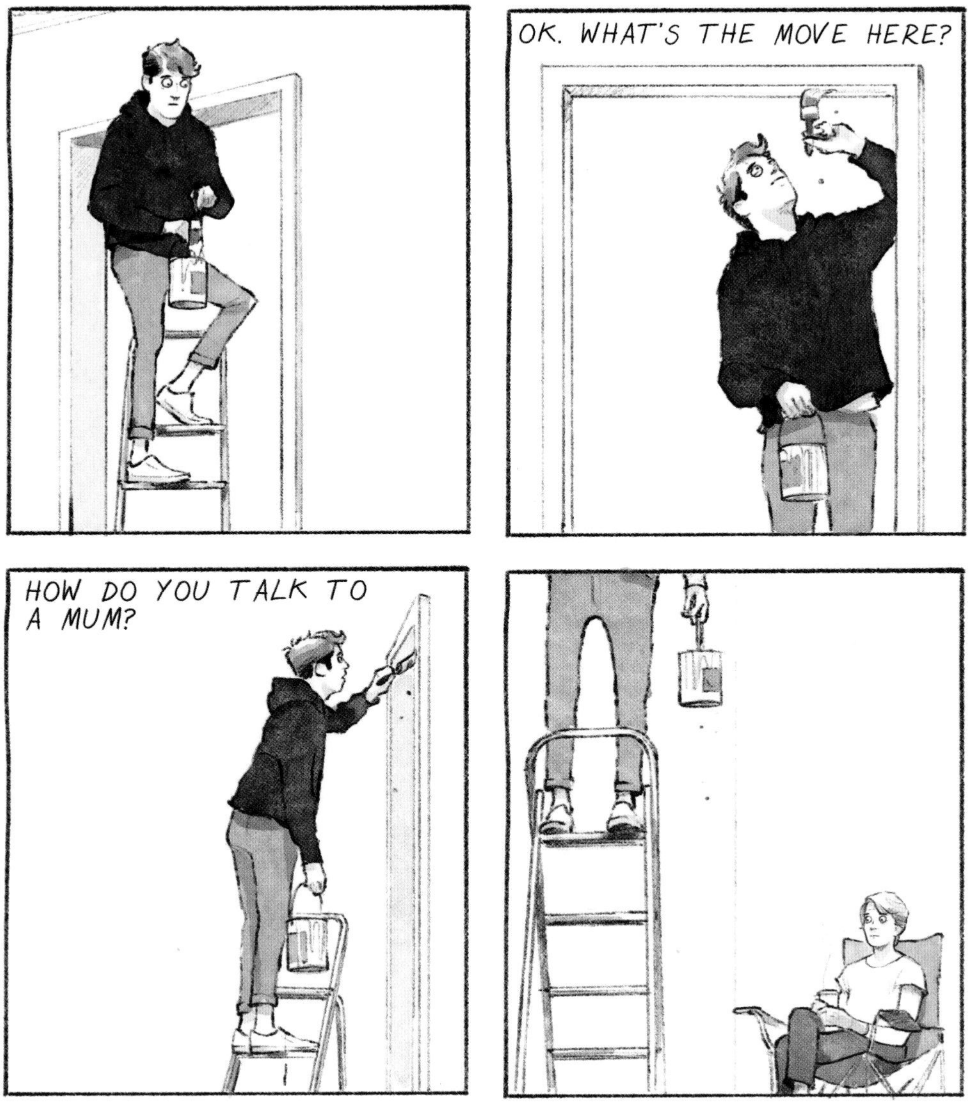
OK. WHAT'S THE MOVE HERE?
HOW DO YOU TALK TO A MUM?

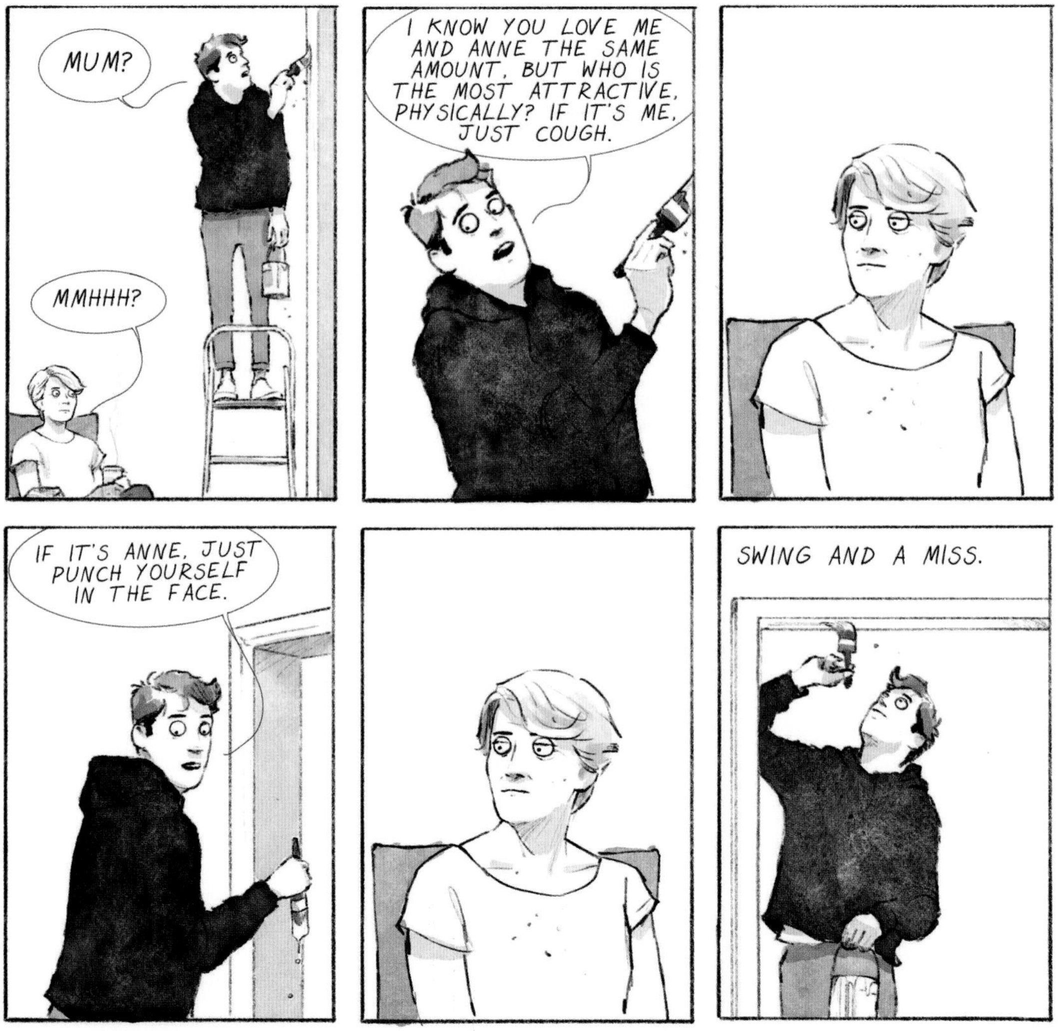
MUM?
MMHHH?
I KNOW YOU LOVE ME AND ANNE THE SAME AMOUNT, BUT WHO IS THE MOST ATTRACTIVE, PHYSICALLY? IF IT'S ME, JUST COUGH.
IF IT'S ANNE, JUST PUNCH YOURSELF IN THE FACE.
SWING AND A MISS.

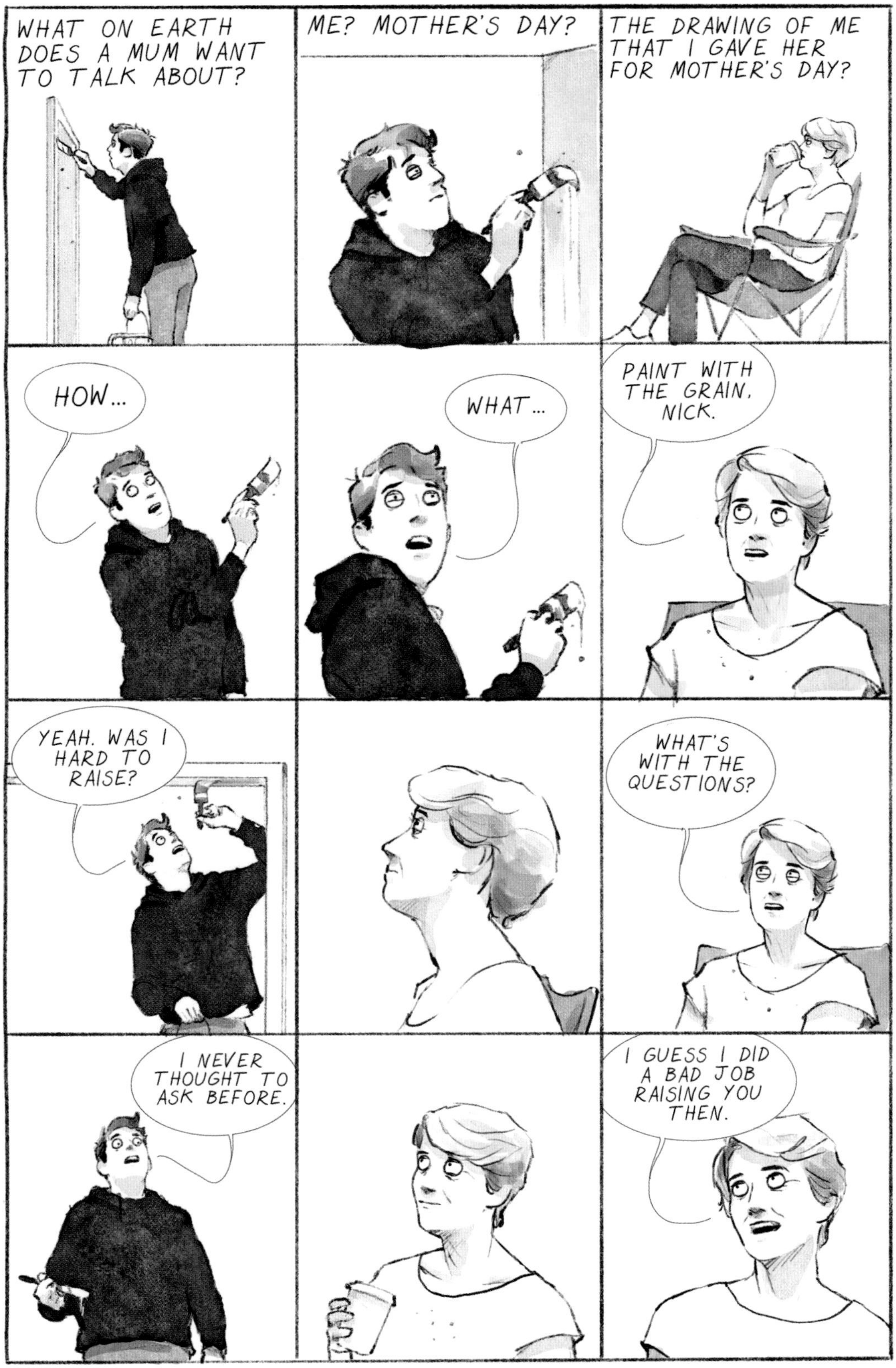
WHAT ON EARTH DOES A MUM WANT TO TALK ABOUT?
ME? MOTHER'S DAY?
THE DRAWING OF ME THAT I GAVE HER FOR MOTHER'S DAY?
HOW...
WHAT...
PAINT WITH THE GRAIN, NICK.
YEAH. WAS I HARD TO RAISE?
WHAT'S WITH THE QUESTIONS?
I NEVER THOUGHT TO ASK BEFORE.
I GUESS I DID A BAD JOB RAISING YOU THEN.

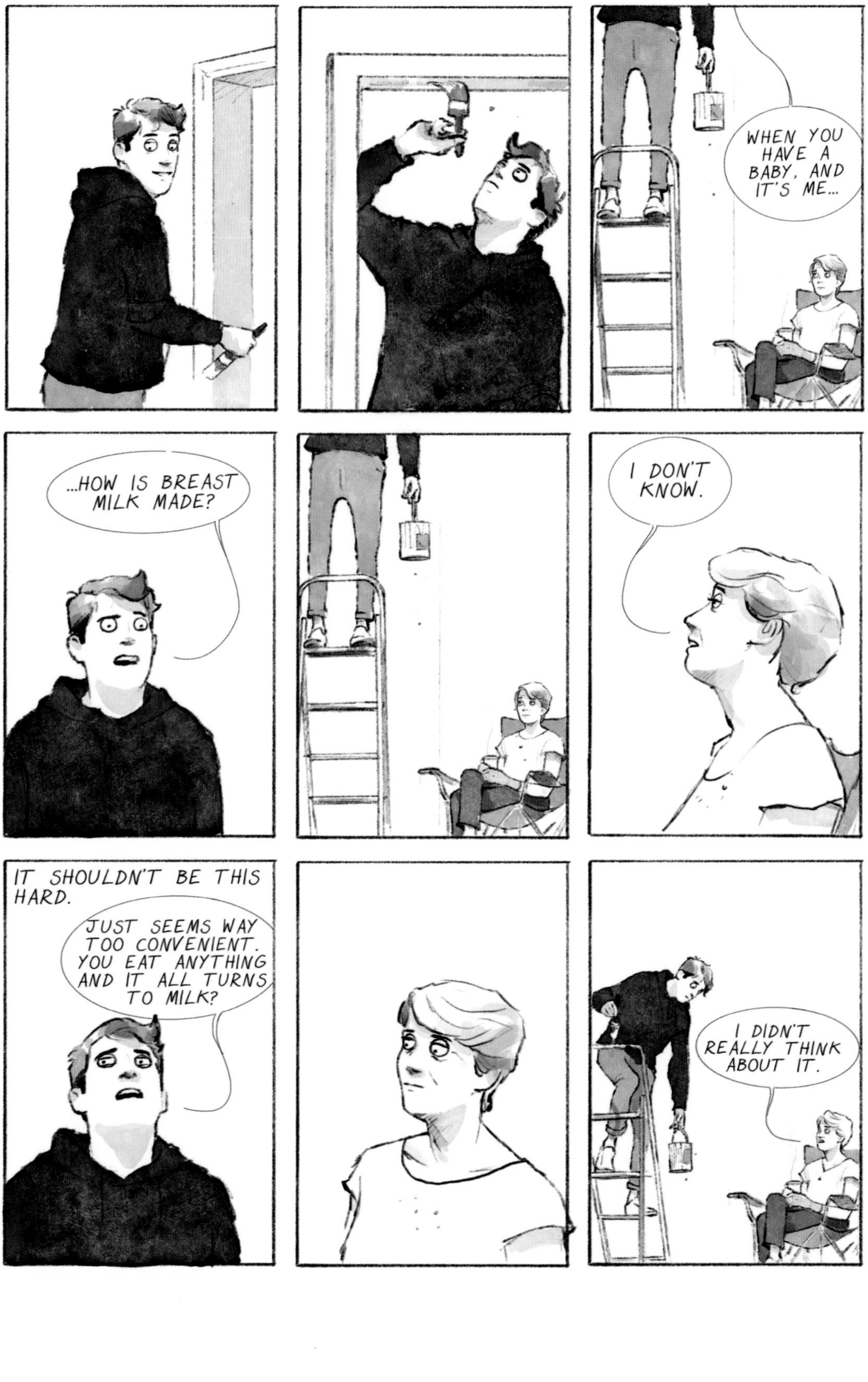
WHEN YOU HAVE A BABY, AND IT'S ME...
...HOW IS BREAST MILK MADE?
I DON'T KNOW.
IT SHOULDN'T BE THIS HARD.
JUST SEEMS WAY TOO CONVENIENT. YOU EAT ANYTHING AND IT ALL TURNS TO MILK?
I DIDN'T REALLY THINK ABOUT IT.

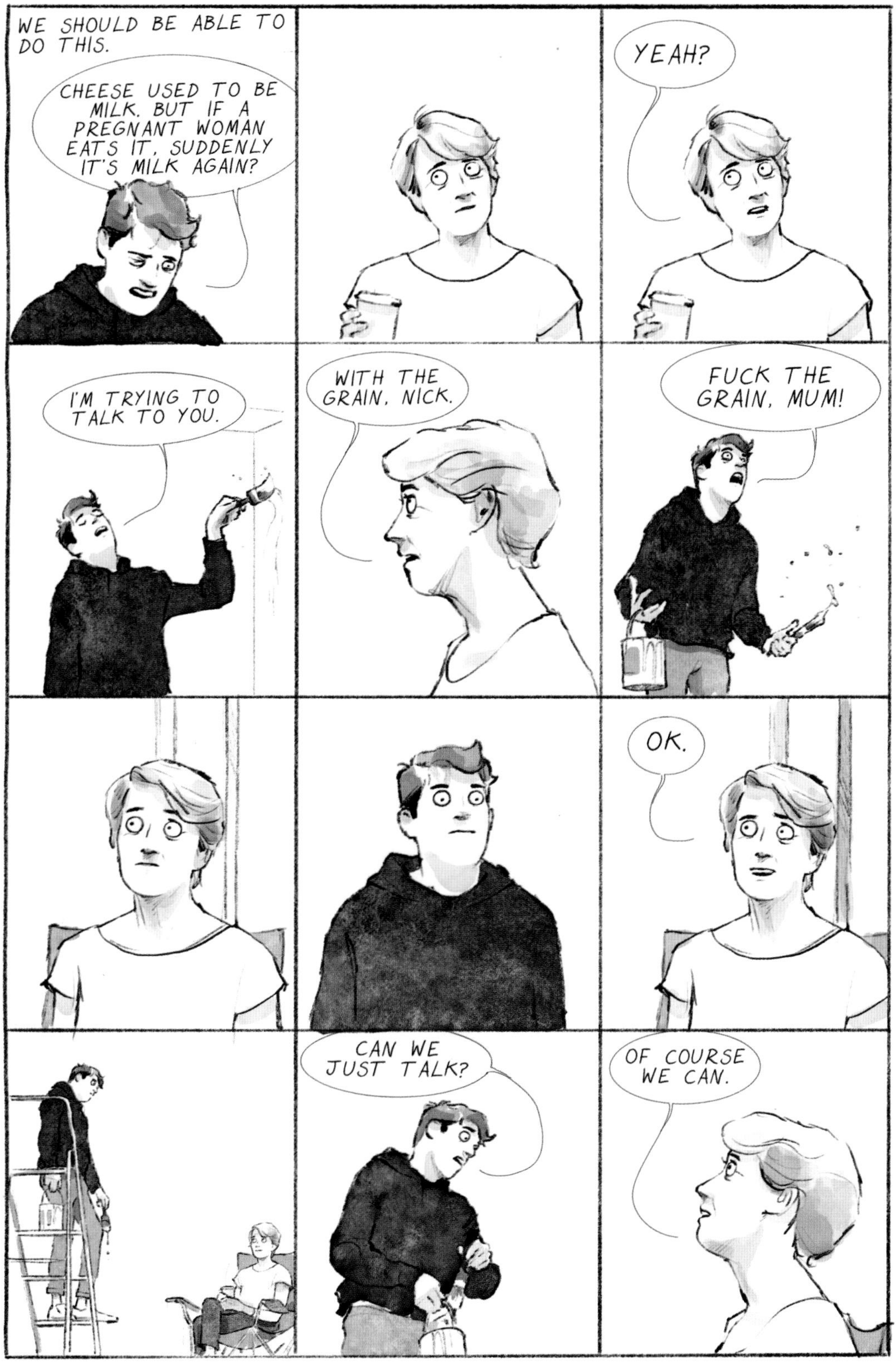
WE SHOULD BE ABLE TO DO THIS.
CHEESE USED TO BE MILK. BUT IF A PREGNANT WOMAN EATS IT, SUDDENLY IT'S MILK AGAIN?
YEAH?
I'M TRYING TO TALK TO YOU.
WITH THE GRAIN, NICK.
FUCK THE GRAIN, MUM!
OK.
CAN WE JUST TALK?
OF COURSE WE CAN.

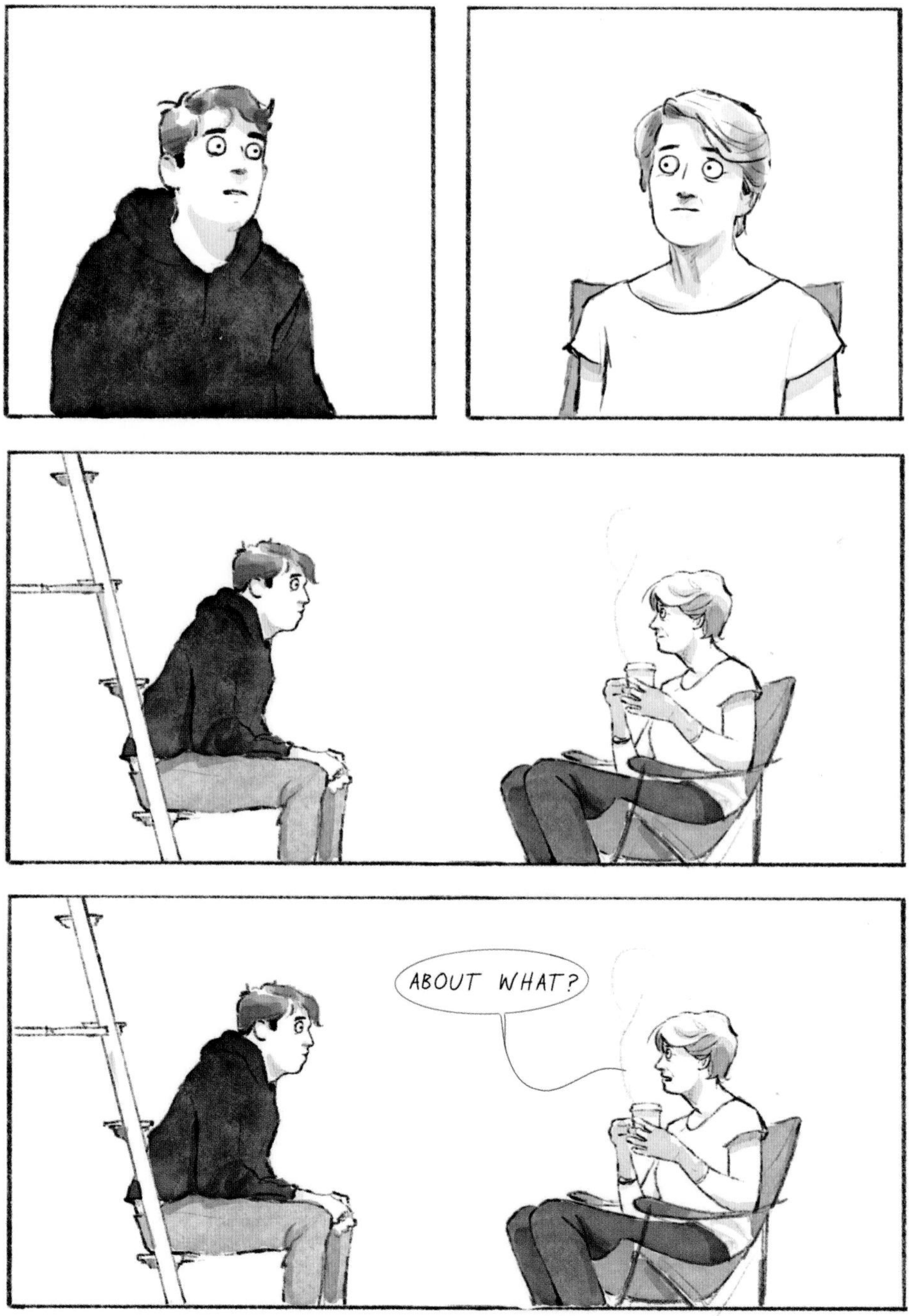
ABOUT WHAT?

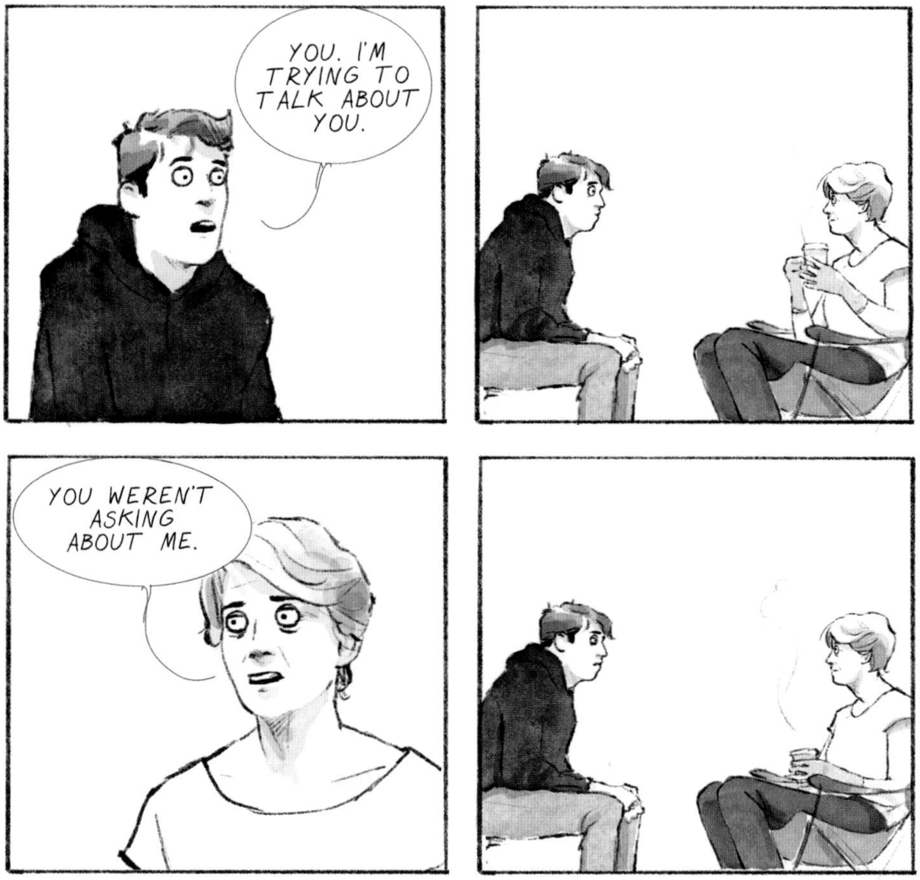
YOU. I'M TRYING TO TALK ABOUT YOU.
YOU WEREN'T ASKING ABOUT ME.

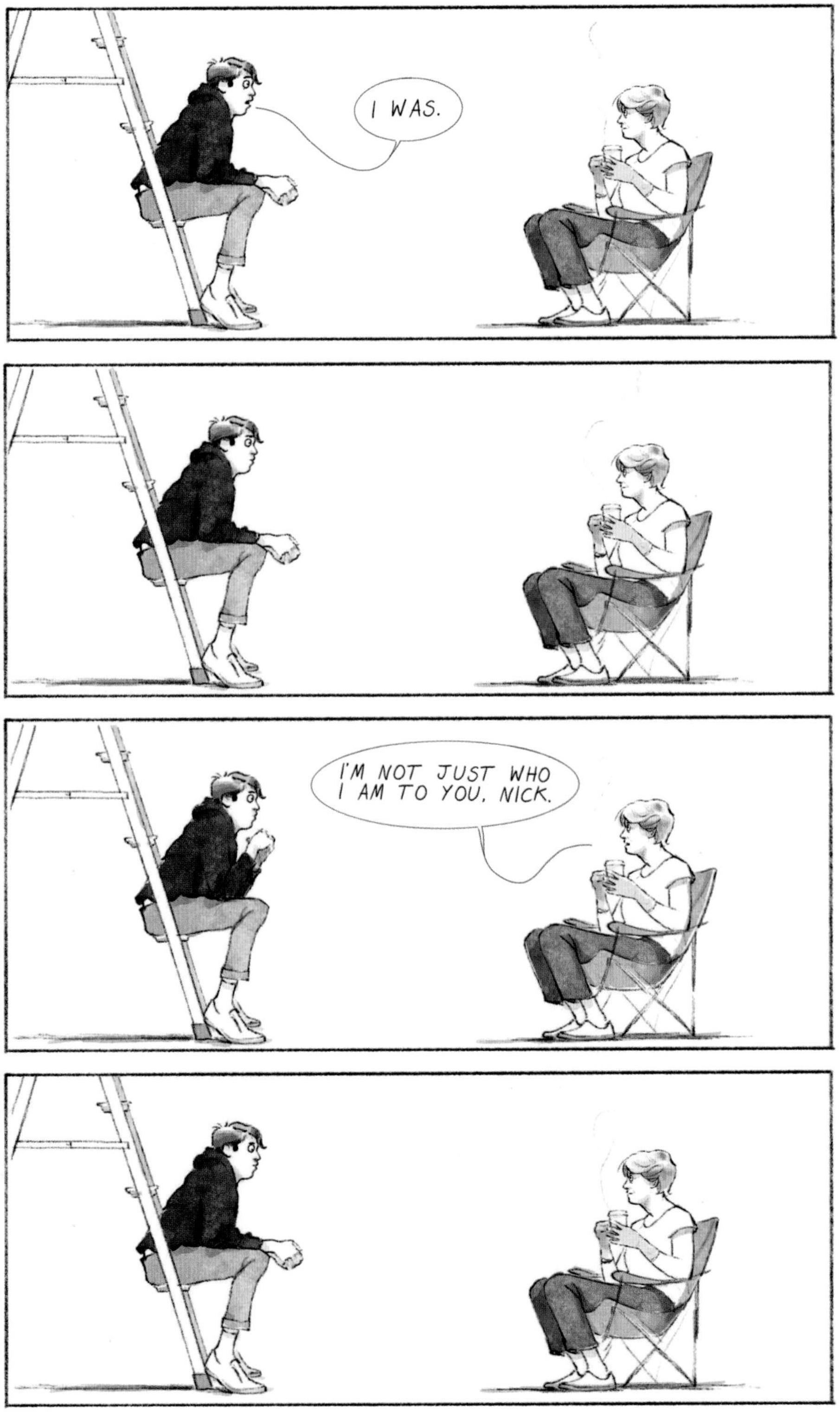
I WAS.
I'M NOT JUST WHO I AM TO YOU, NICK.

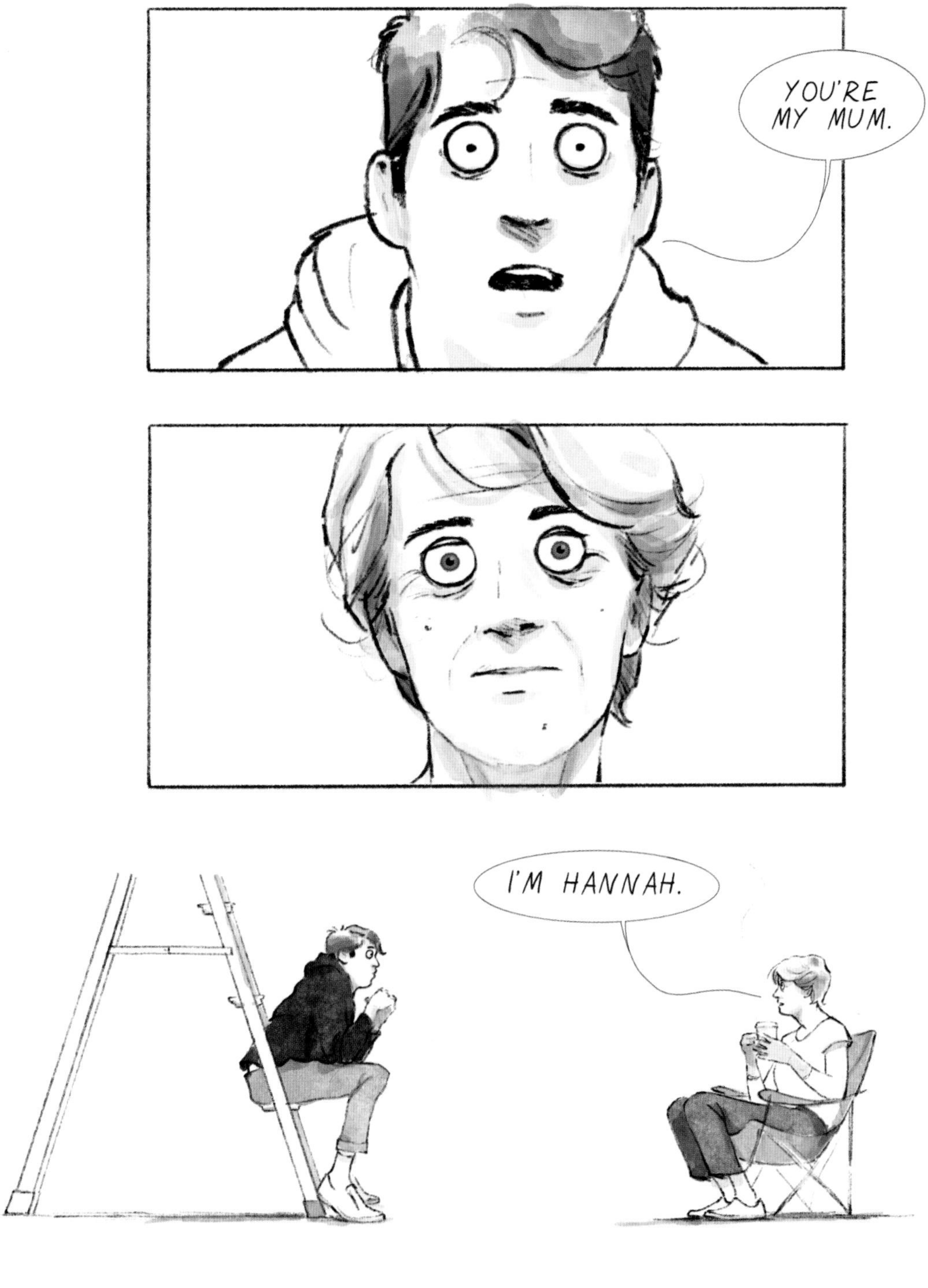
YOU'RE MY MUM.
I'M HANNAH.

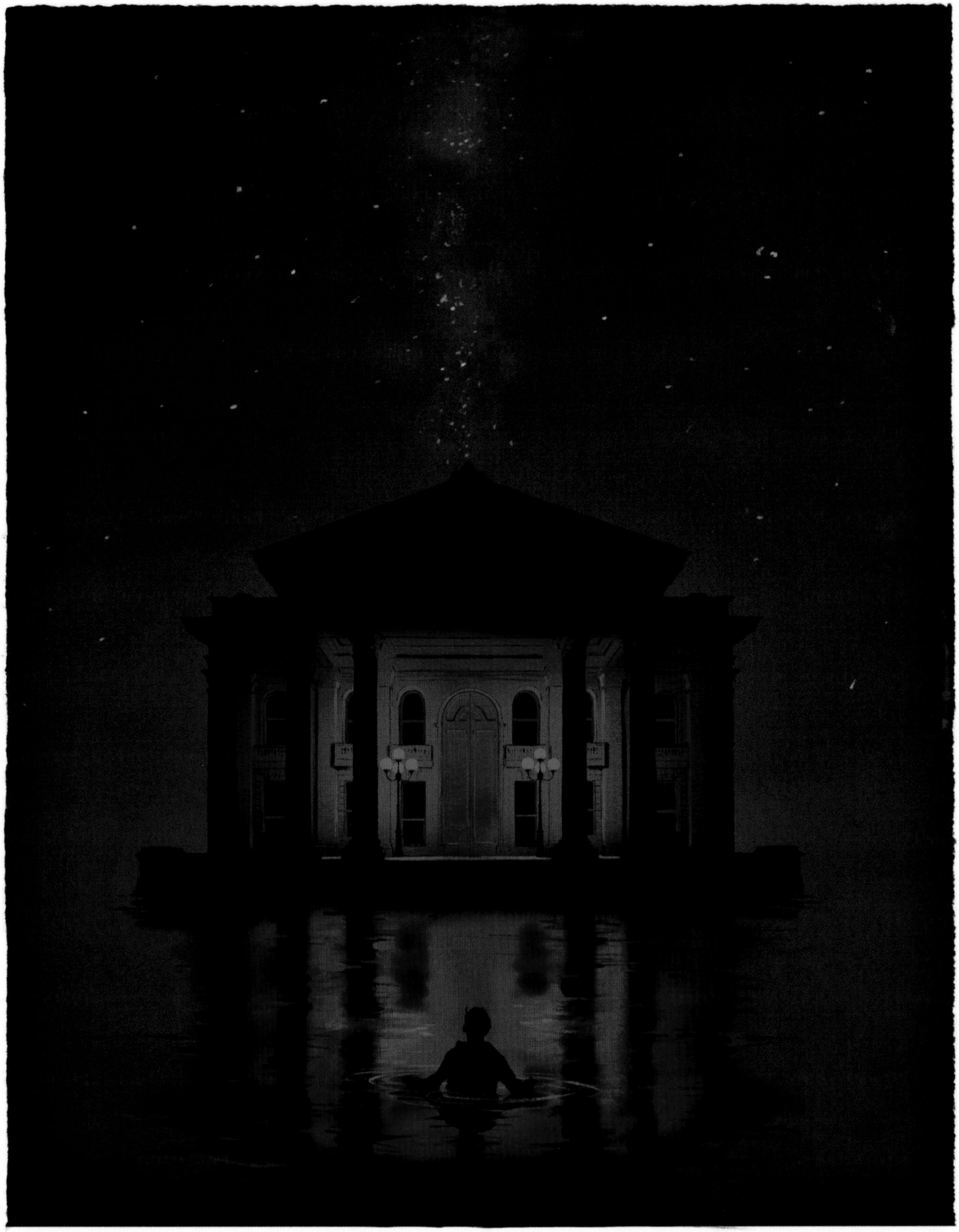

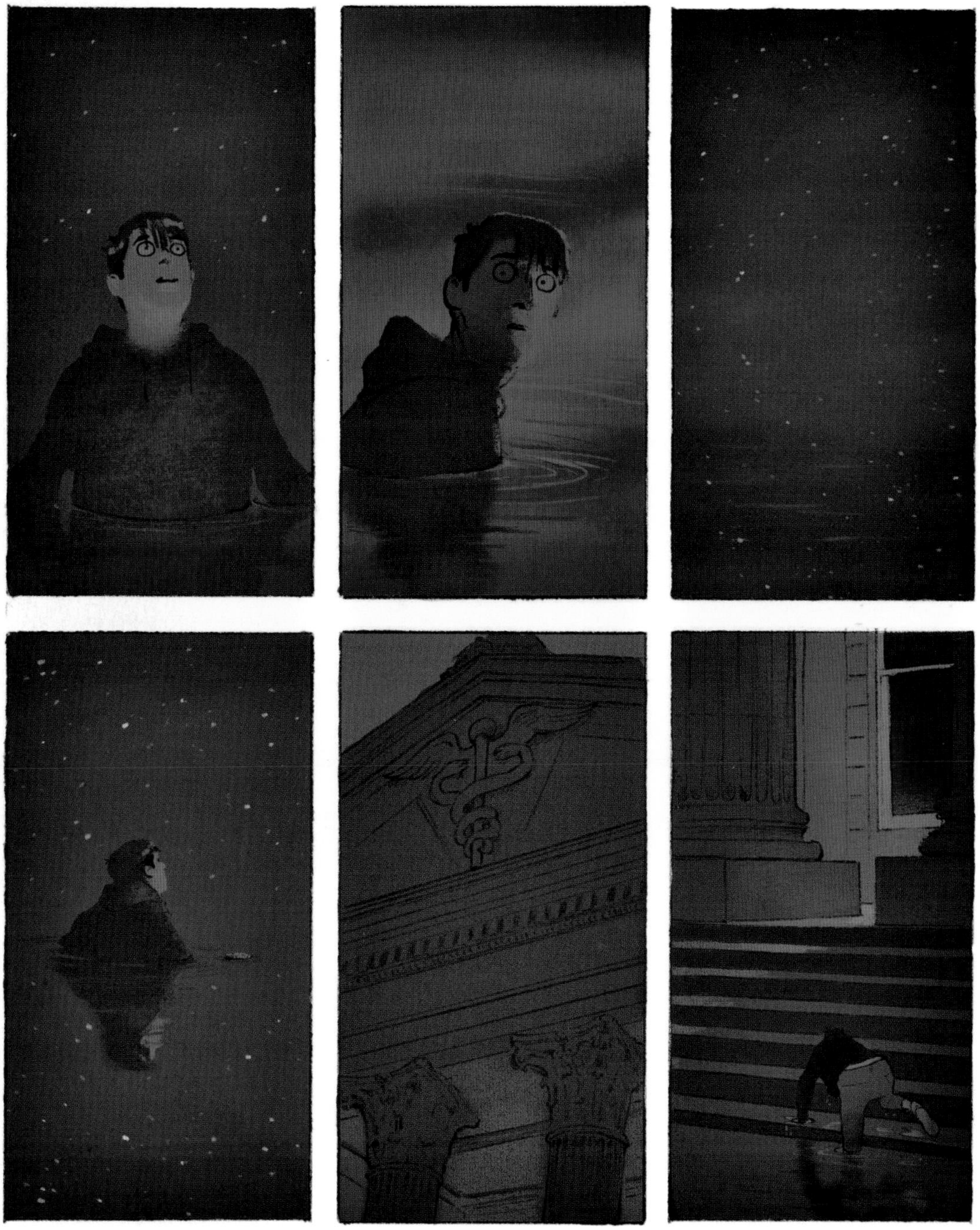

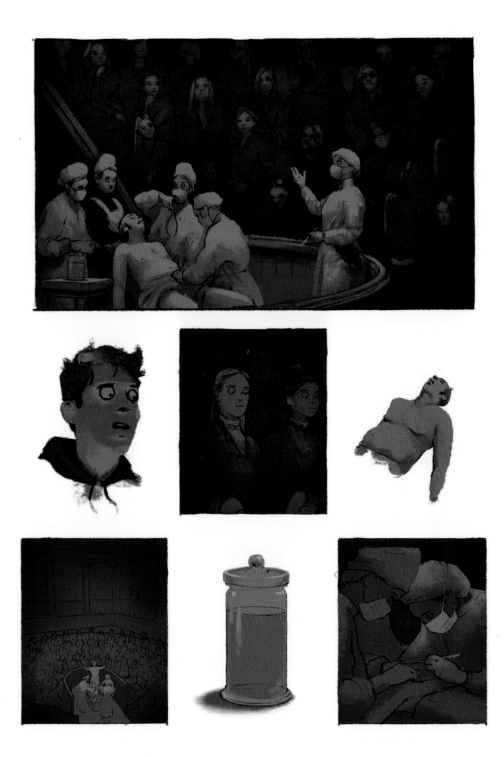

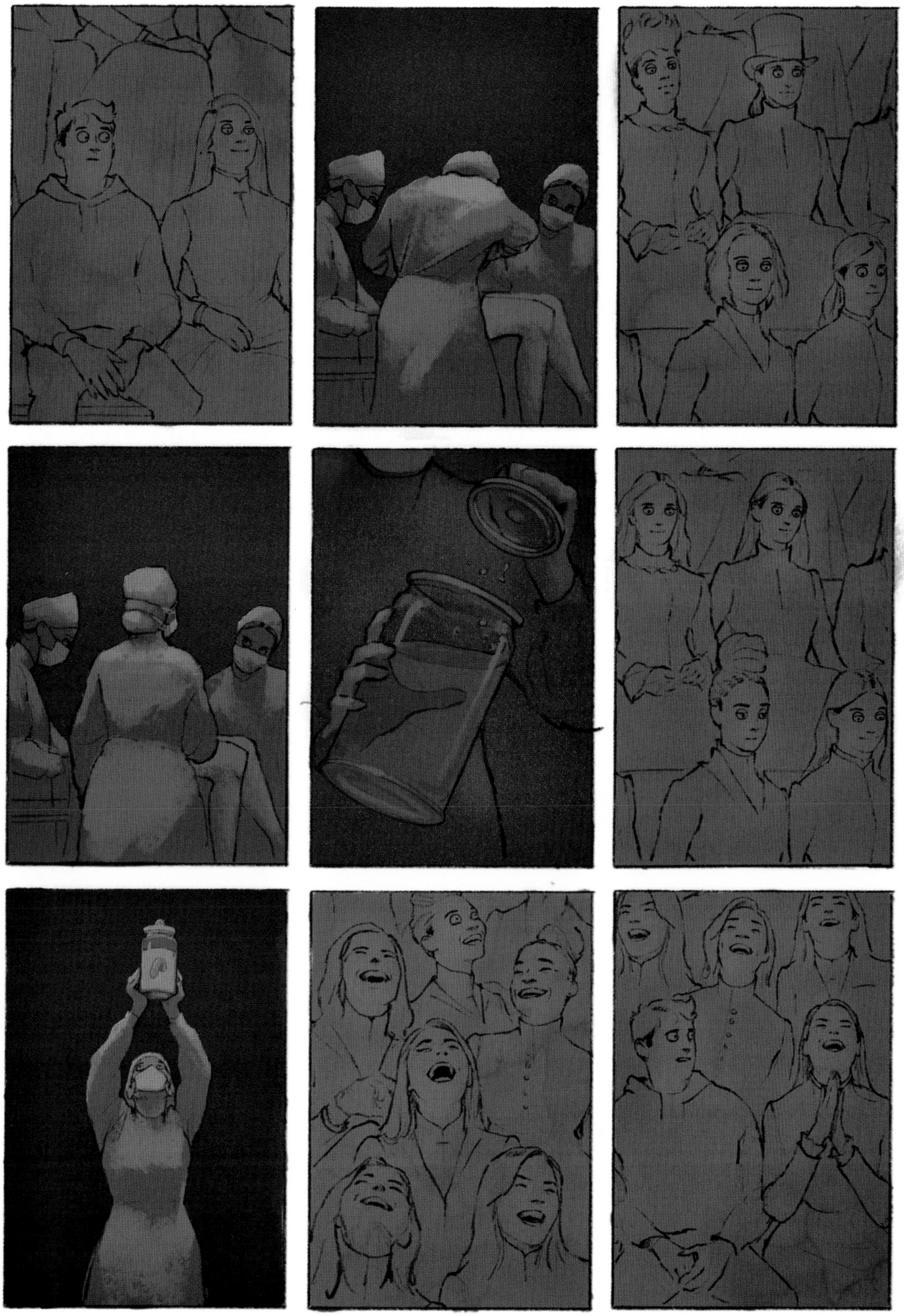

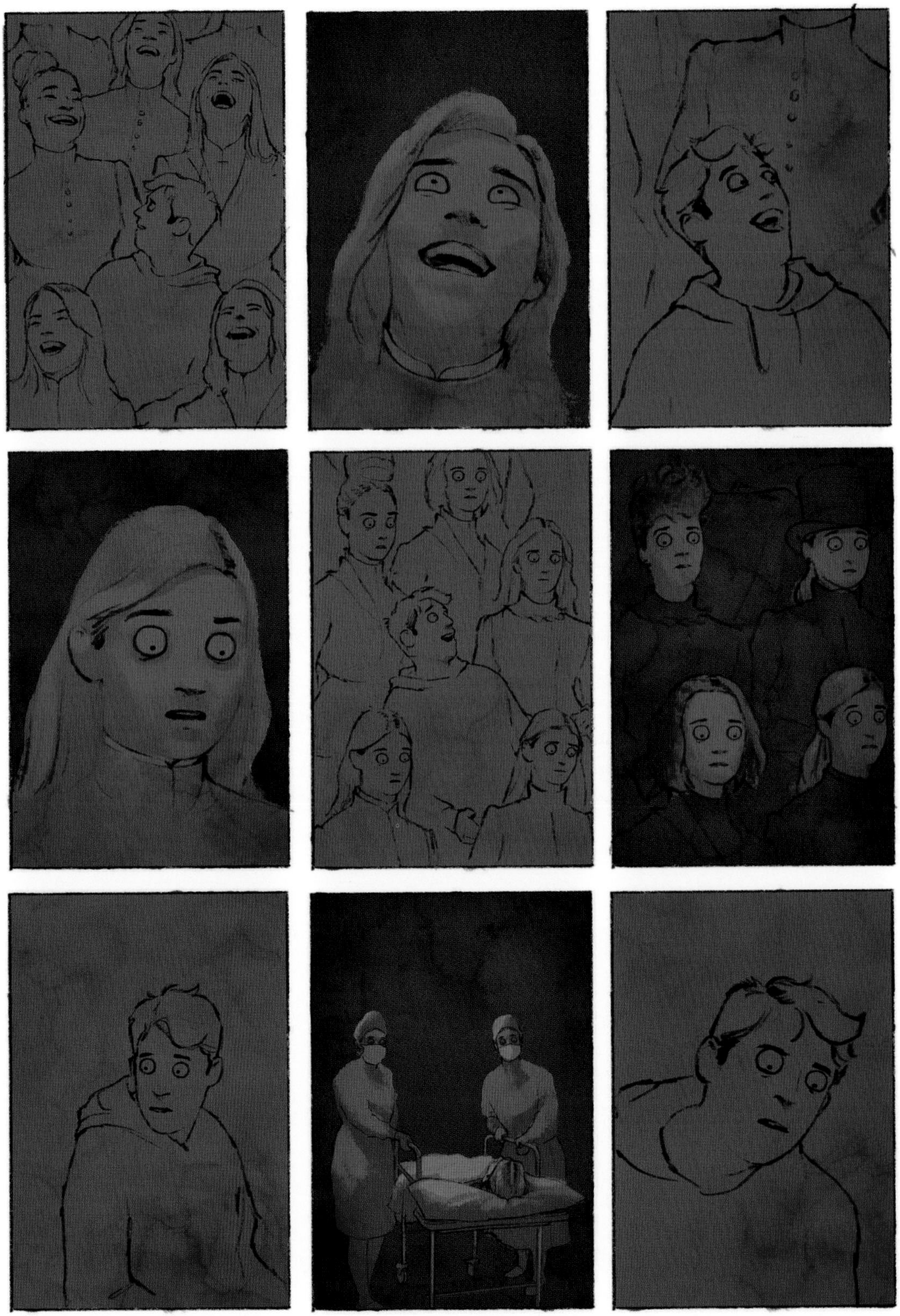

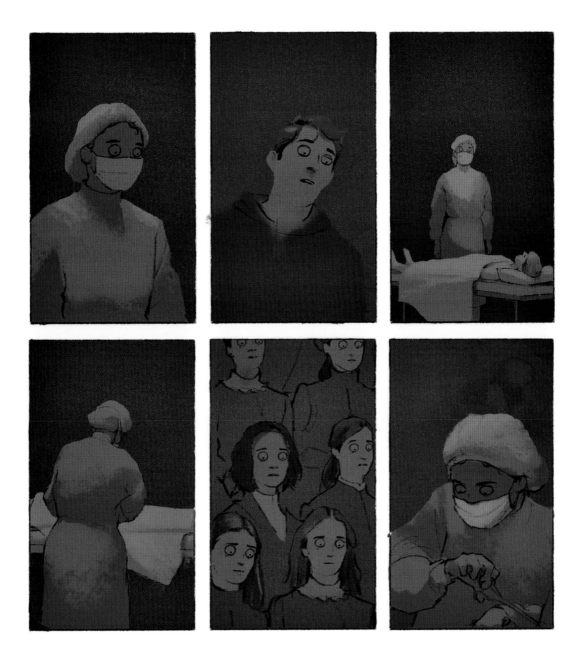

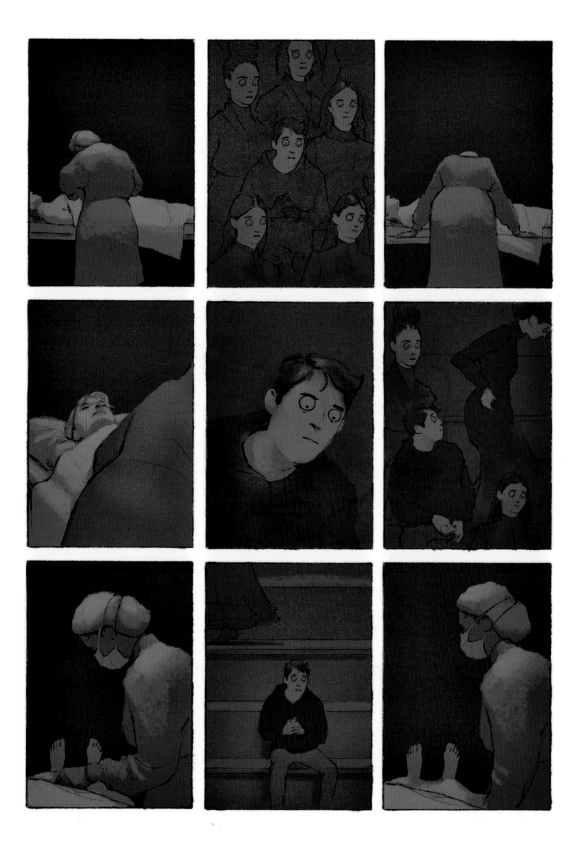

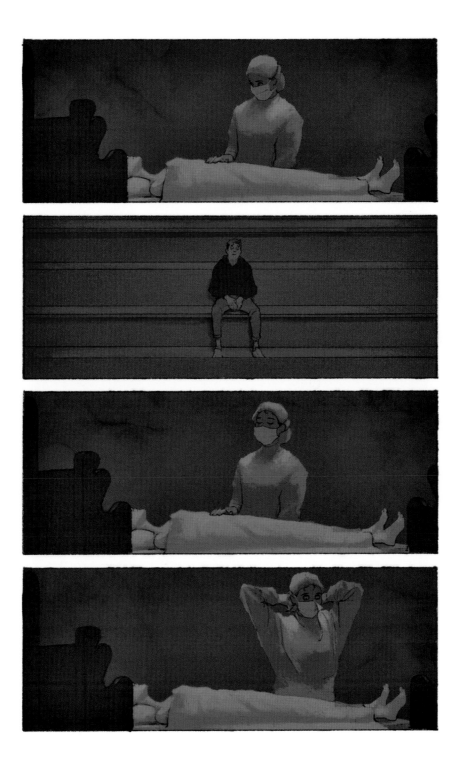

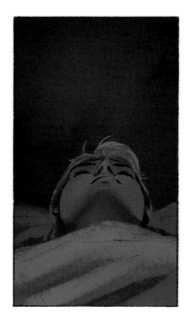

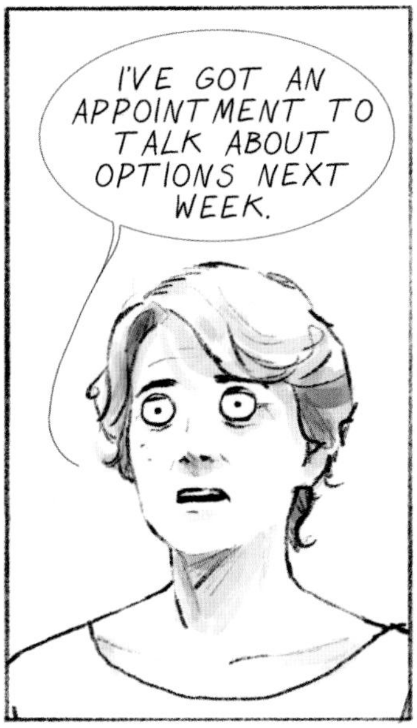
I'VE GOT AN APPOINTMENT TO TALK ABOUT OPTIONS NEXT WEEK.

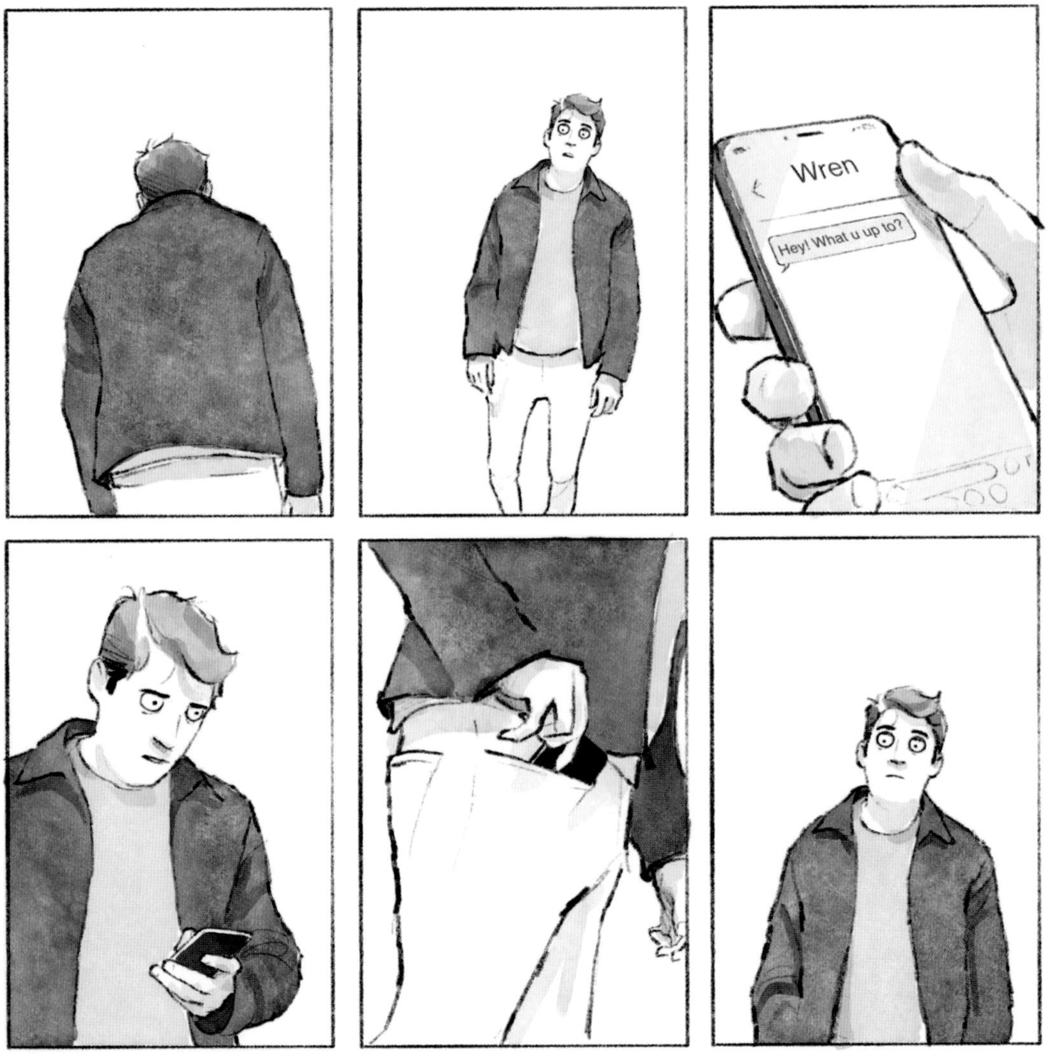
Wren
Hey! What u up to?

graham's bar
CUP OF TEA, NICK?
NO, THANKS.
Anne
What time is mum's appointment?
10:30. Love you x

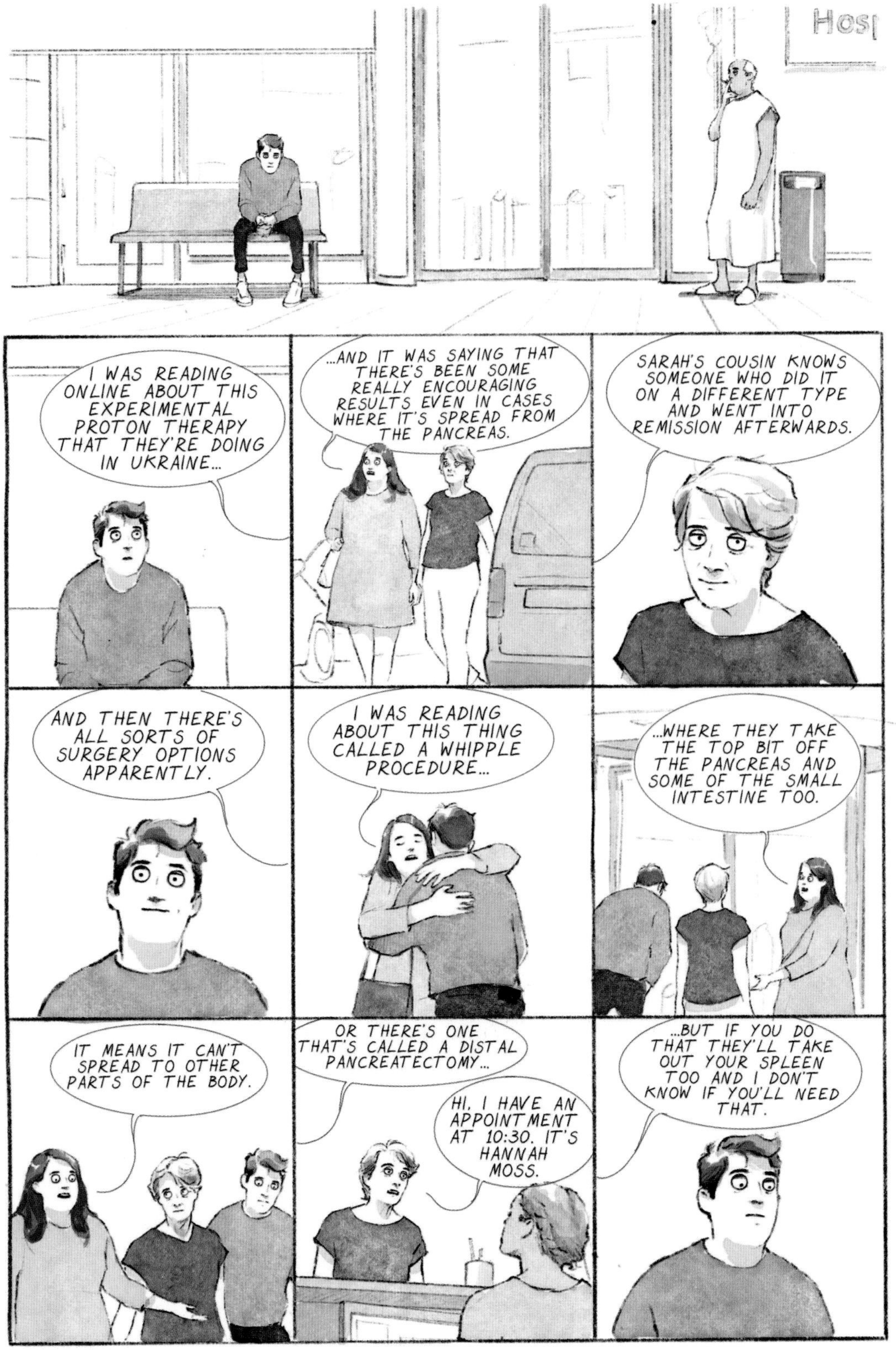
Hosp
I WAS READING ONLINE ABOUT THIS EXPERIMENTAL PROTON THERAPY THAT THEY'RE DOING IN UKRAINE...
...AND IT WAS SAYING THAT THERE'S BEEN SOME REALLY ENCOURAGING RESULTS EVEN IN CASES WHERE IT'S SPREAD FROM THE PANCREAS.
SARAH'S COUSIN KNOWS SOMEONE WHO DID IT ON A DIFFERENT TYPE AND WENT INTO REMISSION AFTERWARDS.
AND THEN THERE'S ALL SORTS OF SURGERY OPTIONS APPARENTLY.
I WAS READING ABOUT THIS THING CALLED A WHIPPLE PROCEDURE...
...WHERE THEY TAKE THE TOP BIT OFF THE PANCREAS AND SOME OF THE SMALL INTESTINE TOO.
IT MEANS IT CAN'T SPREAD TO OTHER PARTS OF THE BODY.
OR THERE'S ONE THAT'S CALLED A DISTAL PANCREATECTOMY...
HI, I HAVE AN APPOINTMENT AT 10:30. IT'S HANNAH MOSS.
...BUT IF YOU DO THAT THEY'LL TAKE OUT YOUR SPLEEN TOO AND I DON'T KNOW IF YOU'LL NEED THAT.

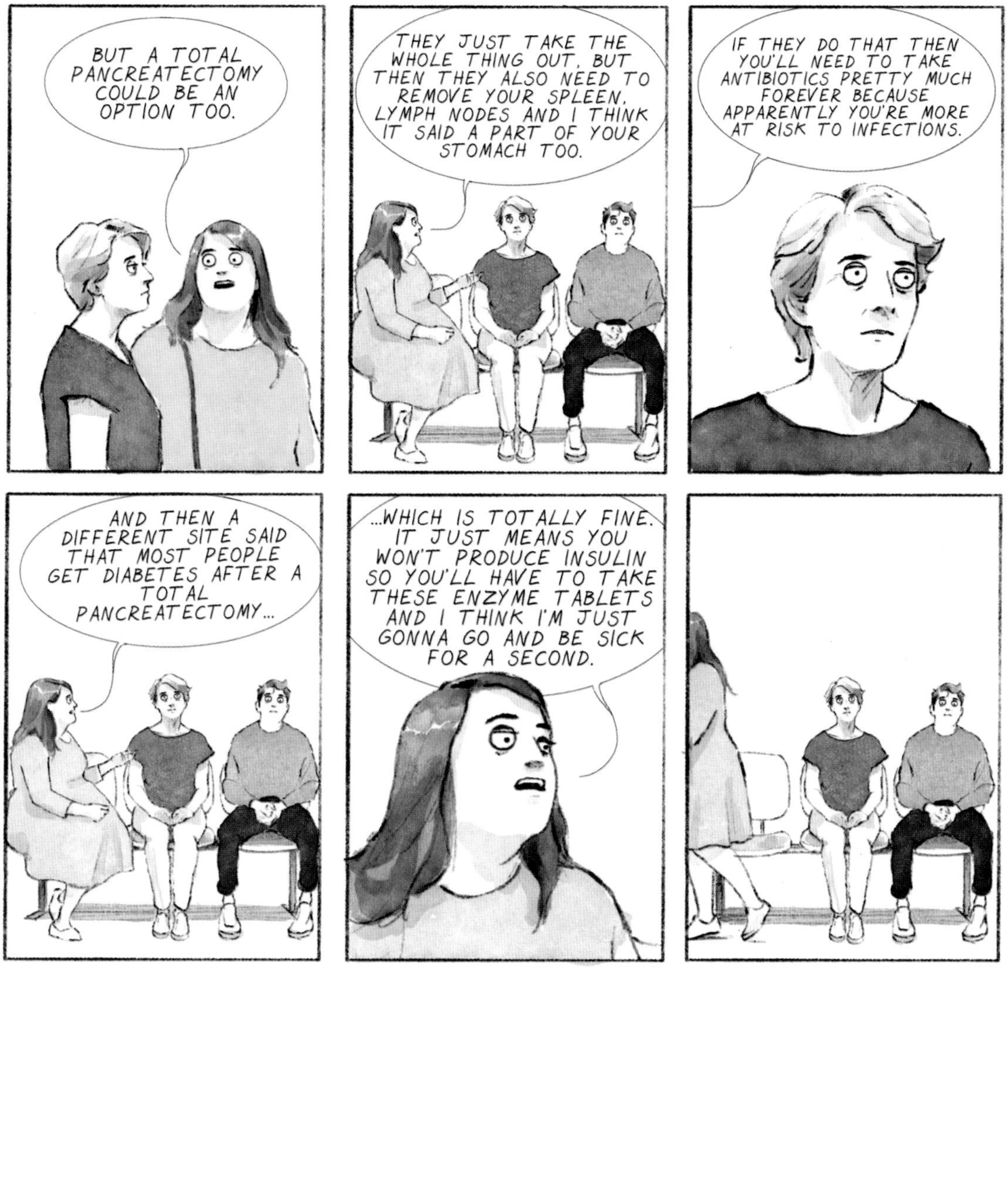
BUT A TOTAL PANCREATECTOMY COULD BE AN OPTION TOO.
THEY JUST TAKE THE WHOLE THING OUT, BUT THEN THEY ALSO NEED TO REMOVE YOUR SPLEEN, LYMPH NODES AND I THINK IT SAID A PART OF YOUR STOMACH TOO.
IF THEY DO THAT THEN YOU'LL NEED TO TAKE ANTIBIOTICS PRETTY MUCH FOREVER BECAUSE APPARENTLY YOU'RE MORE AT RISK TO INFECTIONS.
AND THEN A DIFFERENT SITE SAID THAT MOST PEOPLE GET DIABETES AFTER A TOTAL PANCREATECTOMY...
...WHICH IS TOTALLY FINE. IT JUST MEANS YOU WON'T PRODUCE INSULIN SO YOU'LL HAVE TO TAKE THESE ENZYME TABLETS AND I THINK I'M JUST GONNA GO AND BE SICK FOR A SECOND.

AND I WAS READING ABOUT ANTI-ANGIOGENESIS DRUGS...

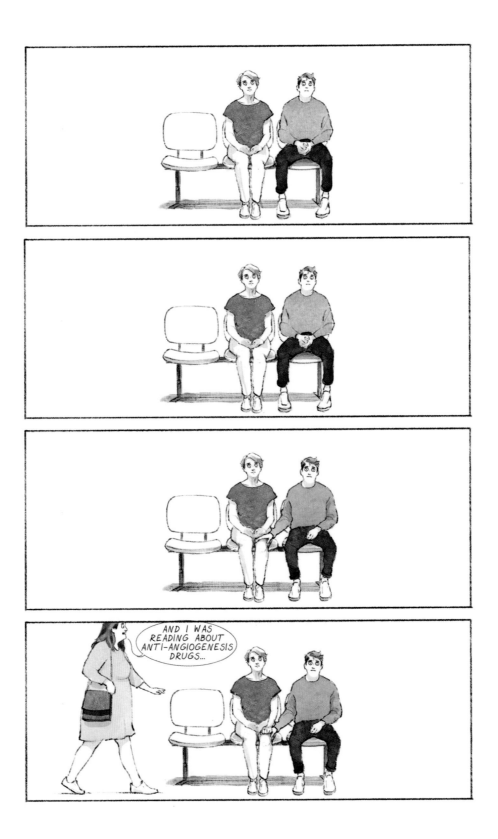

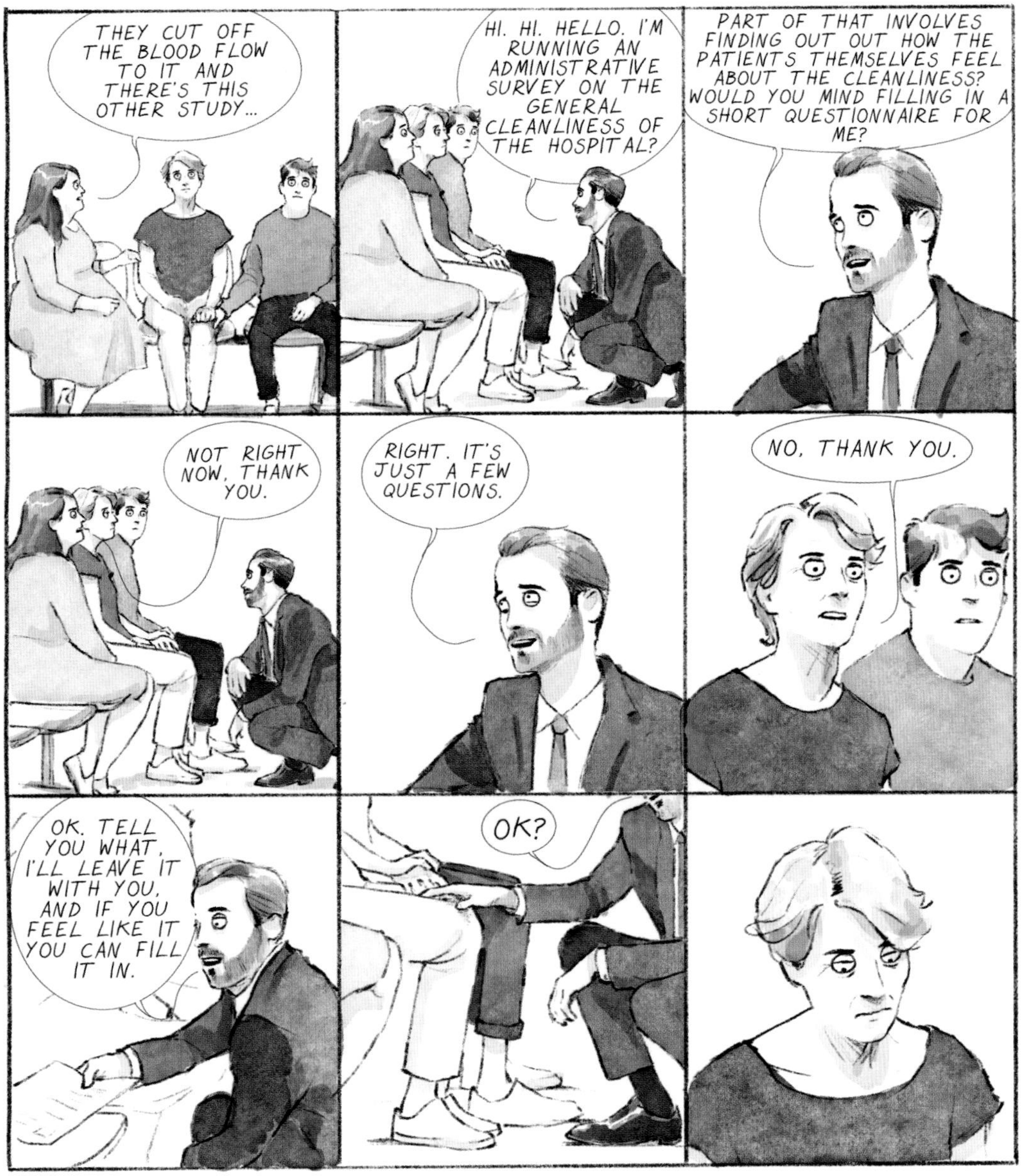
THEY CUT OFF THE BLOOD FLOW TO IT AND THERE'S THIS OTHER STUDY...
HI. HI. HELLO. I'M RUNNING AN ADMINISTRATIVE SURVEY ON THE GENERAL CLEANLINESS OF THE HOSPITAL?
PART OF THAT INVOLVES FINDING OUT OUT HOW THE PATIENTS THEMSELVES FEEL ABOUT THE CLEANLINESS? WOULD YOU MIND FILLING IN A SHORT QUESTIONNAIRE FOR ME?
NOT RIGHT NOW, THANK YOU.
RIGHT. IT'S JUST A FEW QUESTIONS.
NO, THANK YOU.
OK. TELL YOU WHAT, I'LL LEAVE IT WITH YOU, AND IF YOU FEEL LIKE IT YOU CAN FILL IT IN.
OK?

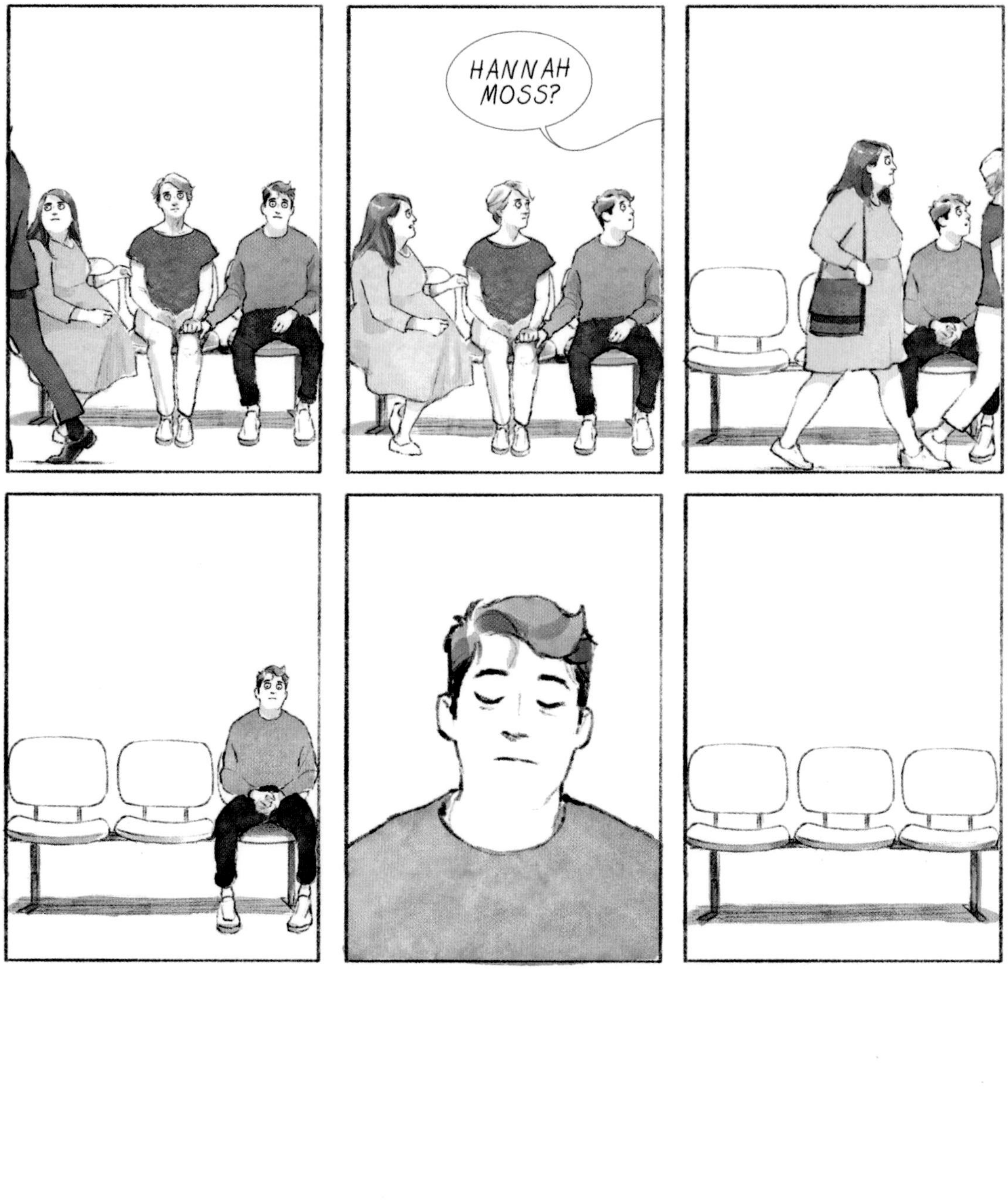
HANNAH
MOSS?

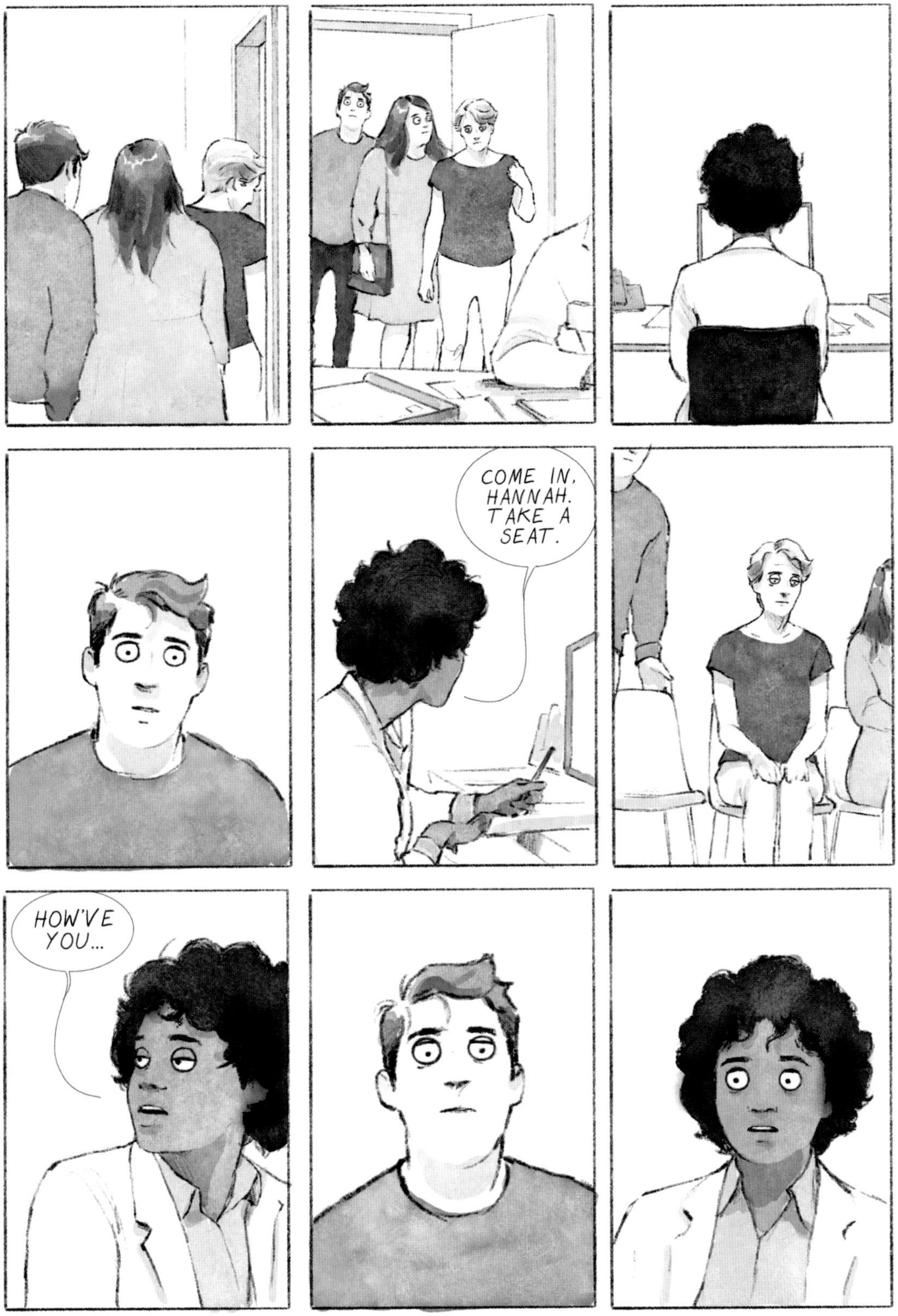
COME IN, HANNAH. TAKE A SEAT.
HOW'VE YOU...

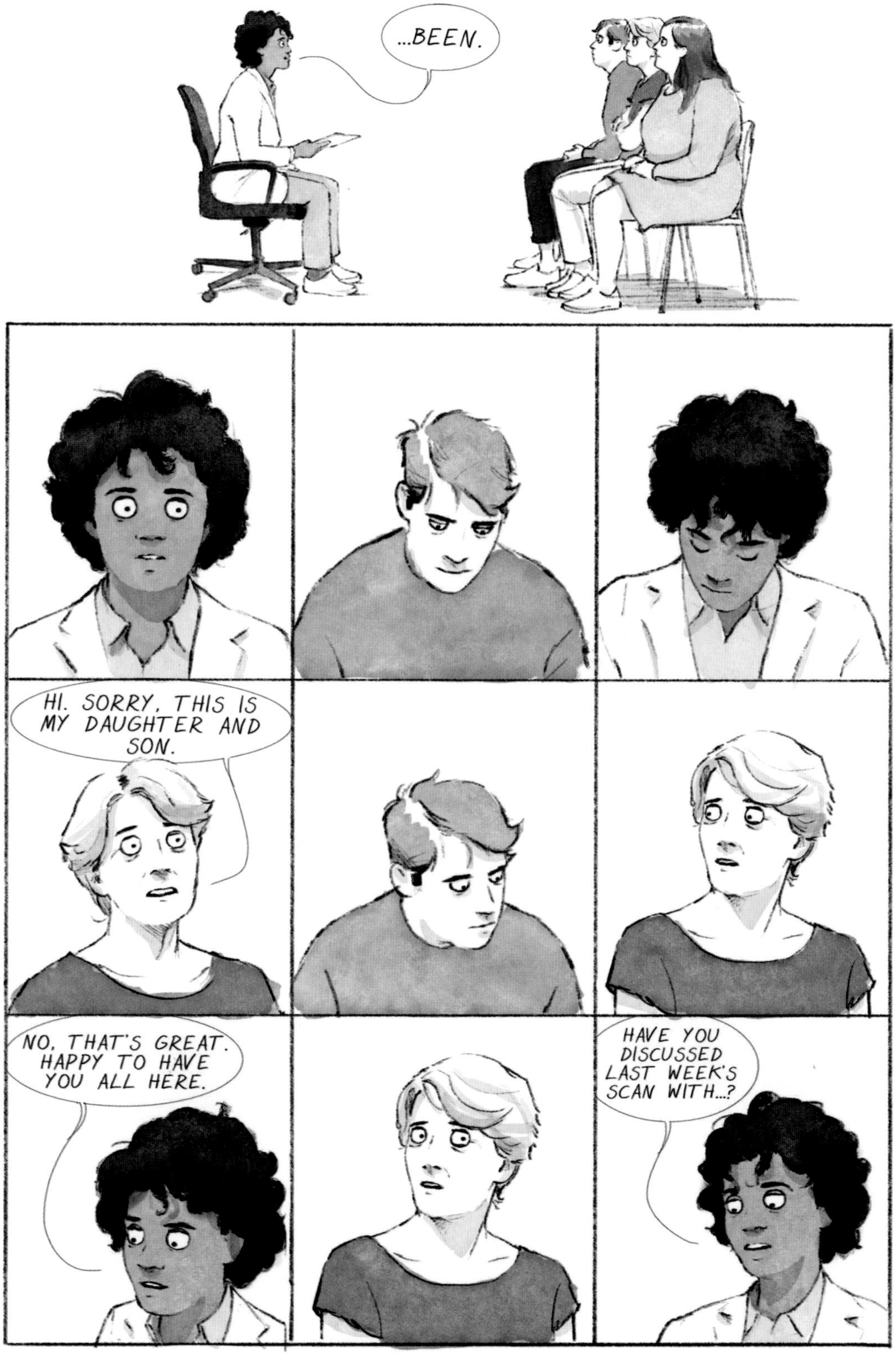

...BEEN.
HI. SORRY, THIS IS MY DAUGHTER AND SON.
NO, THAT'S GREAT. HAPPY TO HAVE YOU ALL HERE.
HAVE YOU DISCUSSED LAST WEEK'S SCAN WITH...?

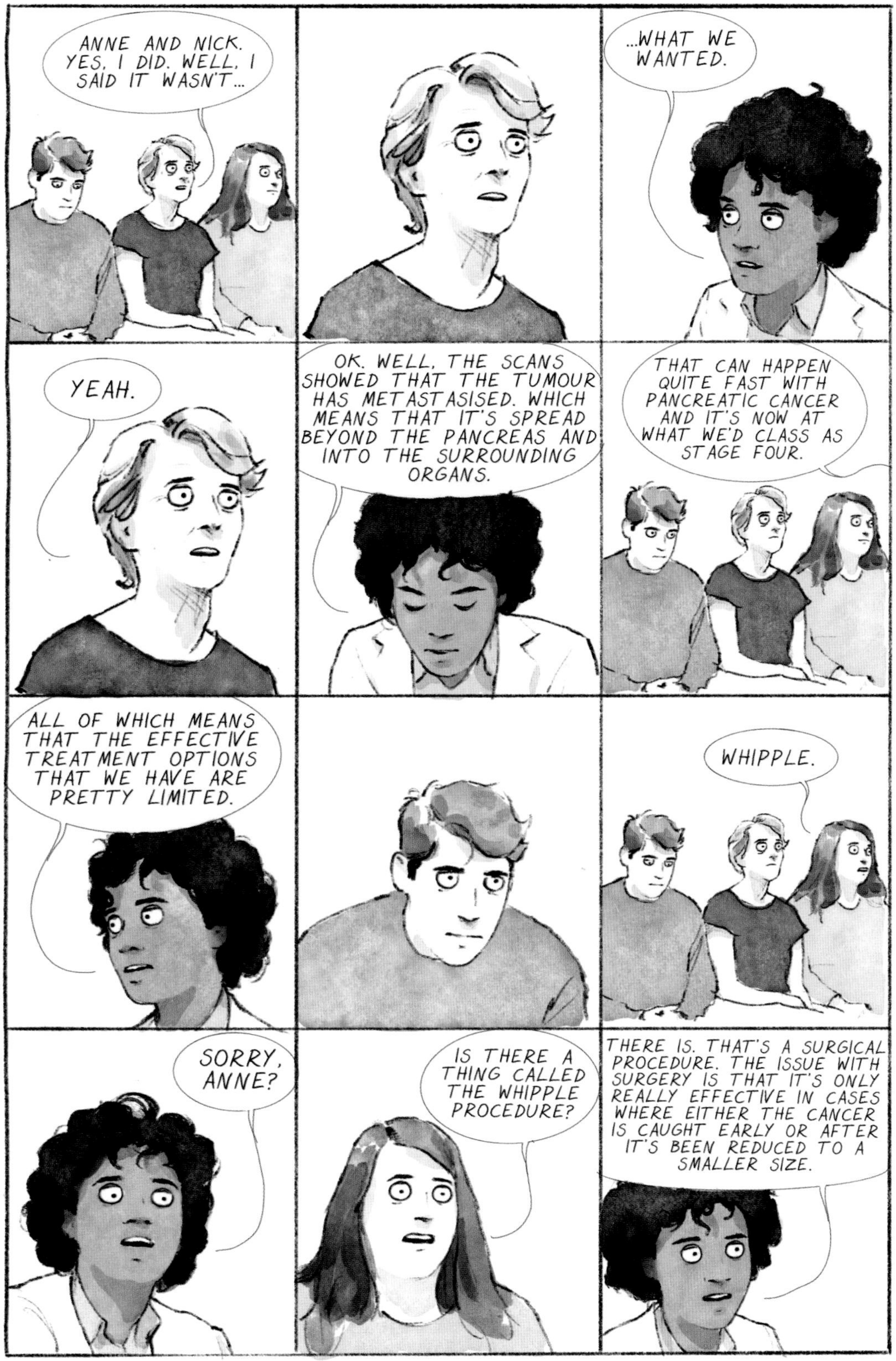
ANNE AND NICK. YES, I DID. WELL, I SAID IT WASN'T...
...WHAT WE WANTED.
YEAH.
OK. WELL, THE SCANS SHOWED THAT THE TUMOUR HAS METASTASISED. WHICH MEANS THAT IT'S SPREAD BEYOND THE PANCREAS AND INTO THE SURROUNDING ORGANS.
THAT CAN HAPPEN QUITE FAST WITH PANCREATIC CANCER AND IT'S NOW AT WHAT WE'D CLASS AS STAGE FOUR.
ALL OF WHICH MEANS THAT THE EFFECTIVE TREATMENT OPTIONS THAT WE HAVE ARE PRETTY LIMITED.
WHIPPLE.
SORRY, ANNE?
IS THERE A THING CALLED THE WHIPPLE PROCEDURE?
THERE IS. THAT'S A SURGICAL PROCEDURE. THE ISSUE WITH SURGERY IS THAT IT'S ONLY REALLY EFFECTIVE IN CASES WHERE EITHER THE CANCER IS CAUGHT EARLY OR AFTER IT'S BEEN REDUCED TO A SMALLER SIZE.

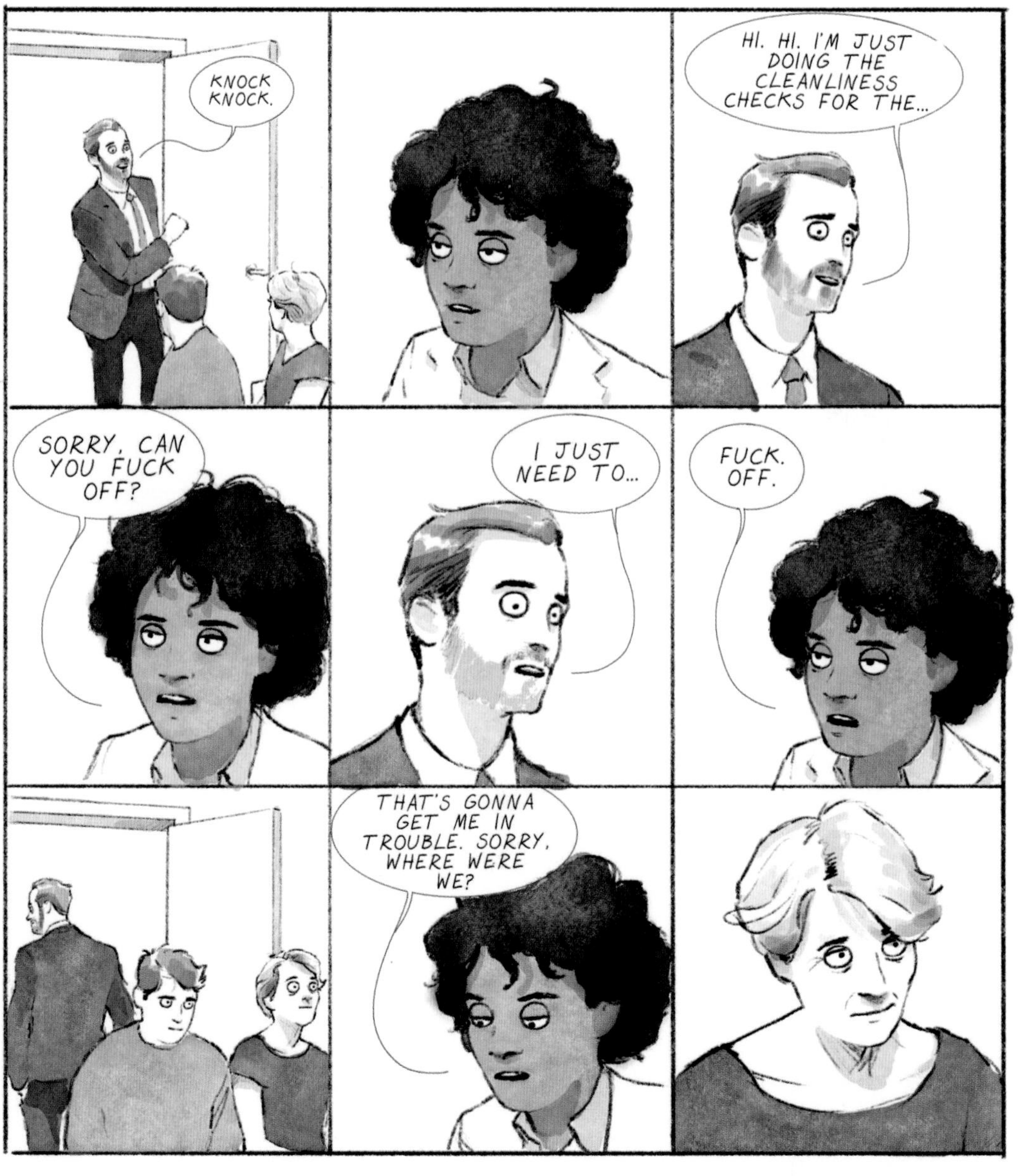
KNOCK KNOCK.
HI. HI. I'M JUST DOING THE CLEANLINESS CHECKS FOR THE...
SORRY, CAN YOU FUCK OFF?
I JUST NEED TO...
FUCK. OFF.
THAT'S GONNA GET ME IN TROUBLE. SORRY, WHERE WERE WE?

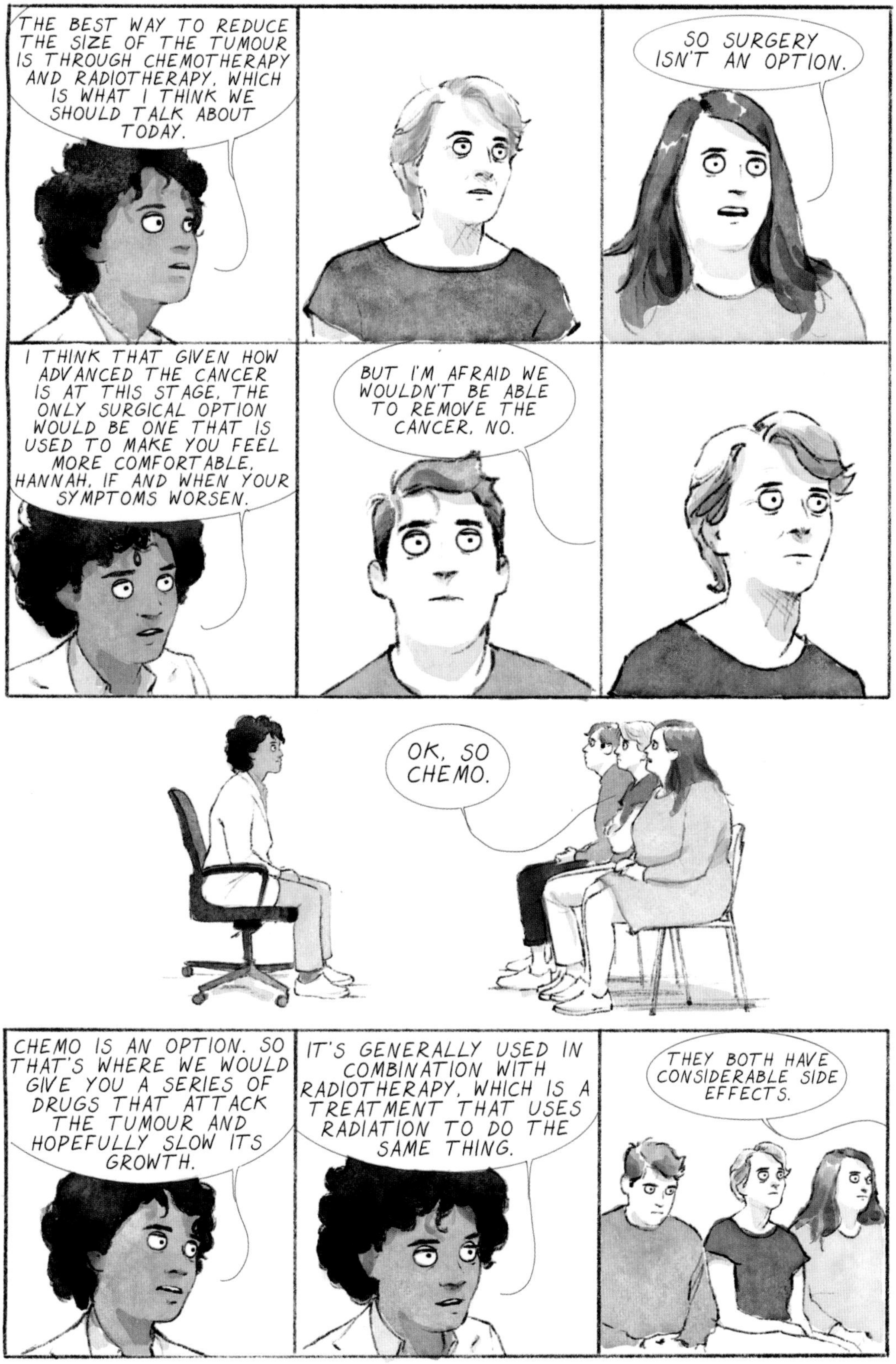
THE BEST WAY TO REDUCE THE SIZE OF THE TUMOUR IS THROUGH CHEMOTHERAPY AND RADIOTHERAPY, WHICH IS WHAT I THINK WE SHOULD TALK ABOUT TODAY.
SO SURGERY ISN'T AN OPTION.
I THINK THAT GIVEN HOW ADVANCED THE CANCER IS AT THIS STAGE, THE ONLY SURGICAL OPTION WOULD BE ONE THAT IS USED TO MAKE YOU FEEL MORE COMFORTABLE, HANNAH, IF AND WHEN YOUR SYMPTOMS WORSEN.
BUT I'M AFRAID WE WOULDN'T BE ABLE TO REMOVE THE CANCER, NO.
OK, SO CHEMO.
CHEMO IS AN OPTION. SO THAT'S WHERE WE WOULD GIVE YOU A SERIES OF DRUGS THAT ATTACK THE TUMOUR AND HOPEFULLY SLOW ITS GROWTH.
IT'S GENERALLY USED IN COMBINATION WITH RADIOTHERAPY, WHICH IS A TREATMENT THAT USES RADIATION TO DO THE SAME THING.
THEY BOTH HAVE CONSIDERABLE SIDE EFFECTS.

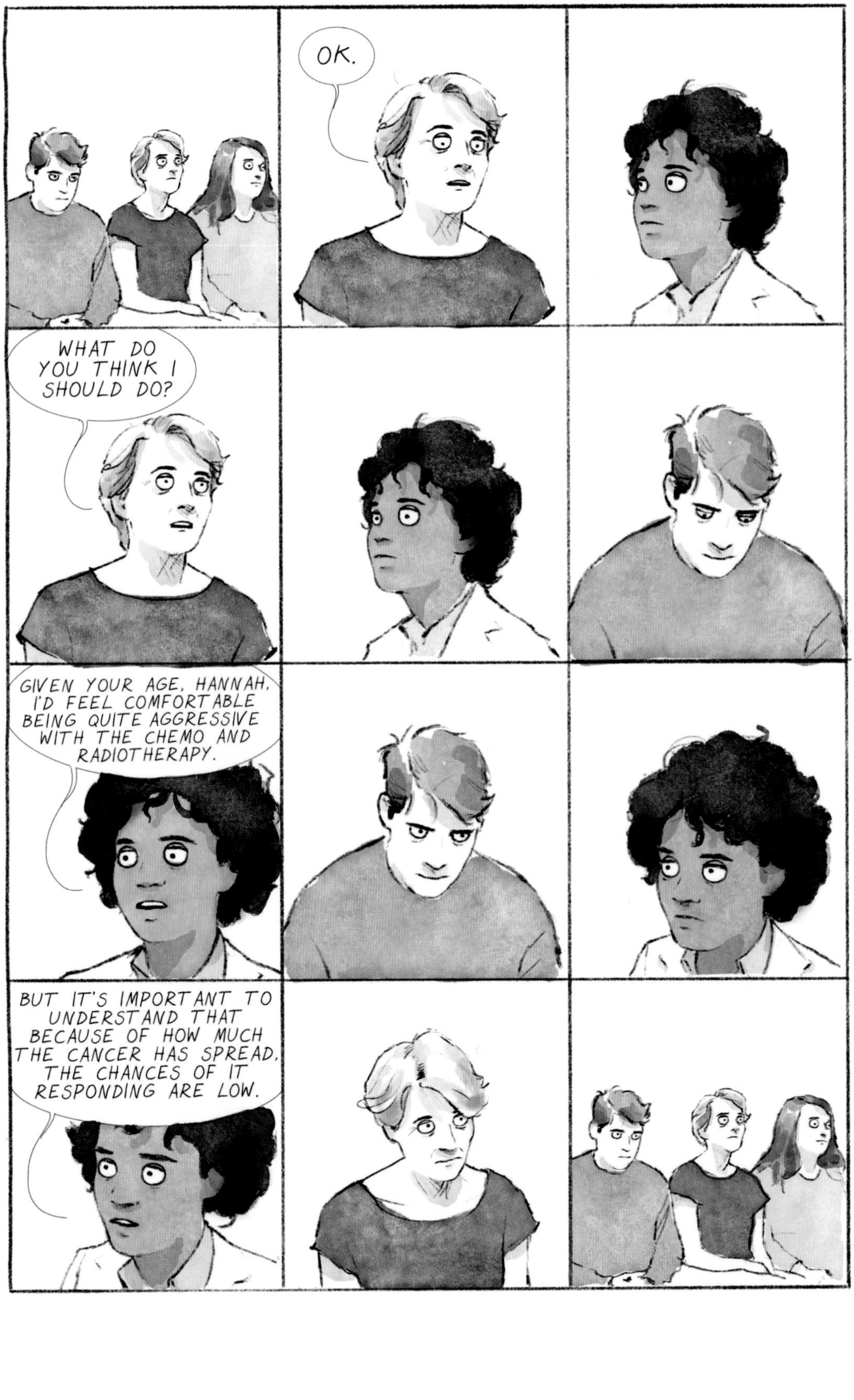
OK.
WHAT DO YOU THINK I SHOULD DO?
GIVEN YOUR AGE, HANNAH, I'D FEEL COMFORTABLE BEING QUITE AGGRESSIVE WITH THE CHEMO AND RADIOTHERAPY.
BUT IT'S IMPORTANT TO UNDERSTAND THAT BECAUSE OF HOW MUCH THE CANCER HAS SPREAD, THE CHANCES OF IT RESPONDING ARE LOW.

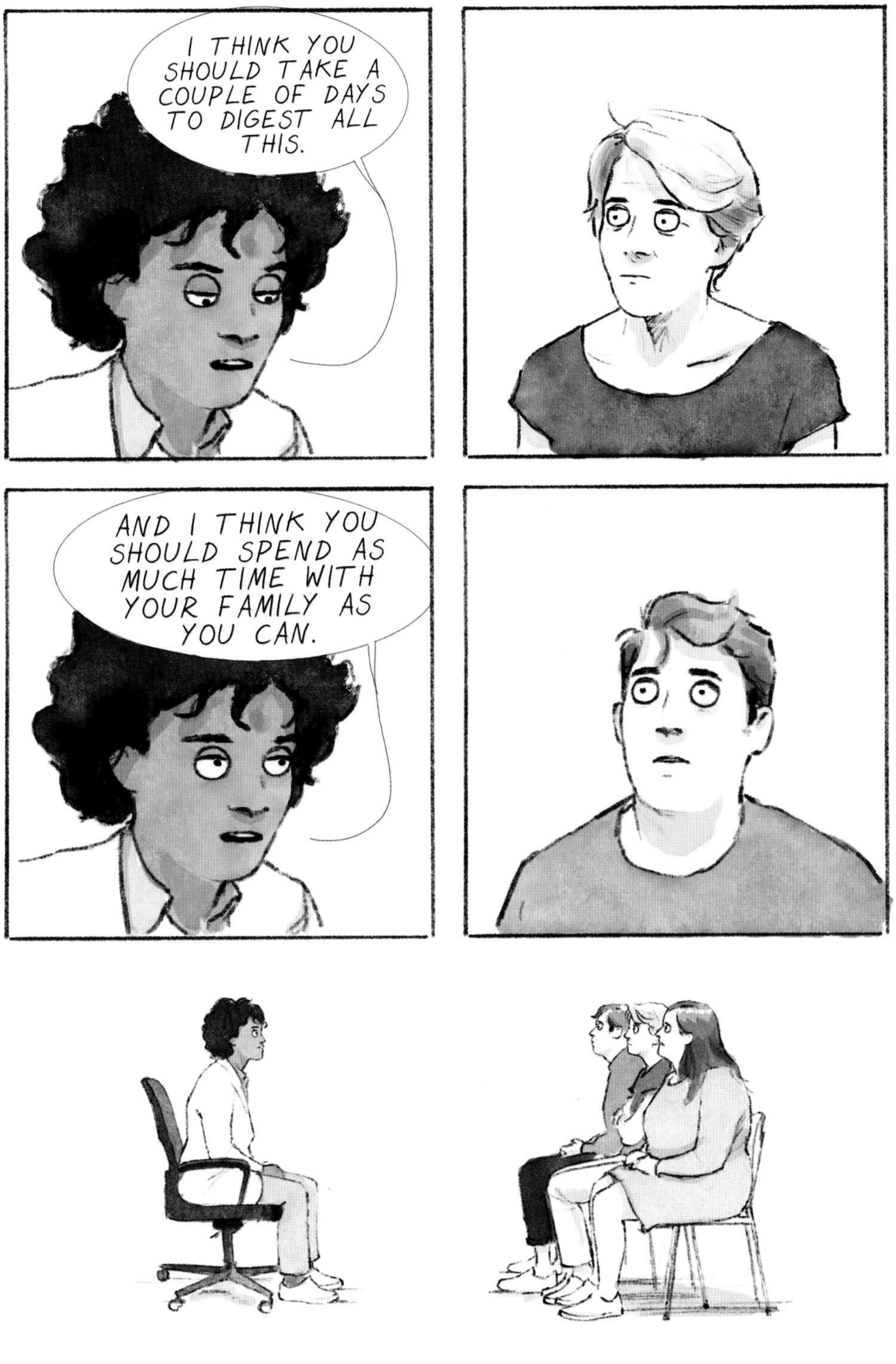
I THINK YOU SHOULD TAKE A COUPLE OF DAYS TO DIGEST ALL THIS.
AND I THINK YOU SHOULD SPEND AS MUCH TIME WITH YOUR FAMILY AS YOU CAN.

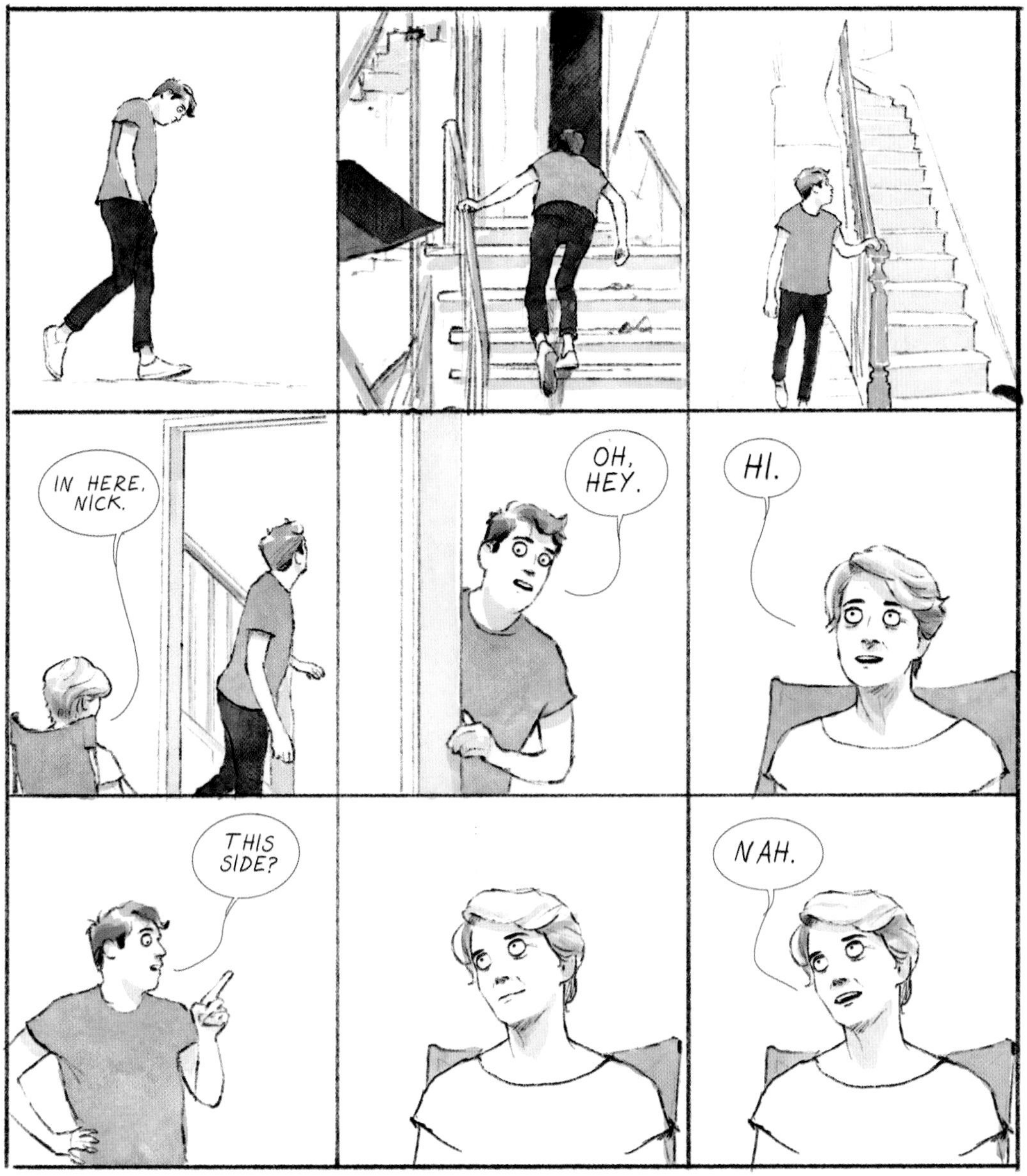
IN HERE, NICK.
OH, HEY.
HI.
THIS SIDE?
NAH.

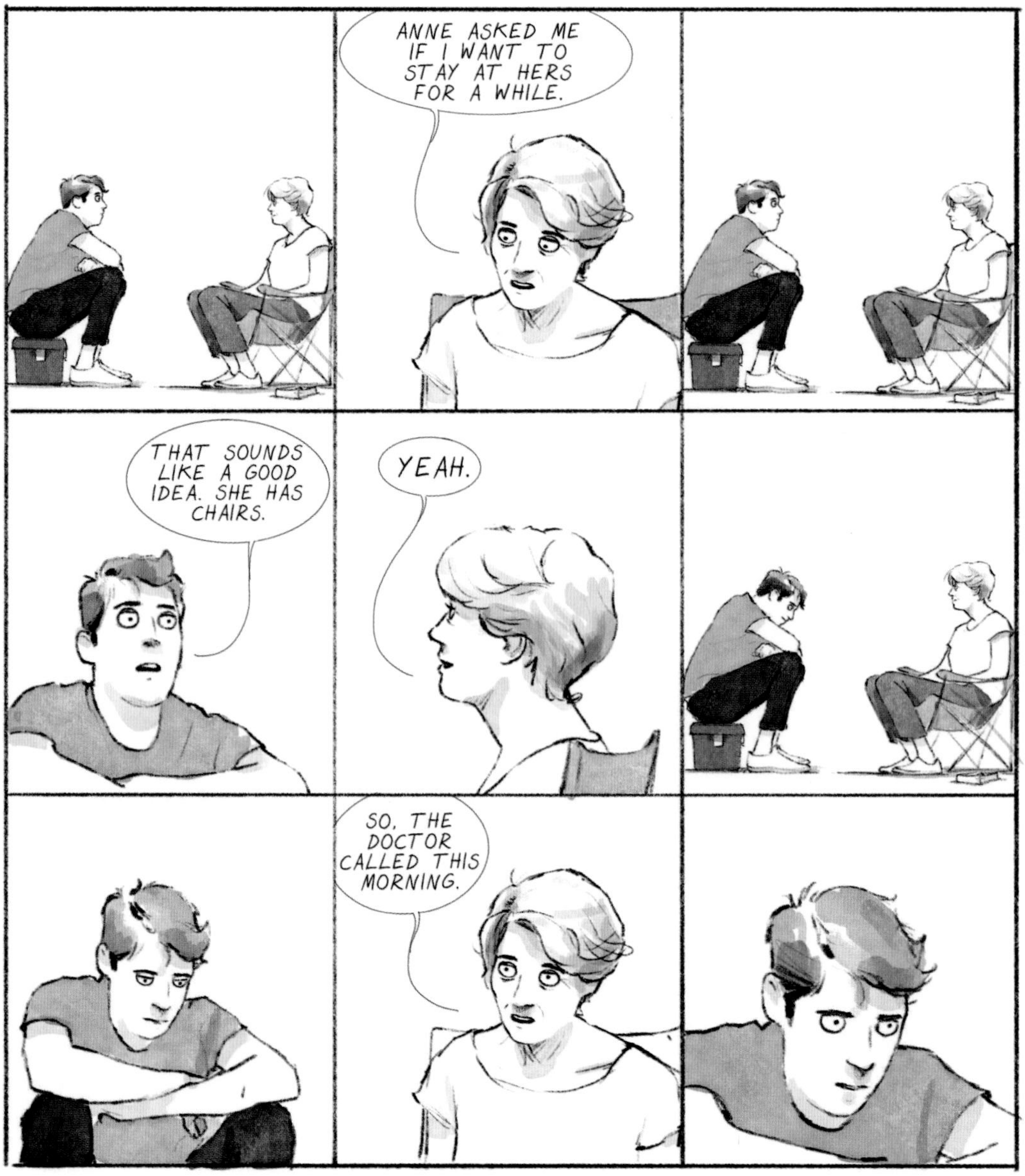
ANNE ASKED ME IF I WANT TO STAY AT HERS FOR A WHILE.
THAT SOUNDS LIKE A GOOD IDEA. SHE HAS CHAIRS.
YEAH.
SO, THE DOCTOR CALLED THIS MORNING.

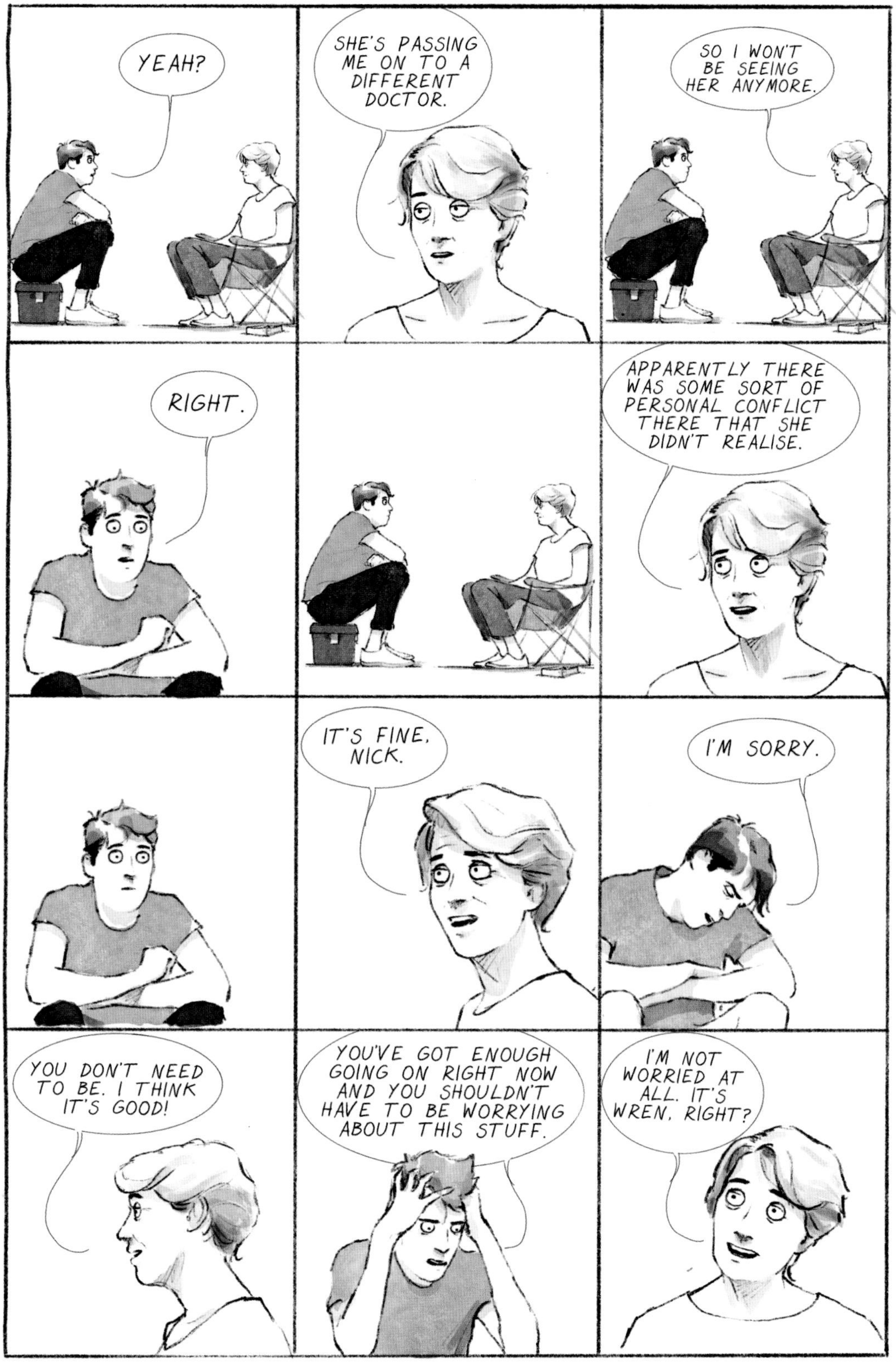
YEAH?
SHE'S PASSING ME ON TO A DIFFERENT DOCTOR.
SO I WON'T BE SEEING HER ANYMORE.
RIGHT.
APPARENTLY THERE WAS SOME SORT OF PERSONAL CONFLICT THERE THAT SHE DIDN'T REALISE.
IT'S FINE, NICK.
I'M SORRY.
YOU DON'T NEED TO BE. I THINK IT'S GOOD!
YOU'VE GOT ENOUGH GOING ON RIGHT NOW AND YOU SHOULDN'T HAVE TO BE WORRYING ABOUT THIS STUFF.
I'M NOT WORRIED AT ALL. IT'S WREN, RIGHT?

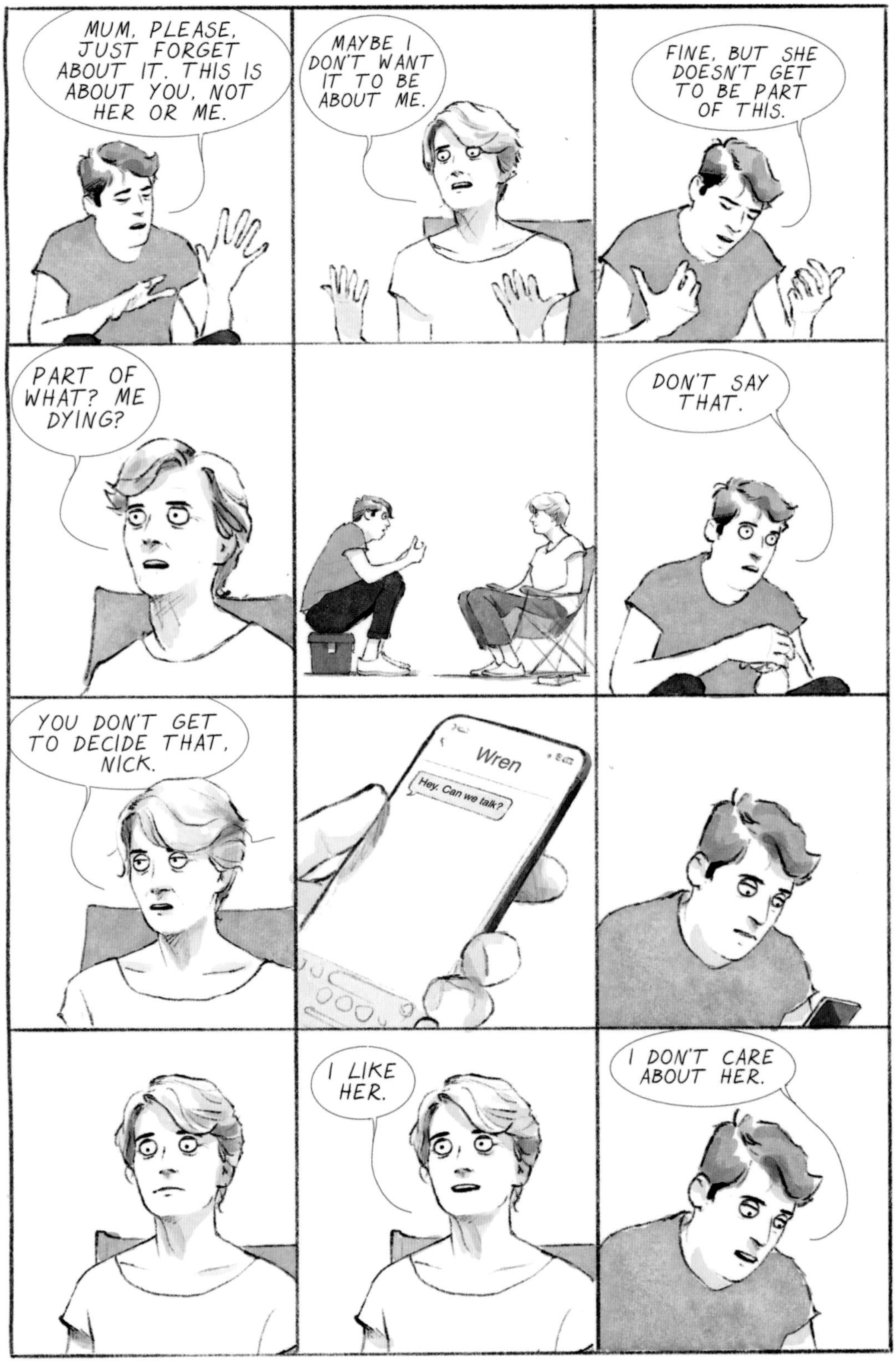
MUM, PLEASE, JUST FORGET ABOUT IT. THIS IS ABOUT YOU, NOT HER OR ME.
MAYBE I DON'T WANT IT TO BE ABOUT ME.
FINE, BUT SHE DOESN'T GET TO BE PART OF THIS.
PART OF WHAT? ME DYING?
DON'T SAY THAT.
YOU DON'T GET TO DECIDE THAT, NICK.
Wren
Hey. Can we talk?
I LIKE HER.
I DON'T CARE ABOUT HER.

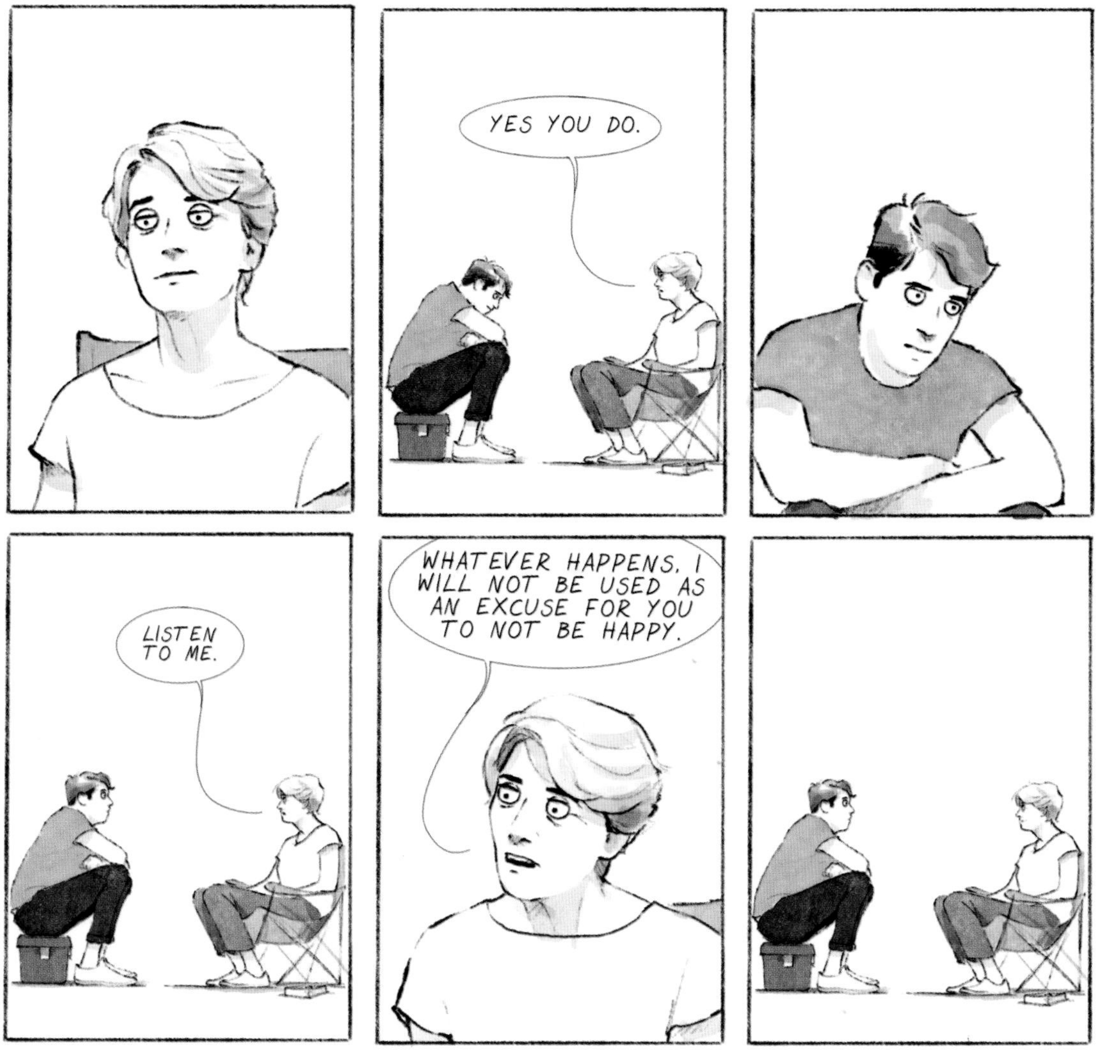
YES YOU DO.
LISTEN TO ME.
WHATEVER HAPPENS, I WILL NOT BE USED AS AN EXCUSE FOR YOU TO NOT BE HAPPY.

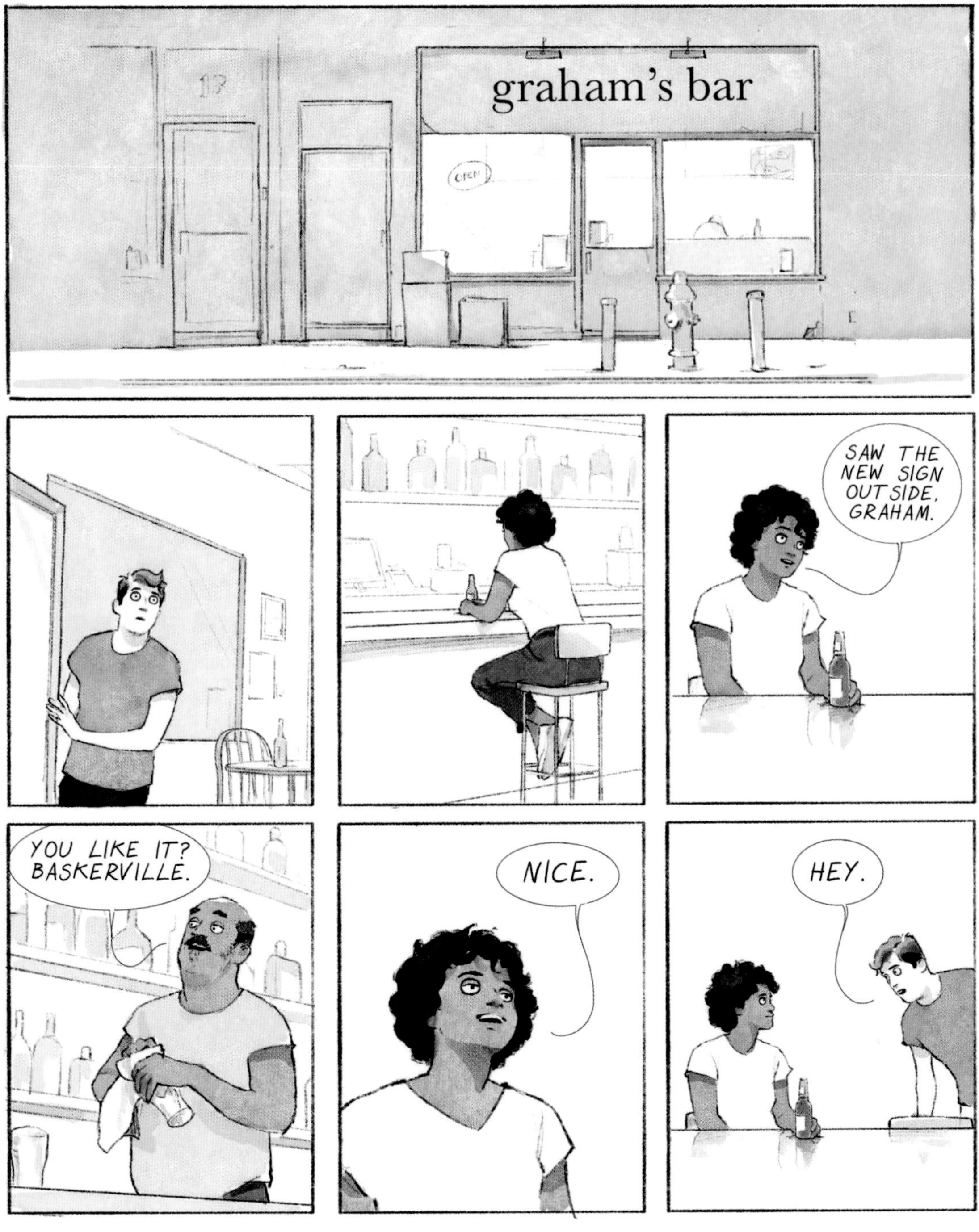
graham's bar
OPEN
SAW THE NEW SIGN OUTSIDE, GRAHAM.
YOU LIKE IT? BASKERVILLE.
NICE.
HEY.

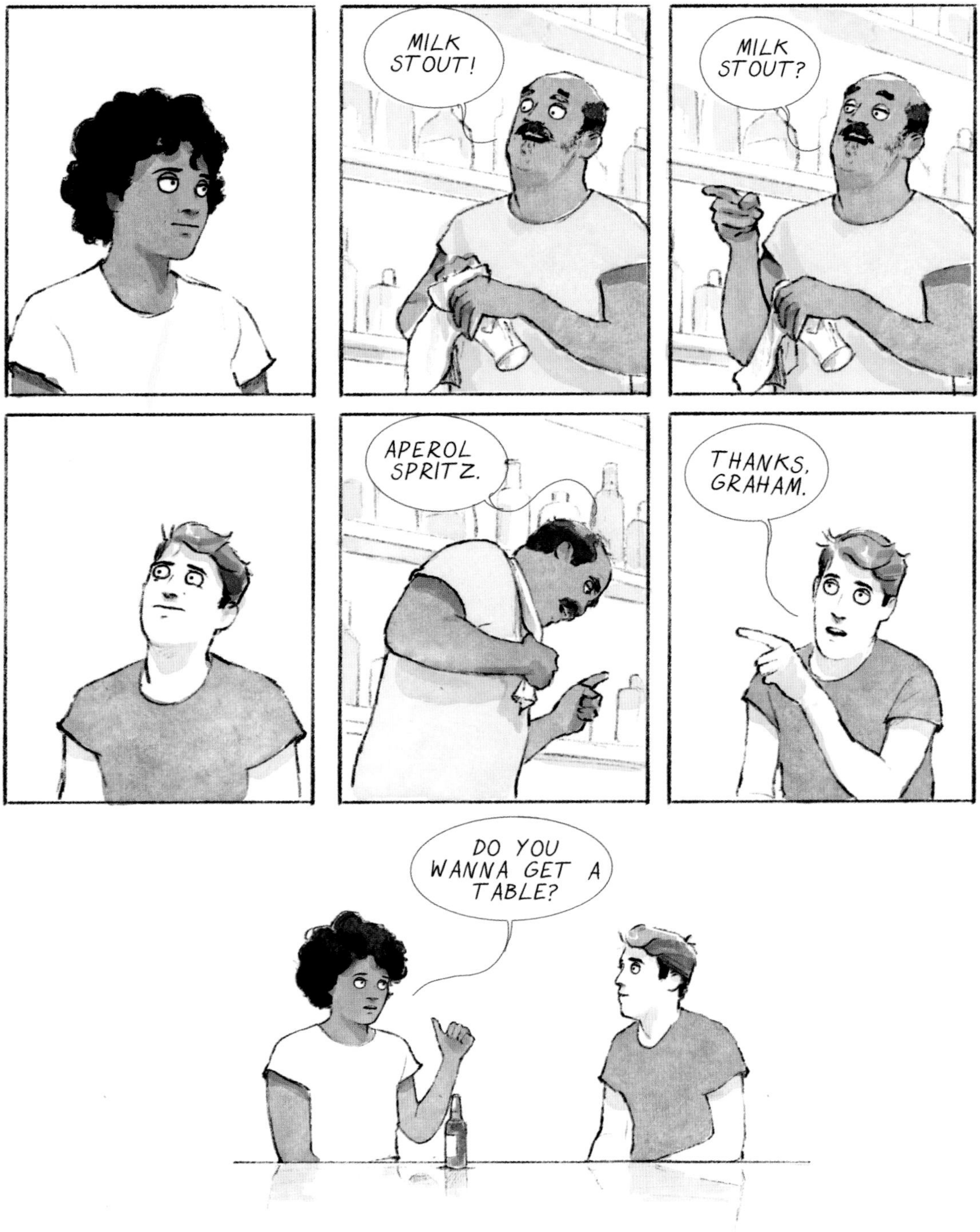
MILK STOUT!
MILK STOUT?
APEROL SPRITZ.
THANKS, GRAHAM.
DO YOU WANNA GET A TABLE?

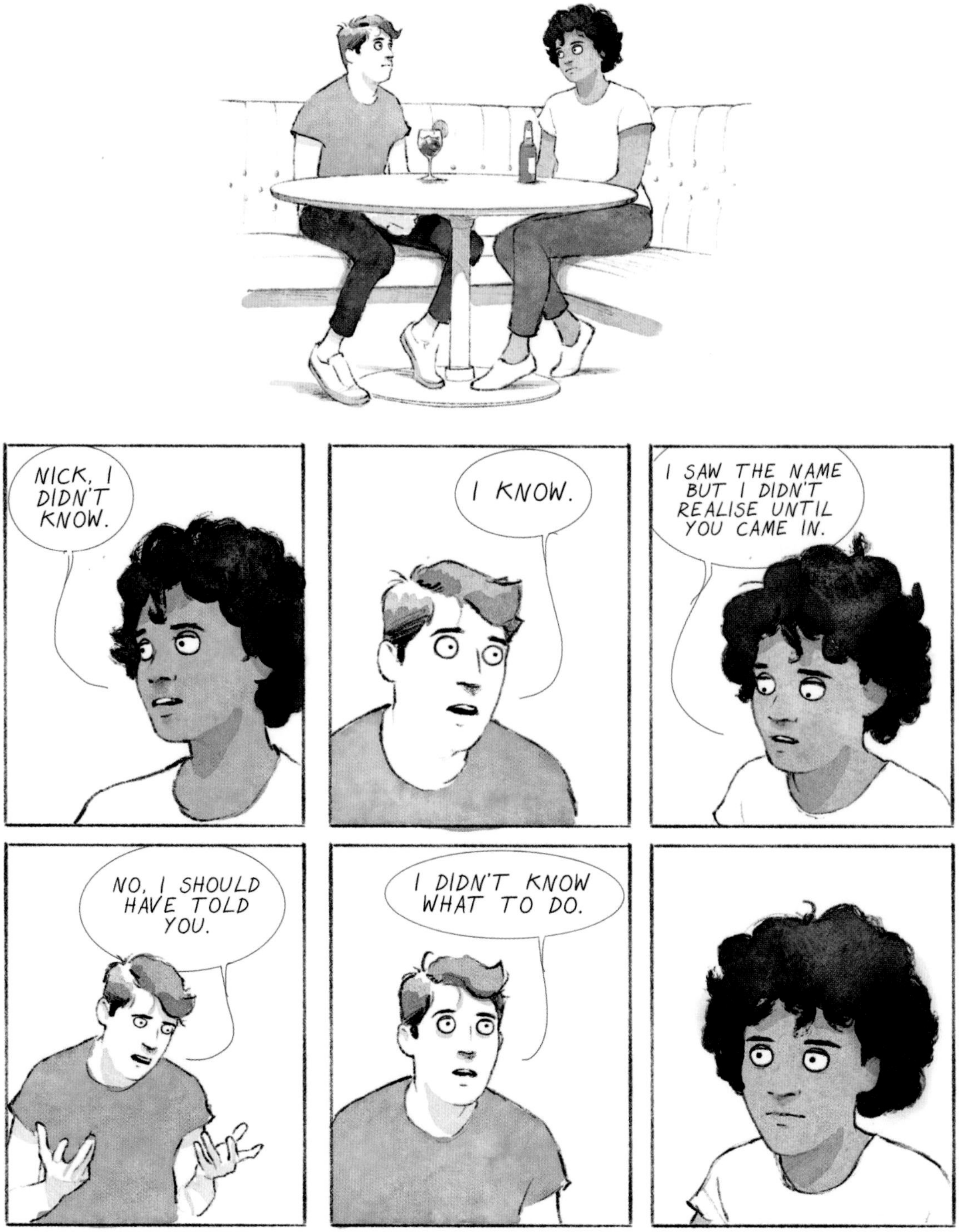
NICK, I DIDN'T KNOW.
I KNOW.
I SAW THE NAME BUT I DIDN'T REALISE UNTIL YOU CAME IN.
NO, I SHOULD HAVE TOLD YOU.
I DIDN'T KNOW WHAT TO DO.

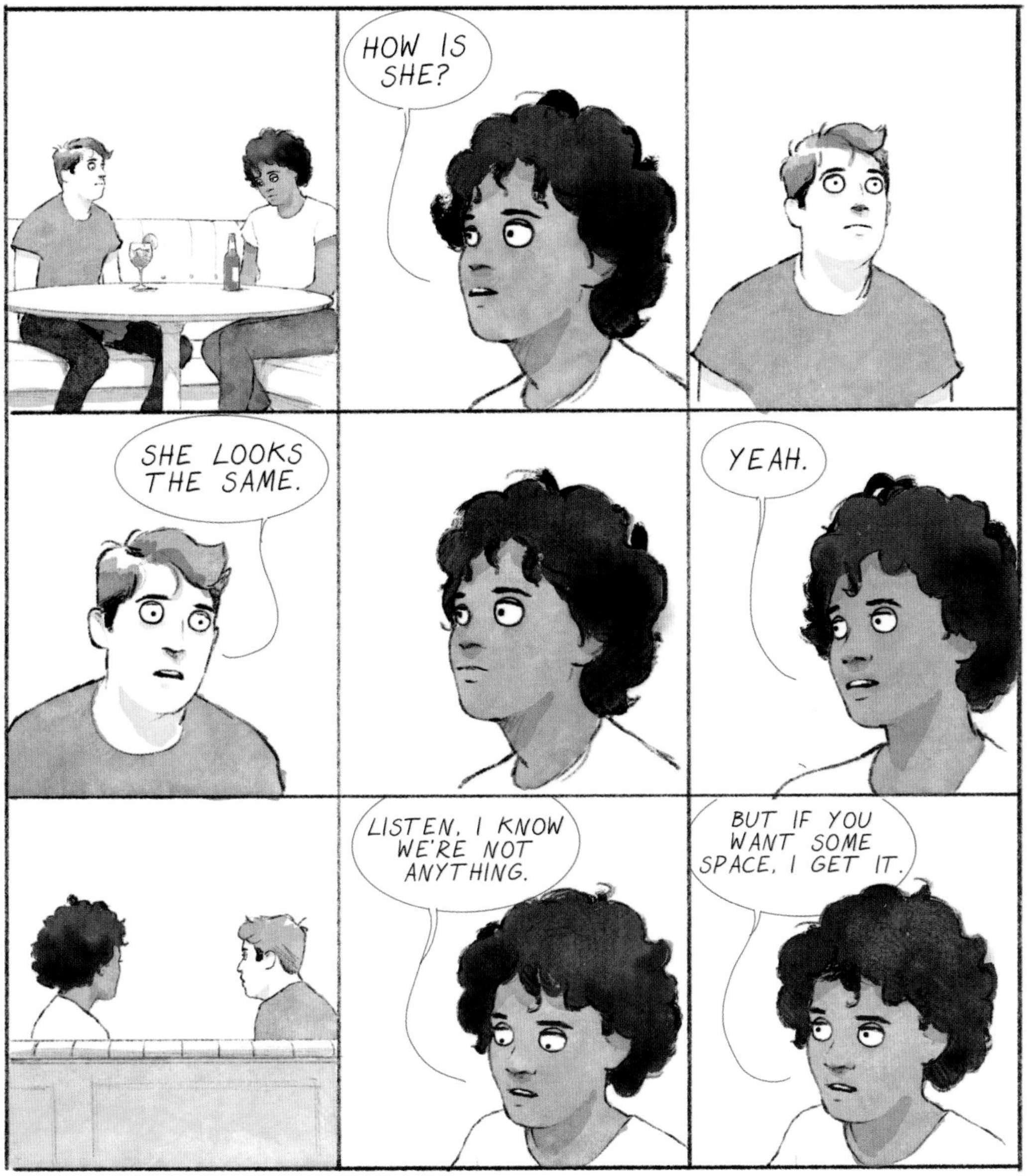
HOW IS SHE?
SHE LOOKS THE SAME.
YEAH.
LISTEN, I KNOW WE'RE NOT ANYTHING.
BUT IF YOU WANT SOME SPACE, I GET IT.

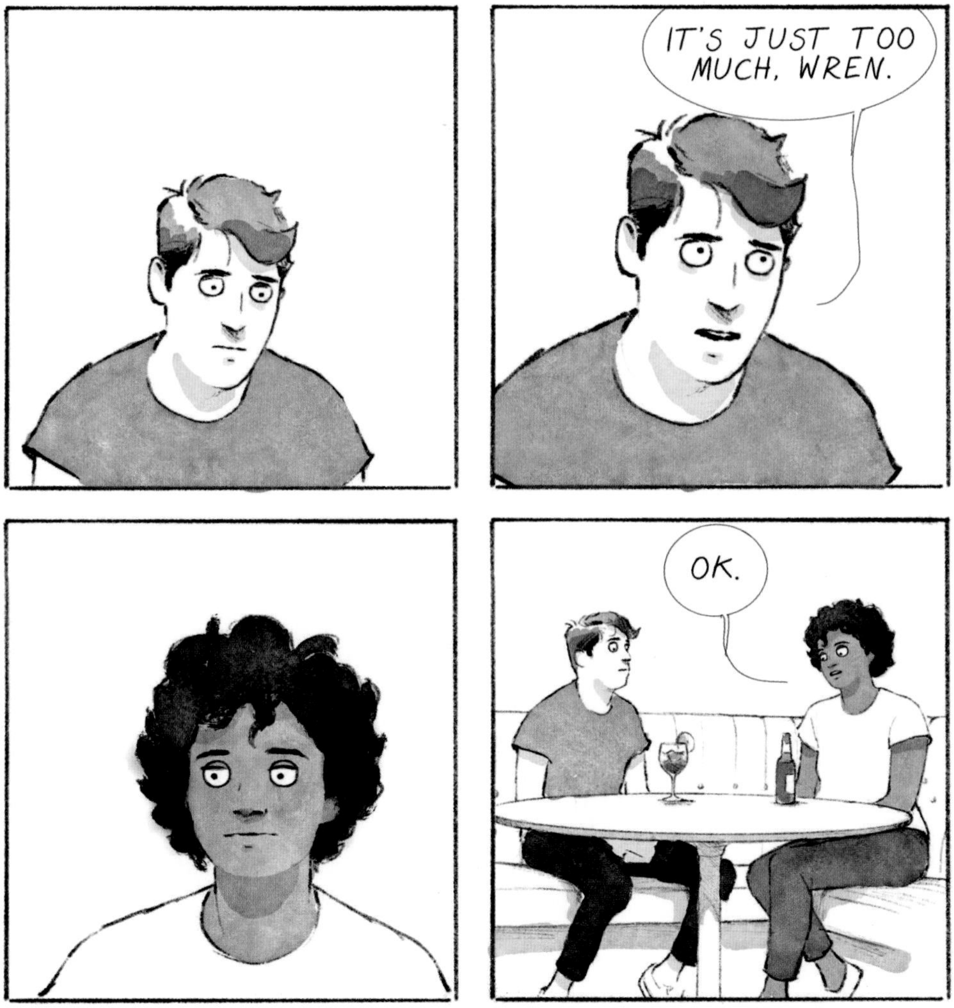
IT'S JUST TOO MUCH, WREN.
OK.

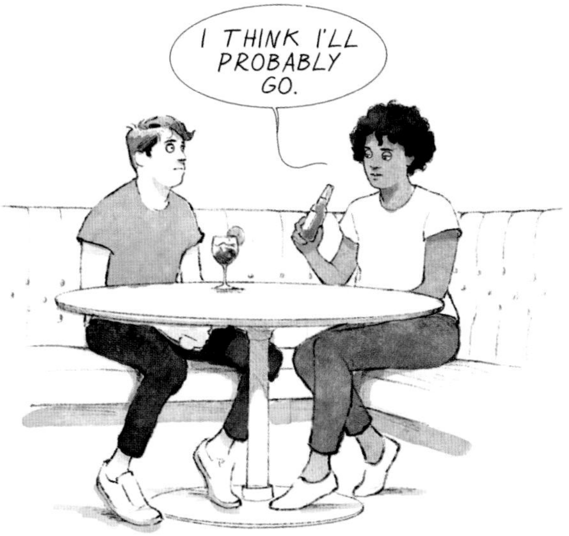
I THINK I'LL PROBABLY GO.

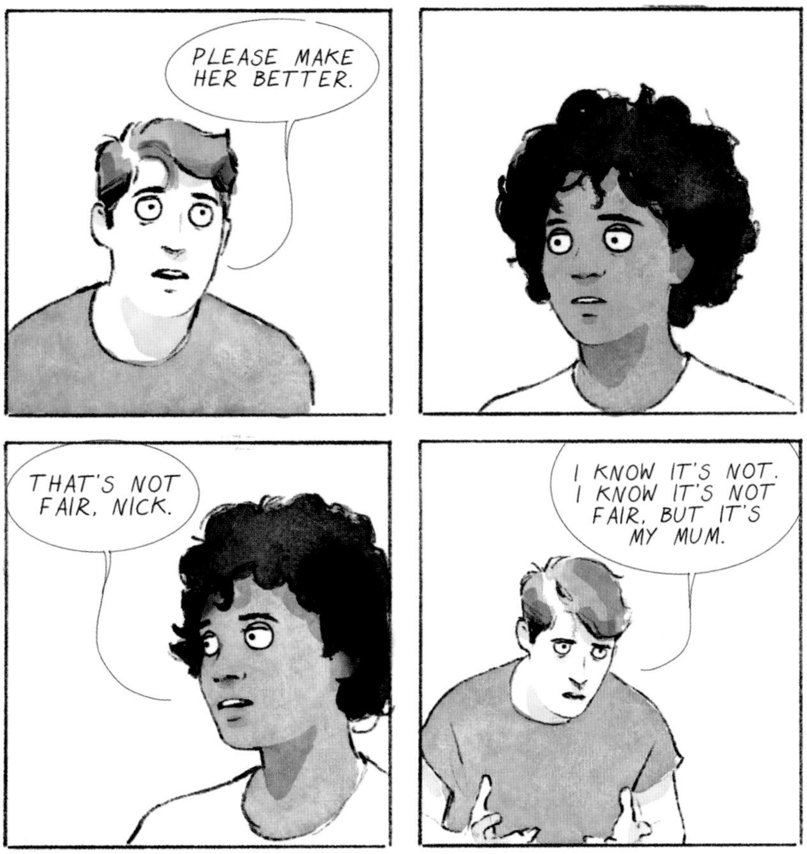
PLEASE MAKE HER BETTER.
THAT'S NOT FAIR, NICK.
I KNOW IT'S NOT. I KNOW IT'S NOT FAIR, BUT IT'S MY MUM.

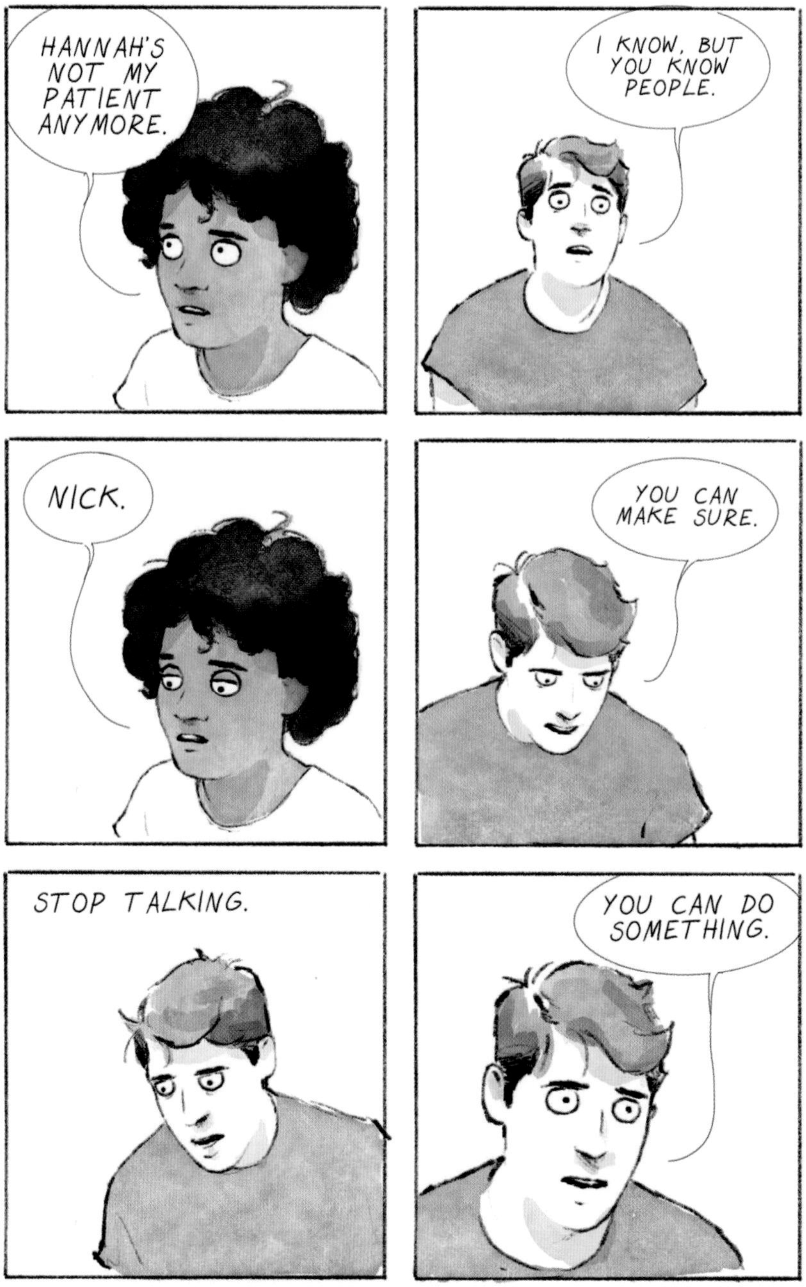
HANNAH'S NOT MY PATIENT ANYMORE.
I KNOW, BUT YOU KNOW PEOPLE.
NICK.
YOU CAN MAKE SURE.
STOP TALKING.
YOU CAN DO SOMETHING.

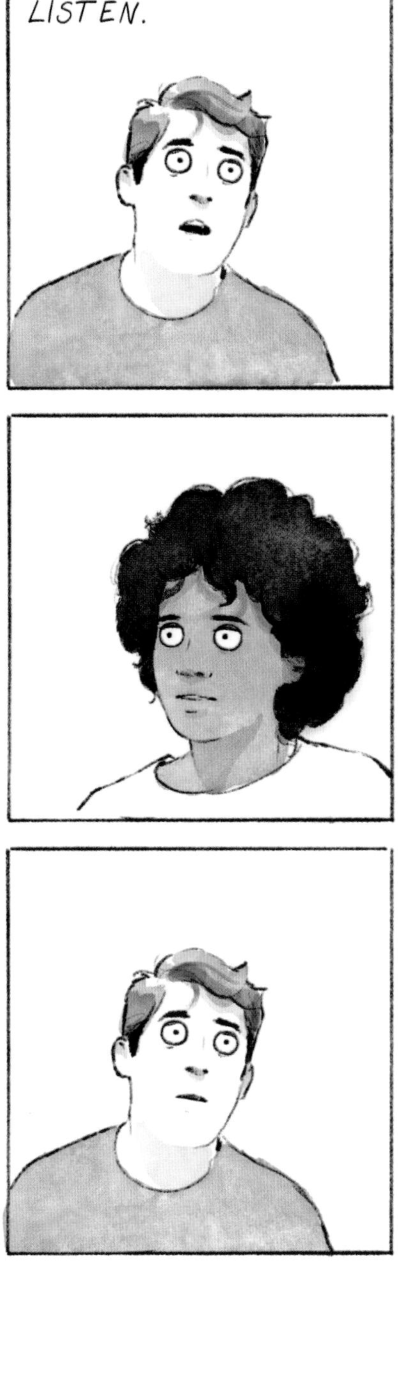
LISTEN.

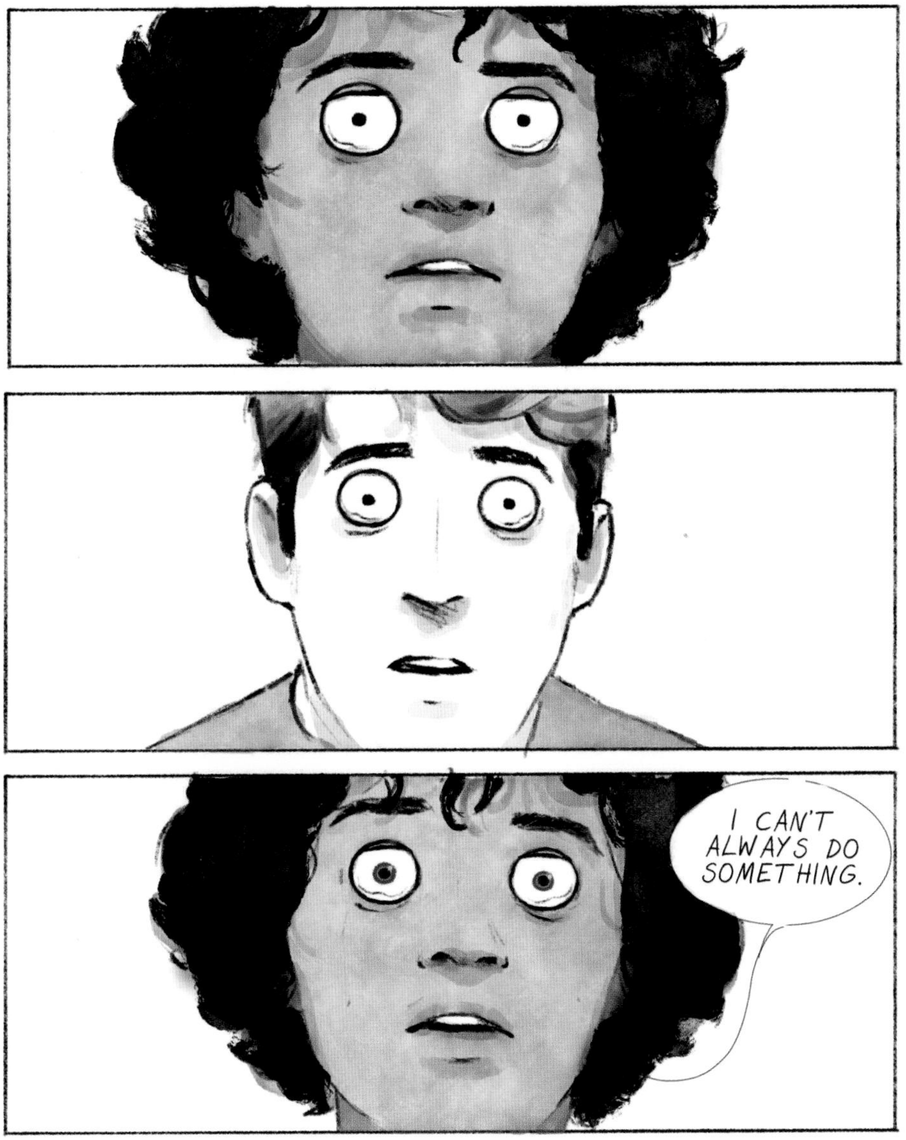
I CAN'T ALWAYS DO SOMETHING.

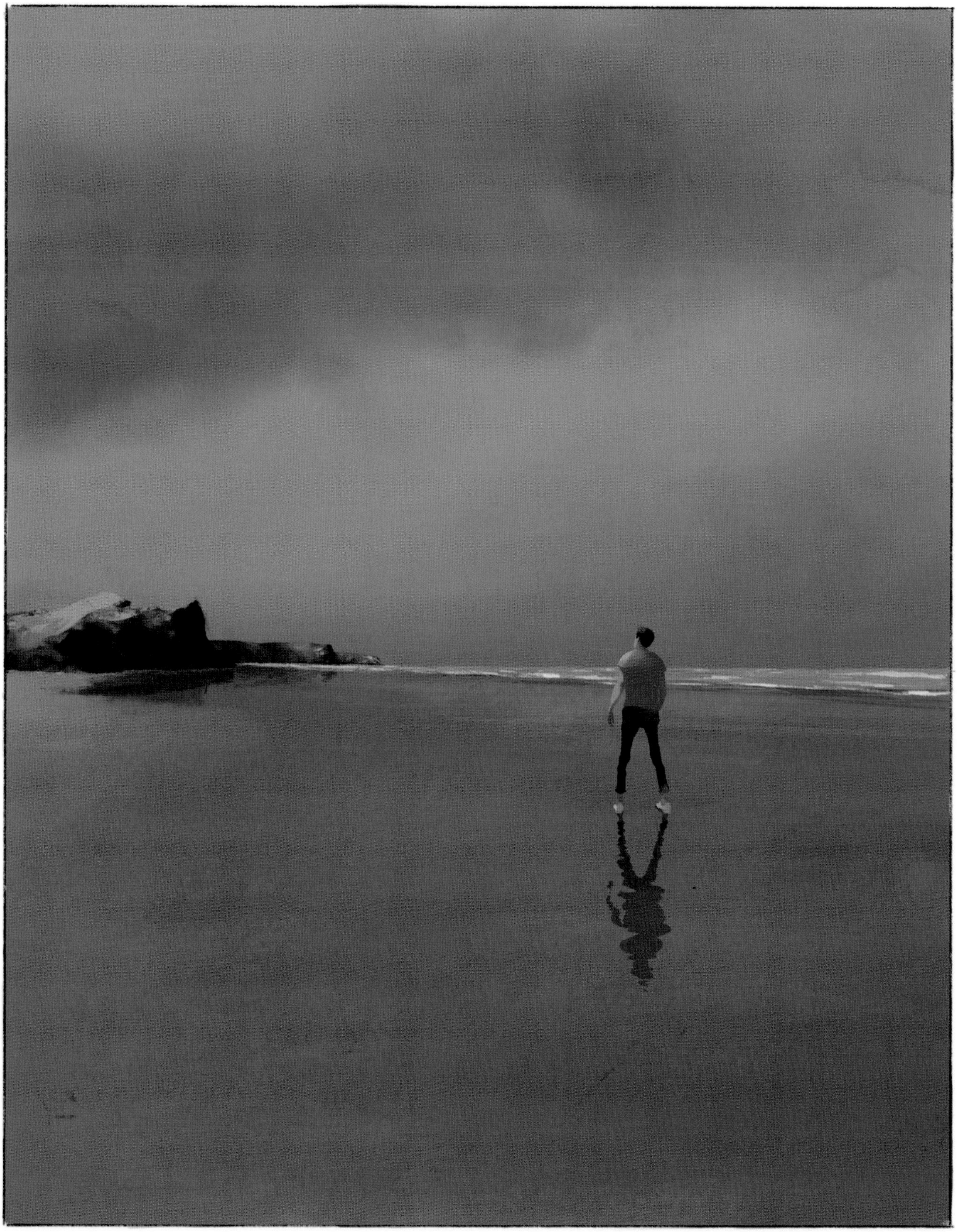

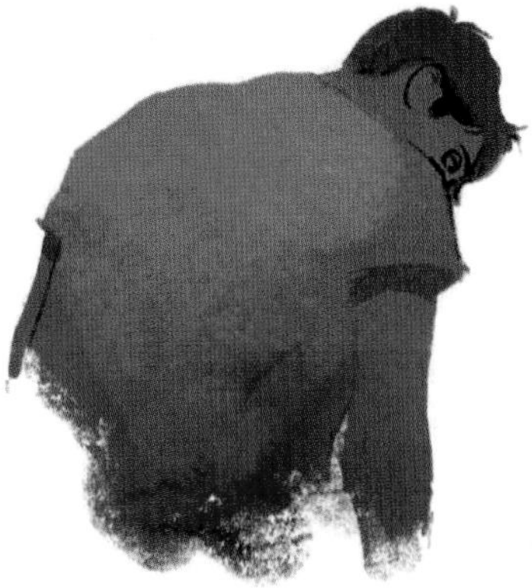
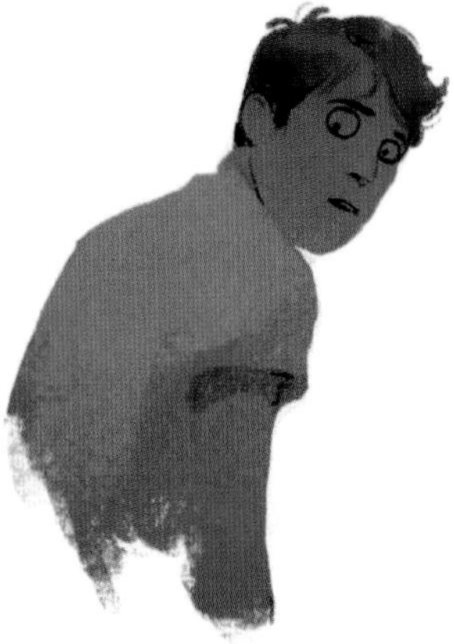
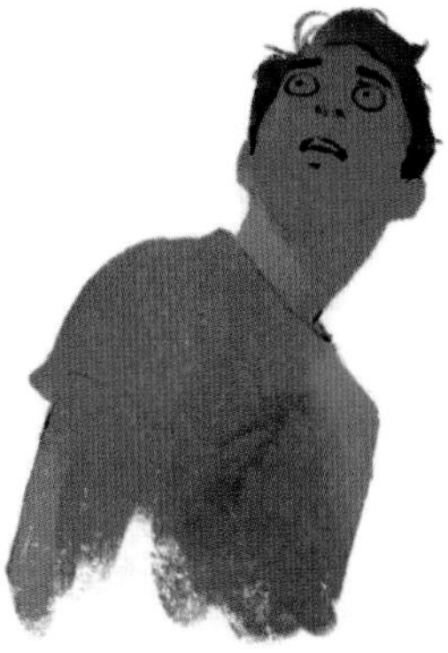
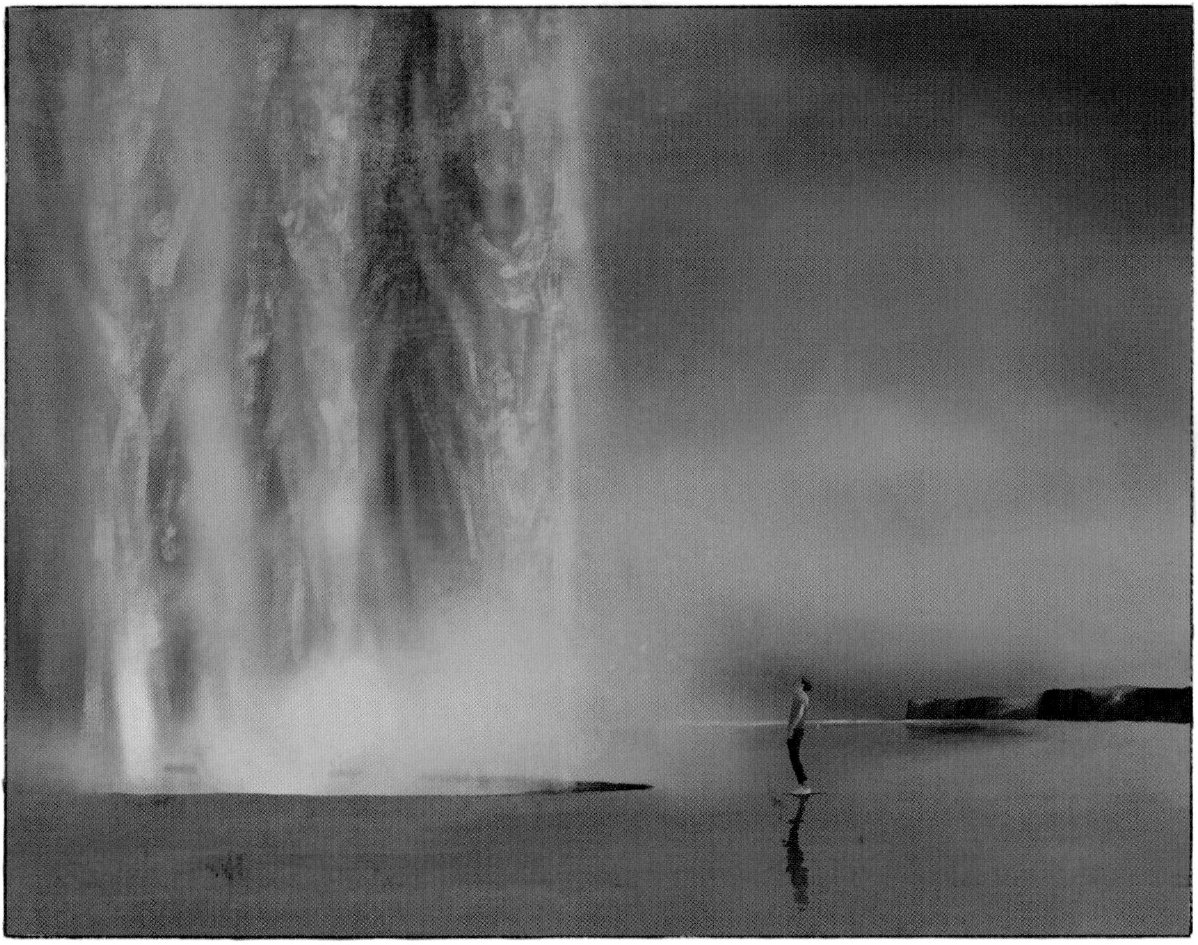

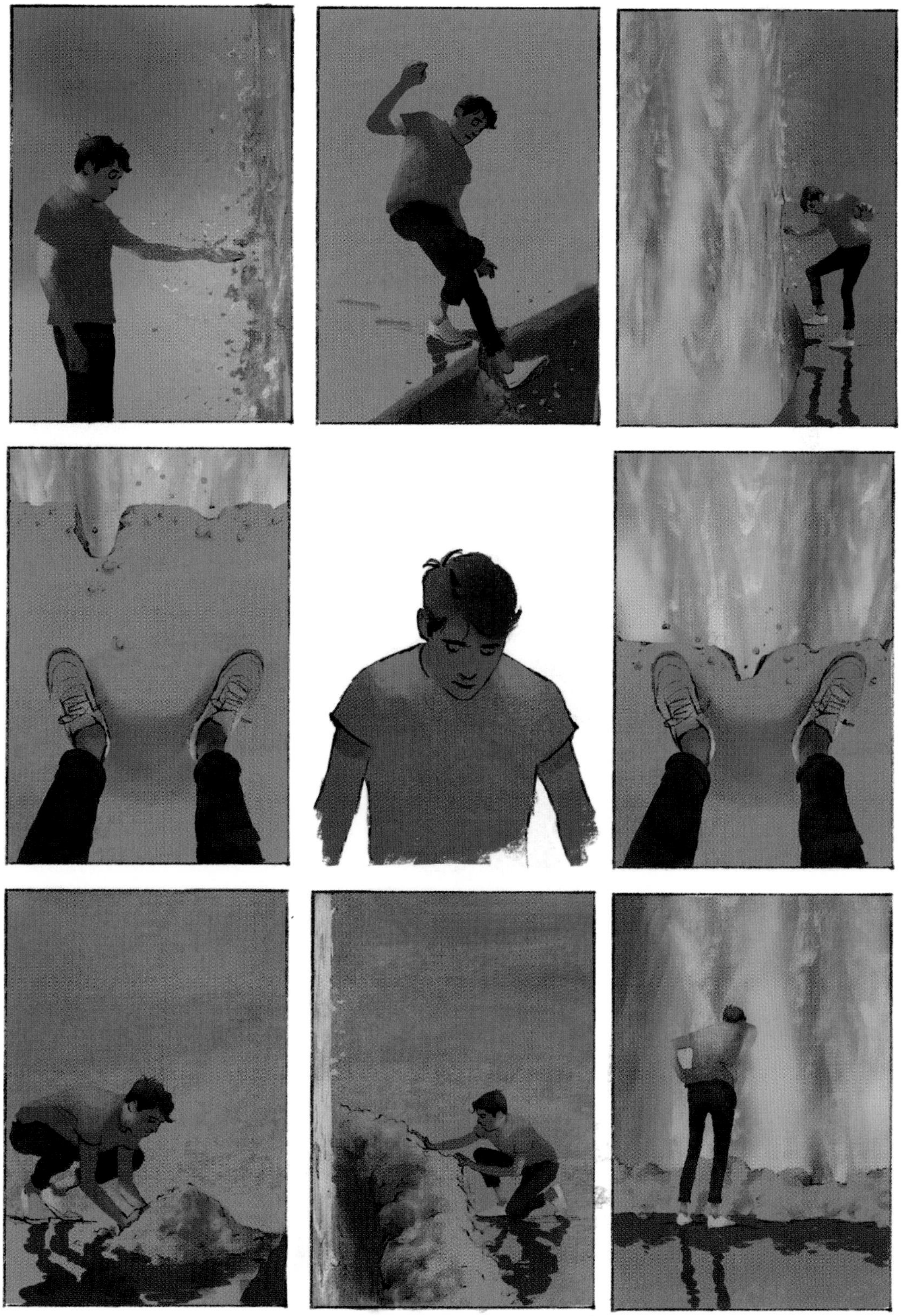

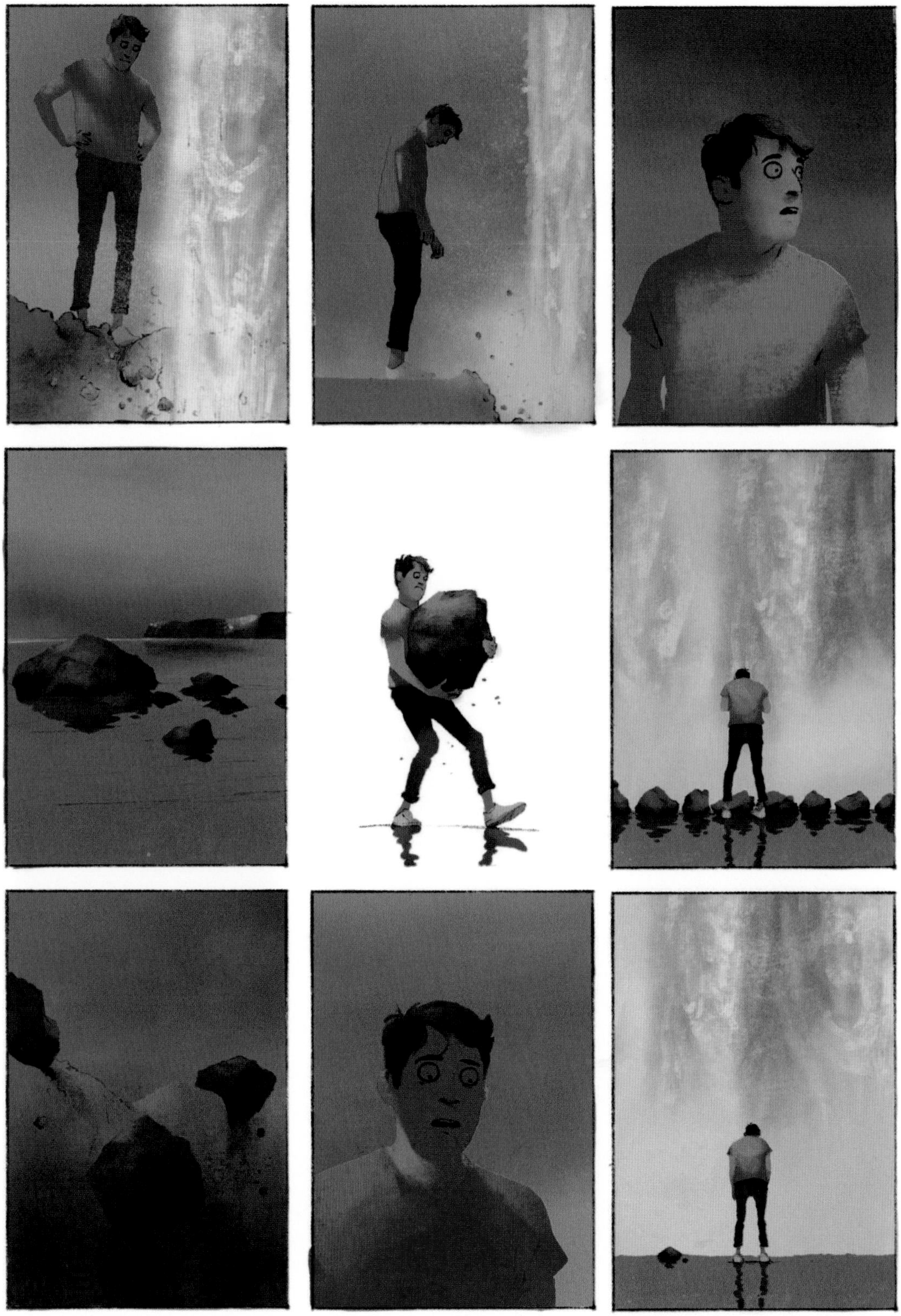

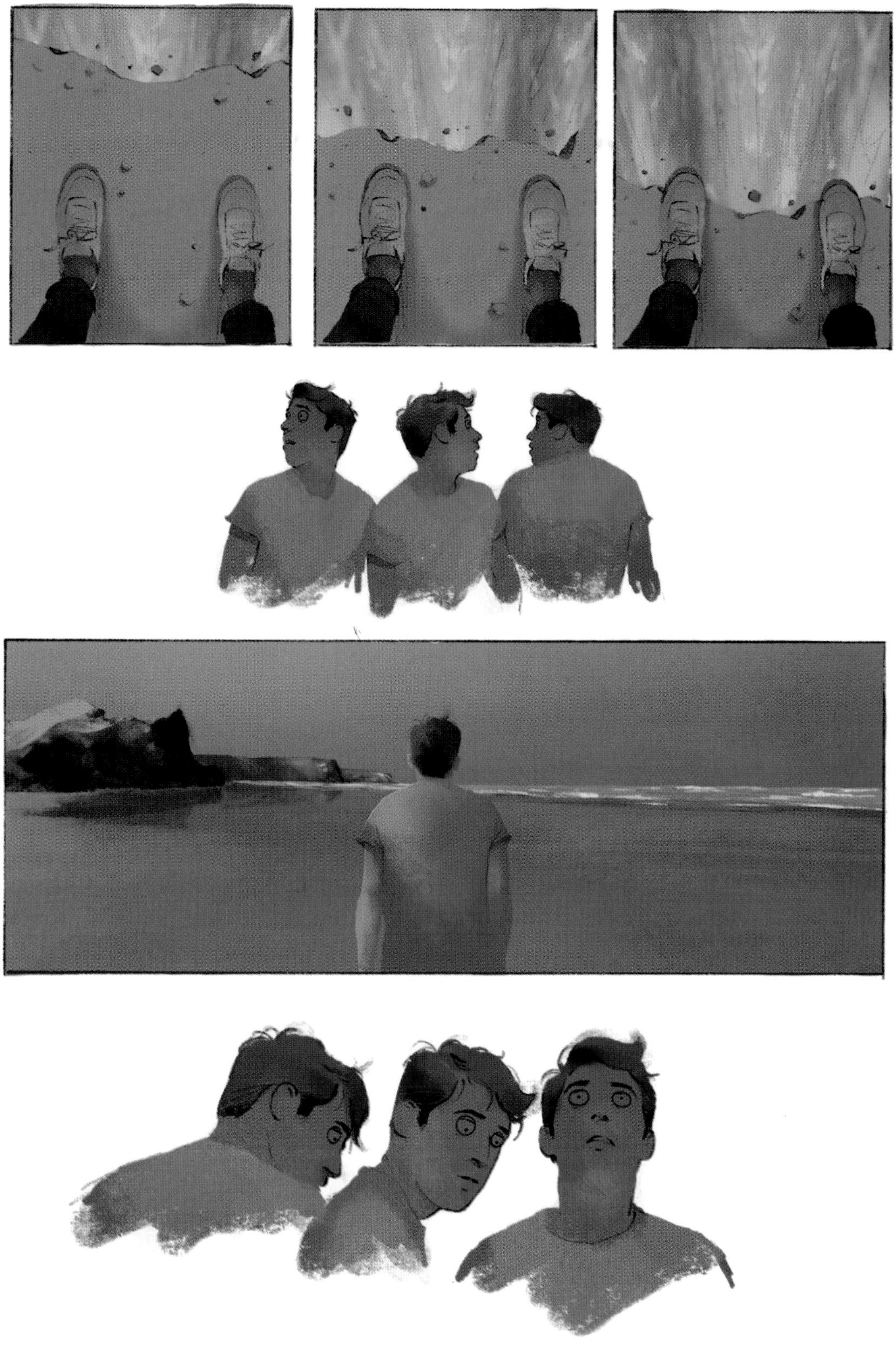

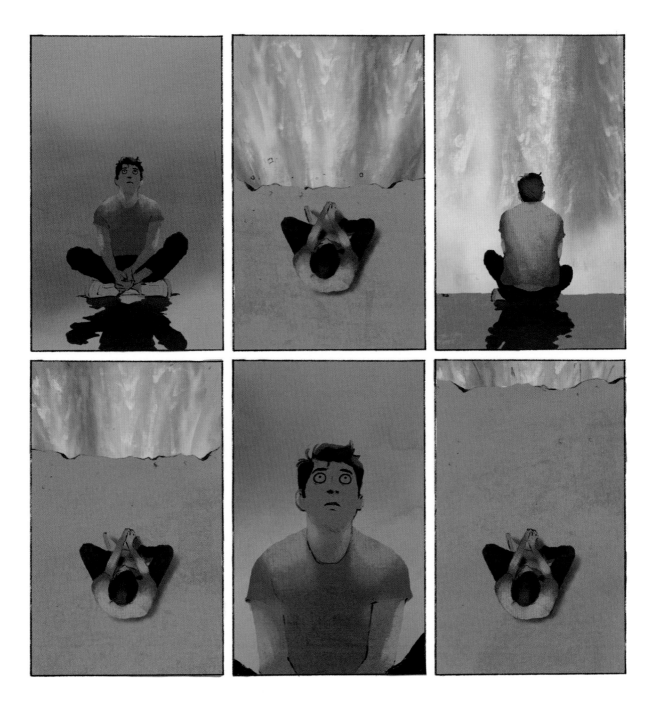

225

232

233

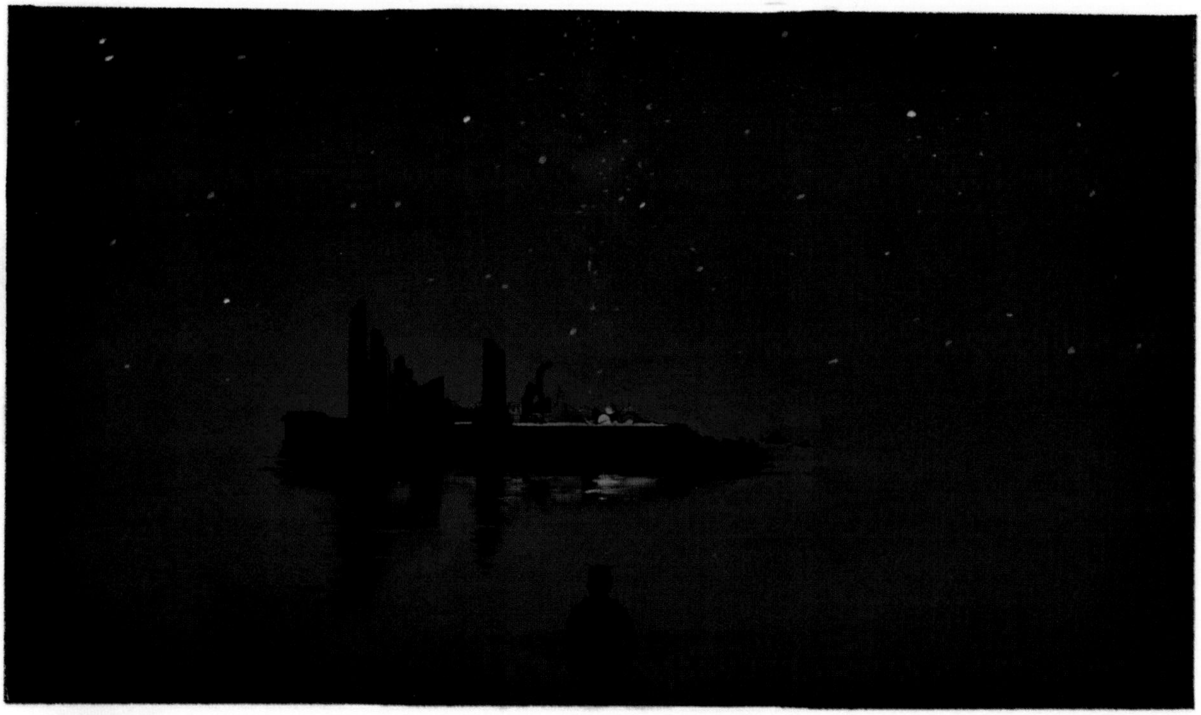

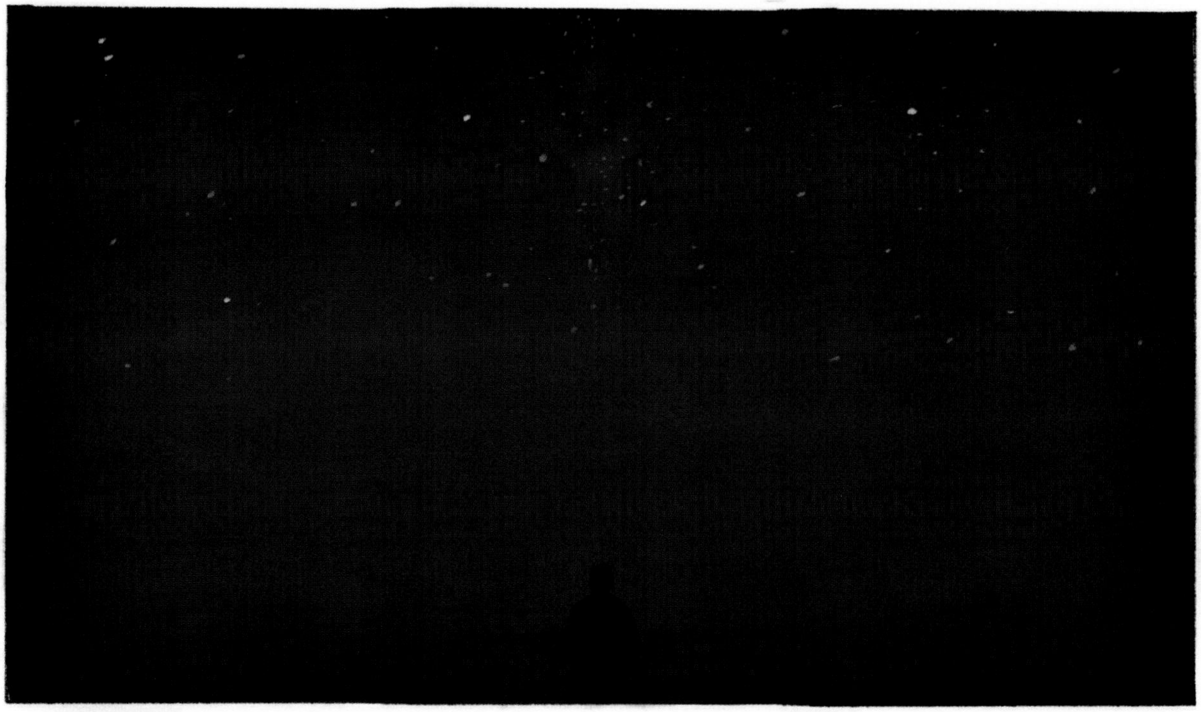

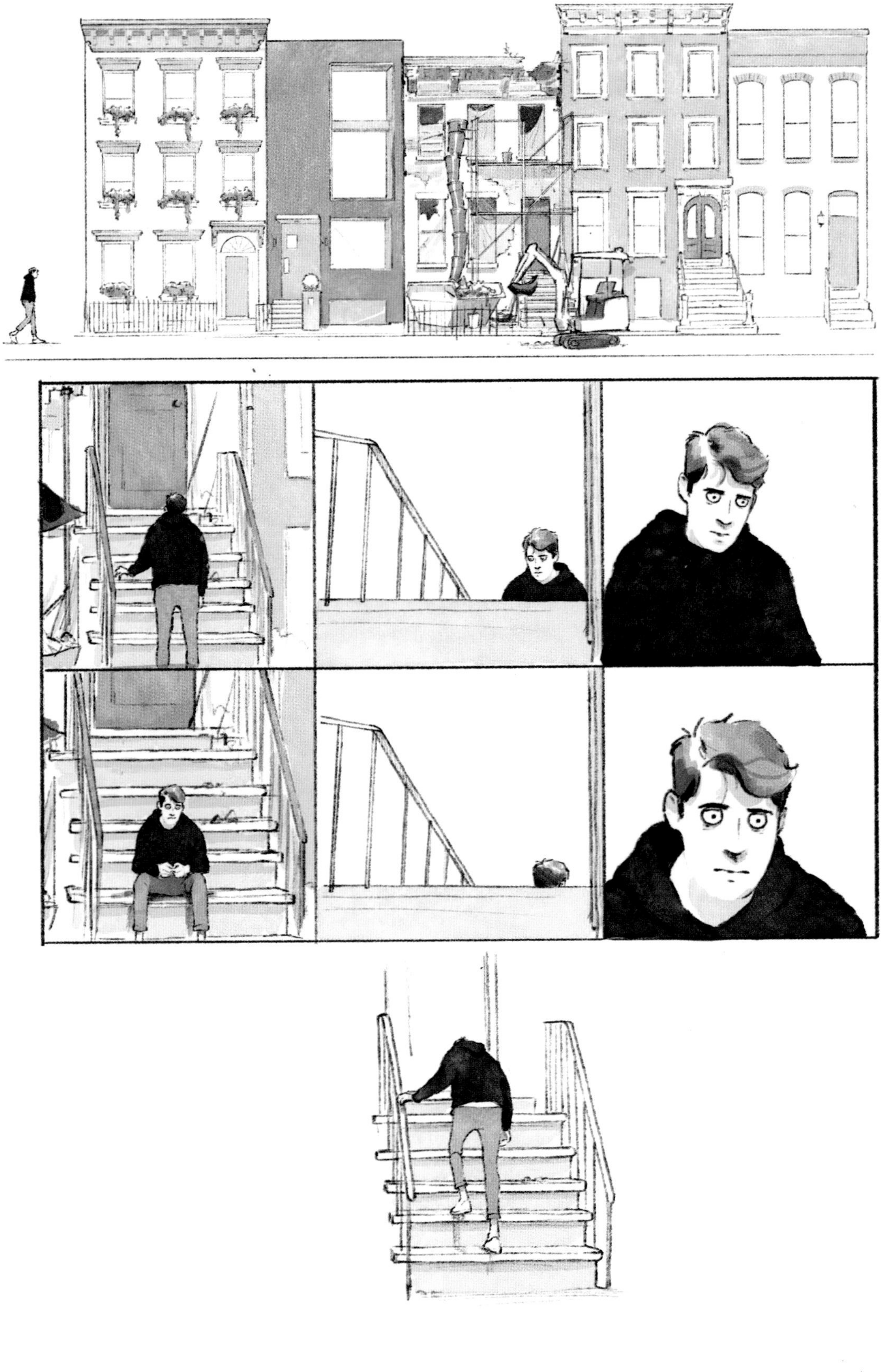

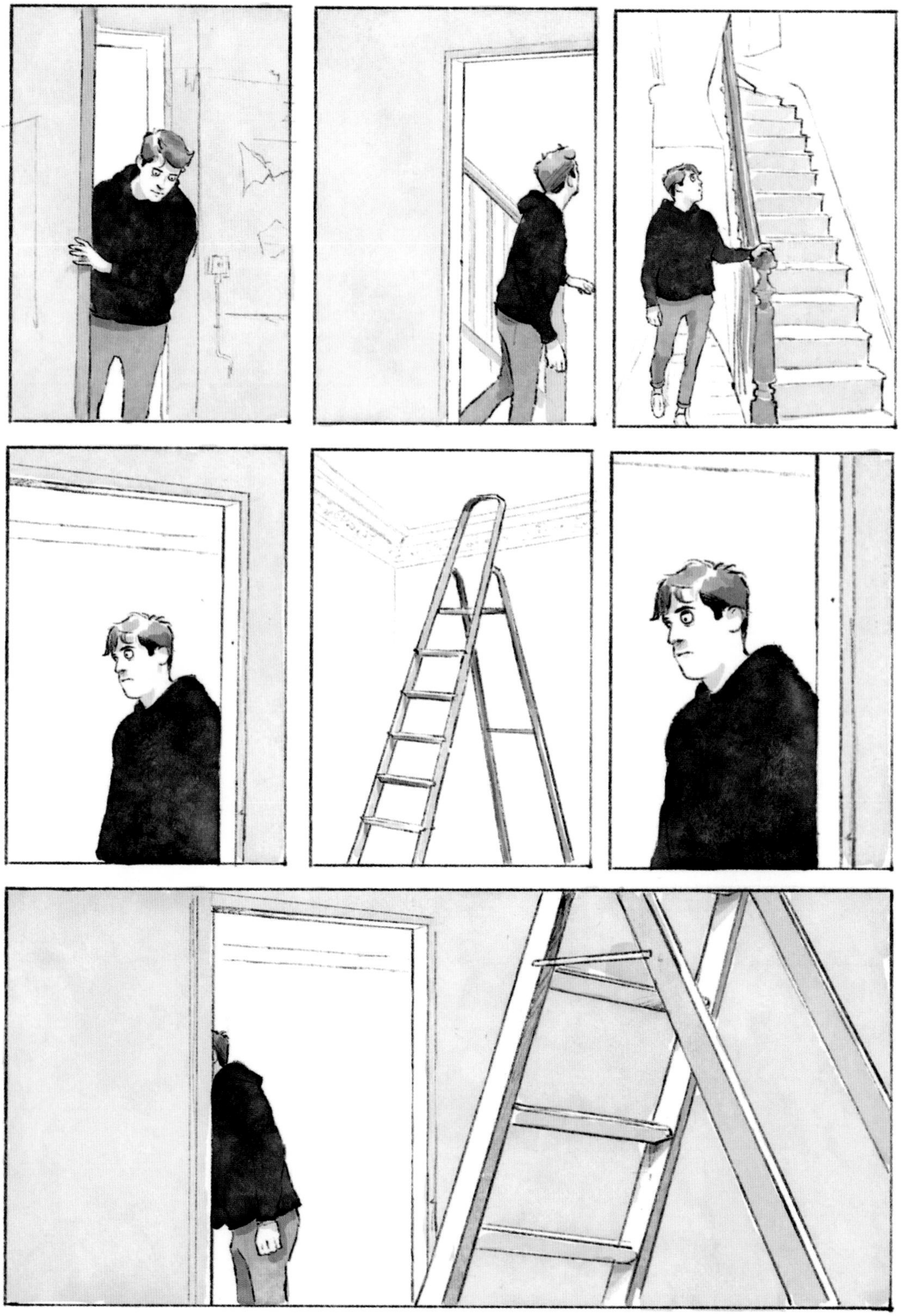

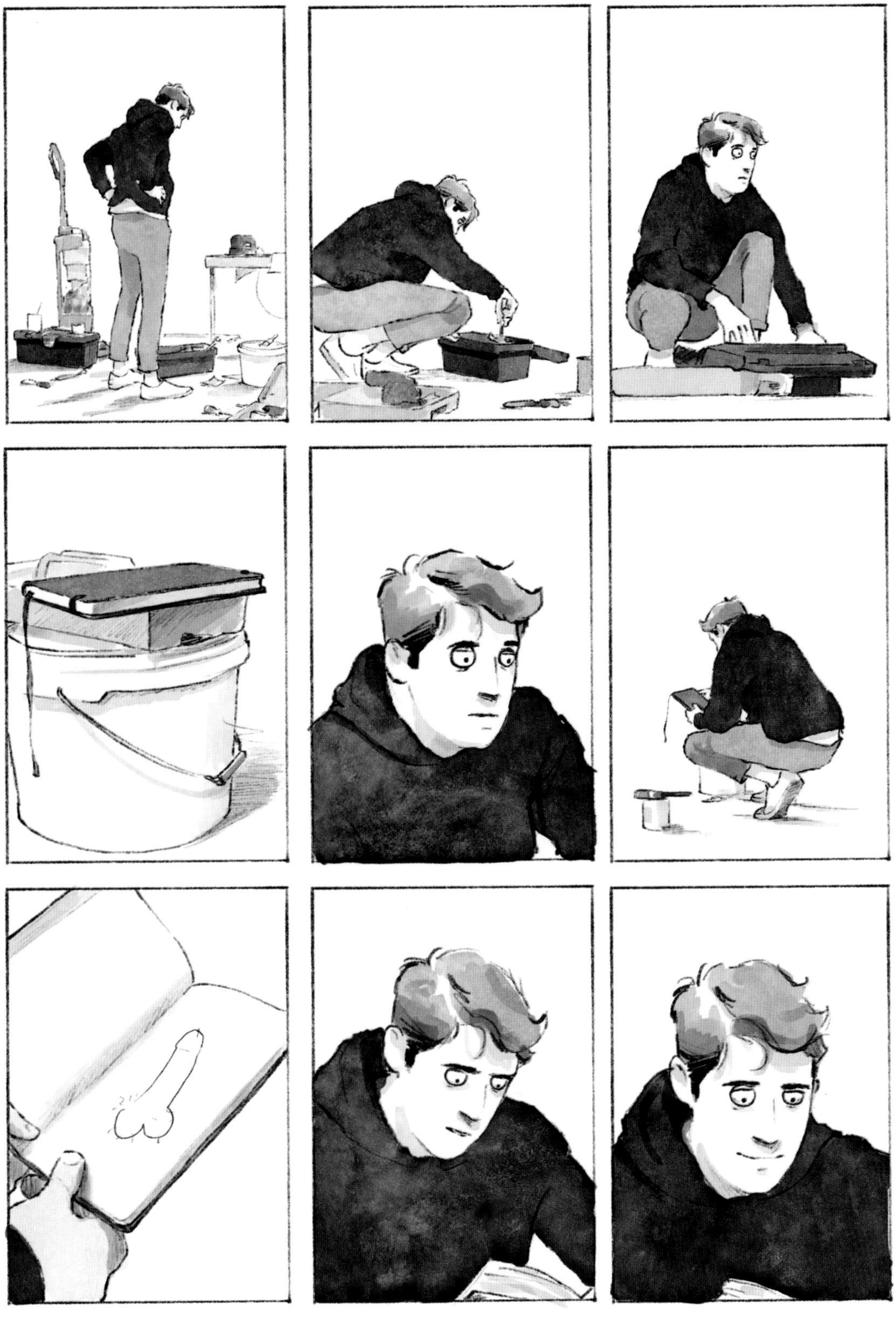

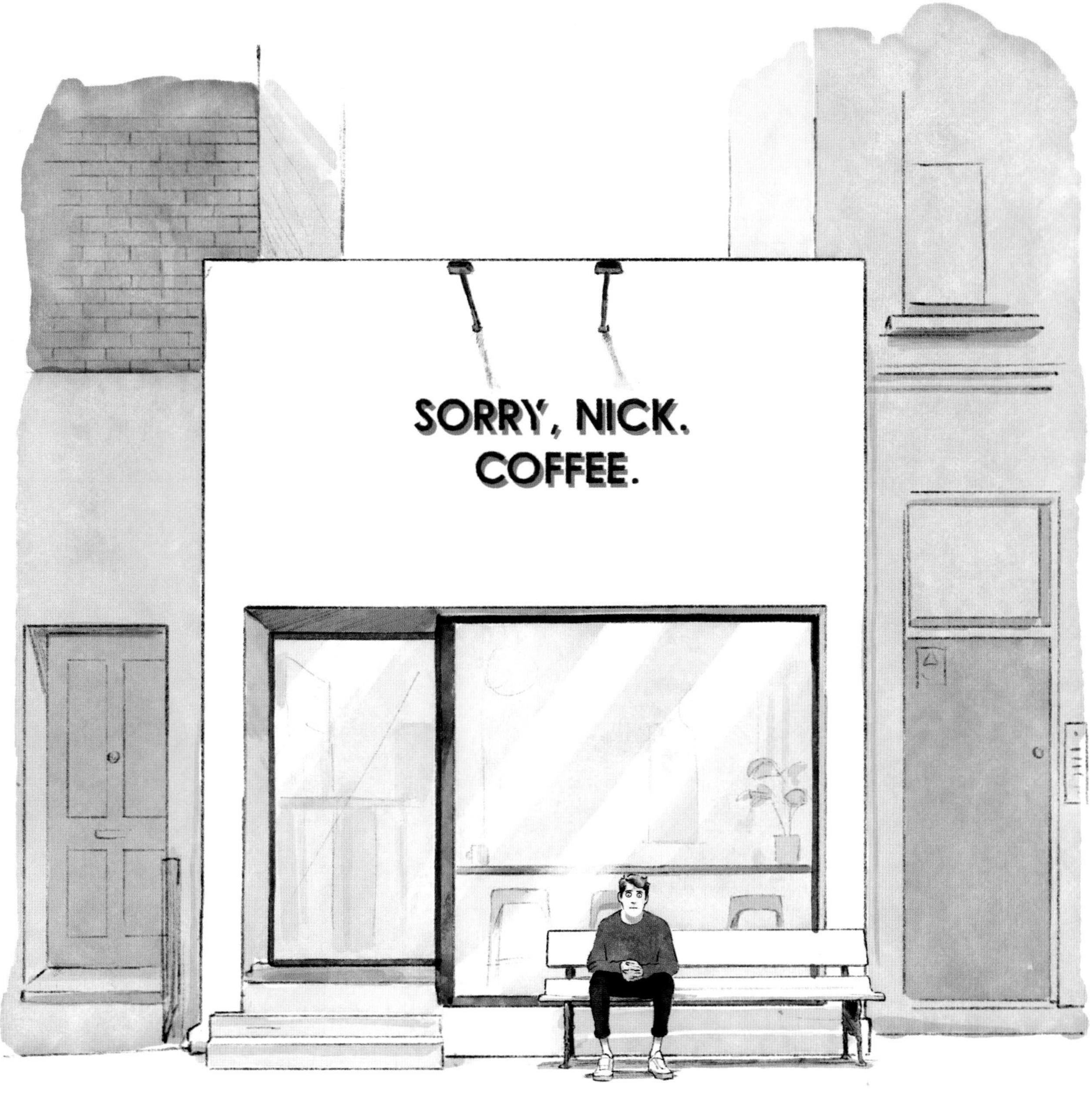
SORRY, NICK.
COFFEE.

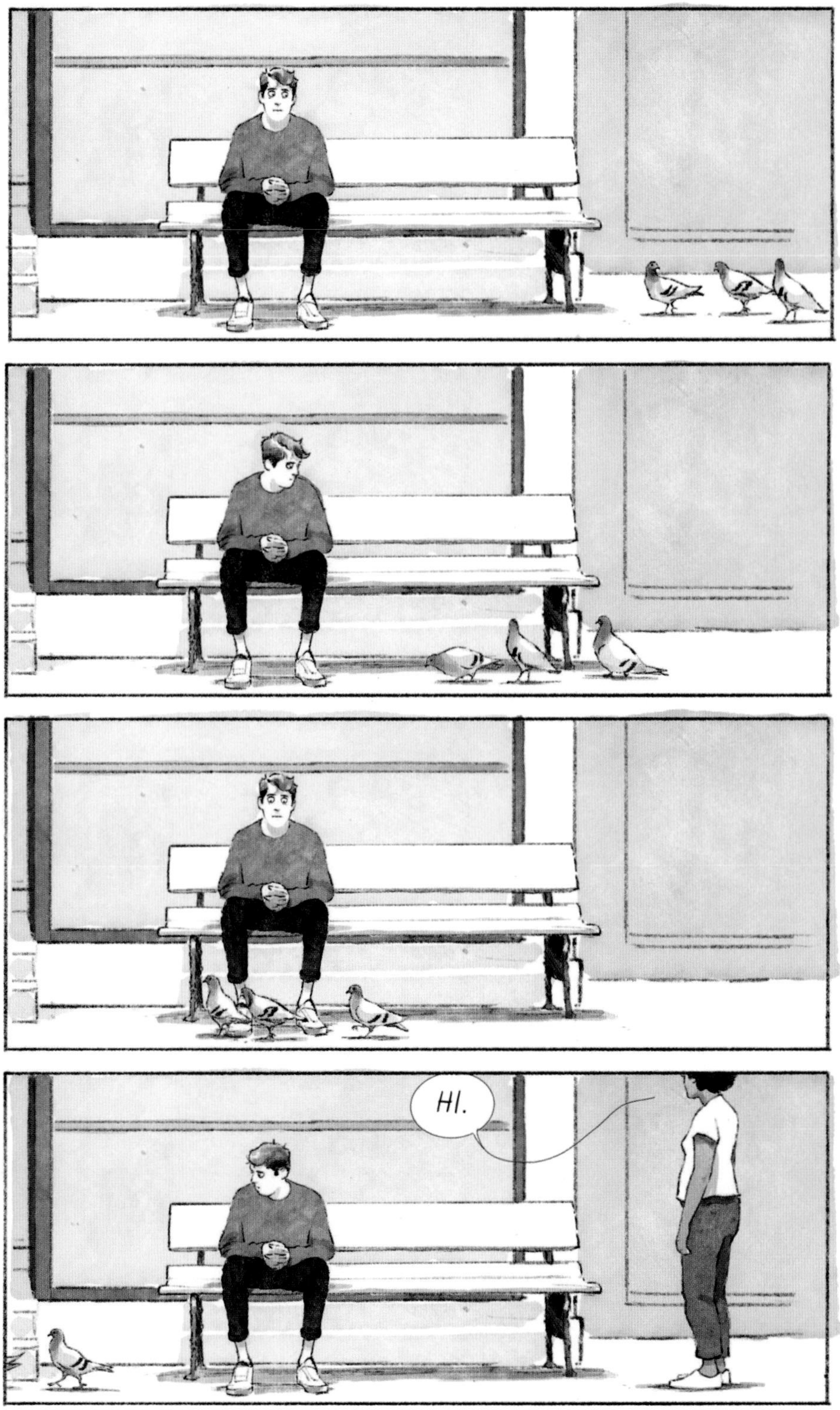
HI.

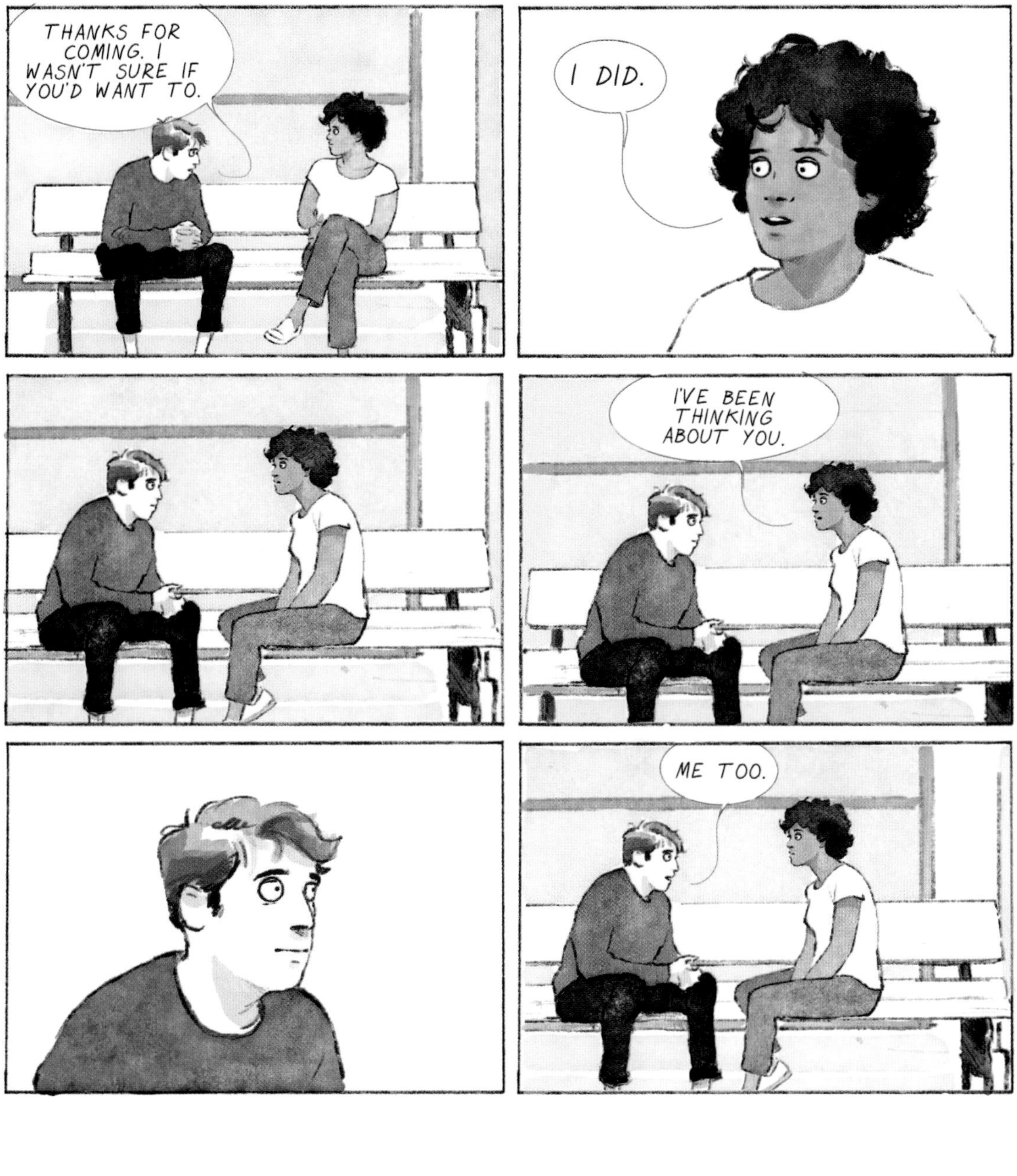
THANKS FOR COMING. I WASN'T SURE IF YOU'D WANT TO.
I DID.
I'VE BEEN THINKING ABOUT YOU.
ME TOO.

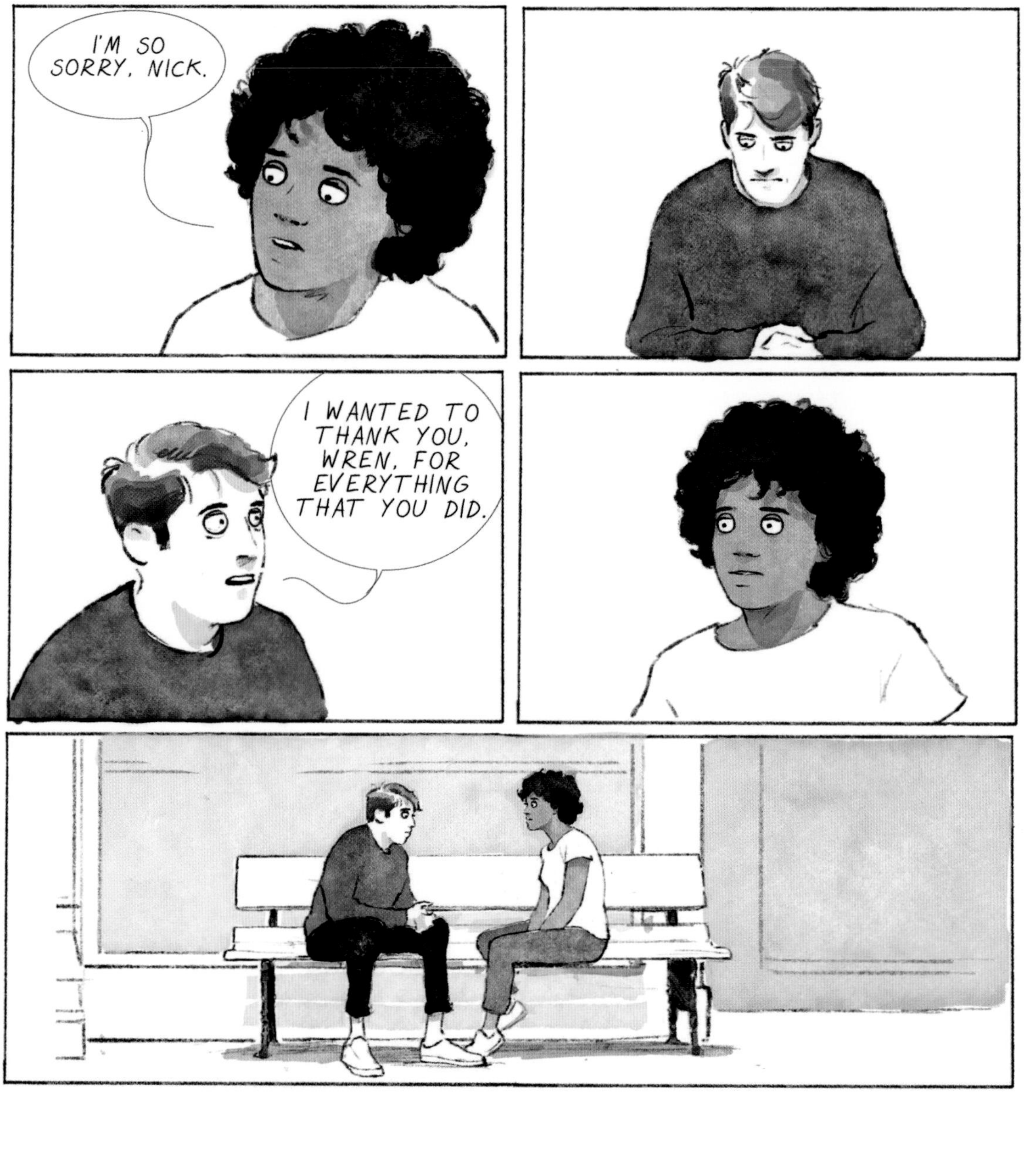
I'M SO SORRY, NICK.
I WANTED TO THANK YOU, WREN, FOR EVERYTHING THAT YOU DID.

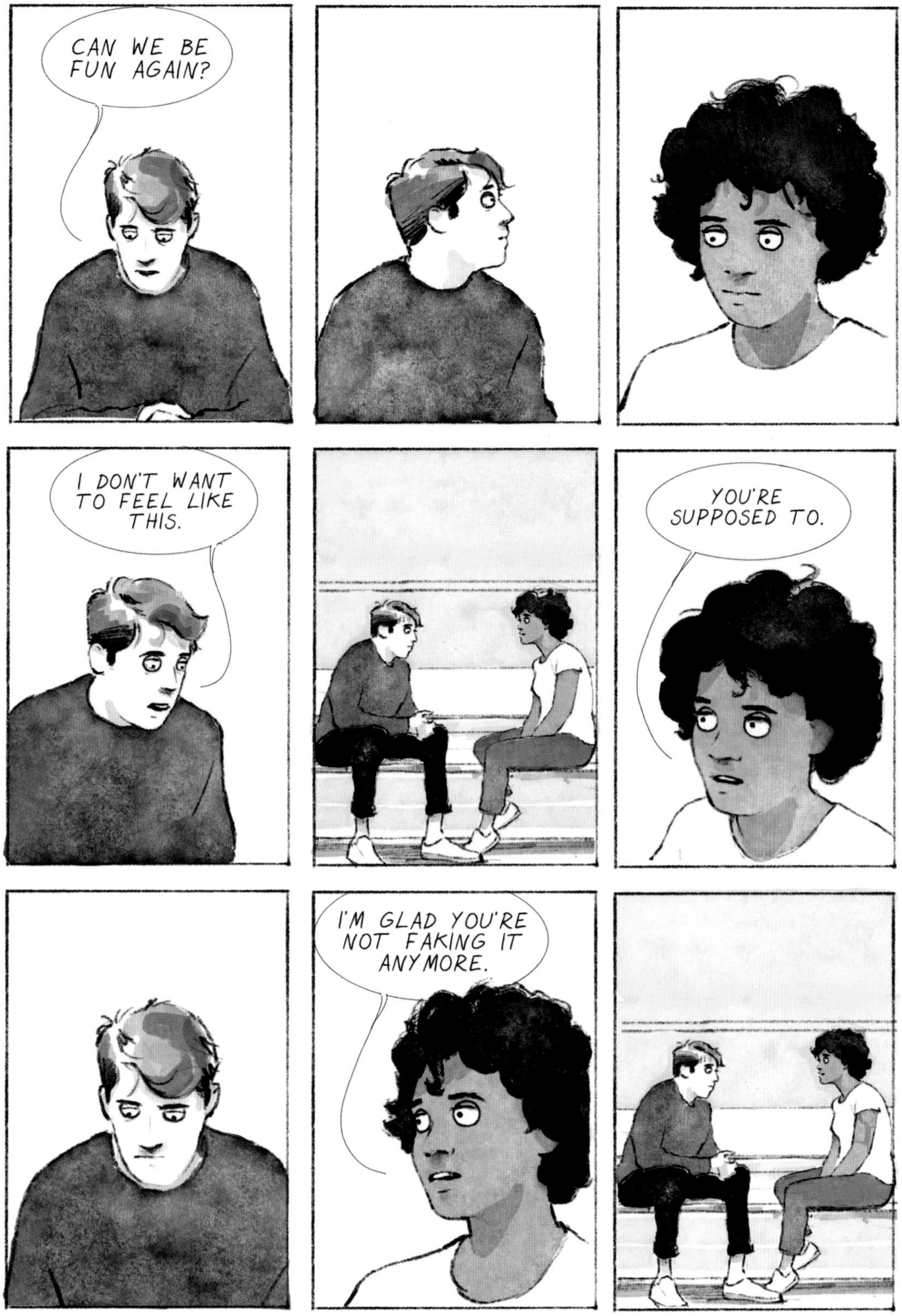
CAN WE BE FUN AGAIN?
I DON'T WANT TO FEEL LIKE THIS.
YOU'RE SUPPOSED TO.
I'M GLAD YOU'RE NOT FAKING IT ANYMORE.

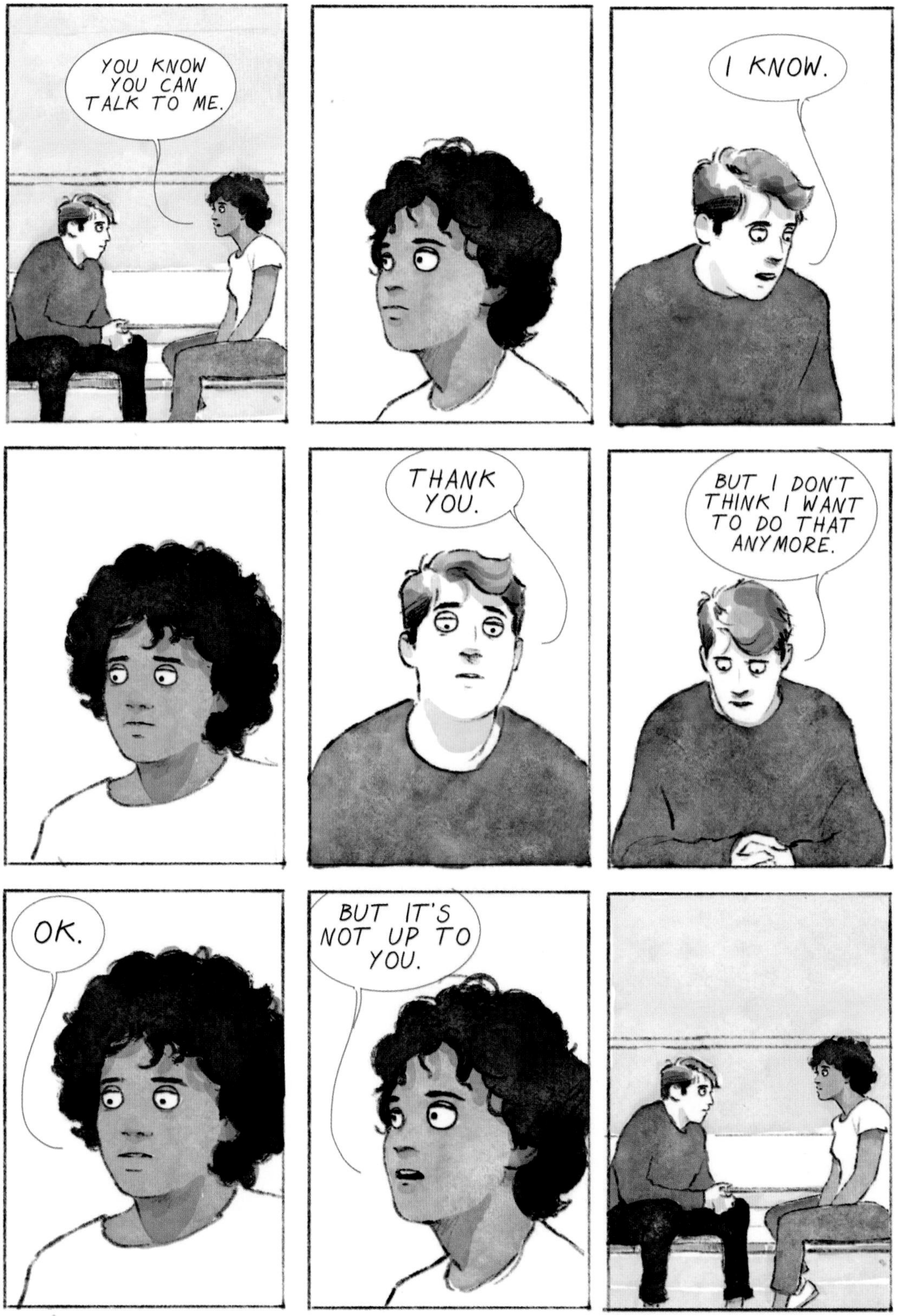
YOU KNOW YOU CAN TALK TO ME.
I KNOW.
THANK YOU.
BUT I DON'T THINK I WANT TO DO THAT ANYMORE.
OK.
BUT IT'S NOT UP TO YOU.

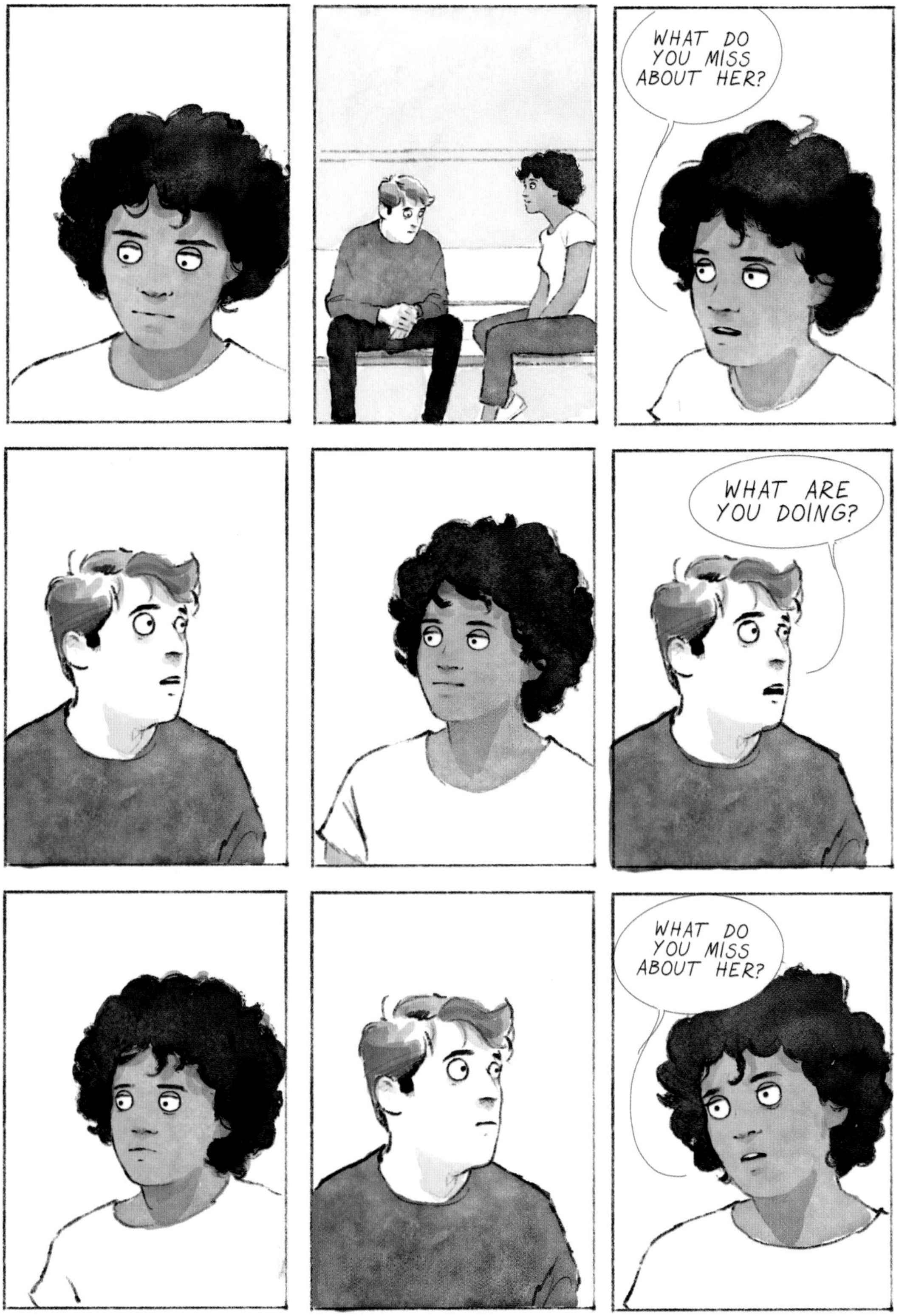
WHAT DO YOU MISS ABOUT HER?
WHAT ARE YOU DOING?
WHAT DO YOU MISS ABOUT HER?

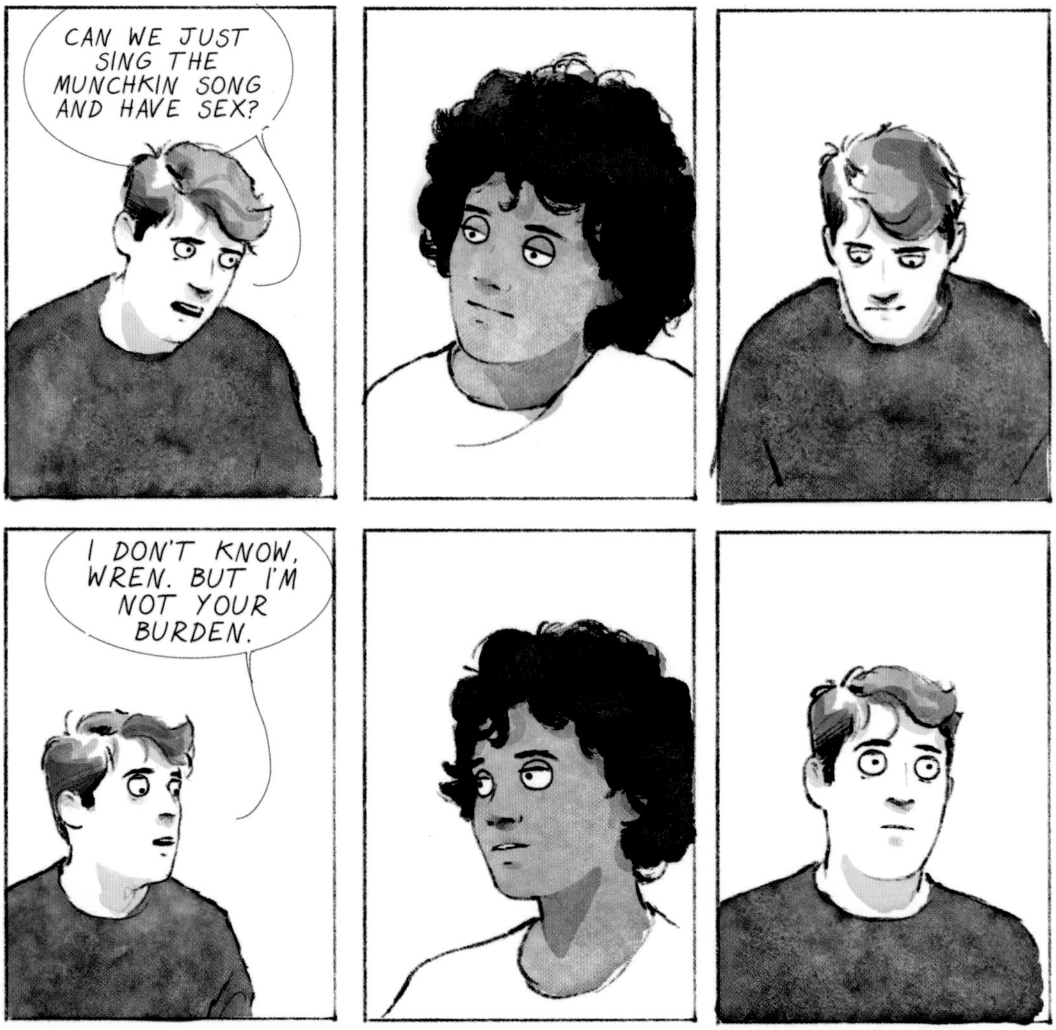
CAN WE JUST SING THE MUNCHKIN SONG AND HAVE SEX?
I DON'T KNOW, WREN. BUT I'M NOT YOUR BURDEN.

IT MIGHT BE NICE TO HAVE SOMEONE IN THERE WITH YOU.

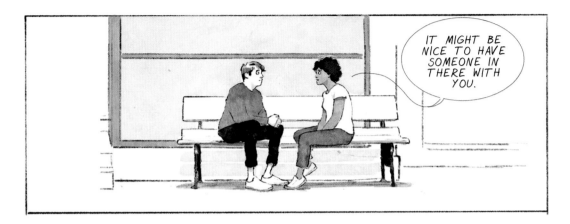

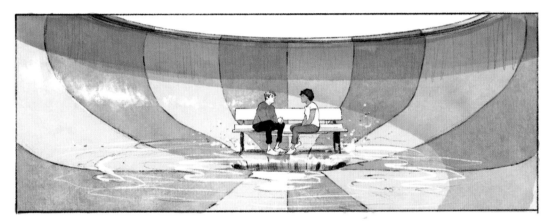

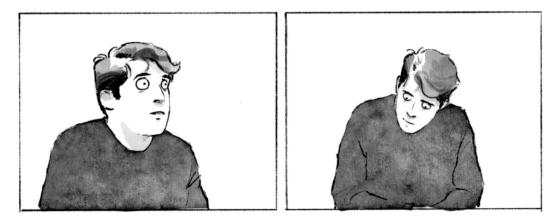

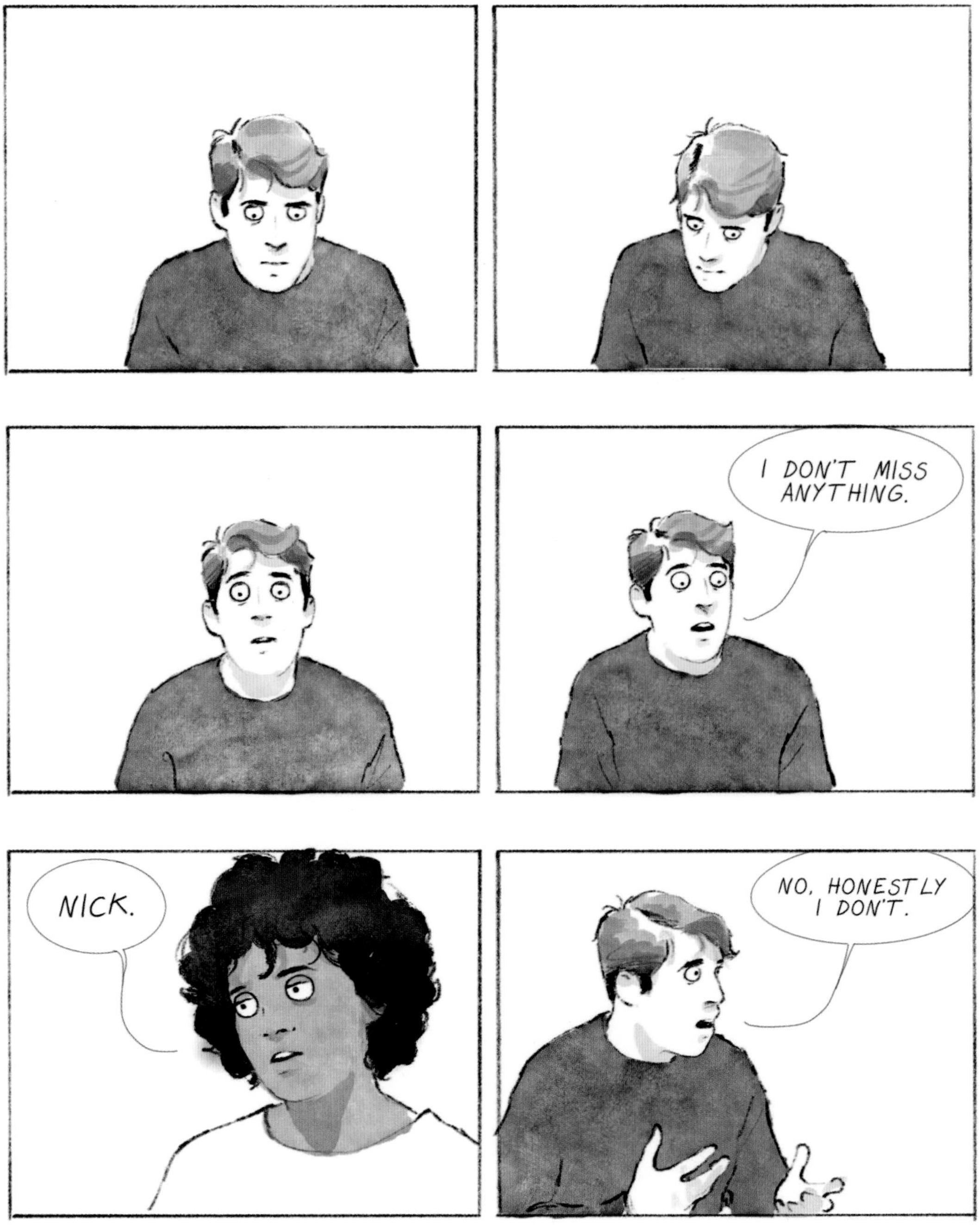
I DON'T MISS ANYTHING.
NICK.
NO, HONESTLY I DON'T.

IT'S NOT WHAT I MISS.
IT'S THE STUFF THAT HADN'T HAPPENED YET.

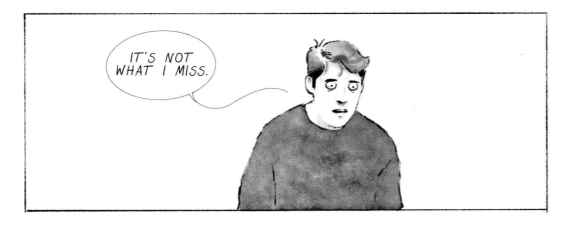

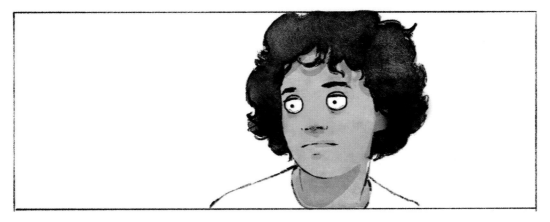

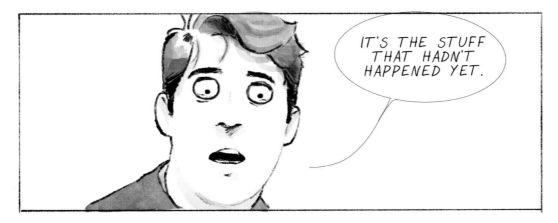

I'VE LOST EVERYTHING THAT I DIDN'T KNOW ABOUT HER.
I WAS GOING TO KNOW HER.

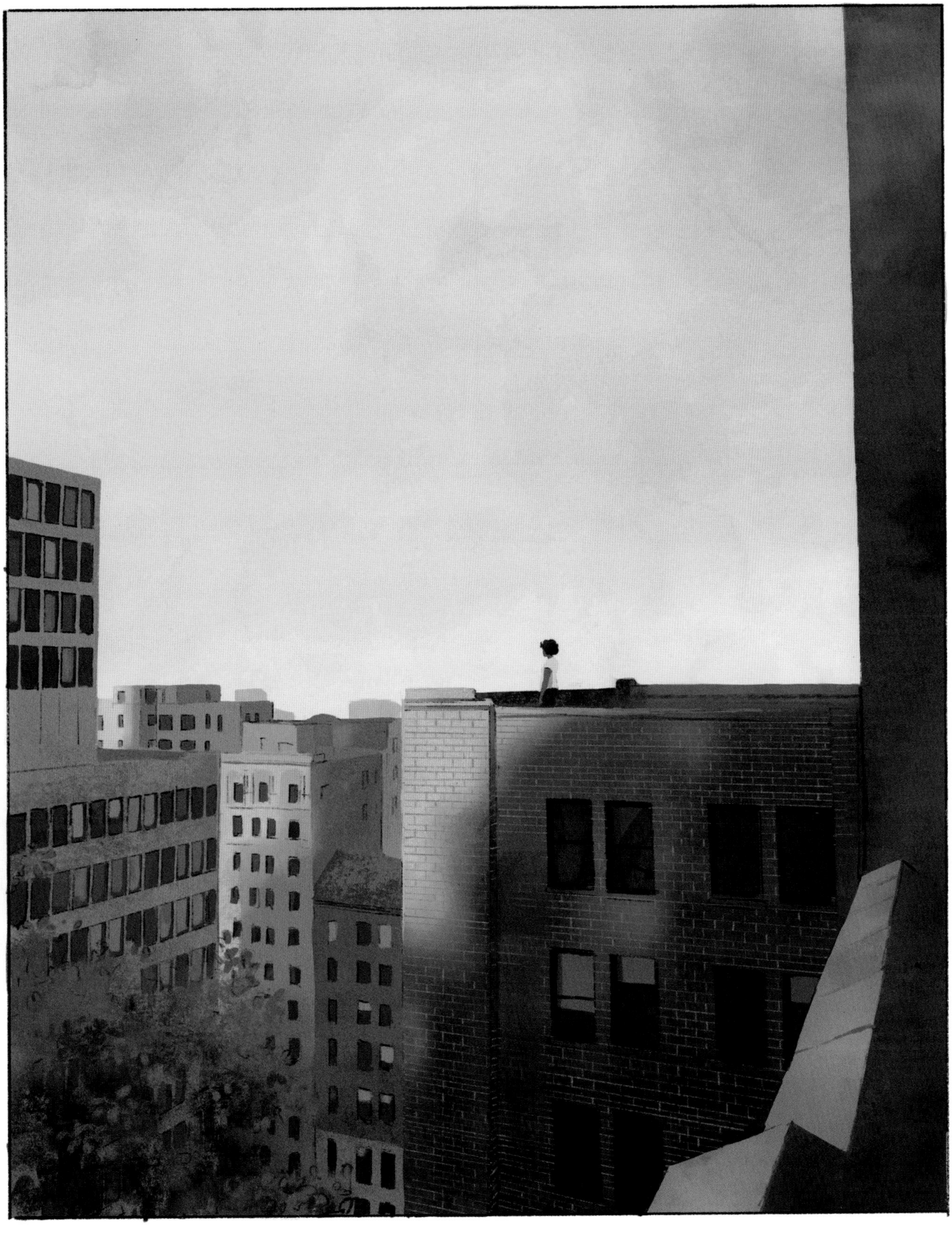

259

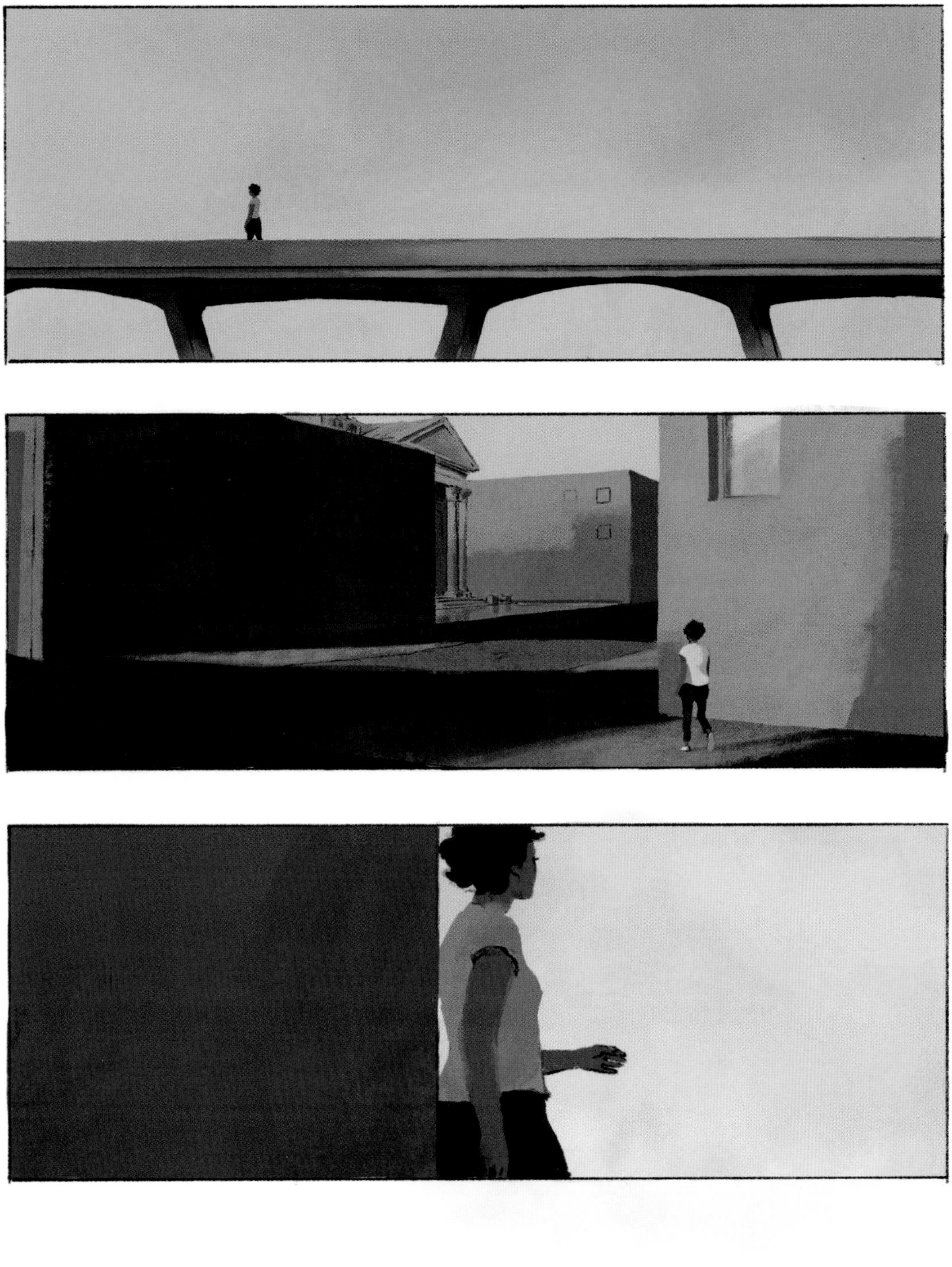

262

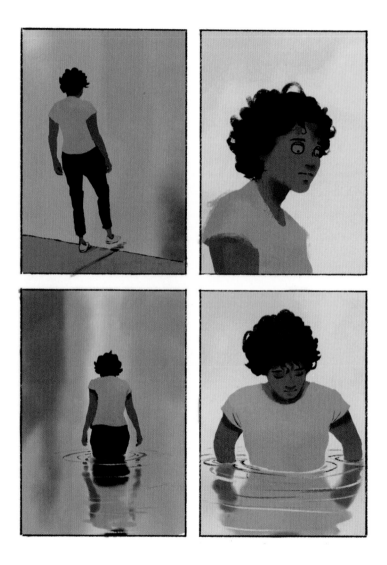

ACKNOWLEDGMENTS

FIRST AND FOREMOST, I'D LIKE TO THANK MOLESKINE. I KNOW THAT THINGS HAVE BEEN DIFFERENT BETWEEN US SINCE WHAT HAPPENED BUT RULED NOTEPAD, PLAIN NOTEPAD, THE ONE WITH THE DOTS THAT I BOUGHT BY ACCIDENT ONE TIME, I REALLY DON'T KNOW WHAT I WOULD HAVE DONE WITHOUT YOU GUYS. PROBABLY USE A LESS EXPENSIVE NOTEPAD AND BE ABLE TO AFFORD MY GAS BILL.

IN A CAREER WITHOUT RECOGNIZABLE STRUCTURE OR DIRECTION, THE NEW YORKER MAGAZINE AND ITS WEEKLY CARTOON SUBMISSIONS HAVE BEEN AN EVER-PRESENT COMPASS FOR ME. THE OPPORTUNITY TO WRITE THIS BOOK IS A DIRECT RESULT OF MY WORK BEING IN THERE AND IT IS MY CONTINUED HONOUR TO DRAW FOR THEM. IN PARTICULAR I'D LIKE TO THANK BOB MANKOFF, WHO BOUGHT MY FIRST NEW YORKER CARTOON; COLIN STOKES, WHO TOOK PITY ON ME AND THE INCREASINGLY DESPERATE SUBMISSIONS THAT I WOULD POST TO THE OFFICE; EMMA ALLEN, WHO CONTINUES TO LET ME SOIL THE MAGAZINE'S HALLOWED PAGES, AND TO ALL OF MY NEW YORK FRIENDS—I'M SO GRATEFUL FOR YOUR KINDNESS AND LAUGHTER.

TO MY AGENT, MY GUARDIAN ANGEL AND MY FRIEND, HEATHER. IN THE REALEST POSSIBLE SENSE, THIS BOOK WOULD NOT EXIST IF IT WEREN'T FOR YOU. I'LL NEVER BE ABLE TO THANK YOU ENOUGH FOR PATIENTLY SHOWING ME EXACTLY HOW TO TURN MY PIPEDREAMS INTO REALITY.

THANK YOU TO EVERYONE AT HOUGHTON MIFFLIN HARCOURT FOR TAKING A CHANCE ON ME. TO DAVID ROSENTHAL, MY EDITOR AND DRINKING PARTNER—THANK YOU FOR SURGICALLY REMOVING EVERY OUNCE OF BULLSHIT FROM THIS PROCESS AND GIVING ME THE WRITING EXPERIENCE THAT EVERY FIRST-TIME AUTHOR DREAMS OF. I AM DEEPLY SORRY FOR MAKING YOU DRINK GRAPPA AND THINK ABOUT OAT LUBE.

THANK YOU TO GORDON WISE FOR SHIELDING ME FROM ALL THE NECESSARY ADULT STUFF SO THAT I CAN JUST DRAW PICTURES. AND TO EMMA HERDMAN AT SCEPTRE, YOUR NOTES, INSIGHT AND COMPANY HAVE MADE ME A BETTER WRITER AND A BETTER PERSON.

IT'S EASY TO FEEL ISOLATED IN A JOB LIKE MINE AND IT IS ENTIRELY THANKS TO MY FRIENDS THAT I DON'T. STEVE, HEATHER AND GABBY, I LOVE YOU. AND THANK YOU TO MY OLDEST FRIENDS: CHAZ, GREG AND DAVE, WHOSE CONVERSATIONS ARE ALWAYS IN FULL COLOUR.

FINALLY: TO MY FAMILY, THANK YOU ALL FOR RAISING ME, INSPIRING ME AND FOR ALWAYS BEING WHAT I CALL HOME. OL AND NELL, I CAN'T TELL YOU HOW LUCKY I FEEL TO HAVE GROWN UP BETWEEN YOU. AND TO MY MUM, YOU'VE GIVEN ME ALL THAT I HAVE AND MADE ME ALL THAT I AM. I'M SO PROUD TO BE YOUR SON.